PRAISE FOR
*SON OF THE BORDERLANDS*

*"If you are in the market for a fantasy novel that will draw you
in and keep you waiting for more, then look no further."*
—REEDSY DISCOVERY

*"It's not often that epic fantasy intersects with intrigue and a
form of suspense more often relegated to the thriller genre."*
—MIDWEST REVIEWS

*"On par with the inviting world of Patrick Rothfus and other
epic fantasy creators, Son of the Borderlands cements action with
moral, ethical, and psychological conundrums to keep the story
fast-paced, the protagonist's evolution believable and wondrous,
and the results unpredictable and thoroughly immersive."*
—MIDWEST REVIEWS

*"This is an excellent beginning to the saga, not to be missed."*
—BLUEINK REVIEWS

# SON

### *of the*

# BORDERLANDS

ISBN: 978-1-967432-00-4 (Electronic)
ISBN: 978-1-967432-01-1 (Paperback)
ISBN: 978-1-967432-02-8 (Hardcover)
ISBN: 978-1-967432-03-5 (Audiobook)

Library of Congress Control Number: 2025913080



www.josephsterk.com
www.sonoftheborderlands.com
www.starwolfpress.com
www.riseofthedragonlands.com

# SON

*of the*

# BORDERLANDS

RISE OF THE DRAGONLANDS

BOOK ONE

## JOSEPH P. STERK

For as long as I can remember, I loved creating fantasy worlds in my head. I could be a major league baseball player, intergalactic warrior, professional wrestler, or magical knight in my favorite video game. In good times, I found extra joy there; in rough times, I found solace. I created a cast of thousands, ergo, it was inevitable that one would break out of my mind.

Agni Kazirian was formed twenty-five years ago, as my avatar in a message-board based fanfiction roleplay. In his first incarnation, he was filled with anger and sorrow; he wanted only to inflict his pain upon the world and die. But other role players felt drawn to him; they saw a nobility and magnetism in him that I could not.

Throughout the years, Agni took on life, like a statue emerging from the sculptor's marble. He developed a heart and depth. He needed companions—of my many creations, Kali was the first that I grew smitten with; Alexander evolved from mere bodyguard and bullyboy to faithful mentor. At the same time, they needed a great world, and one of warring gods shaped by primal fears and desires materialized.

But for years, I buried this world like a seed and pursued other life priorities. I knew one day it would sprout again—it took the water of later life tribulations to do so, to discover my own locked-away power, and to feel worthy of telling such a tale of fortitude and the human spirit. I found a purpose for his first tale, to illustrate "things truer than true."

May it do so in your heart.

As I put the finishing touches on *Son of the Borderlands*, I give special gratitude to those who drew this world out of me.

To Andrew Force and Miles Butler, with whom I co-created the predecessor to this world, and two of the first to see something greater in Agni Kazirian.

To Jen Braaksma (JenBraaksma.com), my book coach, fellow author, and guide along the way.

To my parents, James and Elizabeth Sterk, and all the love over the years. I told you all those hours losing myself in books and video game RPGs wouldn't be in vain.

A special thanks to the tireless and talented artists who brought *Son of the Borderlands* to visual life. View their depictions of characters and scenes at **JosephSterk.com/Art** and a full-color world map at **JosephSterk.com/Books.**

*PLEASE NOTE: No artwork is "official," except the renditions in my mind. Also, it may contain spoilers.*

# Map of the Mortal Realms

The Infinite Sea
The Pine Sea
The Cold Eye
BLACKMOOR
The Pupil
The Blackened Wing
The Roc's Perch
AVIGIA
TERCERA
Stonereach
Wintertown
The Blighted River
THE FEATHERROAD
THE DELTA
Tereera
East River
THE ROC'S WING
THE WINTERROAD
East Fork
Roc's
Bay
Northtown
Roc's Talons
The Feathered River
THE LONGROAD
Southtown
THE EASTROAD
Middleport
Farport
Nearport
Landfall
The Great Sea
Vian
The Vast
Sea
TARKA
Faluania
Adia

THE REACHES
Stinking
Bay
Tonda
THE CAPITAL
LANDS
Lontak
Ralonda
Alara
The Cat's Tail
Prenda
Balarda
The Dragon's Tail
BLEVENIA
THE CENTRAL
PLAINS
The Placid Shores
LEEWARD ROAD
Zarda
The Fine Tailed River
The Steaming
Forest
THE LEEWARD PLAINS
(WESTERN PLAINS)
THE FLAMEROAD
The Lion's Tail
The Wolf's Tail
The Monkey's Tail
PLAINSROAD
THE FIRELANDS
FORBIDDEN ROAD
Erta
The City of Strife
Kaziford
THE DRAGONROAD
Bethen
The Black Desert
The Mountains
of Fury
The Unending Sea

# Fate

*The past is still, but never silent.*
*Never silent.*
*Never silent.*

The gentle voice whispered to young Agni in a dream. It had no face and no name, but it woke him like a dragon's roar across a gorge.

He had barely slept—an hour at most, covered in moldy straw, his left wing wedged against a splintered plank and his right against the manor barn's fattest sow. The welts and cuts that crisscrossed his back, worsened by the rain through the splintered roof, stung like a cloud of wasps.

Why had Papa tied him to the pasture fence and lashed him raw for sneaking a handful of the horses' oats after three days without food? What did he expect a starving boy in his ninth year to do?

Long ago, Papa had taught him to saddle a pony and shoot a bow and told him he would be a famed knight of Solantia. Then, after the raiders came and slew Mama, Papa's love died with her. Even the sound of his breath seemed to provoke his wrath. *Worthless boy*, he would snarl. No reason, no sense.

But tonight, that whisper had stirred something deeper. A thrill. A beckoning. It drew him towards that gargantuan ruin that sat across the old stone bridge. A place forbidden by Azectrai's most sacred law.

*The Ancient City.*

Its true name had been lost to the mists of time, said his tutors. Once the seat of the Empire Kazia, brought low by the Scourge that wrecked the ancient world. He remembered his tutors' words, that the Scourge leveled many great cities. But only refugees from this one founded their city, Azectrai, a mere river's span from the ruin.

He recalled the punishment his tutors taught him: *The offender is to be garroted by the neck, speared through the belly, the corpse set aflame then cast into the river.* They said even a lord's boy would suffer the same fate. This ritual was thought to cleanse the Ancient City's evil air from the trespasser and placate the abominations that seethed against the living.

*Thought to cleanse.*

The lore of Azectrai was rich in death, but never had its threats felt so near. Agni used to think they said that just to frighten him into not skipping arithmetic lessons, but even Mayor Goro, the strongest knight in Azectrai, dared not cross that bridge.

*I do not know why, but I must know what lay beyond.*

Agni wrapped his bleeding wings in a damp sack and shivered as he stepped into the crisp autumn night. His night vision—strangely sharp for a boy of his age—had always guided him through the manor's dark hallways and away from Papa's drunken fists. But tonight, it was not to hide.

His face beaded with sweat as he ran the road to town. He focused on the sound of his boots—splashing and sucking in the mud—to drown out the wave of questions he might have for the voice. Who spoke it? *Why was the past still but never silent, and why did it speak to me?*

Within an hour, the city walls came into view, and with it, the glow of the watchmen's torches who walked atop the walls. With their slow, measured steps, they appeared bored; they watched for raiders, not boys.

The rain had just stopped and the air was still. When Agni slowed his walk and avoided mud puddles, he could hear his own heart.

He stalked a wide arc east around the wall to the majestic river that gave the town its name. Groves of elms lined the river, giving him a cloak of shadows. Soon, he arrived at the western foot of the bridge that separated his world of the vigilant from that of the condemned.

Now still, Agni shuddered, in both wonder and fear. Madmen claimed to commune with the spirits of the Ancient City, their distant tortured ancestors, but their ramblings found no believers.

He turned an ear towards the guard tower. Fifty yards away, he could hear the bridge guards laughing and rolling knuckle-bones inside, seemingly oblivious to the child about to commit a capital offense. *No one tested that law*, he thought; why should they expect anyone to tonight? Even if he crossed the middle strut of the bridge, why would they pursue him only to share his fate?

The Ancient City looked eerily beautiful against the moonless sky, its darkened walls absorbing what starlight reached them. They stretched to the edges of his gaze; it could hold Azectrai hundreds of times over. His gaze swept back and forth between the guard-house and the ominous silhouette of the castle at the city's heart. The guardhouse seemed like a hovel by comparison.

Before that blasted raid, Papa once sat him by their hearth and told him that their family name, Kazirian, meant "dragon of the moonless night," or "dragon of midnight." Like this night.

Like his deep blue hair and wings, the blessing of Varenox, God of Dragons and God of Fates. Agni, dragon of this night, felt the night, without a voice, whisper his name. His heart fluttered and his palms glistened with excitement.

A crude line of river shales, weathered by decades of wind and rain, marked that fateful middle strut. Centuries of rainstorms had washed away blood from past executions—or mud, he could not tell—to a faint brown stain.

He held his breath and leaped across. Nothing happened, no guards, nor shriek of the condemned, not even a cricket. Only his thumping heart. *Has it all been a fable?* He smirked.

He tiptoed a few steps, then broke into a dead sprint until he reached the broad gate at the far end. Chest heaving, legs burning from exhaustion, he looked back west. The guardhouse's braziers looked like embers from that distance.

The Ancients carved the gate out of eastern granite and embedded it with gems of fireglass—*fireglass!*—that withstood the Scourge and two thousand years since. A beautiful, sculpted stallion stood over the gate alongside some ancient script. *What power must have poured forth from this gate!*

The double oaken doors, twenty feet high, were too massive for a team of oxen to move, yet one had been left ajar—just wide enough for a determined child. He took off the sackcloth and then slipped one wing, then a shoulder through.

Now the agonizing part; he gritted his teeth as his raw back scraped against splintered wood. Silver bolts of pain shot through his vision, followed by tears. He bit his lip to stop from screaming. But after what felt like eternity, he scraped through. He collapsed to his knees with a wave of nausea, though he had eaten nothing to vomit. The Dragon God was a god of deeds; if the temple priests spoke truth, he would reward Agni's daring and sacrifice with knowledge. Knowledge that even Emperor Taran's priests did not possess; only the ancient dead.

As the stinging faded, he rubbed the tears from his eyes. Pain gave way to puzzlement. The Ancient City did not respond to him. The voice did not speak. Had he just flayed his back for nothing?

But amazement took over when he took in the full vista. The main boulevard could fit eight carts side-by-side; the fountain was polished fireglass and stood taller than his manor house. He marveled at inns, smithies, apothecaries, just like his town—only larger. Even its hovels were made of stone, like Azectrai's finest manor houses.

Life had not been scorched as much as frozen in its tracks. Agni saw a suckling infant skeleton, collapsed against its mother's right arm; a potter who had dropped his now-shattered wares; a horse skull fallen into a preserved wooden trough. Even the dust stood still, his footfalls leaving little marks.

The city stood outside time.

But where were the shrieks of abominations, driven by hunger and rage? Had his tutors, his family, his priests deceived him? No, so many wise men and women could not agree on such details of a lie, nor keep every madman or fool out.

Unless the voice shielded him.

The great castle beckoned him. It rose like a crown atop the Ancient City, a monument of shadow and stone. Papa said emperors with his name once ruled from it. But if their name held power, like a dragon, how did they fall so far? If he lived before the Scourge, would he have grown up a prince, wearing silk rather than sackcloth, and eating fatted sows rather than bedding down with them?

The castle was as large as the Azectrai town common, with smoky-grey towers that pierced the sky. Its stout walls could repel any invader—that which wiped out the Ancient City did not mar their beauty. But there was no life, not even a crow circling overhead.

The raised castle gate dared him to enter. Where might the voice come from if not the seat of power itself? His upbringing warned him to turn back, but the voice pulled him forward. Agni walked in, past the looming towers, into the great hall.

Giant statues of men and dragons lined the corridor, casting long shadows in the faint starlight. Were the men his ancestors immortalized in stone? They looked powerful, venerable. But why were there statues of dragons? Their god, Varenox, did not take kindly to idol worship, certainly not of the beasts in his image.

Yet in this eerie world he felt a twinge of belonging. Here, he was not a worthless boy, like ale-addled Papa said as he whipped him. He imagined returning home brag to his best friend Balo and Mayor Goro of what he had seen. He would dare them to execute him, the boy to whom the Ancient City opened its heart. *Let them try.* He might die, but he would die special.

Ahead, the throne room stretched into shadow, the fireglass throne shimmering purple in the starlight. Behind it, three giant spires climbed skyward, their outlines jagged against the darkness. A chill coursed down his spine—whomever sat there ruled the Dragonlands, half the Mortal Realms. The throne pulsed with power.

He touched the seat; it felt warm, smooth, alive even. He scrambled up, his muddy boots slipping three times. But he had come too far not to sit on it. With a pant, he pulled himself up by the armrests. Once he mounted the throne, he pretended to command a legion.

"Form up! Attack! Defend the empire!" he shouted, echoing throughout the great hall. And he laughed. The immense space around him swallowed the sound, so he yelled even louder. He felt like the emperor who once sat there.

He spread his wings and stood on the armrests, reaching towards the stars. No wonder they never let anyone cross the bridge; this was his birthright! *Let Papa keep the leaky barn and the dirty pigs.* This home was fit for the dragons of the moonless night.

Light flickered at the edge of his vision. No sooner than he turned did he hear a resounding chime. A great marble staircase appeared before him, descending into the depths of the castle. A faint azure glow—like the breath of a dragon—beckoned.

*Never silent. Never silent.* The voice whispered into his heart again. Destiny. Dragons. Thrilled and terrified, he inched down the stairs.

The staircase seemed to spiral through the layers of time.

The first twenty were smooth and polished, gleaming in the light below; the next grew weathered and chipped, then finally cracked and crumbled, a descent through time, somehow free from the Scourge. The purple throne-light gave way to an azure light, like a dragon's breath or springtime thunder, from whatever lay at the bottom. A rhythmic sound, like the stomping of a hundred feet and the ringing of steel, filtered up the stairs. It sounded like a mass of knights, the thudding of boots and the clangor of armor. His thrill grew stronger.

He descended the last steps into a great chamber, half the size of the throne room and bright as twilight. Great smoky forms of men had lined up along the side. Lifelike ghosts, wielding weapons and wearing steel plate, marched in place.

As he took the last step, they raised their weapons in salute to a frail boy.

*Zaka tai! Ar Kazi go fali chai!*
*Zaka tai! Ar shai hana mokli muai.*
*Zaka tai! Kazirian azakh fa jai!*

Agni gasped in shock. His eyes widened. He knew the Kazian tongue to sound sharp, but this was hoary, jagged, draconic—ancient. Yet every word imprinted on his heart.

The translation leeched its intensity but resembled: "No one stands in our way, as we raise the dragon on high, let our enemies look into our eyes and see a thousand curses. Let the great Kazirian lead us to the skies!" For the first time, he heard his name spoken in awe. A word of power. But what did that mean, to lead an army to the skies?

A marble slab sat at the far end of the chamber, bearing a relief of his family's blue dragon-rampant crest on a tower. The ghosts raised their swords in salute as he walked past. He turned his head but saw no other exit. He stopped before the slab and waited. Nothing happened. Another minute. Nothing happened, the shadows kept marching and chanting his family name. How could the voice lead him here, but not speak?

With an angry grunt, Agni kicked the slab. He jumped as a voice answered. *"Agni, please do not kick."* The deep baritone resonated in his mind. Comforting yet commanding. *What? Papa's voice sounded like that before the drink ravaged his throat.*

Agni stood frozen as vapors swirled in front of the slab. Slowly, they coalesced into the form of a man—tall and broad, with flowing black hair and glistening black wings. His silver breastplate and broadsword glowed with the electric blue of this chamber.

The form placed an ethereal hand on Agni's shoulder. He felt no weight, but a warm pulse radiated through his body and essence. He felt rapture, at one with the ghosts and the stones of the castle. Words of ecstatic worship poured out in the ancient tongue.

*"Blessed Ancestor, your will be done."*

*"Brave, shrewd Agni. It was I who summoned you. I am Anton Kazirian, Emperor of Great Kazia, last child of the Dragon God. You are safe here."*

Agni remembered that whispered legend from his tutors, more myth than man. He would have prostrated himself, had he not felt rooted where he stood. *Safe here. And nowhere else.*

*"Tales of your deeds will ring, even after the stones of this castle crumble."*

*"Agni. My son. For two thousand years have I pained for one worthy man—or it were, boy—to breach these walls."*

Anton's voice radiated power and sorrow.

Agni's mouth grew dry, his mind racing. Two thousand years? The Feast of the Harvest lay a moon and a half away, followed by his ninth name day a fortnight and some later. It felt like an epoch would grind away before his tenth. Two thousand lay beyond comprehension.

His voice trembled as he finally found words.

*"What are you? You are not an undead abomination, yet I sense that you no longer live."*

*"You are correct. A man lives no more than a hundred years. The undead rise under the power of the Netherworld. More than just living and undead walk among us. I am what you see, Agni. A spirit. Lord of a ruin. Fit for neither the Lands Beyond of the virtuous or the Netherworld of the condemned. But I too was a man, and before that, a boy like yourself."*

Agni blinked, fighting a wave of sadness. Anton said he was once a boy. But what a boy Anton must have been. A prince, with retinues of servants, groomed for that throne above.

*"Why this boy? Why am I worthy? Why this night? I am a sickly child, a dishonor to my line fit to sleep with sows. I eat once every four days—see, my elbow bones bulge beneath my skin. You could snuff my life with a thought. Our name means little outside these walls. My mother's bones molder in the ground; my father has squandered our wealth. Where does the mighty maw of Varenox intervene?"*

Anton smiled, a fatherly warmth in his expression.

*"A curious boy. From this ruin, I can do little but watch over the Mortal Realms. For two thousand years, I have watched our line crumble, eroded by time and misfortune. Your pain cried out to me. I summoned you, boy, because the God of Dragons fated you to die in obscurity this night. And I would not accept that."*

The words struck Agni like a thunderbolt.

*"Fated to die?"* He gasped in horror.

*"I—I do not understand, ancestor. Why would a god kill a boy?"*

Anton bowed his head.

*"The gods see not mortal notions of mercy, Agni. Once, the gods bore children with great destinies. I was born to unite the fractious Dragonlands and rule them for a thousand years. I did so, but with prosperity and abundance, our people fell into depravity. They enslaved and stole from one another; but worst, they forgot our god and worshipped statues of the beasts whose features we bear. I could not stop it.*

*"I pleaded for my father to return us to his grace. But his heart was hard, and instead he brought the Scourge—the wrath of the Netherworld—upon the Mortal Realms. It destroyed our learning; it slew our leaders and scholars. Bereft of our greatest, the Dragonlands broke apart. Grieving, I sought the release of death, but he would not grant it. He left me as what you see."*

Anton's face twisted into a snarl that showed millennia of boiling rage.

*"For two thousand years, he has battered our line; tonight, he would end it."*

His voice rose to a bellow.

*"For that, I curse him forever!"*

Agni shuddered at seeing this side of his ancestor. The shriek of pain unseen in the Mortal Realms. His lip quivered and a tear ran down his face. Fated to die, by the god of his people, the god of destiny, the god his family celebrated and bowed before.

*"That is horrible, ancestor."*

Anton's voice dropped to the comforting calm Agni had accustomed to.

*"But boy, you have already proven your worth. You defied the Dragon God's will this night when you crossed the bridge. The courage of a famished boy to face two horrible deaths and question an emperor. That is the Kazirian blood within you."*

Agni's chest swelled with a strange, fierce pride. A fire burned in his heart. *Chosen,* of a being he might never be able to understand.

*"I thank you. But... why do you tell me this?"*

The words felt scant coming off his lips. Gods. Curses. Spirits.

In return, the awesome spirit laughed.

*"That throne you climbed upon."* Agni blushed at the reminder of his own insolence. *"From it, I will rule Great Kazia—the Jewel of Eternity—for my promised reign. With you, my scion, at my side. Then when my time has passed, my father will be forced to hold me dear as a father should. To once again call me his son and his pride. And then, you shall reign for a thousand years."*

*"What?"*

Half exclamation, the question burst from his stunned heart. What Anton promised lay beyond his comprehension, to rule the quarreling lands of Blevenia and Solantia together. His battered homeland would be the beating heart of power. Anton spoke with such sincerity that Agni could allow himself a vision. A land where no father could starve his boy. Where he could personally strike down every raider. Where curious children and animals could frolic in the streets of the Ancient City.

*"That fireglass throne and spires. Were you of unworthy blood, they would sit silent. But no man is birthed with the prowess to rule. For one thousand years, you will learn the art. We will guide the Mortal Realms from darkness into light. In time, your legacy may eclipse my own."*

Darkness into light. What darkness his troubled land knew. And from it, Agni, Emperor of Kazia, astride the Mortal Realms. But why him?

*"But you could have chosen any great lord or priest from the eighty generations that separate us. I sense your power, but you are not a god. How could I survive one day when a god wishes me dead?"*

*"Ours is the god of fate, even the roc-people of Avicia and the orca-people of Tarka and the tiger-people of Aloi acknowledge that. But if fate is a loom, and Varenox chooses the thread, then we cast the shuttle."*

*"I am no weaver's son. I do not understand your riddle."*

The shade flashed a disarming smile.

*"You have already cast the shuttle, tonight. The Dragon God, like his element of lightning, is fickle. You may feel when his thunder is set to strike. You can stand still and accept doom; some of his most faithful seek it in the mountain storms. They call it the Ritual of Ascension and say that it resurrects them at his side. Or you can defy it."*

Agni shuddered. Would he have walked into the night, knowing he would step into a war between a shade and his god? He had stepped into something that might quake Emperor Taran Solant himself. He shook his head.

*"Agni, you chose to heed my call. Even now, I do not hold you fast. You may return to your family's barn and accept fate. Or heed me—I will gift you the wisdom of ages. I will sculpt you into a mighty warrior, a regent, and one day, an emperor. Which will you choose?"*

*"What?"*

Agni tried to speak, but no words escaped his lips. On his darkest night, how could he choose anything—let alone death— over power beyond his comprehension? He bowed his head.

*"Forgive me, ancestor, but hours ago, you were a folktale. Now, you offer me power that dwarfs Emperor Taran's. How do I know you can fulfill your promise?"*

He expected Anton to scowl or berate him—like Papa would—but instead, Anton smiled. Like a father should.

*"I will offer you a sign. Before the sun sets again, you will see how you have defied fate. Do you know what your name means, Agni?"*

*"It means 'living flame' or 'he who burns inside,' Mama said. But the temple priests say it is an ill omen."*

Anton's lips curved into a small smile.

*"In another land, it is the name of a god, he who carries the offerings of the faithful to their heavens. But in any land, a flame transforms all it touches. It burns, yes, but it also lights the way."*

*"Then what will I burn?"* Agni asked in a whisper. The weight of destiny felt heavy.

The azure light in the chamber intensified, reflecting off Anton's armor. A silver mist swirled around Anton's outstretched left hand, materializing into a magnificent sword. The cross-guard, shaped like a dragon's mouth, seemed to exhale the blade like lightning. It thrummed with power.

*"My blade is now yours, Agni. Wield it with the honor of the Empire Kazia."*

Agni hesitated as the sword floated towards him, seemingly daring him to grasp it. Slowly, he reached out and wrapped his trembling fingers around the hilt. The instant it closed, a wave of energy surged through him. The power of ages, of a dragon's breath, awakening something within him.

While lost in his reverie, he caught a foul stench. Something stirred behind him. *A wight!* A rotted, animated corpse animated by nether magic, and the death of any stripling boy who would fight it. He fought the scream in his throat. Then, Anton spoke.

*"It is a sword, the same as your father's. Test its power."*

The undead screamed defiance, maggots falling from its outstretched arms.

*"Strike!"*

Agni drew the sword back with both hands and slashed its right leg. To his surprise, it not only sliced through as easily as air but burned six inches of flesh on either side. The abomination wailed and fell to the ground, crawling towards him, extending a rotten hand. Agni brought it down on the abomination's head. The body burned to fine dust in the same azure flame.

*"This is incredible. The mothers of Azectrai tell of abominations to frighten children."*

*"By what remains of my power, I hold these creatures of the Scourge at bay for you. They would devour or corrupt any who intrude. But not you, my son. Though this city was bathed in the Netherworld, it will shine once more as the splendor of the Mortal Realms. You were born to awaken what has slumbered for an age."*

Agni swallowed, feeling the doubts again.

*"Ancestor—father—but now Kazia is the name given to the poorest duchy of Solantia, the backward land of feral beasts."*

Anton hung his head. Agni could tell this stung him.

*"The Empire Kazia, the land of dragons, encompassed what you now call Blevenia and Solantia. You of this age do not part with names even when they wither."*

*"No, great one. A name carries power, and no beast carries power like a dragon."*

*"Yet no word of our harsh Kazian tongue, which mimics a dragon's cry, nor a man's scaled wing will stop a nighthunter in mid-dive. This was not always so."*

*"Mama said that was an old crone's tale."*

Anton smiled, even as Agni saw hurt in his eyes.

*"We rode them into battle and struck terror into northern invaders. Our mages harnessed the element of lightning, like a dragon's deadly breath. Before the Scourge, we shared knowledge and philosophy and loved one another as brothers."*

Agni's eyes widened. Dragons preferred stags and cows but would not hesitate to feast on an unaware man. He knew the town hall, the guardhouse, the city wall, and any manor worth defending had a ballista mounted on its roof, since no ordinary bow could pierce its scales.

*"Brothers? How can that be?"*

*"Scion. It is the birthright of those of the dragon to rule the Mortal Realms. Unlike the lesser beasts of other lands, dragons built a civilization, throughout what is now Solantia and Blevenia. Together, no army could stand against us. Listen."*

Agni stood, transfixed. For the next few hours, Agni stood spellbound as Anton regaled him with more tales of gods and dragons, blood and conquest, love and heroism—and especially of how Anton grew from a boy like him into an emperor. He felt like his name; his life meant something again. The town, Papa, and the pigs felt worlds away.

*"Not without reason, our dragon brethren faulted man for the Scourge that took their most eminent. They withdrew into the mountains; the nature of their society, we know not. Only that a man in a dragon's domain will perish. Curse our god who cleaved us apart."*

*"Ai, curse him."*

The words did not even catch in Agni's throat. Curse the god he prostrated himself to, for an ancient empire shrouded in myth. Anton's form wavered like a mirage, his voice echoing like in a cave.

*"Your path begins here, Agni, and ends on the throne above. Time will forge you, as fire tempers steel. For now, you must return to the world of life. The city sleeps, and the living must not find you here. This night is your secret. Bury the sword in the great river, and when the day of reckoning comes, you will reclaim it."*

Agni's heart lurched.

*"But why?"*

*"The blade's power is not meant for boys. It will call to you when you are ready to unlock it. Your mind will become your first weapon. Your limbs will thicken into a man's. Many will instruct you; learn from them."*

The sword throbbed in Agni's hands, as if it heard Agni's words, and it too would wait.

*"I will do as you say, Blessed Ancestor."*

Anton smiled faintly.

*"Already you speak with honor. One day, I will guide you in your dreams, in the deepest night, like our family name. I will show you visions beyond your comprehension, but you must embrace them, or they may drive you mad. Your path ends again, by my side, scion, as warlord, as regent, then emperor. In the due time of the Ancients. Let that be your first lesson on the nature of time."*

Agni just stared, unable to comprehend himself as anything more than a boy.

*"Agni Kazirian; the living flame; the dragon of the moonless night. You will light the night."*

Agni could say nothing more. Anton acted on a timeline of centuries, and he was an impatient boy. But he felt flush with power from this wondrous place.

*"I will learn, Blessed Ancestor."*

*"Now go. Your name sits on my heart, just as mine sits on yours. Live and wait in hope."*

The chamber dimmed, and the azure glow flickered as Anton's form sank back into the stone. The ghostly soldiers bowed in one last salute, then faded like smoke in the wind. The power and warmth of the room ebbed, leaving a chill that crept into Agni's bones, like the family larder. He realized he was once more a boy in the world of the condemned. Only the sword remained to light his path.

He pulled back his wings and dashed up the marble stairs, fighting the burning ache in his legs. The throne once again loomed in darkness. Agni cast one final glance at it, a shiver running down his spine. *My birthright, my destiny.* Past the statues of men and dragons, that would one day conquer the Mortal Realms as one.

The city stood silent as he retraced his steps. The mother and child, the fallen horse, the shattered pot. *One day I will see these streets teem with life.*

He took off his burlap sack and forced his body through the splintered gate. The splinters dug into his wounds. He felt his flesh tear further. He bit his lip so he could not scream; he could neither falter nor indulge the pain.

He emerged to find the bridge bathed in the faint light of dawn. His heart pounded as he approached the line of shales, the boundary between the living and the damned. A lone guard paced the foot of the bridge. His heart rose in his throat—even if the guard hung his head low, kicking river rocks, the other side of the bridge sloped back to the earth. And the eastern horizon was starting to lighten. If the guard looked up, he would see Agni standing there—and believe him corrupted by the cursed city. His wings ached; even a warrior would struggle to glide the distance.

He flattened himself to the ground and crawled over the line, like mountain scouts did to creep up on enemy sentries, grabbing a handful of shales. Anton's words echoed: *In the time of the Ancients. Patience.* He fought the urge to dash, or to leap and glide and risk falling into the river's fierce currents. The guard looked dull and exhausted; probably passing the time until he could return home to fresh porridge and a straw mattress.

After some minutes, the sun rose enough to shine into the guard's eyes, averting his gaze. Agni flattened himself against the north wall and threw a shale into the elms.

"What?" the guard said. He squinted into the elms.

Agni hurled a second stone, farther. *Lest this guard think it is only a rabbit.*

The guard followed the crack of the stone.

"Who's there?"

Agni took a final stone, grunting as he put his full strength into it.

"Come out, in the mayor's name!" the guard shouted, gripping his spear.

*Good, he will stay to investigate.* Now was his time. He clambered up to the railing, took two deep breaths and spread his wings. He coiled his legs and launched himself into the opposite trees.

Immediately, his wing muscles spasmed. With no food and no sleep, he had only willpower and memory of a night of glory to keep himself aloft. Did Anton really stay the Dragon God's fate? Or was his fate to plummet into the river? Now that he had something to live for, he strained to reach the bank. His wings shook from the effort.

Five feet from the bank, he could hold out no longer and splashed into a backwater. He gasped and lost his breath, but realized he was safe. He pulled himself over the bank and shook out his hair like a wet dog.

Now came the mundane concern of finding food. He could spear a trout and bring it to Balo's city house, where they would build a cooking fire. He knew Balo loved building fires, even if his mother would slap him for it.

The guard's voice rang out.

"Boy! What are you doing splashing about the river at this hour?"

Agni grunted and continued to cut curls of wood off a long branch. After the night's adventures, one city guard meant little next to Anton Kazirian.

"Boy, answer me!"

The guard prodded him between the shoulders with the butt of his spear. He winced but did not turn.

"Answer me, child, or I'll lash you myself!"

In one motion, Agni stood and spun around, sword at the ready. It vibrated in his hand. The guard jumped back with widened eyes.

"Gaah!"

Agni stared the guard down.

"I am preparing to fish, you brute."

"Where did you get a broadsword?"

Agni sighed. "From my father, Piro Kazirian. Now return to your post before he has your cock sliced off."

He spoke with his new father's confidence but substituted the name of that drunk who sired him.

"You are Lord Kazirian's son, Agni?"

"I just said he was my father," Agni said, drawing out the last word, *faaah-thurrrr*. "So that would make me his son."

"What would he say if we found you at the bridge at this hour?"

"Send a messenger and find out," Agni sassed.

The guard stopped speaking, as if pondering Agni's boldness.

"Catch your breakfast and wander home, Agni."

Agni heard the voice trail off. He knew the guard would do no such thing, lest he confess to the fear of a scrawny child.

Agni stepped into the river, his legs shaking with exhaustion. The sword still throbbed faintly in his hands. It reflected the light of the full dawn. He placed the sword on the bottom, covering it with a layer of sediment and gravel.

"I will see you again, my friend."

That morning, Agni speared a fat trout and roasted it on Balo's fire. They play-fought with sticks rather than mystic blades. By the time he returned to the manor house that afternoon, Piro's chamberlain was peeling off his father's boots and urine-soaked trousers. Father was in no condition to beat Agni for running off—again.

"Boy! Where were you? Did you see the barn? I thought you were cinders. Your father and I searched for you all morning. Did you not sleep here?"

The faithful steward, Agran, waved him to the barn. Or rather, what remained—half of it had burned to ash. He crawled over the fallen timbers and saw the sick black veins of a lightning strike where he slept. The sow had been charred to a blackened form. Agni's heart pounded as Anton's words returned to him. *You will see how you have defied fate.*

"I could not sleep."

Emperor Anton Kazirian had kept his word to a mere child.

He turned and walked toward the manor, his back straight, a smile of purpose on his face. For the first time in his life, he felt power—and a secret that would shake the Mortal Realms.

C H A P T E R   I

# *Justice*

Twenty years after that encounter in the Ancient City, Agni slipped into a dark dream. A billowing black cloud surrounded him like a blanket. Anton's familiar, ghostly figure appeared—the only thing Agni knew to be real.

*"Where am I, Blessed Ancestor?"*

*"Your body lays in a bedroll off the Median Road. But for a few moments, I brought your mind beyond the Mortal Realms. Only in this stillness can I answer."*

Agni felt little, his emotions dampened by the strange but comforting cloud.

*"Twenty years, and you have not stopped speaking in riddles."*

*"This is no riddle. Only now can I show you your world and your life, as the gods see it, as I see it, from the vantage of millennia."*

*"Why would you bestow this gift?"*

*"It is both a blessing and a curse. As one draws closer to the gods, one must forsake the realms of men."*

Closer to the gods and the reborn Empire Kazia. Mortals played their games of power, but only Agni knew the greater current that would sweep them up.

*"And why would you have me forsake the realms of men?"*

*"Because without the short-sightedness of men, you would rule from my throne. Mankind is ruled by the moment's passions; its hot heart and pride lead to misery. You would be wasted in the realms of men."*

Passion radiated from Anton's eyes.

*"Yet by your design, I am High General of the Empire of Solantia, your chosen land, and Lord Guardian of the East. From my boyhood dream, you crafted my purpose, to stand between Kazia and those who would do it harm. I know no other path."*

*"Remember, Agni, what you call Solantia, my chosen, and Blevenia, my accursed, are but constructs of mortal men. True peace will come when our empire subsumes them both. Our time to strike draws near."*

This sent a chill down Agni's spine, like an autumn gust off the Spires.

*"If we are wayward brethren and Great Kazia will encompass both, why have you allowed me to snare our mountain roads against raids?"*

*"My son, peace between brethren must come on Great Kazia's terms. Your snares will ensure that. But one day you will disarm them; your children shall tug on their ropes alongside Duke Harkon's grandchildren. Your dragon whistles will summon our sacred beast to frolic, not to kill. Our prodigal brethren of Blevenia will see the superiority of our ways. Today's fragile peace will pale against our glory."*

Another image pierced the darkness, a burning, bloody one.

*"You saw my sword—our sword—strike down their fathers and burn their lands. They, too, are a venerable people. They remember."*

*"Ai, scion, they do. But soon, they will count the cost as worthy."*

*"Until then, my heart is unquiet."*

*"You are a ship built for winter seas, Agni. You overcome. Too many of your grandfathers accepted their lot. Were you the man who*

*sired you, you would have mounted your mother's ravishers' heads on spikes, then burned their farms to ash. But it broke him. In truth, he died years before he stumbled into the river."*

Agni cringed, even through the darkness. He could only muster a simple word.

*"Mother…"*

The memory still stung. Anton said nothing for a minute.

*"She must watch you with joy from the Lands Beyond. You still burn bright. Soon I will bid you awaken. I command you: let not your flame diminish; let neither your arm nor your tongue grow dull. Protect your peace; just know that it will one day give way to greater."*

*"Blessed Ancestor, your ways are still strange to me. But as Lord Guardian, I will give my all for this fragile peace."*

*"Just know, one day the maw of Varenox will turn on you once more. Denial of a god is a continual act. Together, we will reshape that fate again; or alone, you will fall to it."*

*"You have guided me well. Your will be done, Blessed Ancestor."*

He felt the swirling blackness start to part. In place of numbed emotions, he felt a stirring in his limbs, a resolution to further the Ancient's will.

*"Now awaken, Lord Guardian."*

Agni felt his mind fall backwards and into his own body. He felt the bed of pine needles under his back and wings, and a blanket over his body. The first rays peeked over the horizon. Five minutes later, the chirping of robins stirred him.

———

Agni bolted upright and blinked his eyes twice. He tapped his face and chest; the strange daze of the dream still felt more real than his hide tent, two days east of Azectrai. On instinct, he reached for his sword—his most faithful companion—and steeled himself for the Mortal Realms and another day of inspecting garrisons. He tapped his legs twice before he regained enough sensation to don linen trousers and boots.

The sun crested the eastern Spires, casting beams of red light along its peaks. Crisp gusts rushed through the pines. He spread his wings and shook back his hair to take in the wind. He rubbed his muscles, still unnaturally relaxed after Anton's dream. His soldiers could sleep another hour while he performed his morning exercises, a throwback to simpler days. *The body disciplines the mind,* so the Solantian garrisons taught him.

He ran three miles up the mountain towards windswept peaks, near where the speaking stone relayed messages from one mountain to the next. For his first exercise, he grabbed a boulder and threw it overhead. Recover, lift, press, and throw again. He savored the strain in his shoulders and thighs. Next, he latched onto a sturdy overhead branch and pulled himself up to his chin thirty-four times—*three better than yesterday.* Then, five-minute rounds of shadow sparring with punches and kicks, gymnastics and calisthenics. The thin altitude air challenged him, but the tautness of his muscles made him feel alive and fierce, like a soldier should. *So many commanders neglect the basics of soldiery.*

Satisfied and dripping with sweat, he removed his trousers, found a mountain stream and splashed handfuls of icy water over his body, then wings, then head. His tiger-tribe lover had introduced the joy of bathing with soap, but he did not pack this luxury into the mountains. *Sweet Kali,* he thought, *I miss your touch,* he thought.

Then, a high voice intruded upon his peace. He grunted.

"Lord Guardian! Lord Guardian!"

A ragged boy who appeared no more than eight years dashed down the rocky incline, wings pulled back in a sprint. Judging from the dirty blotches on his tunic and dirt-smudged cheeks, he must have spent several nights at the watch point.

"Yes?"

*What is this stripling boy doing at a watch point?* Agni thought. *He should be throwing rocks on the common.*

"We had intruders!"

Agni, still unclothed, stared up and knitted his brow. He wondered, was this a misunderstanding, or did some brash young raiders test the still-fragile peace? He rose to his full height, ignoring the prickle of frost on his feet.

The boy snapped into a rigid salute, wings twitching like a restless crow's.

"What is your name, boy?" Agni crouched down to look the boy in the eyes.

"Qualo, sir."

The boy's lower lip trembled like a leaf, but he spoke with pride.

"Qualo, what do you mean 'had' intruders? Where? How many? Were they armored? What crest did they bear? In what direction did they ride? At what pace? What are the trail conditions?"

"I-I don't know, sir. My brother sent me to report at once, but I did not know the Lord Kazirian made camp there."

Forgetting his annoyance, Agni felt a slight smile pull at his lips. He had not expected an innocent boy's excitement at sentry duty. How many soldiers grumbled about it when they thought Agni stood out of earshot?

"Qualo." Agni softened his tone, knowing the near-mythical Lord Guardian stood opposite an eager child, not a recalcitrant sentry. He placed a hand on the boy's bony shoulder, nearly engulfing it.

"When you relay such a message to your commanding officer, you ask those questions. Your brother sits at a stone half a mile up, but next time he might mount you on a horse and send you to a captain half a day's ride where a stone cannot reach."

"Yes, I will, sir!" Qualo sprang into another salute.

"How old are you, Qualo?"

"Ten years, Lord Guardian."

He puffed out his chest.

*Ten.* That was the year that Agni pestered the Solantian garrison to train him in the sword and fist. For a moment, he remembered his longing for an older brother to whisk him into the Spires and away from his father's wine-soaked rages. The boy looked eight at best; he must not have eaten well for years.

"You have spirit to spend your days here, Qualo. Let us not keep your brother waiting. And let me not meet him with my arse out."

Qualo laughed. Agni slipped back into his trousers, and they began the trek to the peak. Judging by his shabby tunic, Qualo was a field worker's son, or at best, a craftsman's. He scratched at his shoulder-length hair. It looked tangled and full of fleas. His wings looked mite-bitten. Agni could walk briskly while Qualo had to jog to keep up.

"Qualo. Are you from Azectrai? How long have you and your brother been in these mountains?"

"Yes, I am, and ten days, sir."

"Like you, I rode these paths at ten years. Only, we had no stones and no snares, and Blevenia claimed these trails for their own. We learned how to spot riders from afar, by the movement of sparrows. How to make pace along rocky trails. And even how to lure bears and mountain leopards to Blevenian campsites. Learn the land well; you never know when it might serve you."

"But aren't you a manor lord? I live out here because I must."

"Wealth did not shield me from my father's fists. If I had not spent my days out here, his blows might have left me the town imbecile."

"I cannot imagine the Lord Guardian fearing any creature."

Agni chuckled right back, decades distant from fearing his father.

"Fathers are supposed to protect their children from their fears. Boys lose innocence when they realize their father cannot. Or will not."

"My father died a year ago, Lord Guardian," the boy confided with a downcast head. "He fell from his horse and his head struck a stone. My mother occasionally washes for a lord. But mostly, she works the taverns."

"Works the taverns?"

*Poor lad.* Agni understood what he meant.

"*Ai.* That's what she tells me. Some mornings she only returns with a couple credits. Or bruises on her face and chest and can't work the next night."

Agni cringed; he felt for the boy. He and his brother would have to split one man's rations of dried pork and hardtack and forage the rest. And there was little to forage at this height—Agni's arms were thicker than Qualo's thighs.

"Is she beautiful?"

"Yes, Lord Guardian, more than any friend's mama."

Agni sighed between breaths. He saw a spark in this boy. Pups like him grew into strong wolves.

"Listen, boy. Thank Varenox that your mother still lives. When you return to the town, you and she are to come to my city house, at the corner of East Street and Knight Lane, at the fifth hour past noon. My manor produces the finest bacon in Kazia, and my cook, Dona, prepares it like none other. We can use another maid."

"A maid? For Lady Kali? Mama told me she sings of faraway Aloi at the Potter's Lane Tavern."

Agni chuckled. "No, for Lady Sara, the Duchess."

Qualo's ears perked like he could not believe such a high noble existed, let alone lived in his home.

"Mama can serve a duchess?"

"Yes, one of her maids caught the river fever. She will be bedridden for a moon or two, and her joints will swell two more after that. In the meantime, your mother will have fine perfumes and silks with which to dress her."

"But Mama said Her Grace called her a nasty name at the tavern and struck her on the cheek. What is a str… strump… strumpet?"

Agni laughed. Qualo had five years to learn the ways of women and might never learn those of nobility. The latter still mystified him, a minor lord by birth and a commander of a decade. He felt a twinge of pity—he knew Sara could never make a home in the provincial East, having known the splendor of the capital.

"Ladies do strange things when envious of one another. If your mother can pour the occasional cup of wine, or prepare her wardrobe, she will earn her way into Sara's—Her Grace's—heart."

Qualo looked taken aback.

"That's kind, Lord Guardian. But why would you aid me?"

The two could now see the summit. Agni stopped and placed his hands on Qualo's shoulders. He thought, *poor boy, subsisting on half-rations that could not grow him.*

"You are a curious boy, Qualo. The youngest in my command, though we have no record of you. Emperor Taran asks much from Kazia and wishes that none that would shed blood for the land go hungry. It is his command—and mine—to uplift our people as brothers."

"Have you ever met His Imperial Majesty?"

He closed his eyes and let the memory flood back. How could he describe meeting the emperor to a boy who might never travel west of Azectrai? The emperor stood six-four, almost half a head taller than Agni, with the hard gaze of a man who had felt enough pain for three lifetimes but refused to crumble.

"I prostrated myself to him when he declared fulfilled my mission as High General of Solantia and anointed me Lord

Guardian of the East. But even in his age, I could see kindness and strength in his eyes. Noble is the man who can act in both."

Qualo's eyes widened. It might be a farfetched dream to him, but Agni could still feel the chill down his spine.

"Prostr—what?"

"Lay on my belly before him. The mark of deepest respect. Now let us do our duty to him, Qualo, and learn the nature of these intruders."

The speaking stone, a foot of granite polished to a mirror sheen, stood on a hewn pillar at the apex. It gleamed red in the sunrise. Next to it stood a crude hut—a wattle-and-daub roof and walls over four stout wooden posts. The wind still whipped through it.

Three men, each wearing boiled leather jerkins, rushed out and raised a fist in salute.

"Hail, Lord Guardian!"

"At ease, men," Agni patted Qualo on the shoulder. "Qualo here tells me you caught news of intruders from the stone."

One stepped forward and blurted forth. Chin out, Qualo beamed at him.

"Three knights, crushed in one of your snares. They work, Lord Guardian, by Varenox they work! The Spires are safe. I heard the message, as sure as the winds."

"Calm, soldier. Where and when did this occur?"

"Half a day's ride to the east, not even an hour ago. They lie crushed."

Agni smiled; this news would please both the mayor and duke, whose treasuries funded his handiwork.

"What crest did they bear? You are sure they serve Blevenia?"

The lead sentry, who bore Qualo's features but looked several years older, glanced at his companions, "They bore the crest of boulders and stumps!"

They all laughed; Agni bit back his irritation.

"Enough, you jesters. Their crest, on their riding gear. If they ride under a Blevenian crest, then this is an act of war, and you shall see more crushed under boulders than you care to. Now answer me, what crest did they bear?"

Qualo's brother, chastened, bowed his head and wings.

"I beg the Lord Guardian's pardon. I received only voice from the next stone east. He told me little, but that they wore mail, and their hair was cropped. No self-respecting Solantian warrior would bob their hair in the Avician style."

Agni glared. He needed to know if these were errant fools, or a scout party that could rekindle the war's embers.

"They cropped their hair and wore mail. Therefore, they are knights sworn to a Blevenian duke, if not King Vardon. Are you certain? If they are, Duke Harkon will send an armed party in search of them."

"Yes, Lord Guardian. The sentry repeated that three times."

"I advise you, on pain of a day's wages forfeit, to ask further questions of the next sentry. As is, Duke Hauran—to whom we are all sworn—will need to know of this. How far in did they ride?"

"Thirty miles into the Spires. A morning's ride from base camp, sir."

Agni paused and looked up at the stone: his masterwork of the last two years, the magical stones that could send messages across peaks, communicating to manned snares with which boys could crush seasoned raiding parties. Snares did not eat, sleep, shit, take pay, or complain. His heart beat fast from his rapid ascent up the mountain, the excitement of potential conflict, and fear for his homeland. *Is Kazia more, or less, secure for this?*

He squared to the next youngest sentry, after Qualo.

"You."

The boy jerked backward, as if physically struck by the Lord Guardian's word, but recovered to salute.

"Sir!"

Agni smiled.

"Your name, boy?"

"Yali, sir."

"By my orders, all sentries must learn the history, as well as the practice of war. What have your superiors taught you about the incident that sparked the Black Moon War?"

The sentry inhaled deeply.

"Lord Guardian, ten years ago on the plateau north of here, six of Duke Harkon's knights, their retainers, and footmen crossed into the west to sortie against Kazian lords who refused to pay them the grain tax. A patrol of Kazian boys, led by the future Lord Guardian, set fire to the forest around them, burning them to death."

"And do you know why we ask that you learn this?"

"So we may learn the Lord Guardian's deeds?"

"No, so you may learn how mere boys, aided by the land, can fell several times their number. I am pleased, Yali. Ten extra credits when you rotate back to town." He turned from the now-beaming soldier to the rest. "Once, raids were so commonplace that my father's steward would budget for them. For the last two years, we have not seen a single lord brave these mountains. Now, one has. Do you see why this should chill all of us?"

One looked like he was about to pipe up, but Agni held a finger to silence him.

"No answer is needed. Today, from this lonely peak, for well or ill, you were our first line of defense. Now, you know that duty—and opportunity—may strike at any time. You performed your duty to Solantia, to Kazia, and to your Lord Guardian today. Be vigilant and man this stone until relieved."

"We will, sir. With our lives if necessary."

Agni looked deep into each of their eyes.

"We appreciate your zeal to serve the empire. Just know that you cannot serve us from the Lands Beyond. Now, I must return to my guards."

He patted Qualo on the wing.

"This one shall dine with my retinue today and return in two hours."

Qualo's eyes lit up.

"Thank you, Lord Guardian!"

"The next of you to show such merit will dine with us upon my return. Strength lies not just in the sword, but in the eye."

Agni raised a fist in salute—none so excited as Qualo—and they responded in kind.

"Hail, Lord Guardian!"

"Come along, Qualo."

Agni and Qualo wheeled for the long walk back to base camp.

———

As expected, when Agni arrived, his entourage was boasting of conquests in distant lands over honeyed biscuits and butter-fried bacon. He heard Qualo's breath catch as they caught the scent of roasting bacon. The boy lowered his shoulders into a sprint, but Agni's long, easy strides caught him.

"Calm, Qualo. You shall eat your fill. But men of rank eat first."

"Apologies, Lord Guardian."

*Poor boy,* Agni thought. *He must not have eaten bacon in several moons.*

"If your mama serves Her Grace well, you shall eat the best bacon in the valley."

Qualo just beamed, as if already savoring his share.

Below, three armored knights sat on logs around the cooking fire, probably laughing at some bawdy joke. A servant boy flipped thick strips of bacon in an iron griddle. That was his retinue except one, whose giant paw slapped Agni between the shoulder blades.

"You did not even flinch your wings, Lord Guardian," a deep voice sounded.

Agni grinned at his top bodyguard's voice.

"I know your greeting anywhere, from the burning fields of Blevenia to the rolling hills of Avicia, Alexander. And I know oxen stealthier than you."

"Though none more handsome."

"You have me there, my friend," Agni said, smiling.

"And who is our little visitor, today?"

Alexander patted Qualo on the head.

"I am Qualo, sir. My brother and I watch the stone at this peak."

Qualo's squeaky voice sounded even higher after Alexander's low bass.

"Do you, now. Can you fight, boy? Scout the land? You're quite young to ride this far into the mountains."

"My mother cannot feed all her boys on a tavern lady's wages. I came here with my brother to split rations and forage for fruit."

Alexander cast his eyes downwards. Agni knew the giant's heart to be larger than his thighs.

"I am sad to hear that, Qualo. But the Lord Guardian here does not bring every hungry boy to eat a knight's rations."

"You are not a knight, Alexander. A knight's rations are a third of yours."

Agni smiled and motioned them towards the fire, both he and Qualo in the shadow of Alexander's huge black wings. The half-Tarkan behemoth could devour a whole hog, given the opportunity. Agni ripped a piece of biscuit and savored the sweetness, handing the other half to Qualo, who devoured it so fast he nearly choked.

"Ay, Lord Guardian, who did you drag down from the mountaintop?" the eldest knight said.

Agni prodded Qualo on the wing.

"I'm Qualo, good sirs."

All the knights nodded while ripping at their breakfast.

"Now tell them how you found me."

Qualo looked at Agni as if pleading for help in delivering his message. Agni just stretched an arm out, like he was introducing a guest.

"I came to deliver a message to this camp but found the Lord Guardian bathing after morning exercises. The next stone warned my brother of enemy knights caught in a snare half a day east. Three of them, mailed and horsed, with short hair, crushed under boulders."

Agni chimed in. "And we shall ride east to make their acquaintance."

"Crushed under boulders, eh? Unfortunately, that saves us the pleasure," one beamed.

These hard men had fought with him on both sides of the Spires and in distant Avicia; he knew such men grew restless without combat.

"Calm, Lord Frazi. If they ride under a ducal banner, this portends more death to come," Agni replied.

"We have grown soft, eating these luxuries deep in the mountains." Frazi held up a torn biscuit.

"We have grown soft in any case. Two years since we fought proper soldiers in Blevenia and Avicia. Not even murderers hide in these peaks. But those days may be past. Varenox help us if the Black Moon rises again."

*Let neither your arm nor your tongue grow dull,* Agni thought. *Blessed Ancestor, is this what you meant?*

"Varenox crafted me to fight, not farm, Lord Guardian. We all filled our chests ransoming noble whelps back to their fathers. Now we grow fat and dull. I hope we can sell today's captives—or their corpses—back to their duke."

While he listened, Agni grabbed the last rasher and started to gnaw at it.

"We will dispose of them in the manner that best protects the peace, Frazi."

Frazi just grunted and picked at his beard.

"I was raised to fight, not farm."

Agni said nothing—battle might find them today. Instead, he caught Qualo in a slight frown, looking at the empty griddle.

"Something catch your eye, Qualo?"

"Uh, no, Lord Guardian."

"You wanted more bacon, did you not?"

As Qualo's face flushed red and his eyes turned downwards, Agni pressed his piece into Qualo's hand, closing Qualo's scrawny fingers around it.

"Take it, boy."

Qualo's eyebrows raised in surprise and his jaw dropped. "Wha—"

Agni patted Qualo on the wing. "Kazirian manor bacon spoils a man. Besides, you have worked these mountains without pay for some time. It is the emperor's justice—and the Lord Guardian's— that you eat your fill today."

*Justice,* Agni thought. *Justice would feed every boy off the soldiery's rolls.*

"Justice," Qualo repeated, as if pondering the word.

"It means to give everyone what they deserve, Qualo. When you return to Azectrai, add your name to the quartermaster's ledger. I will see you paid for your service."

"Thank you, thank you," Qualo replied.

"Now, run back to your fellows at the peak. The men and I need to ride east. In the meantime, keep a watchful eye. Lord Guardian's orders."

"Yes, sir!"

Qualo grinned and raised his right fist in salute before running off with his newfound enthusiasm. Agni and his men watched Qualo disappear up the trail and into the high pines with a long silence.

"Now, Alexander, aid me into my armor. I pray that no knights come to investigate their fellows."

*Justice may have a second face today,* Agni thought, *whether knights come or not.*

—

For the first three hours eastward, the clapping of hooves and idle chatter of his men blended into the background while Agni's mind raced at full gallop. *Kazirian. Dragon of the moonless night,* a night of power, but one of change and terror. Two identities warred within him—the Lord Guardian dealt in reason, but Kazians dealt in myth and magic, and their land suffused in both.

He strained to recall any armored Blevenian knights seen along this road in the last two years. *God of my people,* he prayed to the god who hated him, *let not a black moon shine.* The dark sky stirred the Mortal Realms.

But like a sweet vapor, another voice crept into Agni's mind. He knew it would come slowly in the noonday sun; but it demanded attention. Today, he welcomed it.

"Pause, riders," he called over his shoulder, "we have less than a quarter hour to go. Let me collect my thoughts."

He rode ahead thirty paces, reining back on his giant white destrier as he crested a hill, his hooves grinding into the rocky trail.

"Hold, Ark." He patted his big white stallion's flowing mane. *Arkama,* "white giant," he thought it fit him, for his presence as well as size. Ark acknowledged with his usual sputter.

The Voice of Ages grew thicker, pulling his focus inward. Tendrils of mist coalesced into the apparition of Anton Kazirian, wings spread, arms over his chest, and armored as if ready to battle.

In whatever plane he lay, Anton's hair fluttered in an unseen breeze. His lips moved, but the voice sounded in Agni's mind.

"*Scion,*" Anton began, words laden with reproach, "*you still pray to the god that loathes us. Do you believe you can pray our way into his favor?*"

"*No, but it calms me.*"

"*Then let this calm you, Agni. You slept under half a moon last night. I do not see your blade striking in wrath today.*"

"*Only the Chosen of Varenox see what is to come.*"

"*I need no prophecy to see the follies of mortal men. Blevenian and Solantian, their paths are predictable. I have seen empires rise and crumble from the vantage of eternity.*"

Anton's voice sounded peeved, but Agni knew that Anton had seen empires grow and crumble. A scholar of two thousand years.

"*If I will not draw my blade, why do you appear to me? I need no guidance to police even knightly cripples.*"

A deep, resonant laugh echoed through the corners of Agni's mind.

"*I said it will not strike in wrath, not that it will not strike.*" Anton's wings flared, radiating the command he carried in life.

"*It represents our might, our majesty. Your drunken sheriff can police. You came to parley, like you did with King Theodore of Avicia. And our sword carries fear. The fear of ages. They will know it by sight, and by word.*"

Agni's fingers brushed against the hilt. It throbbed warm on his hip. Its glow cut through will as easily as flesh. How much blood had it spilled, how many noble lines it had extinguished.

"*It is not needed, Blessed Ancestor. They have nothing to parley with. These roads are lined with thickets of death. Their crushed limbs will deter their duke.*"

Anton laughed again.

*"They know our thickets, boy, but they wish to leave as the Lord Guardian's equals. In ten days, they will tipple their wine in Duke Harkon's hall and boast of how they, bereft of their sword arms, faced the Lord Guardian without fear. Rats, all of them. This passes for bravery in the East. Brand them such that their faces speak your message—that the Spires are ours—and that the Kazirian take personal notice."*

Agni's stomach tightened.

*"You ruled a different era. Is that honorable, ancestor? To scar helpless men?"*

Anton's lips curled back like a dragon's snarl.

*"Bah. When we restore the Empire Kazia, you will learn that the nature of men changes not with the era. Neither does the nature of rats. How would a dragon answer a rat's challenge?"*

Anton's will surged into Agni's mind. The scent of burning flesh, of knights cowering at his feet, their branded flesh singing of the Lord Guardian's wrath. *Rats.* The word swept over him like the Great River's current, pulling him deep.

*"Rats are beneath blade or arrow. But they can scurry into crevices that a dragon cannot."*

*"Very good, young Kazirian. Deal with them as an emperor would."*

Anton's phrase branded itself on Agni as his image faded.

*Rats in a trap. They are rats in a trap.*

A voice from the Mortal Realms broke his trance. "Lord Guardian, are you well? You stopped on the trail and mumbled something about rats."

Agni's face flushed as he shook off the chill he always experienced after an encounter with Anton. *What escaped my lips?* No one, not even Alexander, knew Anton as more than history. He recomposed himself and smiled at his retinue.

"Rats. Rats. We have a nest of them."

*Rats must feel fear; let them see the dragon.*

At midday, Agni stood at the edge of a shattered pass. The rockfall, carefully set into the cliffs above, crushed the intruders where they had stood. Splintered stumps, jagged boulders, and pools of blood told the tale. Beneath the fall lay boots and hooves—what remained of three men, jerking like half-squashed earthworms in the rain. Atop them, two footmen taunted and kicked at the boots sticking out of the wreckage.

"Ride behind me. Wedge formation."

He motioned back to Alexander. While his chestnut warhorse could have been Ark's brother, he looked like a pony beneath the giant's muscles and fireglass-black wings. Agni stared down the ridge and beamed.

"Alexander, it appears we snared some rats, and our relay of speaking stones brought the word to last night's camp. Let this be known as the day we secured the last of the Spires. Let Kazia rejoice."

Alexander's deep voice rang back, somber.

"Indeed. If peasant boys can work your web, then engineers, not knights, will secure the land. Would fighting men lose who we are in peacetime? Even boys can deal the mercy blow to maimed knights."

"*Na*, Alexander, this is not peacetime. Knights in the Spires have no peace in their hearts. We will brand them and free them to tell their brothers-in-arms. I would that they ride to every manor and hamlet ten days' ride from the Spires. It will save us the bother."

He heard Alexander sigh.

"Agni, is that justice? The snares have already maimed them. They bear your mark."

Agni stared thunder through his subordinate.

"You will address me as Lord Guardian while in formation. And as your commander, I order you not to leave enemy knights fit to regroup and strike. We will free the rats, but none leaves this trail fit to point a sword westward, if we must sever their fingers ourselves. That is justice."

Sever their fingers—*and brand their faces.* They would suffer in shame. Agni forced feelings of admiration for his captain's honor and decency. *But commanders—and emperors—must commit lesser cruelties to prevent greater ones.*

With the midmorning sun reflecting off his armor, it was time to announce his presence. Agni flared his broad blue wings and drew his blade; time to look the avatar of war.

"Soldiers!"

The footmen whirled.

"Hail, Lord Guardian," they shouted back, fists raised in salute and wings pulled back.

"Guards, ride down."

"Yes, Lord Guardian," they replied in unison.

The footmen looked like twin brothers, earth-flecked from crown to leathers to boot, each leaning on their spears. They grinned like troublemaking children. They looked even rougher than the sentries at the summit, possibly conscripts from south of Azectrai sent to fulfill some manor knight's obligation.

*New to war, new to blood. Let them see it.*

Agni rode Ark near a boulder, dark gray and streaked with gore. Beneath it lay a man's caved-in ribcage, his tunic so blood-drenched that Agni could not identify its original color.

One footman stomped on a victim's stray hand. The owner of said hand screamed. Quick as a flash, Agni struck the footman's shoulder with the flat of his blade, drawing a yelp. A puff of mystic smoke rose from where the sword met leather.

"Behave, you brat! You wear Emperor Taran Solant's crest!"

Chastened, the footman bowed his head and lowered his wings.

A peeved Agni turned to the second footman and pointed with his sword.

"You. Tell us what happened."

The second footman held up a length of severed rope.

"Lord Kazirian, by Varenox's eyes, it worked! Tono—my fool brother, there—spotted four knights riding down this canyon. I nicked the rope, and our wrath tumbled down upon them. They squealed like wounded boars. Three of them lie here crushed, and the fourth—a boulder threw him and his horse clear over the side."

"Calm, boy. Of course, the snare worked; the best engineers in the Empire designed it."

Agni looked over the precipice—a sheer fifty-foot fall to the tops of the elms below, thirty more to the ground. At best, the fall crushed their chests; at worst, they would feed a dragon and her brood, slowly.

Agni dismounted Ark, slowly swinging one leg then the other over the giant destrier, who snorted and stomped. The watchful Alexander rode behind him.

Agni cringed as he saw two maimed horses—handsome destriers, too—their hindquarters crushed, bones poking through their hide, their forelegs swinging at air. The third must have run off. *Poor beasts, victims of their owners' recklessness.*

One knight lay still, his head and helm crushed. One lay unconscious, head intact but his hip crushed. Agni thought he saw an arm twitch. The last, pinned down by his forearm and wing, looked older and vigorous, perhaps forty-five years, with blue hair cropped in the Terceran style that Blevenian nobles saw fashionable. His surcoat bore three mountain leopards rampant.

"How long have these intruders lay here?"

"Since the dawn. Four hours?"

He turned to Alexander.

"They chose quite the morning ride, this deep into the Spires," Agni spat.

Alexander kept his face still.

Four hours. The leader would lose his arm at the elbow or gangrene and fever would set in. The land itself—at Agni's command—struck him down.

Agni licked his lips, then turned to the fallen man. He wheezed several times.

"And you."

The knight wheezed twice and spat blood towards Agni, but it only dribbled down his jaw.

"Well met, Desolator," he rasped.

Agni felt a laugh in his throat.

"You are addressing the Lord Guardian of these mountains, knight, and will give your name, your lord, and the purpose of your intrusion into His Imperial Majesty's lands."

Chest heaving, the pinned man responded between gasps. "I am Jeron, knight of Blevenia, sworn to Duke Harkon. We did not ride under a banner of war. We came to map your snares, the weapon of cowards."

Tono cut in. "Liar! They came to rape Kazian women and pillage our wheat fields! Let's douse them in oil and set them ablaze!"

"Silence!" Alexander shouted.

Agni ignored them. But was the boy right, that this devoted elder knight came to pillage across the mountains? Images of his mother, slain by a gray-haired Blevenian knight, flashed before his mind. They would never fade.

"Cowards?" Agni drew his blade, feeling it pulse with power. "Warriors who refuse to protect their land are cowards. Any merchant to whom we permit passage could tell you that we snared these roads, and only with our escort could they pass. And even were that not so, commanders send peasant boys to scout trails, not," Agni's boot prodded at Jeron's torn chain, "mailed knights. Does your lord test our resolve a mere two years after he surrendered the whole of the Spires?"

Jeron growled again.

"Desolator, we blasted well know your treaty, written in the blood and tears of our kingdom—"

Agni held a hand up to silence him.

"Jeron, you and every other lord of Western Blevenia know that Duke Harkon surrendered the whole of the Spires—from where the hills stand higher than a stallion's head—to the Emperor of Solantia, for the care of his governor, Duke Hauran of Kazia, in the treaty that ended the Black Moon War. What is Duke Harkon's interest in these peaks that yield neither grain nor iron? Does he want a mountain leopard cub for his next festival? Or does he wish to test our resolve? I assure you we will beat you back until the Spires crumble to dust."

Jeron snarled again. Agni allowed a flash of admiration—even maimed, Jeron did not break.

"If the Lord Guardian would let me finish. Do you believe the only marauders in these mountains cross east-to-west? Your own knights sortie eastward to ravish and burn, then hide behind these snares. You, too, have noble blood. If you were my lord, would you let this go unanswered? We know what set you on the path of war, how a raid on your homestead turned the son of a minor lord into the Desolator. Did you believe we would not answer? I assure you, after the war, Duke Harkon would cast any raider off his tallest tower."

*Brand them.* Anton's words clanged in his mind; the vantage of eternity, from a time when cruelty united the Dragonlands. *He will do the Lord Guardian's bidding in body and mind.*

"This is your answer, intruder."

Agni twirled his sword and flared his wings. It let out an angry hum.

Jeron's face twisted in terror.

"No! You would not—"

Agni pressed its flat to Jeron's right cheek. The knight's scream echoed through the pass, along with the hiss of searing flesh. *It smells like roasting ham.*

The footmen laughed again before Alexander raised a burly fist. Something rose in Agni's chest. An angry wind whipped down the trail, mimicking his mood.

Agni hissed.

"Lie to me not, Jeron. One more false word, and I press this blade to your tongue so that you may lie no more. Now, speak the truth of why you have ventured a half day into the Spires. If your sortie was not brazen nor stupid, it was both."

Jeron's voice rose in pitch.

"I obey my lord without question, Lord Guardian."

Agni watched tears form in Jeron's eyes. His lower lip trembled. Tono yelled something again, before his own brother placed his hand over his mouth. Alexander did not even flinch.

"Sir Jeron, you may never lift your sword arm again, indeed if it were not crushed, I would sever your last two fingers, but perhaps we can both win this day. Hear every word of what I am about to tell you, and pass it not only to your lord, but to any Blevenian who knows which end of a sword to stab with. But first, be a lord and collect yourself. Do not face your enemy blubbering like a boy."

Agni waited for Jeron to breathe deeply and calm himself. He squatted down, eyes starting knives through his enemy's, his own lips curled in a snarl.

"Since the day the King of Blevenia pleaded for peace, we have mined every Spire backtrail on which even a goat may pass. We will crush you with granite, impale you on spikes coated with horse shit so that you might die of lockjaw. Our flute-maker in Azectrai even designed what we call a 'dragon whistle,' a flute that mimics a dragon's mating call. Whether the randy beast slices you to ribbons or buggers you, you will be in no condition to progress. Do you understand, Jeron?"

"*Ai,* Lord Guardian."

"Our footmen will strike down their number in knights. Three men will wreck your convoys. Your boys will find neither fortune, nor adventure, nor maidens across these mountains. You are to mount a pig's skull at the trailhead from whence you came. Even imbeciles and children will understand that. And you will speak no more nonsense about Kazian raiders."

"But—"

Agni lowered his blade again, a foot from Jeron's face. This rat would burrow deep into the crevices of Western Blevenia. He pulled a knife out of his belt. Lifting the surcoat from Jeron's body, he sliced off the front portion with his mountain leopard crest. He held it inches from Jeron's face.

"This is now property of the Azectrai garrison. Within days, every soldier in my command will recognize it, with a five hundred credit bounty to any man who brings back a like crest. That will feed a soldier's family for two moons. Please tell Duke Harkon that the Lord Guardian was most merciful to let you walk away. You would do well to question such self-destructive orders. Will you do so?"

Agni watched Jeron's lip tremble again. He knew Sir Jeron was sworn to Duke Harkon, but Duke Harkon did not just brand his cheek.

"*Ai,* Lord Guardian."

Jeron finally looked broken.

Agni beckoned the footmen. "Retrieve your palfreys and lead these survivors back to the East."

Tono wrinkled his nose in displeasure. "Then who will—"

"Obey!" Agni shouted. "They now serve me as messengers. Should they walk back on their own, the next snare might end them before they can pass my message."

Agni turned to the other footman, "Go back to the stone outpost and saddle four horses. Pass the message back to Azectrai, to add a patrol along this span. No Blevenian knight should ride thirty miles into the Spires whole."

He saluted and ran off, presumably eager to outdo his mouthy brother with deeds. Let him instruct the other.

"And you three, pry the boulders from our distinguished guests."

For half an hour, the footmen disappeared, and Agni and his guards removed maple stumps and angular granite from the pile in silence. The giant lifted the largest boulder like a pebble.

"Alexander, leave that boulder on the trail side. Let it serve us again." Alexander heaved it downward, shaking the earth.

The other knights worked in silence, throwing bodies over the ridge so as not to stench up the trail.

Agni patted the mauled horses on their heads, then released them from their pain. As he did, he thought about what he brought that morning; opportunity to an eager boy, destruction to foolish knights, a chance to redeem himself to the last of them and now release these noble beasts who suffered for the latter's foolishness. All in these mountains out of duty.

*The justice of Kazia, great and small.*

C H A P T E R   2

# *Summon*

She dreamed of Father's last feast, of sweet honey cakes, crimson wine from Lesdran in the southwest and meaty fish from the cold northern waters of the Great Sea. What delicacies Father brought! She and Agni had sat arm-in-arm, wing-in-wing at Father's table, cackling at bawdy songs and swooning over tales of Agni's valor in distant Avicia and Blevenia.

Father had just commissioned her to the East with Agni for some moons—not just to embody the capital's devotion to the East, but to lead the Azectrai Valley's levy while Agni fortified the border. Even as a little girl, sums and ledger entries danced before her eyes, dazzling Father and his treasurers. Agni had spoken of Kazia as a lush land of history and dreams, and her heart had raced at the thought of living the noble life in the cradle of the Ancients. She could practice the arts of rule and return west with newfound skill, one step closer to ruling the capital duchy.

Then a rooster crowed.

Her Grace, Duchess Sara Ristana of Artania, rubbed the sleep from her eyes, realizing once again that she awoke one thousand miles from home. That Artanian goose feather bed was one of the few mementos she had of the capital, and the blessed life held out of her reach. She felt the pang of loss in her chest, real as a knife. The day would only crumble from here.

Her head thumped in rhythm with her heart. *How much did I drink?* she thought. She had resolved to limit it to three cups, until her lack of sleep forced a fourth. Was that the last? Or had she had another? A ray of harsh red light interrupted her self-flagellation, assaulting her eyes.

The rising sun cleared the horizon, and a shirtless Agni opened the shutters. He spread his wings and arched his back. His morning vigor felt like a taunt.

"Blast you, Agni, close those shutters," she spat.

Immediately, she regretted her harsh tone. Country folk awoke early, most to feed their stinking beasts, Agni to swing iron mauls and harden his body for a war that ended two years ago. Men like Agni created strife in the home when they could not find it on the battlefield.

Agni chuckled back.

"Do not sleep the day away."

She pulled the blanket over her face. Again, her mind flashed back to a happier time, when her noble father pressed her delicate hand into Agni's sword-callused one. She saw not just a dashing warrior—so unlike the soft boys at Father's court—but a lord whose eyes gazed into hers with awe and passion. For that moment, at least, she felt his kindness.

*A Kazian will wither in foreign lands like a yew in the desert,* so he told her. How could he not understand that this was her desert? Until that day Father would recall to the capital, that day's pot of wine would be her solace. She lapsed back into a blissful sleep.

Sometime later, the clatter of pots and ladles and the sharp sounds of spoken Kazian roused her again. Every word seemed to end in "ai" and "akh," and to her Western ear, that made every conversation sound like it would come to blows.

"What in blazes are you two screeching about?" she shouted.

Again, Sara regretted her harsh voice.

"Apologies, milady," Dona called meekly from below.

Agni huffed in response, and continued in their "screeching" language, his voice carrying upstairs. She thought she heard, "Sara is learning the Eastern tongue." Then, some unfamiliar phrase elicited a stifled laugh. Then, "Please prepare her a platter and retrieve a jar of cider; she has had a long night."

At least today, Agni showed some concern.

The front door creaked. One of her maids crept up the stairs, holding a fresh linen chemise and a shimmering white silk tunic. Wordlessly, she helped Sara out of her nightgown and into her day clothes before handing her the silver circlet of a duchess. She thanked her with a nod and descended the stairs.

"Apologies, Dona. I did not mean to speak so harshly," Sara said as the entered the kitchen.

Dona smiled, unfazed. Despite her hunched form, wispy hair, and mottled wings, the old woman radiated warmth. She treated Sara like her own daughter and not some stuck-up noble, unlike the other maids who grumbled when they thought Sara out of earshot. Perhaps they could put this morning's quibble aside.

Sara smiled and turned to Agni, who had picked up a rasher and torn off a piece with his back teeth, his lion-like mane shaking side-to-side.

"And this one should apologize for learning table manners from wolves," she quipped, forcing pleasantry into her voice.

Agni bared his teeth, flecks of bacon stuck between them.

"You would do well to learn from them, too. Unlike Her Grace, wolves prosper in this land."

Sara winced; that jab landed hard. Though Agni had never struck her with his hand, his words hit just as fierce.

"But you love wolves," she replied, her voice sharpening. "I had thought you would feel flattered by the comparison."

Agni slapped his palms on the table, the force rattling his pewter mug of cider.

"First, you insult our tongue, then you compare us to beasts. If you cannot embrace this land, at least hide your disdain for us. Your father sent you here to learn our ways."

Her face flushed. *Have I not tried for two years?* she thought. *Has he not seen my efforts?* Now, she wanted to land her own blow.

"As few moons as we will make our home here, it will not merit the trouble," she scoffed back. Even if neither she nor Agni knew how many moons—or years—they might stay.

Agni recoiled. He puffed out his chest and flared his wings, nearly knocking over ahis mug. His voice lowered to a growl.

"I have been chained for moons in rock hollows and slept in frozen Avician mud. I will find a way to prosper among swaggering peacocks if I must. You will bear Kazian children, and they will yearn for my home—the land of dragons," he huffed.

*Was this how it feels to cut down a foe in battle?* She felt the rush of scoring a blow, against his constant barbs that he and not she held power here.

"Yes, your bumpkin myths," she scoffed. "If I did not myself have the wings of a dragon, I would be sick to the back teeth of your prattle about them. Why my father saw fit to craft a low Borderland knight into a duke, I do not understand."

She braced for him to storm out, but instead, he threw back his head and laughed, open-mouthed. This unnerved her more than his anger.

"Dear, your father sent you here to keep this 'bumpkin land's' accounts, lest you spoil his own. Such that he raised armies from the Aloi borders to the southern coasts to shed blood for it. Your father did not betroth us to craft me into a duke; he did so to infuse the capital with Kazian blood. And I will, even if the thought of living in that damned palace makes me retch."

She dropped her own voice to a bitter growl.

"Then stay here with your tiger clan whore and come to the capital once a year to put a baby in my belly and keep the facade."

She saw Agni hold his smile.

"If only your father did not covet a Kazian puppet, I would accept that. But enough of this, love," Agni announced, mercifully ending the exchange. *Love?*

"You show affection strangely, Agni."

"I was speaking to Dona. I will eat my midday meal with my warriors and return for dinner."

Agni stormed upstairs, leaving Sara to stew in silence. *Every time we converse, it goes netherward so.* At least their destiny lay in her homeland, not his. Would Agni be the withering yew? Would he turn to drink and she to other men? She hated the way Agni's eyes softened when Kali's eyes met his, her easy charm and grace, and especially Kali's kindness towards her even as she raged inside. Taunting. Humiliating.

Chagrined, she bit into her own rasher. She would miss Dona's cooking. She fried the bacon to a perfect crisp. Perhaps Kazian merchants would bring manor bacon, along with summer apples, to the capital, the only fond reminders of Kazia at home.

She saw Dona had kept diligently at her work, retrieving water from the well and scrubbing pots. Sara felt lucky that Dona had no appetite for imperial politics; from these arguments alone, Dona must have known more gossip than any of Father's courtiers. Unlike Father, Agni surrounded them with simple folk whom they could take at their word.

With a sigh, she turned to the door and walked off to the keep, looking forward to the simple routine of the town's tax accounts. Even if Mayor Goro and his slob of a son stole glances at her tits.

—

The counting-house was a cold, cramped room in the undercroft of the town hall, lit and warmed only by torches in sconces, except for a rush of heat whenever the door to the upstairs hall creaked open.

Still, she found comfort there; in the order of the twice-yearly count, the fragile calm amidst the rancor of home. Clerks rolled out their counting cloths, dutifully opening padlocked chests from every manor lord in the Borderlands. They placed gold hundred-credit pieces, silver tens, and copper ones in rows on checker cloth for her to record on parchment rolls. In two days, she would present her sums to Mayor Goro, and in several more, an armored convoy would shuttle the chest to Eltrazan, provincial capital of Kazia, and sometime later, to the imperial capital of Artania. One day, she imagined herself settling accounts for the capital lands, the weight of rule balanced in her ledger.

A clerk waved her over to his table, with rows of coins neatly arrayed on a checkerboard cloth. "Your Grace, from the manor of Lord Kolu Kazinata, the sum of seventeen thousand, six hundred and fifty-three credits."

Sara checked her rolls and beamed back at the boy.

"That is a quarter above his levy from this time last year, and ten per hundred above the spring levy."

"Yes, his wool trade and summer orchards have blossomed."

"Very good. I know him to be an honest man. I will record this."

"A pleasure to serve you, Your Grace."

Sara put down her scroll, procured a quill, and recorded the name, amount, and comment. The cool precision of numbers provided calm and order amidst the chaos and loneliness elsewhere.

Sara advanced to the next table, where ten rows of coins were laid out. The clerk continued.

"Your Grace, from the manor of Lord Agni Kazirian, the sum of thirty-two thousand, nine hundred and seventy-nine credits."

Taken aback, she gasped and placed her hand over her mouth.

"Child, say again?"

With a smile, he repeated himself.

"Thirty-two thousand, nine hundred and seventy-nine credits, Your Grace."

She laughed.

"I knew his—our—lands flourished, but last levy, we only paid twenty-seven thousand credits, not nearly thirty-three."

"Yes, the Lord Guardian is a great man."

She let a delighted smile tug at her lips. *The boy does not need to know what happens within our city house,* she thought.

"*Ai,* clerk, he is."

Again, she pulled out her scroll and quill and made the recording. Grasping the two ends of the cloth, the clerk funneled the coins to the center and deposited them back into the chest.

"Your Grace!"

The sudden voice startled her. There stood the herald boy, wearing Duke Hauran's dragon-and-chevron crest. Without that crest, he was a gangly boy in his fourteenth year who ran minor errands for the mayor; with it, he conveyed the duke's—Father's peer's—authority.

"Yes, herald?"

"I speak the following message from Duke Hauran of Kazia. He wishes your presence, and that of your betrothed, the Lord Guardian, at a feast to honor the second year of peace and victory over Blevenia in the Black Moon War. He will hold the feast a fortnight from today."

Sara's eyes widened. The morning's quarrel felt like a moon ago.

"That would be lovely."

The dutiful herald repeated himself.

"Yes, Your Grace. All of Kazia will celebrate our victory with song and laughter. It sounds grand. Your father, too, will be in attendance."

His voice held a tinge of longing; Sara guessed the boy had spent his whole life in the valley.

Images flashed through Sara's mind, mixed with excitement at the comforts of her old life. She closed her eyes and imagined wrapping her arms around Father and hearing a familiar voice recounting courtly intrigues. She imagined a handsome Agni in the silk waistcoat he wore when her father pressed their hands together, symbolically uniting them. Agni would hate to hear this, but he could cut a noble image.

Finally, the thought that warmed her most: would Father end her two-year sentence to the distant East? Even if she had to return after the celebration, the memories would warm her through a few more moons of isolation.

"Yes, yes, of course we will attend. We will begin preparations immediately. For how long does he desire our presence?"

"Ten days, Your Grace."

Ten wonderful days. The jousts, at which she would sit in the seat of honor alongside Agni and Father. Barrels of fine wine and ale, troubadours from East and West. The re-enactments of the Battle of the Ports and the Siege of Tercera; maybe they could provide a glimpse into Agni's distant, hardened heart, the source of his fits and nightmares that lay somewhere beyond her comprehension.

Again, she collected herself.

"Very good. Have you told the Lord Guardian?"

"Not yet, but I will today, Your Grace."

"I am sure he will be equally honored," she lied.

*Agni hates feasts more than fleas in his hair or ticks on his wings,* she thought. Still, she would savor the sight of him in her element rather than his own.

"Please tell him and then return to the stone. I must return to the levy here."

"As Her Grace wishes."

The boy bowed, as if himself practicing for Duke Hauran's court, and climbed back up the stairs.

For the first time in moons, she felt excitement. Today, she would raise a cup of wine in celebration.

C H A P T E R   3

# *Duty*

That same day, Agni had just dined with his soldiers on a midday meal of dried pork, cabbage, and hardtack. Coarse but hearty, it would hold him through the hot hours ahead and a ride to his manor, though he craved Dona's mutton stew with onions and carrots for dinner. Sara loved it too—could it smooth over her cutting remarks from this morning?

He shook his head. *Wolves. On another day, I might smile at the comparison to such a noble animal. Why not this day?* Their betrothal burdened them both, yet neither could end it.

He had only started across the common when a shout rang back from the roof of the town hall.

"Dragon! Dragon! Take cover!"

*Death from above.* Boys across the common dropped to their haunches and covered their ears. But the Lord Guardian, trained and unflinching, acted on a different instinct. He whirled and dashed back toward the town hall, where the only armament that could pierce a dragon's hide—a ballista, mounted with a spear-sized arrow—sat on the roof.

He scanned the sky as he ran but saw nothing; that did not mean the danger had passed. No one shouted "dragon" in vain, under pain of fifty lashes. He burst back through the door.

"Away, away!" he shouted, cutting through the din. The crowd parted as he dashed up four flights.

On the roof, two men nocked the giant arrow, winching it back with a click-click-click. Two more returned with an arrow under each arm. Then, Agni saw a dragon gliding over the north of town. A majestic creature, its wings barely moved to hold its height. This was a large one, an older female, at least fifty feet across. But whatever her intentions, the dragon flew east at eight hundred yards, dead across the line of fire. The best archer in the empire could not hit her at that distance.

"Hold!"

Agni's shout froze the arrow carriers, but the boys manning the ballista—barely old enough to grow stubble—shook with fear as they turned the ballista on its pivot. Agni sprinted faster, ready to bowl them over if they lined up a shot.

"I said, hold fire!"

With a startle, the boys jumped back. Agni grabbed the nearest by the shoulders. A slender, stripling lad of thirteen years, he felt soaked with sweat. He reached for the second boy's wrist, pulling them together.

"Who trained you in the use of this weapon?"

"I saw my older br—" the first boy replied.

"Stop. Who trained *you* in the ballista?"

"No one, Lord Guardian."

"Then what thought is lolling about in your head to operate it?"

"My apologies, Lor—"

Agni shoved the boys to each side and looked back towards the dragon. It circled back over the river and northeast.

"Silence," he snapped. "Any man trained in this blasted weapon knows you will never down a dragon at this distance. Doubly so when it flies at this angle to the line of fire. Did Mayor Goro not post one trained bowman in this rabble?"

The four boys gazed at one another, as if deciding who should next face the Lord Guardian's wrath.

"I am most displeased. While the Lord Guardian's remit is to secure the eastern border, it seems I must also guard the skies. If, by some extraordinary act of our god, you were to hit the dragon, the arrow would bounce off its scales like a pebble. It would wheel around and blast this roof with thunder before you could load a second."

He tracked the dragon to the south, where it screamed and broke into a dive. He heard a crack of thunder and a distant, muffled scream. A horse, perhaps a cow.

"This ballista is not meant to down every dragon in the Spires. If it wants a cow, you leave it its cow. If it strikes your younger sister, and you cannot shoot it through the heart, you leave it and mourn with your mother."

The boys bowed their heads. None dared reply.

"Now, send for an archer immediately. This town needs a better shot than even I. Go!"

Agni waved them off. Two of them dashed back down the stairs. He turned back to the sky, shielding his eyes against the sun's glare. The other two boys lingered, motionless. He ignored them, instead patting the arrow to ensure it was securely nocked. He turned the ballista south, in case the dragon returned.

It was not an archer, but a familiar voice that broke his watch.

"Lord Guardian! Lord Guardian!"

Agni squinted into the sunlight. He recognized the high voice as the young herald's. The boy's waistcoat bore Duke Hauran's dragon-and-chevron crest. Agni sighed; the herald's stringy hair and gangly frame made him look barely older than the boys on the roof, but that coat outranked the Lord Guardian—he carried the duke's authority.

Agni steeled himself. He thought about his distant relationship with the duke—he sent Agni credits and men; Agni used those to deter marauders and, in doing so, sent larger tax chests west. *Blast it,* he thought, *he would not use a herald to ask about mountain snares.* Already annoyed with the commotion, Agni took a breath and forced pleasantness into his voice.

"Yes, herald. How shall I serve His Grace today?"

The herald looked up to Agni—a full head taller—and cleared his throat.

"Lord Guardian. I carry a message from the His Grace Duke Hauran of Kazia, received from the town hall speaking stone this morning. He requests your honored presence and that of your betrothed Lady Sara, at a feast to honor the second year of peace and victory over Blevenia in the Black Moon War. He will hold the feast a fortnight from today."

Agni stifled a frown. A feast? Why now? The duke held no feast last year; why mark the second anniversary and not the first? No feasts honored the Dragon God or his chosen, Emperor Taran Solant, for two more moons.

"A feast, is it," he replied with a flat voice. "Who spoke this message to the stone?"

"The duke himself, directly from his palace. I recognized his voice and direction," the boy answered.

Agni sighed even deeper. *Blasted speaking stones.* Agni had hounded Mayor Goro to install one thrice the mass of those in the Spires to send messages westward. Today, it served as an ankle chain, and Duke Hauran had just yanked it.

"I suppose I could use the diversion, herald. My traps and relays over the Spires are nearly complete," Agni spat, sardonically.

The herald bowed, ignoring Agni's bitter tone.

"I too am your liege's obedient servant, Lord Guardian. I do not know why he requires your presence."

"Very well then. Tell His Grace that the Lord Guardian, Her Grace Lady Sara Ristana, his aide Alexander, and a convoy of guards and drivers, would be delighted to attend. All guards armored, on destriers. He will need to stable them."

The herald twitched, clearly unprepared for such a request.

"I beg the Lord Guardian's pardon, but destriers? They are slow. Could they cover the journey in that time?"

"We will leave at a proper time, herald. The Median Road is not safe to the west."

"Who would dare attack the Lord Guardian and Lady— Duchess—Sara."

Agni forced a humorless smile.

"Boy, have you ridden the Median Road?"

"No, I have not."

"There are more brigands than rabbits on the road. By the time they identify the Lord Guardian's crest, my sword will have saved the executioner the trouble of the pinion-and-drop."

"What if you encounter a dragon, Lord Guardian?"

His voice trembled as he spat the word "dragon." Duke's crest or not, he seemed like just another boy again. Agni chuckled, despite himself.

"Boy, did you not just hear that thunderbolt? That was not the clouds."

"I heard something," the boy said, with a nervous nod.

"We are fortunate that it struck in the noonday. If it waited until nightfall, an owl could not pick it out against the night sky. Once one sees you, it drops into a full dive, then breathes a bolt of lightning which stuns and knocks down its prey. Do you ever hear a crack on a clear night?"

"*Ai*, Lord Guardian." The boy sucked in a breath.

"A dragon's breath will kill a foal, or even a small man at once. That is mercy, rather than if it sinks its claws, sharp as banded swords, into your back. If it has mercy, it will bite through your neck; if not, it may carry you screaming for its young's three-day feast. I saw one carry off a palfrey. If a dragon wants your life on the trail, it has it. Blessedly, they prefer stags and mountain goats."

The boy stood frozen, taking in the story. City boys loved dragon stories, even if all knew a dragon would devour one just the same. They only knew what the priests told them—that Varenox, God of Dragons, blessed them with their blue hair and wings along with his gifts of prophecy. Only Agni knew Anton's tales as truth—that men and dragons once lived as kin. Would that they could again.

"Spectacular," the lad replied.

Agni smiled and patted him on the shoulder.

"Now go. I have waistcoats to prepare."

The herald smiled.

"As you wish, Lord Guardian. I will relay this message immediately."

Agni turned back to the town, bracing himself for the ordeal ahead. Feasts were vanity, not valor; pomp and pretense for the effete and comfortable. Worse, this felt ominous.

On instinct, he ran his fingers along the seam of his shirt.

*At my last feast, I scratched under my waistcoat until my skin wept. But at least Sara will enjoy the finery and spectacle—it might give us a moon's peace.*

# Servant

News of the feast had lightened her step; she got to regale the levy counters with tales of troubadours from across the empire, and fatted goose with plums. The thought of a moon away from this backwater dulled her headache to a faint throb.

At the fifth hour of the afternoon, Sara arrived back at the corner of East Street and Knight Lane. Her mood buoyed, she stepped lightly through the door and removed her boots when she heard another pair of steps.

"Good day, Dona," she called out.

But a different voice rang back—young, smooth and sonorous.

"Dona is in her shed. I am Nira, Your Grace."

Surprised, Sara turned around to see a woman her own age. The new maid had a striking beauty, more sensual than graceful. She had plump lips, and her commoner's wool tunic could not hide her buxom figure. Sara addressed Nira with a mixture of suspicion and puzzlement.

"Hello, Nira. Are you my new chambermaid while Fala suffers the river fever?"

"Yes, yes, Your Grace. The Lord Guardian met my sons in the mountains and asked me to meet him here at this time."

Sara nodded slowly.

"Ah, Qualo's mama. Agni took to him, called him a wolf pup. That is flattery; Agni loves wolves."

Her gaze lingered; where had she seen Nira? *Yes, the Potter's Lane Tavern.* The poor lady, low-cut tunic showing off her breasts, batting her lashes and flicking her wings at a young man. *I slapped her and called her a strumpet,* she recalled, chagrined. A wave of heat rose to Sara's face. Shame pricked at her; she envied neither Nira's looks nor station, but her carefree demeanor. It had taunted Sara, even if Nira's flirtation had only been a means to feed her boys. She sighed; once again, she had fallen short of a duchess' duty.

"Ah yes, we met at the tavern, did we not?"

Nira lowered her eyes in silence.

"I believe I called you some vile names. Please forgive me."

Nira's eyes rose to meet Sara's. Sara laughed at her genuine surprise, pleased she could atone for her rudeness.

"Yes, milady," Nira stuttered, pausing as if debating to say more.

"If there is more you wish to say, Nira, speak freely." Sara spoke in a gentle tone.

Nira's full lips widened into a bright, genuine smile.

"A duchess asking a washing woman for forgiveness—I never thought I would see that day. We all speak words we regret."

Sara felt a flicker of warmth. Her earlier envy felt petty and misplaced. She remembered that she had lashed out at Nira on the same night Agni had gone to his mistress. Her hurt needed a target. Nira had simply been the closest. Though it helped that Nira covered her prodigious breasts today.

But then, Nira's first words came back to her.

"Wait, Nira, you said the Lord Guardian asked you to meet him here at this time?"

Nira's eyebrows perked up.

"Yes, Your Grace. I know I arrived early, but I had thought—"

Sara's mind raced. *The herald could set the town's clock by Agni's comings and goings.* He ran the household and manor as rigorously as his soldiery. Did he really ride out to his manor? Did he tarry to walk the manor's hounds? Or did he sneak off for a midday tryst with Kali?

*That feral bitch.* The thought of that she-savage's hand between his thighs spoiled her light mood. No matter how often Sara reminded herself that their union was neither's choice, those trysts degraded her, the hundredth as much as the first. And he paraded Kali, not Sara, before his soldiers. A thief and entertainer. The herald must have seen Agni that day and conveyed the summon. Might he seek comfort in Kali's arms?

"Did he mention a visit in the northwestern quarter, near Potter's Lane?"

"Why, no, Lady Sara, I have not seen him in some days."

Sara's face flushed. While she had just met Nira, tavern girls always knew the movements of the menfolk—even those like Agni who never partook.

"Nira, do you know Kali, the Aloi clanswoman?"

"Why yes, Your Grace," Nira replied hesitantly. "Some nights she sings for the patrons, and keeps the peace when it requires a gentle touch—"

Nira broke off, her face reddening.

"Please, again, speak freely. Have you seen her and Agni together today?"

"They often walk about the common at sunset, Your Grace, but I have not seen them in ten d—"

Sara cast her eyes downward, fighting a sniffle. The reminder of Agni's genuine affection for his lover—affection he rarely showed Sara—stabbed at her chest.

She failed at a tender gesture this morning, just as she failed at winning his heart for two years. Kali felt like a third resident of this house, a shadow over what should have been a happy day. Now, even the feast felt tainted—a whole moon with this distant man to whom Father had sentenced her. She raised a hand, her voice shaking.

"Enough. Please pour me a cup of wine."

Without a word, Nira scurried to the back, returning moments later with a pewter mug of wine. Overwhelmed, Sara placed her head on the table, breathing deeply.

"Are you well, Your Grace?" Nira sounded concerned, motherly even, as she placed a gentle hand on Sara's shoulder.

"Please bring me my harp from my maid's quarters. It lightens my mood."

Sara heard Nira's footsteps diminish in the distance.

Alone again, she buried her head in her arms. Did Agni truly ride out to the manor, or had he gone to Kali? Her mind churned with unwelcome images: their hands and mouths roaming over one another, Kali's feral charm drawing Agni away from her yet again.

*When we return to the capital,* she thought bitterly, *I will have him flogged if he so much as smiles at that bitch.*

C H A P T E R   5

*Return*

For the hundredth time that afternoon, Agni felt sweat sting his eyes. He dabbed his forehead with the corner of his riding tunic. But despite the unrelenting sun, the journey cleared his head. The ride gave him space to think after spilling his heart to wizened Steward Agran, who, despite his hunching back, still carried the manor's weight on his shoulders. Agni reacquainted himself with manor gossip—dukes trafficked in whispers.

*If I am to be a duke someday, I had best accustom myself.*

He stabled his rented mare and stopped to feed Ark a sweet apple, which the destrier devoured in two bites. Feeding his horse felt simple and grounding; horses had no guile. Now for the comforts of home. He smiled faintly as he reached the entrance to Knight Lane.

Agni walked around the front garden and to Dona's kitchen shed. She had begun boiling a cauldron of water for the evening meal. Without a word, he wrapped an arm around her shoulders and kissed the cheek of his longest confidante and grandmother-in-all-but-name.

"And how is my favorite lady?"

She giggled.

"Careful with the sweet words, Lord Guardian. Would Lady Sara or Mistress Kali approve of them?"

"Are they here to protest?" Agni replied with a grin, baring his teeth.

"Lady Sara sits inside, playing her harp."

Agni strained his ears to hear a lilting melody. Its light, high tones floated through the air, reminiscent of the western cotillions Sara had so often waxed about. Both his women possessed the gift of music—Sara for the refinement of court, Kali for the earthy tales of alehouses. One for duty, one for companionship, love, and pleasure. *Why could they not reside in the same woman?*

He hoped for a bit of warmth from Sara tonight, fleeting as it might be. The harp was a welcome sign—she could bring such beauty into the house. Perhaps one day, in the capital, he might take joy in it too.

"Did she spend the day at the keep?"

"Yes, she did. Though I don't have letters and figures, she seems quite skilled with accounts."

"Indeed. Are you sure it was the keep, and not the vintner's?" Agni spoke with a teasing edge.

Dona laughed.

"A duchess' words carry heft, even in distant lands. I'm sure she spoke your regards to Duke Hauran through the herald."

"I see she told you. Yes, we head west in several days' time, though I none too gladly." Agni sighed.

"If only a simple maid could travel. I hear Eltrazan Keep is incredible, with towers that touch the stars."

Agni smiled at the awestruck twinkle in Dona's eyes. Though in her eight decades she had never ventured further than his northern manor, she loved his stories of exotic lands, claiming to have never doubted that he would return a hero, even if not on a duchess' arm.

"I shall record the sight on one of my seeing stones, though it is less impressive than you might believe."

"I would love that, Agni. Never fear, I won't let this house go to rot."

"You did so for five years without me. A moon will be a pittance." Agni tapped Dona twice on her left wing, "I will don a fresh tunic."

Dona nodded and returned to chopping onions for her stew. Agni grabbed a dish rag, dipped it in water, and wiped the sweat from his face and body.

He turned and headed back through the front door. Passing Sara, he greeted her briefly, noticing how she seemed lost in the harp's melody. Upstairs, he exchanged his sweaty leathers for a fresh silk tunic. In his mind, this cleansed the day and ended his watch. For a few hours, he could try to be her betrothed.

But as he descended, he spotted a striking beauty at the base of the stairs. Her sleek wings and flowing hair caught his attention, even against a poor woman's tunic. He recognized the curve of her cheekbones from her sons' faces.

"Lord Guardian!" a familiar boy's voice exclaimed, darting out from behind her wings before his mother could catch him.

He bolted up the stairs and into Agni's arms, all pretense of soldiery gone. Agni patted him on his freshly washed head.

"Qualo, boy! What an unexpected pleasure. Did you and your brother stay vigilant at the stone?"

"V... vi... what?" Qualo stumbled over the unfamiliar word.

Agni pointed to Qualo's eyes, then his own.

"Vigilant. Keeping a watchful eye without fail, like the emperor commands. Did you?"

"Vi—li—gant! Yes, Lord Guardian!"

Agni smiled; for now, the boy's enthusiasm was enough.

"Good. A sentry's greatest weapon is not his blade; it is his eyes."

Agni turned to the woman at the foot of the stairs.

"And you, my lady, must be Qualo's mother?"

"Yes, Lord Guardian, I am Nira," she replied in a soft voice, curtsying.

"Rise, Nira. You have strong boys. I apologize for the delay—I tarried departing my manor."

In the background, Sara continued to pluck at the harp, a pleasant coda to the day.

"Thank you, my lord. Dona and Lady Sara have granted me a warm welcome."

"A cup of wine please, Nira. And one for the lady."

Agni gestured to the back alcove, which held the pot of fine Lesdran red. Imported from the Far Coast, the wine fetched a hefty price but brought Sara joy. He hated to admit he had developed a taste for this luxury.

Nira procured two cups with a hearty pour. Sara still had not spoken. Agni noticed a second used cup off to Sara's side. *Blast it, how much has she imbibed already?*

"Sara, are you well?"

She looked engrossed in the music. He savored the wine's rich earth tones.

"Ah, prime vintage," he spoke to the air. He closed his eyes and focused on the harp's melody. It was delicate, flowery, urbane, like Sara herself. She once said it reminded her of the moon over Artania.

Sara stopped her melody to take a swig.

"Surely, the herald boy found you today, Agni," she said, her tone rising.

He sighed and rubbed his temples; her excitement grated against his growing irritation.

"*Ai*, the lad did. As if the peace at the eastern border maintained itself."

"You have ably trained your engineers and captains. Besides, you must learn how to comport with the highborn while Duke Hauran's treasury funds your work."

Agni folded his hands. The statement stung, but he resolved to let one pass. Yet another reminder that, even with the Duke of Artania, he would remain an outsider.

"I can 'comport with the highborn,' as you call it, though I would rather be useful than charming."

Sara cocked her head, narrowing her eyes at him. Suspicion flickered across her face. What did she read into that statement?

"What do you mean by that?"

"I mean that I prefer citizens' warmth and openness to nobles' duplicity. What is a feast but a chance for us to jockey for unearned favors? We enjoy the same wine here as we will in Eltrazan, and thanks to my—our—manor, finer pork."

"Like our citizen that you spent the afternoon with?"

Agni's heart sank at that cutting remark. He knew any denial would ring hollow.

"I reviewed manor affairs with Agran, and stopped to feed Ark a golden manor apple," he said flatly.

Sara's voice deepened, taking on a snarl.

"Manor affairs? Do not lie to me, Agni, I know your accounts. I recorded your levy this morning. And Ark could devour a bucket of apples in seconds."

"I assure you, I was not—"

Sara cut him off, voice trembling with rage, "—with your Aloi whore? And to think I had hoped to spend a pleasant evening together and even lie with you like a husband and wife should."

Agni stiffened as her words struck true. He caught Nira's shocked expression in the corner of his eye.

"You have martyred me with her since your northern campaign. Tell me, are her striped nethers that tight? After all, we make love once a fortnight faster than stray dogs, while you rut with her loud enough that every drunkard and servant on Potter's Lane hears her moan. A shame Father has not sliced off your wings for it."

Agni slammed his fists on the table.

"Watch your tongue! You do not know that of which you speak—"

"You would forsake your marital duty for a woman who should be off wearing leathers and hunting plains behemoths with the rest of her kind."

Agni's eyes narrowed. Her insult to Kali's race burned hotter than her accusations. The Aloi, too, had bled for him in the war, yet she reduced them to savages.

"And she would still be twice the lady as she who sits in front of me," he growled. "If only I could send you back to Artania alone, capital duchy be blasted! You should thank the Dragon God you are not betrothed to another. Any other man would strike your insolent mouth!"

Sara maintained her glare.

"And in some moons, you will abandon her here. You will dishonor me no more."

That truth burned like a red-hot poker. Unless Kali made the perilous journey to Artania, their lives would part ways.

"After we dine, duchess," Agni spat, "I may as well do what you have already accused me of."

Just then, Dona walked in with a bowl of mutton stew. These venomous exchanges must blend into the air like the clucking of chickens. Nira, on the other hand, looked mortified, stood frozen, her wings pressed against the woven Kazirian crest on the far wall, matching the shade of the cloth dragon's.

"Lord Guardian, Your Grace, is there a problem?" Dona asked.

"Only the usual," Sara replied icily.

Agni muttered, "Yes, Dona, there is a problem. Please serve me my bowl. I will be going soon."

Next, he turned to Nira.

"Nira, dear, clean my cup and bowl, then return tomorrow an hour after dawn. See to Her Grace."

Agni wolfed down his stew and wine without saying another word. No matter how exquisite, it all tasted like wormwood in his mouth.

He turned upstairs to his chest and retrieved a leather pouch of seeing stones—*my friends.* He opened the thread that held them; one gold, one crimson, one blue. Treasured images and words of days gone by, before this constant strife. *Without them, I forget who I am.* Parts he locked away from the world. *Someday, I may show even you, Sara. And you will see why my future title is a living death.*

He took his sword in hand and stormed off—to find a happier home.

# *Heart*

Agni's anger dissipated over the quarter-mile walk to Kali's house; the familiar path had become a ritual. Along North Street at the edge of the common, he spotted boys jumping off an earthen mound and spreading their wings. Occasionally, one glided a few yards before landing chest-first in the dirt. Undeterred, they laughed and tried again.

Agni smiled at their easy delight. Someday, he could teach his own boys to tuck their hips and land on their feet. Dragonlanders could only glide—how he envied Avicians' true flight, their fanes perched in unreachable heights—but these boys needed grit even to glide. It would serve them well.

Kali's house came into view. He admired its construction—half the size of his own house, paid for by war spoils. Close enough to the northwest hovels to avoid whispers of favoritism, but still in the company of guildmasters. Smoke wafted from the chimney, carrying the welcoming scent of cinnamon and cloves.

Agni rapped at the door. A pair of emerald green eyes stared through the slit.

"Who is there?"

"Constable Avro, come to drag you off in irons for theft of a man's heart!" Agni teased.

A latch lifted, and the door swung open to reveal a young lady fit to be her god's consort. Lit by the glow of the fire, her radiant face was framed by deep-red hair. Her three tiger-like facial stripes marked her as Aloi, her ample chest barely hidden beneath a linen tunic and leather apron. A tail, the length of his longsword, swayed behind her. Her clawed feet, strapped into leather sandals, hinted at her desert homeland.

"Love!"

She threw her arms around Agni's neck and pulled him into a deep kiss. He returned the embrace, her warmth already making the strife in his home feel distant.

"My Dear Tigress," Agni replied. The title, once used by men on his campaign, felt especially fitting tonight. In a way, it made her equal to a duchess.

"How has the Lord Guardian's business fared today?"

Kali re-lowered the latch and returned to the fire pit, where she was mulling the same fine wine that Agni drank earlier. Sara would slap them both if she knew Kali was "debasing" it with spice, but that thought only made Agni crave it more. He inhaled the rich smoke.

"I would rather forget this day, so far." He sighed.

"Then I will need a second pot, knowing how you imbibe."

"Spiced wine is a winter drink, dear, to warm your heart against mountain blizzards."

"Not in this house. The Aloi deserts grow chill by sunset. It reminds me of home."

Her free spirit always delighted him. Even thousands of miles from home, she preserved her roots: an altar to her god, traditional food and drink, and the occasional Aloi idiom slipped into proper Kazian.

"That will not be all that warms you, tonight, dear kitten."

"It had best not be." Kali tugged on his right wing and kissed the edge. "I love how this falls over me at night, like a second blanket."

Agni took a deep breath; time to sour the warmth.

"It will for another night or two. Then I must depart for a moon. Duke Hauran has summoned me to a feast in Eltrazan, celebrating the second anniversary of our victory in the Black Moon War."

Kali's ears drooped, but she looked more surprised than disappointed.

"A feast? There was none last year. Why celebrate the second anniversary but not the first?"

"Duke Hauran wants to parade the duchess and I through the streets of Eltrazan. To what end, I do not know," Agni mused. "Perhaps his grip on power wanes. Or he wants a spectacle to impress Sara's father, Duke Verlan."

"Will he attend?"

"I expect him to. He cherishes two things above all: his daughter, and reminding all of Solantia, especially Hauran, that he alone financed the Avician Campaign. He would append that to his title if he could."

Kali laughed, her bright voice lifting his mood

"He would slice off your tongue if he heard that."

Agni lowered his head; he intended that as both truth and humor.

"I might prefer that. This feast feels…wrong. The timing, the occasion. The dukes will watch me for ten days. They may whisk me westward to Artanport. Or find a pretext to assassinate me, yet I cannot refuse. I feel the Dragon God's maw turning towards me."

"You have not said that in years."

Agni stared downwards. Anton forbade him to share their communion, yet here he was, speaking of fates and visions.

"I feel it. Another cycle of wrath and fate begins. I have often told you of my unease with the Dragon God. Since my ninth year, the temple air felt heavy, like a boulder on my chest. Priests recoiled from me and told me that I had affronted him. Many times, I would scream and run outside. How could a boy anger the god of fate?"

*I allied with his most accursed,* he thought. *I chose greatness over death; my family name over the god who torments us.*

The Dragon God cursed his last child but left him with great power—enough to wield but never to escape.

Kali's hand cupped his, the light fur of her palm a comforting touch.

"A curse, but a sure one. Do you think Verlan will recall you and Sara to Artania?"

Agni sighed.

"Duke Verlan may pass the title of Lord Guardian to Baron Goro, then imprison me in Artanian silks. But the Dragon God is unpredictable like his thunder."

"You often tell me that power and skill can defy fate. You have done it for decades."

"I know no higher calling than to guard the Borderlands, even if I must keep an uneasy peace between a woman of duty and one of love. But this cannot endure. It could never."

Kali glared at him, her tail swishing. What compassion yet what ferocity in her emerald eyes.

"If the Dragon God pries us apart, I will follow you if I have to ride the Median Road on a pony and live in a wattle shed."

A lump rose in his throat.

"You are stronger than any noble, my tigress. You did not accept your birth lot either. But I would feel stricken if you were to die on the journey. You have coins; you could live the life you please here with another."

"Agni, you dolt!" she snapped. "Bugger your coins! I want *you*, not some craftsman or knight. I traveled five hundred miles from Charoi to Arteva while still a girl. Do not presume me helpless."

Her passion overwhelmed him. She loved without reservation, and he cherished her for it. But she did not know dreams and fates like a Kazian. Her god rewarded sacrifice and endurance. Could she set those gifts against the malevolent whims of Varenox? Her voice continued, softer but no less determined.

"And I know more of fate than you believe. You know I would fight every god for our fates to lie together as man and wife. Before you, I never saw myself as a wife. But that is my dream, and I will not part with it lightly."

Now, a tear fell from Agni's face. Her love offered hope he could not share. Was she ignorant of nobles' schemes, or did she see a truth he could not? Never one to hide her emotions, Kali did not love easily, but when she did, she loved as fiercely as the desert sun.

"And it is the one thing I cannot give you," he replied, his voice wavering. "I have no more power over Duke Verlan's will than the Azectrai's currents. This lovely land runs deepest in my heart, but the duke will wrench it from me, too."

"I still hold hope," she replied, her voice steadier than his. "Perhaps because I have little else."

"I know, love. Just know how bright your flame burns. Even if the Dragon God takes my life, you will be a power in your own right."

"But if your god does not," she countered, her eyes piercing his, "what power could we wield, together? Every time the Dragon God moves to strike you, you transform it into a greater destiny."

He saw beauty in her worldview—the boundless optimism of a lowborn girl with nothing to lose. Yet it also unsettled him that her faith in him was greater than his own.

"My desire is to end this all. The endless squabbling of dukes. Raids, invasions, and wars of gain. The night of my mother's murder, fate placed me on a runaway stallion, riding down a path of endless war. Let it end with me, even if I must throw myself off and become a cripple."

"You want to stop history, Agni." Her voice softened. "With that dream, you will never know peace."

Agni felt his shoulders slump, exhausted in spirit; he knew she was right.

"And I have never. Bringing to heel the two strongest nations in the Mortal Realms only strengthened these ambitions."

A gentle hand nestled against his neck, her warm fur reassuring him like a blanket.

"Agni, remember my words and never lose hope. We spent six moons apart when your army sailed north to Avicia. Even you thought you might not return. Many nights, I prostrated myself before my god until the sun peaked, praying for your victory. And you returned with only a dent in your breastplate."

He recalled those difficult nights. She could only pray, but he planned, trusting his own skill over any god.

"Your faith gives me strength, sweet Kali. I will try to remember your words."

She placed her forehead against his, her breath warm against his face.

"Tonight, forget the feast, fate, all of it. Rest your burdens with me."

"On my honor, love, I will. But this would rest me further."

He wrapped his hand around her head and pulled her close for another, longer kiss. Her face smelled earthy, like spices and cooking flame. Her tongue flicked at his like a sensuous snake's. She rested her head on his shoulder, her tail flicking playfully against his side.

"I feel so small and protected in your arms," she murmured.

He stroked her hair, pressing a kiss to her forehead, without a word. Together, they watched the wine simmer in the firelight.

"The wine is ready."

Kali filled two pewter cups, her movements graceful even in an apron.

"A toast, to that which was, is, and may come to pass."

Agni rose alongside her.

"Hear, hear."

They clinked glasses and drank deeply. Her words, though full of hope, could not ease his doubt, but her presence—her fire— offered a unique solace. If they could defy the gods together, raising children with both wings and tails—even bastards—would feel easy. They sat down in a warm embrace, her head on his shoulder as they watched the cooking fire fade.

"You like this, Agni," she whispered.

"This moment is complete, darling. I want to feel only the flame and your touch."

He felt her right hand rub his knee. His loins stirred. She knew how to soothe him as much as Sara knew how to inflame him.

"Like this, love?"

He ran his fingers down her spine to the base of her tail; it flicked in response, their bodies attuned.

"Since our first night, I never knew you to hide your desires, Kali."

She laughed and squeezed his knee.

"Since then, I never saw a reason to."

"If you want this night to feel like our first, we can ride to my manor and make love on a pile of hay. We have two hours of riding light."

Kali inclined her head and purred, low and teasing.

"No, no more piles of hay." She licked at his ear and whispered, "But a table in my hall, in front of a dying flame. I would like that."

"It would not be the first time," he replied, capturing her lips in another passionate kiss, then his open mouth, pawing at her full breast over the apron.

"Consider that an order, Lord Guardian. Just take me. Right here."

——

Hours later, covered in each other's musk, they collapsed. She curled in his arms, her forehead against his, her hand on his chest, their hair dancing blue and red on the bolster.

"Is that a fond enough memory to take to Eltrazan?"

"I will return for another. We do not leave for four days."

"You have a moon with the Duchess; do not anger her. Perhaps you will rekindle a flame."

"That flame burned but a night. Duke Verlan pressed her hand into mine; then I campaigned in the River Axis for five years. By the time I next saw her, I had you. And when the three of us traveled eastward here, I knew I could not love both. I care deeply about her, but our bond is duty, not love. On the rare occasions that Sara and I make love, I feel like I dishonor you."

A feeling of shame washed over him, even if most nobles took three lovers and most ravished servant girls. Kali understood his duty towards another, but Sara never could.

"I pity her. But you know I could never forsake you. I feel condemned to hurt her because of our love," she spoke in a resigned tone.

"She does not hate you, Kali. Only the loss of her station that you represent. High nobles do not make homes here. Duke Verlan said he sent his daughter here to administer the land, but I believe he did it to humble her."

Again, he felt their uneasy coexistence. His betrothed and lover stayed civil but strained in front of the town.

"Your god and mine both revere deeds, and we are people of deeds. That gives me hope."

"I want more than hope. I want to bend fate."

"Yet we only have this night."

Agni admired her ability to lose herself in a moment, unlike his mind, which could never stop calculating.

"Then let us savor this night together, love. Good night."

She pulled the silken sheet over them, her hips against his, his left arm under her neck and his right against her bare belly. He moved her hair to the side and gently kissed up and down her neck; it relaxed both of them. Soon, her breath trailed off into slumber.

———

Agni closed his eyes, but sleep eluded him. He concentrated on her soft belly, tracing the line below her navel where skin met fur, and her tail rubbing against his thigh.

That might have stirred his loins again if not for that chill. Deeper than sleep. Uninvited.

Tonight, he did not welcome the Voice of Ages.

The silver specter cracked a rare smile.

*"Ancestor, you advise me on matters of war and state, not those of the heart."*

*"People of deeds you are,"* Anton intoned. *"Would that your lover were born a man, minstrels would write plays about his valor. I, too, took an Aloi lover. Her spirit of the tiger delighted me, even if I could not place our mongrel brood on the throne."*

*"Father,"* Agni replied, anger absorbed by the unnatural gloom. *"Do you visit tonight to compare lovers? I have had Kali for six years. You rarely speak of her. She drinks a tea to keep her moon flow; we have no brood and no throne."*

*"She is a speck of dust in the wind. I will not stay the Dragon God's hand for her."*

Agni's fury flared again, but he steadied himself. Anton did not brook insolence.

*"Ancient One. You told me that those of great merit have defied our god for millennia. Why not her?"*

Anton spread his wings and let out a malicious laugh.

*"Scion, he will tread her underfoot like a man does an ant— without taking notice, let alone ill intent. The Kazirian fell from power but never from his eye. Not even a worthless boy."*

Agni snarled under his breath, his back bracing for the lash like it once did. But Anton continued.

*"Boy. Soldier. Commander. High General. Lord Guardian. As your power grew, so did that of his wrath. When the time comes— soon—to seize our power, we will face his full wrath together."*

The memories flooded back. Every battle, every misfortune, every blow. How many deathblows had Anton turned away?

*"I will not stray, Blessed Ancestor. But while you are my guide, I am your arms. I will need a woman of strength; I count it as fortune that I know Kali—and Sara."*

Anton chuckled at their names.

*"One of love, one of duty, you say. You have drawn them into your fate, like a stream feeding the Great River. They cannot escape."*

*"Perhaps they—or at least the one I lie with—do not wish to escape, ancestor. And I will need strong blood to propagate our line. Whom would you have me wed?"*

Anton solemnly bowed his head.

*"Boy. Your addle-pated father made foolish choices, even for a mortal. But he chose a strong wife, even if a Chosen of our accursed god. They bred a good son."*

A wave of sadness swept over him.

*"I feel Mama's absence every day. I dream of her dying moments more than any flame or blood since."*

*"Just know,"* Anton growled, though without malice, *"that night, your pain cried out to me. Had I my body, I would have sliced the raiders' wings off."*

*"And I see her fire in Kali, Blessed Ancestor. She has great merit,"* Agni begged.

*"Scion, perhaps I have forgotten the desires of the flesh, and a lover can satiate them,"* Anton said with a sigh. *"But soon, nobles from across the Empire Kazia will vie to lay in your bed and bear your heir. You can choose the finest."*

*"I will never see Kali as a mere lover."*

Anton spat. A mortal might have shaken his head.

*"Bah. She is not of the dragon; her god is fierce but guileless. You tempt her with the promise of a life together. I will not stay you—yet. You learn through pain and consequence. When your fate strikes her, you will learn."*

Anton faded, his parting words echoing.

*You will learn.*

*You will learn.*

*You will learn.*

Agni returned to his body with a shudder. He felt Kali's hands squeezing his. A cold sweat drenched his tunic.

"Love, are you well? You had a night terror."

"It was a dream of the Battle of Zarda," Agni lied, kissing her hand. *I lie out of love. The truth is more terrible—and speaking it would endanger us both. Would Anton forsake me, leaving me to Varenox's wrath? Would he strike you dead? Or…would he rouse the Ancient City to march on the Mortal Realms?* Kali existed in the realms of men—of which Anton slowly drew him away.

"You lie poorly, Lord Guardian," she spoke with narrowed eyes, her tail twitching against his.

"You know I cannot take you to those recesses of my mind from which terrors come. Just be, love. Just be. Let that be enough for tonight."

She placed a palm over his heart. Her warm touch steadied him, even as he knew that answer would not satisfy her.

"I can feel your heart racing. You know I cannot bear to see you so."

Her touch eased some of his tension, the fine fur on her palms warming the sweat on his chest. Slowly, his breaths slowed.

"Then let me step outside. The night air calms me down."

Agni got up and slipped back into his tunic and trousers.

"You want to look at your stones, right?"

"Yes, Kali. Please stay here," he implored.

"Someday, you must show them to me."

"You would not recognize me. Even I see a man—and a boy—long gone."

"And I was once a thief and a girl. I promise, I will only love you more for it."

"I am exhausted. Someday, love. Someday soon. Perhaps after this stupid feast."

"Do you swear that before Varenox?"

Agni laughed at Kali's invocation of his god, but he sensed truth in her voice. "I do, love, when the time is right."

"I will wait right here. But too long without your warmth and I may suffer a chill."

With that, Agni walked down the stairs and into the still night. The stones were not just relics to him—they reminded him of who he was before Anton, before dukes and wars. In their glow, he could find a fleeting peace.

———

Agni stepped out into a pleasant breeze, just enough to tug at his wings. The crescent moon gave but a sliver of light, but the stars above formed a shimmering canopy. Bless Kali, she loved him fully even as he hid so much of himself. Yet showing her those stones would feel more intimate than lovemaking. *Someday.*

He walked around to the back of the house, near the privy and out of view. The oak overhead rustled. He reached into his pouch and pulled out three stones, polished to a sheen, each the size of a silver coin. They glowed faintly, holding secrets of simpler times.

He placed one between his left thumb and forefinger and lifted it up to his eye. It glowed a pale gold as an image moved within.

*The scene unfolded in the grand banquet hall of Duke Verlan's palace. Banners fluttered along the ceiling, stirred by the faint breeze through peaked stone windows. A vibrant waltz played in the background—one, two, three, one, two, three. And at the head table, a younger Agni and Sara sat at Verlan's right hand, laughing and toasting the ascendant Empire of Solantia.*

*Verlan clapped his hands. "Cupbearer! Another for my darling daughter and her betrothed!"*

Agni whispered, as if undoing time itself. "General."

At that moment, Duke Verlan had been his benevolent sponsor; not ambition personified. Agni and Sara, smitten with the innocence of youth had met one hour, been betrothed the next, and kissed for the first and last time in five years. A pleasant, fleeting illusion.

Now, the memory carried a pang of guilt. *Would Sara still have loved me, had I not found solace in Kali's arms?* he thought. *The desires of young warriors; eighteen moons and no woman had warmed my bed.*

Yet since, she understood his duty to Sara, even if Sara could not understand his love for Kali.

He placed the stone back in his pouch and took out the second. It glowed a deep crimson, casting light over his hand.

*The vision revealed the Azectrai guardhouse, its beaten-earth floor covered in rushes. On the makeshift table—three planks of wood across two trestles—the guards tossed knucklebones with a laugh. Smoke lingered near the ceiling; they would not build a chimney for years. A ten-year-old Agni held the stone at arm's length, recording the scene.*

*"You again, boy? Shouldn't you be feeding your chickens?"*

*"I already did. I want to wield your blade."*

*The four guards laughed, the sound echoing off the rough stone walls.*

*"Are you sure you can swing a longsword, boy? You'll slice your wing off!"*

*The leader drew his blade with a zing and handed it to Agni, probably expecting him to struggle and drop it. Instead, he executed a flawless parry and counter.*

*"By Varenox's arse, little Agni thinks he's a knight. Give that back, boy, and show up on the common tomorrow at midday. We'll make a knight of you."*

Agni intoned again. "Soldier."

He grinned at the memory. Where would he be without that knight captain who saw his station in Azectrai as a punishment, and his earthy footman who saw Agni as a diversion? They struck his face when he dropped his hands, or his hand when he exposed his sword arm, but unlike Papa, they did it to teach, not harm. Unlike Anton, they asked nothing in return—they were his first family beyond blood. On campaign, Kali laughed and drank with men like them—she might find this scene precious. *One day.*

The final stone glowed deep blue as he held it to his eye.

*The front room of his family's manor house appeared. His mother, her face framed by long blue hair, pulled on a pair of well-worn leather boots. Beneath her beauty lay a warrior's hardness.*

*"Mama, when do I get to ride out with you and Papa?"*

A six-year-old Agni recalled that day he had just discovered seeing stones.

*"Boy, enough with that question. You are no longer than Papa's horse's legs. We will be back by nightfall. Dona will prepare your mutton stew, and you'd best eat every last bite."*

*"But papa can carry me on his dest… dextri… his war horse!"*

*"A destrier, Agni. And you will need to master a pony first. Wait, you found a seeing stone? Where did you get that? Give it here—"*

Agni whispered, his voice breaking, "Boy."

And the memory faded. Mundane yet cherished, it was his last clear image of her before her death in a Blevenian raid. A mother and a warrior to the end.

That day set his life on the path of endless battle. The Ancient City, Anton, the soldiers, his command, the dukes, Sara, Kali, his current posting, his impending feast. The Dragon God fated him to die desolate, but now his name was etched on the heart of every imperial soldier.

Echoes of who he had been: General. Soldier. Boy. The current of his life ran deeper than Anton, a reminder that he belonged to the realms of men before the schemes of gods.

Content, he returned inside, divesting his boots and tunic. Kali had lit a candle and watched the flame's shadow dance against the wall. She turned to him but said nothing.

"Someday, love, someday," he whispered in her ear as he pulled the sheet on top of him.

Her ear flicked in acknowledgment as he stroked her tail.

"Be gentle, Agni, it likes you," Kali cooed, resting it against his leg. "I like it, too."

He wrapped an arm under her neck and the other around her belly. She kissed his forearm and sighed, her breathing slowing as she drifted off. Her warmth anchored him to this world as they drifted off together into sleep.

# *Mercy*

Five days earlier, Azectrai had given the convoy, twenty men and three maids deep, a grand send-off, complete with trumpeters and a cheering throng. Sara had walked arm-in-arm with Agni, past rows of bowing men and curtsying women. A pleasant illusion of unity—a rehearsal of the façade they would wear for a moon. She pretended to ignore Kali, who waved and blew kisses like any other citizen.

Sara had climbed into an ornate seat atop the newest wagon, padded to absorb ruts and rocks. The convoy set off with the raised banners of the Kazirian and Ristana families. For the first few hours, this journey felt like an adventure.

By today, the sheen had worn off. The Median Road, so grand and broad near the capital, had become just another winding mountain path. The banners were long since stowed. If she did not turn her neck to see the endless trees, she had to face the stench of horse arse. For three nights, they had slept at local manors; for the last two, she had crammed into the wooden bed of the wagon, her wings pressed against molding canvas. She hoped her maids did not hear her whimpers of frustration at endless days of dirt, sweat, and stale bread.

For years, she had regarded her god as an indifferent being, but today she prayed for some end to the boredom.

In the late afternoon, the vista finally opened onto a stunning view of the western plains. Hawks circled against the dipping sun, brown against red, diving for unseen prey. For the first time in days, she felt a thrill of wonder. Agni often said that dragon blood yearned for the skies. For once, she felt it too, longing to glide again.

A bump and a large crack shattered the moment. The driver screamed a Kazian curse that she did not recognize but must have been so vile that two knights whipped their heads around in shock.

"What is the matter, driver?" Agni's voice rang out as Ark trotted up, his hairy white hooves kicking up clouds of dust.

"We broke a wheel, Lord Guardian."

Agni dismounted to inspect the front-right wheel, almost directly beneath her. Then he laughed—that infuriating, inappropriate laugh that always set her on edge.

"*Ai*, did we ever. Replace it and prepare to ride by torchlight. We will send a rider ahead to secure lodging with Baron Lazo."

He glanced up at her with a small jerk of his head, as if above asking her to dismount. She stifled her irritation that he could not spare a hand to help her down. She took a deep breath to berate him, but before she could speak, his voice boomed out over the ridge, barking orders to his knights.

Sara swung a leg over the side and glided to the ground, wings spread for a soft landing. She walked a few steps into the beeches to take in the circling hawks. *What I would do for minor comforts—a warm bed, a wool blanket, maids brushing out my hair before laying out my evening gown,* she thought.

Suddenly, a shout broke the peace.

"Brigands! Brigands on your right! To arms!"

Her heart seized. Cries erupted from beyond the ridge, the zing of drawn swords mixed with sharp commands. Precise as dancers, two knights flanked her, their faces grim but calm, and two more surrounded the wagon.

"Protect the duchess!"

*"Ai,* captain!"

She felt as helpless as a mouse. She fumbled for the small dirk sheathed to her thigh, gripping it as if it would turn the tide if four of Agni's best fighting men could not. Her knuckles whitened as she hissed a desperate prayer to the god of fate, her second of the day and that whole year. Mid-prayer, she switched to her basic Kazian, as if it might better supplicate her god.

Peering around the nearest knight's stallion, she saw only billowing clouds of dust. Her ears rang with the shouts of men and the pathetic screams of the dying. She bit her lip hard, fighting a rising tide of panic. Her guards and their horses stood indifferent—it calmed her. These were bandits fighting masters of bow and blade.

Above the cloud, a white-blue flash caught her eye. Agni's sword—the blade said to hum with their god's will—sliced downward into the chaos. In that moment, pride swelled in her chest. He looked every bit the hero she had admired, the knight who had charmed her at her father's court.

But she also felt pity. *How desperate must those brigands be to attack such a formidable convoy? In Artania, Father would have given them alms, perhaps even invite them to feast at Midsummer.* Her ladies carried coins for such occasions. Why instead did they raise blades?

The cries began to subside. Alexander's voice cut through the din.

"Finish and form up!"

The dust began to settle. Now, she heard only a few screams; the mercy blows for men whose life force leaked into the mud.

When the clouds settled, a wretched-looking man stumbled onto his face, rolling twice in the dirt before he could arrest himself. Looking closer, Sara saw that one of his wings had been half-cleaved off, as well as his right arm at the elbow. The skin around the remaining arm sagged, perhaps because it once held knots of muscle; scabies encrusted the remaining wing.

The poor bandit grunted, struggling to his feet. One knight poked a sword between his shoulder blades, drawing a yelp.

"Keep walking, worm!" a knight barked.

Four knights surrounded the bandit, swords drawn. The front two parted for Agni atop his warhorse. *I have never seen a battle this close. What reduced this man to this state?*

Two of Sara's protectors rode up and fanned out to surround the bandit. Four armored knights pointed their swords at him. Soon to be five, as the front two parted for Agni atop his warhorse. The rear knight raised his voice.

"Your Grace, it is dangerous. Remain—"

Sara raised her hand and silenced him.

"No. If this is battle, let me see its fruits."

He only nodded back.

Agni's wings flared wide, catching the last rays of the sun. He looked like an avenging god, merciless and unyielding. He dismounted Ark with a flourish, his breastplate only showing a speck of dirt.

"You. Your name," Agni demanded.

"R-Rolo," he stammered back. He cowered, eyes robbed of both malice and hope. "Your sword… are you… th-th-the Lord Guardian?"

"You will address me as such. And you will answer what madness gripped you to attack an armored convoy."

Rolo fell to his knees, clutching his cleaved arm. Blood dripped from his nose and mouth.

"Lord Guardian. W-we thought the messenger carried rations. We've not eaten in five days."

Agni froze, his jaw tight, his eyes fixated away—Sara recognized that he was having one of his spells—his body, like a viper, coiling to strike. How would he emerge? Snarling, babbling about gods and destinies? Even his knights looked uneasy.

"Agni—" she began, but the word barely left her lips before he pounced.

With a guttural roar, Agni's fist crushed Rolo's cheekbone. The man crumpled, but Agni struck with relentless fury—a stream of curses on his lips as fists and elbows rained down like a storm. Blood spurted from each wound.

"Stop, Agni, stop!" she screamed in vain.

Alexander and two knights struggled to restrain him, holding every limb.

Sara rushed to his side, placing a trembling hand on his chin. His sweat drenched her palm. His body shook with unnatural rage.

"Agni, please. Be still. The battle is over."

Sara's mind raced. He fought something deadlier than bandits within. The first time she saw him have a fit, he bellowed in rage and overturned a cart laden with turnips. Neither physicians nor priests could cure nor pray him free of them.

But only today, she felt a needle of fear.

"Sara," he intoned, chest heaving.

For a moment, he looked dazed, like a child waking from a nightmare. He stared deep into her eyes. She met his eyes with a soft but trembling resolve, desperate to pull back from whatever fit consumed him. Her heartbeat thundered in her ears. Then a flash of motion caught the corner of her eye.

Agni's right shin arced towards her head at deadly speed.

"Ah!"

The third knight lunged forward, his steel-covered arm deflecting the kick just in time. But the redirected blow still struck her left shoulder like a war hammer. She crumpled to the dirt, her arm numb before she realized what had happened. Globes of light flashed before her eyes. Then a hideous wave of pain. Her scream echoed in her own ears.

"Ahhhhh!"

"Your Grace!"

The familiar voice was Nira's, shrill with panic. Dazed and gasping for breath, Sara lifted her head to see Nira scrambling from her rear wagon in wide-eyed shock.

Sara could do nothing but stare at the ground, a sharp throb radiating up to her neck. Numbness gave way to pain with every heartbeat. Her breaths came short and sharp. For a long minute, servants and knights alike stood over her, mute.

"Ah…ah."

She felt violated. Unsafe. Her betrothed had struck her—not out of malice, but some unnatural rage. Were the whispers true that he had grown more erratic, more dangerous? Might he strike her again—hard enough to kill her?

Agni gurgled and thrashed as Alexander tightened his massive forearm around his neck, still struggling. A fourth knight had rushed in, pinning Agni's striking leg, though his convulsions shook four strapping men.

Nira dropped to her knees, cradling Sara's head and brushing dirt off her wings.

"Your Grace," she whispered, voice trembling. "Can you stand?"

The words froze in her throat. She stared at the horizon, her body trembling. *No. No. Five more days to Eltrazan. What if this madness overtakes him? What if this is my true betrothed?*

Nira's fingers brushed Sara's shoulder, sending a fresh bolt of pain through her arm. She gasped, jerking away. The sharp pain jolted her back to reality.

Her lip quivered as she bit back tears.

*It is time to be a duchess, not a frightened girl. Have resolve,* she said to herself. *Let him see that I can rise above this.* Agni might command fighting men and inspire fear, but she carried ruling blood.

She clambered to her feet, every heartbeat sending a new ache up her shoulder. She steadied herself with a deep breath, straightening her back and spreading her wings, forcing herself through the pain.

Agni grunted and growled, but his struggles were weaker now, his body spent from fighting his captors. Sara approached him but dared not come too close. Her voice was soft but firm.

"Calm, love. It is I, Sara."

For a moment, his gaze locked on hers, his face twisted. Half aggressive, half confused, whatever foul force grasped at his mind was weakening.

"Sara," his voice rattled.

His mouth moved as though trying to form more words. His limbs twitched. Whatever tempest raged within him had not yet cleared.

*He is not lucid; I must show him that I can thrive in the realm of blood.*

She swallowed hard and turned her attention to the bloodied man on the ground.

"You, bandit. You say you have a family. Are you lord, citizen, or outlaw?"

The man coughed and propped himself up on quaking forearms, his voice weak but steady.

"I was once a lord, my lady. But I returned from Avicia to find my wife and son vanished, and my manor seized by my cousin. He paid mercenaries to fight in his stead. My slain men were loyal servants. Now, I eat tree bark and raised a sword against a man I once pledged my life to."

His words carried a hollow sadness that pricked at her heart. Rolo had sinned, but he had suffered. Agni's fury had already stripped him of dignity—surely there must be a better way to resolve this.

"Had you approached us with open hands, we might have fed you from our wagons," she said, voice rising with confidence. "Had you petitioned us in Azectrai, we could have granted you a land forfeiture and honest work. Instead, you stand accused of robbery and assault on high imperial officials. How do you plead?"

Rolo bowed his head. Tears streaked through the blood and grime on his face.

"Guilty. I submit myself to Her Grace's mercy."

Sara drew in a breath to respond, but the sound of armor clanking in lockstep interrupted her. Her heart sank as Agni, his breastplate heaving, drew near. His eyes still gleamed with an unnatural flame.

"And as the ranking official of the law, I deny it," Agni snarled. "Your life is forfeit."

Sara's fists clenched at her side. *How dare he? I, not you, am sworn to Emperor Taran himself!*

"Lord Guardian, I am—" she began, but Agni silenced her with a raised hand.

"Alexander, gag our criminal. I tire of his babble."

Alexander obeyed, wrapping a thick rope through Rolo's mouth and pulling it tight.

"Out of respect for your service, Rolo, I offer you two choices," Agni continued, his voice sharp and cruel. "Tap your chest three times, and my guard will cut your throat cleanly. My guard will place some credits in your jerkin. I will instruct the sheriff to bury you in your manor. Some of those coins may return to your kin, if the sheriff forgets to line his pockets. Or…" Agni leaned in, his face inches from Rolo's, "we drag you to Eltrazan, stab thrice through each wing…"

Agni tapped three places on Rolo's right wing.

"…weave a rag through…"

Agni poked the makeshift gag.

"…and throw you off Duke Hauran's eastern rock. It is a short drop; you may live to feel buzzards pluck out your eyes. And if Varenox smiles upon you, a wolf's teeth may grant you mercy."

Her stomach turned at the vivid threat. This was barbarism, not justice.

"Agni, I must—"

"Sara, return to your maids. You have no business here," he snapped.

"No," she replied, back straight and wings spread. "I am Duchess Sara Ristana of Artania, and this man has put himself at my mercy, not yours."

Agni turned to her with a bone-chilling smile, as if this were a game. She shivered in fear; she had the title, but Agni brought two potentates to cower—and had just brutally struck her.

"Then command Alexander to release him, duchess. Alexander, I order you to hold him fast. Let us see who holds the true power."

Sara's voice broke as she pleaded.

"Alexander, let him stand. Please."

Alexander's grip shook, but he did not release the man. His loyalty lay with his commander, no matter how his conscience might waver. Agni once told her that power flowed through blade and fist—now, she understood.

Agni's hand went to his sword.

"Your father would do the same, Sara," Agni said, tapping the hilt of his sword.

"H-h-he would not delight in inflicting terror like you, Agni," she countered, lips quivering.

"And my father, ogre though he was, trained his son into the emperor's loyal subject. Tell me, will Rolo serve him if I grant him mercy?"

Sara breathed deeply. She looked into Agni's eyes and realized he had not blinked once since he approached Rolo.

"He just may."

"Let me show you the true meaning of mercy."

Agni drew his enchanted blade—it looked like a thunderbolt in his hands, gleaming with hatred—and thrust it into Rolo's belly.

"Gah!" She jumped back in fright, covering her mouth.

She smelled charred muscle and fat on the wind. Bile poured forth. The wound would fester and he would die in agony. Agni was no longer the gallant knight who just protected her, but a butcher who delighted in pain.

He turned to her, his voice calm and flat.

"End it, Sara. Thrust your knife beneath his ear and cut forward. That is mercy."

Her skin crawled. She had never killed so much as a rat. The blade felt as heavy as Alexander's greatsword.

"Blast you, Agni," she hissed, tears spilling down her cheeks. "Blast the day I was laid before you."

She thrust the blade beneath Rolo's ear. Blood spurted over her hand, warm and sticky. Her hands were too weak to cut forward. Soon, Rolo's breath left him.

Agni had turned away, barking orders to his soldiers as if nothing had happened.

"Soldiers! Prepare to depart. We have another hour to Baron Lazo's manor. Let us reward a loyal Solantian lord appropriately."

Sara stumbled towards the woods, then dropped to her knees. At least her tears could stain the forest floor rather than her face, reminding her of her shame. She scrubbed the blade with fallen leaves, but no matter how hard she tried, it would not come clean.

# *Triumph*

As the dark granite skyline appeared over the horizon, Agni's breath caught. The midday sun lit Eltrazan's towers gold and orange. Eight years had passed since he first entered the city as a captain; six moons later, he left at the head of a column. Today, he returned as the conqueror of Avicia and Blevenia.

"Make way! Make way for Duchess Sara of Artania and the Lord Guardian of the East!" shouted his advance rider.

The crowd outside Eltrazan parted like a tide, eyes locked in wonder, their murmurs rising in waves. Agni straightened his back, his cloak billowing behind him like a banner, the rising sun catching its silver threads. A chill rose up his spine. The best theatres in Kazia would re-enact the surrender of King Theodore of Tercera, and the actor who portrayed Agni could bed any woman in the city that night.

With that thought, a flush of shame darkened his cheeks. Since the bandit attack, Sara would not look him in the eye. Last night, she stared at him agape until she thought he fell asleep and then crept out to bed with her maids.

*What have I become? I felt Anton's hatred of the world of the living—the world that denied him. Sweet Sara, forgive me...*

That thought made his hands clench on Ark's reins. Anton's presence sent lightning through his veins, and he lashed out blindly at the first shapes he saw, the bandit, and then Sara. Since then, her eyes widened in terror, like a rabbit's for a wolf, every time she saw him.

He twisted in the saddle to glance at her. She sat atop the carriage, her wings arched gracefully, waving at children who lined the road. *At least she seems happy outside my presence,* he thought. *I hope her father's presence soothes her wounds—the wounds I inflicted.*

The horns atop Eltrazan's walls sounded in unison, three long blasts that echoed across the sky. A pause, then another three. A wave of silence fell over the crowd before it erupted into a deafening roar.

"Hail, Lord Guardian! May your enemies bow before you!"

"Long live the Empire of Solantia!"

"Hail, the Son of the Borderlands!"

Agni watched fists rise into the air—farmhands clenched rakes, maidens waved scarves, even crippled veterans raised stumps. Many might have thrown themselves under Ark's hooves, for a glory they only knew by name. The roaring tide of adulation dulled his inner tumult, if only for a breath.

Two guards banged the hafts of their spears on the ground, then raised their right hands in salute.

"Lord Guardian, state the purpose of your visit," their captain shouted.

Agni grinned, recognizing the brusque captain fifteen years his senior. Despite the constable's protruding belly, he still moved with a warrior's grace.

"For fine cuisine and western hospitality, Constable Cavan, you old dog," Agni said, beaming.

Cavan smiled back and patted Ark's nose, "And may the Lord Guardian and this fine beast find our western hospitality most pleasing. Please tarry a moment. I will not have you arrive at Duke Hauran's gates without a proper escort."

"Of course, constable."

While they waited, a crowd gathered around them. A father and two young sisters approached Sara's carriage. Their faces glowed with awe as Sara dangled her white silk scarf for them to touch. She moved with willowy grace—Agni marveled at her poise. Where he stirred men's hearts to battle, Sara could remind them of what they fought for.

"Mama, look!" a young voice shouted.

A boy of eight ran up to Ark, a seeing stone clutched in his hand. Ark snorted but lowered his head. The boy touched Ark's face and pinched the stone, immortalizing the memory, his delight pure. Agni patted Ark's mane—he welcomed the easy delight of childhood before the coming schemes of nobles.

Minutes later, they approached Eltrazan Keep. It still took Agni's breath away—it stood taller and darker than he remembered. *This city was first designed to repel the Kazian people's invasions,* he thought. *Never forget, this is a city of Westerners.*

Constable Cavan whistled, and a fleet of attendants rushed in. Like bees, they zipped back and forth, carrying chests of clothing, food, and wine to their appropriate quarters. Only the levy remained.

Moments later, the gates to the main hall opened, revealing Duke Verlan and Duke Hauran at the entrance. Verlan carried a commanding presence, his broad shoulders and royal blue hair mixed with gray. His surcoat of two proud dragons against a bar dexter spoke of an ancient lineage and power. *One might mistake him for a man fifteen years younger and ready with his sword,* Agni thought. *Even an urchin could tell which of them holds power.* Hauran stood behind his guest, slightly shorter and thinner.

Sara broke decorum, dashing up.

"Father!" she cried, embracing him tightly.

Verlan's expression softened as he wrapped his arms around her, their wings pressed together.

"My darling Sara," he said, his voice warm and paternal. "I have missed you so."

Meanwhile, Hauran strode toward Agni, clasping his hand in both of his own.

"Welcome, Lord Guardian," Hauran intoned. "Eltrazan and Solantia welcome one of our very finest.

"His Grace is most generous," Agni said with a slight bow. "I live to defend Solantian home and hearth."

"And for the next ten days, we will celebrate your deeds. You remind us that every Kazian lad carries greatness within him."

Agni's stomach tightened. What veiled intent lay beneath the flattery? He forced gratitude into his smile.

"Without His Grace's patronage, this boy from the Azectrai Valley might still be prowling the Spires like a wolf seeking prey."

"Yet thanks to you, Solantia stands prouder than ever."

Agni's mind churned with suspicion. Eight years ago, Hauran honored Agni's ancestral claim to a company of knights, a calculated move to share in his glory. His words seemed to honor his own image as much as Agni's.

"And thanks to your engineers and craftsmen, we will know peace."

Verlan's voice rang out, silencing the courtyard.

"Sir Agni, Lord Guardian of the East, for ten days and nights, we shall honor Solantia's greatest victory in a hundred years. Emperor Taran has declared Days of Joy throughout the empire. Feasts will be held from here to the Axis, and ours will rival Artania itself."

"Everywhere but my hometown," Agni muttered under his breath, "we do not have that luxury."

Hauran laughed heartily.

"Prepare yourself for barrels of fine wine, my lad."

"It seems I have no choice," Agni said through another forced smile, "but for now, my men and I are roasting under plates of Kazian steel. Let us rid ourselves of the dust and heat of the road."

"Yes, of course. You must be weary. Let us meet here in an hour," Hauran replied. "Gervo will see you to your quarters."

Hauran waved down a slim adolescent in a silk tunic. The boy walked with a flowing gait, like a lord's son. *This is part of Hauran's spectacle,* he thought. Gervo smiled and bowed at Agni, who returned it with a nod.

"Lord Guardian and esteemed guests, I am Gervo, and it will be my pleasure to make your stay comfortable and memorable."

"Thank you, Gervo," Agni replied, his skin prickling.

As they followed Gervo down a side corridor, Agni ran a hand along the cool, rough-hewn walls of Eltrazan Keep. It lacked the opulence of Artania or the mystique of the Ancient City, but it radiated a cool power.

"Azectrai, yes? The Ancient City must be quite a vision," Gervo opened with an easy tone.

Agni stiffened. What possessed Hauran's servant boy to lead with questions about the Ancient City?

"Less than you might think, boy."

Gervo continued, undeterred.

"They say the sunrise over it rivals the Lands Beyond. Have you ever set foot inside? I would stand on the battlements and spread my w—"

Agni's jaw clenched at that brazen remark; who put those questions in his head? Did Hauran—or worse, Verlan—suspect that Agni had breached the walls? Sara could not yet have told either, who would tell Gervo, about Agni's recent "spell."

Agni dropped his voice.

"Boy, every lad in Azectrai knows that ruin is a beautiful den of foul magic, that anything—or anyone—that enters and returns must be purified with fire."

Gervo's eyes flickered with either curiosity or fear.

"The Borderlands fascinate me. My grandfather came from Artania and married a Kazian woman who taught him the tales of Emperor Anton Kazirian, who ruled the entire s—"

"Silence!"

Gervo stopped, visibly stunned.

"We have been baking in the sun all morning and stink like cows. Prattle later."

Gervo nodded, but his posture remained too poised. Agni's unease deepened; this was no mere page boy.

Pack servants trailed after them. Like a line of ants, they filed into a room, dropped their bundles, and left without a word.

"Lord Guardian, you and Her Grace will sleep here," he said, pointing to the largest room bathed in natural light. "Her Grace's maids will occupy the next room. Captain Alexander, you and two of your men will sleep here. Privies sit next to the staircase we came up."

"Thank you, Gervo, you are quite hospitable. Now leave us for one hour."

"I will be near if the Lord Guardian wishes anything."

"I wish you to return with rags, buckets, and soap, so that we might remove the stench of the road and oil our armor. Then return in precisely one hour."

Gervo bowed and scurried off, footfalls fading into the distance.

Agni motioned Alexander into his suite; his presence reassured him.

"Hauran's little charmer, is he not?" Alexander said with a faint smirk.

"Yes."

Alexander grinned back, saying nothing.

"Now attend me out of this oven of a breastplate. I will do likewise."

No sooner than their plate mail clanked against the ground, Gervo returned.

"Lord Guardian, your supplies, as asked," Gervo said, motioning a line of similar-appearing youths to place buckets on the floor.

For the next fifteen minutes, Agni and his men stripped off their riding clothes and tended to their armor. Yet Agni's unease bubbled up again. Gervo's gait, his words—everything about him felt too refined. No Kazian boy spoke of the Ancient City or Anton Kazirian to strangers.

"Thank you, Gervo," Agni replied, avoiding the boy's gaze, "now give us some time to dress ourselves like your lord."

"Yes, sir."

Gervo wheeled towards the door. But as the light spilled in from the hall, a strange shadow flickered—a boy's pressed against the wall just out of sight. Alexander lumbered towards the door, still in his linen breeches.

"Boy," Alexander growled, his voice low but firm, "the Lord Guardian says to leave, so we had best not see your shadow for another hour. Begone."

Gervo slinked away down the hall, his footsteps echoing. Undoubtedly, a lord's eyes and ears. But for whom?

He turned to Alexander, raising a finger to his lips. With a thumb and forefinger, he mimed *you and I*, followed by an arse-wiping motion, inviting him to the privies for a private conversation.

The narrow latrine stank and forced them to stand head-to-chest, wings pressed against the sharp stone.

"This will be a long ten days, Agni," Alexander muttered.

"*Ai.* These walls have ears. Trust no servant, no manor lord that you do not know by face, and especially neither duke." Agni's eyes glinted in the dim light. "Do you understand the meaning of that boy's questions?"

"An imbecile could understand his snooping outside your quarters after he said he would depart."

Agni nodded with a hard expression. "More. He is no Kazian. Eastern boys do not speak of the Ancient City; they murmur of it with reverent fear. And no Azectraian—not even a priest—speaks lightly of Varenox's last child."

"Your ancestor, yet even you only whisper his name. I only know him from myth. Many question whether he truly lived."

Agni's lips pressed into a thin line. His true father. The thought gave him a familiar chill. Anton gave him a power he dared not to reveal, even to his most trusted friend. A secret tied to his own blood.

"I have little reason to speak it," Agni deflected, voice cold. "But Gervo's questions reveal his Kazian name is a ruse, a mask. Tell me, Alexander, why do you think we were invited to this celebration of strutting peacocks? I would expect Verlan to call us westward for good to Artania. They want us here, under their eyes, then to return to Azectrai. This bodes ill."

"To what end, Agni?"

Alexander spoke in a curious tone. Had he shielded his captain too well from the schemes of nobles?

"Ten days under their scrutiny means more than keeping us close. Perhaps Hauran, the Westerner by blood, loses his grip on his people. Nothing had united Solantia like the Black Moon War. This feast does both. But Gervo..." Agni paused, cracking a smile, "might be the worst spy east of Artania. Watch the boy, miss the dagger. He is a lure, a diversion."

"From what?"

Agni's voice dropped even further. "I wager my wings that our rooms have speaking stones; assume the dukes will hear every word. Tell the men to stay vigilant and share nothing of import outside our ranks. Share none of our suspicions—not to the men, the maids, and certainly not to Her Grace."

"Sara?" Alexander frowned.

"She will always be Duke Verlan's daughter before my betrothed. Her father will turn her ear at every opportunity. I fear she has already told him about my… spell… in the mountains. It galls me that I struck someone dear, even as fraught as we are."

Alexander placed a firm hand on his commander's shoulder.

"I can only imagine."

"It was as if struck by lightning and pulled from my body," he spoke, fighting bitter tears, "then fury beyond any battle, hatred against the living. The wretched bandit. And then my betrothed. Spell or not, I failed as Lord Guardian, and as a man."

"Do you think her father suspects your spells are worsening?"

"If Sara tells him, beyond a doubt. And I fear they may be," Agni said, shaking. "I know the citizens of Azectrai whisper about them, even if they do not question my command. Some call me mad, others touched by our god. I do not know what the dukes believe."

"They fear what they do not understand," Alexander said, his gaze steady.

"Dukes care not for the gods until they feel Varenox's maw turning towards them," Agni's voice darkened. "They may fear a Lord Guardian with a column of knights wielding dark magic. Gervo's questions about the Ancient City suggest that they suspect its power within me."

"They know it as folklore. Would they act on an old tale?"

Agni shook his head.

"You show yourself the Westerner, Alexander, half-Tarkan, given an Avician name, raised on the Great Sea. You have seen more of the Mortal Realms than I. You did not see Azectrai until your seventh year as my aide. You were not raised in its fear."

*I carry its fear—and one day, its power,* Agni thought. *And the latter frightens me more.*

Alexander chuckled.

"I have never claimed otherwise, but the tales still sound strange."

"Let it serve our purposes, my friend. Nurture it and stay safe. They play their shadow games; let us play our own. Sing their praises where their ears—or that oily boy's—can hear."

Alexander grinned, the wheels in his mind turning.

"This conversation never took place."

"What conversation?" Agni smiled back. "Now let us squeeze into surcoats. When Gervo returns, let him find us jesting with the men."

Agni peeked out of the privy, his ears straining. Only the distant clatter of dishes and bawdy laughter filled the hall.

"Now, follow me at the count of thirty."

Agni slipped into the hall, shadows at his back.

The familiar sting of soap cleansed the grime of the road, but it reminded him of Kali.

Gervo returned precisely on time. Agni greeted him with a mask of calm gratitude.

"Lord Guardian, your midday meal awaits," Gervo spoke with a polished bow.

Alexander stepped forward, fully dressed and composed.

"I beg your pardon for my harsh words, earlier, Gervo. His Grace has been most hospitable."

"No matter, sir. It is our pleasure to host you."

Agni inclined his head slightly, hiding a smirk.

*Let us all play the shadows, Your Graces.*

Sara and the two dukes entered Hauran's private study, the banded oak door closing behind them with a thud. Shelves of worn books and tightly rolled scrolls lined the back wall, darkened by time. Hauran made a beeline for a thick, leather-bound tome and flipped it to a marked page.

Sara hesitated. Freed from the gaze of the court and jubilant throngs, her composure wavered. The throbbing in her shoulder from Agni's kick still flared with each heartbeat, a painful reminder of her fragility in the face of his monstrous strength. A bruise the size of her palm had formed; even the touch of a silk gown hurt.

She bit her lower lip, trying to steady herself, but her wings betrayed her, trembling faintly as she fought back tears.

"Yes, Sara, please open the scroll with the levy from the Azectrai Valley," Hauran instructed, breaking the silence.

Sara's fingers brushed the coarse parchment as she unsealed the thick scroll. But before she could unroll it, Verlan's firm hand clamped over it.

"Oh, the levy can wait, lovely daughter," Verlan exclaimed with a wide smile. "I have not seen your face in two years. Two long years. Do you agree, Hauran?"

"I suppose," Hauran harrumphed, clearly displeased at being upstaged. "We will have some days together yet."

Verlan pulled her into a tight embrace. He buried his face in her shoulder; *did a tear just dampen my sleeve?*

"Father," she whispered, her voice shaking. Her wall of dignity had started to break.

"Not a day has passed that I did not dream of this moment," Verlan murmured. "Your tutors, your nurses, indeed the very walls of the capital duchy miss their shining jewel. My only solace is that you have grown so strong in the East. Soon, you will return to Artanport. You will overlook the Great Sea again—it is as magnificent as ever."

Sara stole a glance at Hauran, who stood awkwardly by his desk with a furrowed brow. Father's affection warmed her, yet it also loosened the flood of two years of longing and despair. Her breathing shook. She wanted to beg Father to take her west, to wed her to anyone else. She had once hoped to civilize Agni the brute, to rule by his side as a capable governess. But now, she recoiled like a whipped dog around him. The next blow might end her.

"And I count the days until I might return west, Father. To learn at your side again. To the only life where I have ever felt whole."

Father released her, gently taking her hands.

"My dear daughter. I would bring you—and Agni—back west after this feast, if I could. But I feel you growing stronger. Commanding the levy is no steward's task. Every missive from the East praises your judgment."

"But I cannot—" Sara began, her voice cracking.

Father cut her off with a joyful tone, seemingly unaware of the coming flood tide of tears.

"Sara, Agni—and all Easterners—are strange to me as well. Their tongue, their myths, their taboos, their very language frozen in time. Yet its people will fight to the last for their land—and for Agni Kazirian. With him, we unite Solantia. The dukes of the Far Coast and the River Axis would not dare challenge an alliance between Artania and Kazia. If they did, we could break their treasuries with a tax to transport goods through our lands. Emperor Taran may rule in name, but we will stand behind the Crystal Throne. Your children may sit on it."

Sara took a ragged gasp, her chest tightening as tears began to pour. Did Father not see her pain? Or the danger Agni posed to her?

"Father. Please," she sobbed. "Deliver me from him. I cannot return east. He—he—struck me, Father. I fear I may not survive the next blow."

Verlan's body stiffened, his arms tightening around her.

"Struck you?" His voice perked.

Sara slowly nodded before burying her face in his shoulder. Her fears spilled out without conscious thought.

"On the trail… he had a fit. His leg struck me. If not for Alexander and three strong knights, he might have torn into me like a mountain leopard. I fear his fits worsen. I fear for my life."

She felt Verlan swallow a lump in his throat as he gently stroked her hair.

"Oh, Sara…" he moaned.

Her voice broke again as she recounted the bandit's execution.

"He ran a bandit through with his blade, then—then ordered me to slice his throat. I—I had no choice. I see that man's dying face every time I close my eyes. May the Netherworld take him!"

Verlan held her tighter but said nothing—his silence felt ominous. She could sense Father weighing her words, his ambitions against her safety. He could not sacrifice her for his vision of power—or could he?

As the tears subsided, out of the corner of her eye, she saw Hauran, impassive and motionless, his hands folded neatly on the desk.

"Please, Father," she pleaded, her voice a whisper. "Deliver me from him."

Father sighed deeply, patting her wing as he had when she was a child.

"My dear, you have endured two years of hardship. Give me a few short moons. Artania has the finest healers—physicians, priests, wise women. They will cure him."

"If it is our god's work, no healer will suffice," she said with a weak nod.

Father smiled, his tone soothing but calculating. As always, balancing love and ambition.

"Legends, Sara. Nothing more. The Ancients, the Empire Kazia, the Scourge, even if they existed, what do they mean to us? We *are*. Solantia *is*. Remove him from that land of whispers and myths and let him occupy himself with western matters. The Dragon God will find another soul to haunt."

*His tone can calm a rabid dog. But he will return me to the East,* she thought.

"Father, I need to be free of all of it—Agni, the East, the last two years. Let him wed his mistress and guard the Spires. He does not want the West. Wed me to Duke Rowan of the River Axis; he prefers young Aloi boys and will see me once a year, to put a child in my belly. Or Danan of the Far Coast. We will hold half of Solantia without Kazia."

Verlan frowned and sighed. She felt ill in her stomach—did she admit too much? But she felt compelled to lay it bare. That striped bitch could absorb his fits, his blabber of dragons and spirits, and his lusts which had almost completely bypassed her.

"Sara, it pains me to see you like this," he said softly. "But I have faith in you. You have a rare gift of command—Baron Goro speaks glowingly of your leadership on the levy. A duchy runs on coin, not on battle orders. Agni commands men, but you," he pointed a finger at her chest, "command the future."

She forced a smile, though her heart remained heavy.

"Thank you, Father. Your faith is my anchor, even when I feel adrift. I should have known the nature of men like Agni sooner."

Verlan chuckled, mischievously.

"The most spirited stallions make the strongest warhorses."

"I suppose so," she said, trying to mask her doubt.

"Let us mull over how to train up this horse; we have ten days to watch him. Now, let us enjoy this grand city, dear. You have earned respite."

Sara nodded, leaning into his embrace once more.

"Let my maids clean these tears. I have not danced in two years," she said, her voice soft but determined.

"Then dance, my jewel," he said warmly, his hand grasping hers, gently guiding her in an Artanian step.

"But the levy, Verlan," Hauran interjected, his patience clearly tapped.

"It can wait, Hauran," Verlan said firmly. "We will account for every credit in two days. For now, let us celebrate."

"Yes, let us," Sara said with a faint smile. "I shall return to my maids; the noonday meal awaits."

She bowed at Hauran and turned towards the door.

*Ten days to savor,* she thought. *Can Father's tongue tame Agni's steel?*

# Feast

With a grunt, two servants swung the immense oak doors to the banquet hall. Agni's breath caught in his throat—the dukes must have bled the treasury dry on the banners alone. Banners of silk draped from the ceiling, vibrant reds and blues shimmering in the setting sun. His family's crest prominently hung side by side with the duke's and even the emperor's—*the emperor's!* His mind spun. What did this mean?

Then he saw something even more stunning—the painting. Agni, rendered in vivid oils, mounted on Ark. In one hand, he held his gleaming sword aloft; in the other, the severed heads of the kings of Blevenia and Avicia. The scene exuded primal power; Agni the all-powerful, all-consuming—was this a test of his ambition? It thrilled and unsettled him.

A deafening roar brought him back to the moment.

"Agni! Agni! Agni!"

The assembled nobles banged the hilts of their daggers against the tables. Lords raised goblets, and ladies blew kisses while lowering their necklines, their eyes full of promises. He smiled as he walked the long aisle to the head table, his heart pounding in time with the chants.

"Ag-ni! Ag-ni! Ag-ni!"

Each duke heartily embraced him, the chants surging anew. Sara, glowing and radiant, stepped forward and planted a lingering kiss on his lips, their feigned passion drawing another cheer from the crowd. *The longest kiss we have shared in two years*, he thought. *A pleasant façade.*

Taking her hand, he led her to their seats at Verlan's right hand. The chair beneath him, padded with down, felt like a cloud. He let his wings hang back, interlaced with Sara's. Even the harsh stone walls were draped in soft fabric, creating a cocoon of luxury. The world had been reshaped to comfort him.

Sara clasped his hand in hers.

"Agni, is this not wonderful? When we return to Artania, we will dine like this in the emperor's palace."

Her eyes sparkled with unrestrained joy, a stark contrast to the burdened expression she wore in Azectrai. For a moment, he envied that joy; he forced his own smile to hide his suspicions.

"I will accustom myself," he said. "Though I could eat a rat."

A plump servant boy, his silken tunic sky blue, approached, wings tucked in deference. Even the servants dressed like lords here.

"Pardon me, my lord, my lady. I am His Grace's cupbearer, Mani. May I fill your cup?"

"Yes, Mani. Wine for the Lord Guardian and me." Sara nodded graciously, with a genteel tilt of her wings.

The boy's eyes twinkled. He bowed so deeply that his wings scraped the table.

"Yes, Your Graces."

*Your Graces.* Agni winced; it felt oppressive. They chose him as a warrior, not a politician. Again, he glanced at the painting. Did they see him as their hound, a conqueror to fill their coffers?

Sara's voice cut through his thoughts. "Have some cheer, Agni. They came from all corners of Solantia to honor you. You will address them, no? You can rouse armies with your speeches—this will be a trifle."

"I am glad that you are happy."

Agni grunted, taking a long swig of the rich wine. He remembered addressing knights in this very hall a decade ago—his nerves taut, his words rehearsed to exhaustion. Yet he put two knights to sleep and had to cuff their heads awake. *Let the passion flow*, Hauran had admonished. Tonight, he would remind them what greatness flowed from the East—and his own blood. He swirled the wine in his goblet and smiled. *Let them see the fire of the Borderlands.* For a few minutes, he lost himself in the lutes and pipes.

"And how is my future son enjoying the revelry?"

Verlan's voice boomed as he slapped Agni between the shoulder blades.

"His Grace will spoil me for life in Artania." Agni grinned.

"Please, call me Verlan," the duke insisted, his own grin wide. "We owe you more than we can repay. By your strength and cunning, Solantia stands unshaken. We have enjoyed prosperous harvests. What good are our coffers if we never open them? Tonight, we honor your deeds and forge even tighter bonds between the East and West."

"I suppose." Agni shrugged. Verlan's words felt honeyed, as usual, yet he never spoke a word that did not further his ambition. *The Borderlands do not feast like this.*

"Some see coincidence, but I see Varenox's will. Are we of Solantia not his favored children?"

"One can never rely on his favor," Agni intoned. *You regard no god, Your Grace,* he thought.

"I believe he will elevate us skyward." Verlan's voice brimmed with conviction. "My boy, I see so much more than the Lord Guardian within you. By your wits, we will pay our foes back threefold, by the ancient standard. You say Blevenia still tests our resolve; Avicia contests land in the Axis. Their rolling hills cannot hold your mountain snares. Would that the North had a Lord Guardian, we would take back our land and blunt the roc's beak."

The words struck Agni like a lightning bolt. Verlan did not want a successor yet; first, he wanted a High General. An attack dog to fill his coffers.

Agni clasped Verlan's hand. No sword-calluses marred his fingers; they were as smooth as Sara's. Verlan's ilk sent boys to die for ambition disguised as duty. He felt urgency to pry those lords away from this grasping man.

"Perhaps," Agni replied, keeping his voice neutral. "Let us feast tonight and discuss grand strategy some other time. We will have some moons for such talk."

"*Ai*, lad." Verlan leaned closer, dropping his voice to a whisper. "Now look at these fat little partridges." He gestured subtly toward the room. "They live lives of plenty; most have not seen their cocks in ten years."

Agni let out a low chuckle but noticed their bulging bellies as well.

"I see."

Verlan continued, his voice brimming with mischief. "Yet they fancy themselves warriors—heroes, even. Most bought out their service to the emperor with silver. At best, they tell their strumpets stories of valor from thirty years ago. Sell them a grand dream, make them feel like sturdy youths, and they will pledge you whatever you wish."

Agni arched a brow. "And their wives?"

"Oh, a dashing young lord sitting at the head table could bed any one tonight."

Agni looked at Sara, who was looking away.

"Your daughter might not approve," he said, smiling back.

Verlan sighed, waving a dismissive hand.

"She will never understand the ways of menfolk. These fattened hogs have ravished half of their washer women. Though she will never speak it, I suspect my dear Sara appreciates that you take only one lover. What was her name, again? The Aloi woman?"

"Kali," Agni said, tersely, fearing where this conversation was headed.

"Yes, Kali. A sweet girl, I am sure. But in Artania, you will find beauties beyond compare. Exotic courtesans, noble daughters, servants alike."

Agni bit his lip, forcing a tight laugh.

"Indeed."

Verlan clapped him on the back again.

"Anyways, I shall leave you to your thoughts. Be memorable."

Agni wrinkled his nose as Verlan stepped back. Those words grated him like salt in a wound—how dare he equate Kali to a tavern girl. But before his simmering rage could surface, Sara tapped his elbow.

"What did Father just tell you?"

Agni's jaw tightened.

"He joked about our noble guests. Called them fat little partridges. Nothing important."

He looked away hoping that she might not press further. Out of the corner of his eye, however, he saw her lean close to her father, whispering something. *Any of their murmurs could spell my death. Do they think me so blind or stupid as to conspire next to me?*

His fists clenched beneath the table. He would never be their dog.

Never be their dog. Never be their dog. Never be their dog.

*Never be their dog.*

The phrase resonated in his head.

*Never be their dog.*

*Dog. Dog. Dog.*

Vertigo swept over him, terror mixed with ecstasy. The banquet hall dissolved, replaced by a vivid vision—the Ancient City bathed in golden light, its towers bright against the noonday sun. Dragons circled above, their wings beating in harmony. No fear, only triumph. Was this the dream of an aggrieved spirit—or his future? An intoxicating vision—what would he sacrifice to bring it to life.

A voice rumbled in his mind, deep and commanding.

*"Scion. I have waited twenty years for this night. Your rebirth begins now and with it, our lost due."*

*"What?"*

Agni's heart pounded.

*"Rebirth,"* Anton repeated.

Memories raced through his mind. Boy. Soldier. Commander. High General. Lord Guardian. What would follow? The air vibrated with Anton's will.

*"Lord Regent of the Empire Kazia."*

Anton's promise—for Agni to rule at his side for one thousand years. A mere Lord Guardian could not do that. Agni stiffened.

*"Lord Regent? Ancestor, they know not the Empire Kazia—only their silks, gold, and wine. You would have me speak treason."*

*"Only two at this feast possess vision—Duke Verlan, the lesser, and yourself, to whom I have granted the greater,"* Anton calmly replied. *"Do not dismiss him; his ambition serves us. But know that his arrogance will be his undoing. He believes that he can rule the*

*Dragonlands, that Kazia will content itself as a mere province. He deceives himself."*

Agni's breath quickened.

*"What would you have me say?"*

*"The true power in this hall flows through you, not him. For now, use ambitious men like Verlan. In time, he will rally to our side—or die."*

The strength in Anton's voice surged through Agni. Anton spoke truth; the dukes had no one else to parade before their lords. Agni alone embodied the East's might and mystique.

*"How shall I bring him to our light?"*

In his distant body, Agni felt his mouth dry with fear. Great Anton laughed with an emperor's confidence.

*"Once, you doubted you could humble King Theodore of Avicia. Yet you did,"* Anton said, his voice like thunder.

The vision shifted—to the Avician king, his blonde hair caked with mud and sweat, fatigue pulling at his eyes. The tent's air stifled that day, but victory buoyed him.

*"Yes, Agni. The nether cannons—the threat of magical destruction by which a backwater boy could speak as a potentate's equal."*

*"But I possess no such weapon."*

*"Wrong, boy. See that painting where you hold King Theodore's head by that foppish yellow mane. These lords heard embellished tales of that day. You have their fear and wonder. Plant the seed of our lordship. Let it grow."*

Anton's images faded to a lightning blue. He felt it penetrate his body. No herb or tonic felt like this.

*I am the thunder.*

*Seed. Seed. Seed.*

The banquet hall shimmered back into focus as Hauran rose, clapping his hands. The song and chatter stopped, and all eyes turned to the dais.

"Noble guests," Duke Hauran began, his voice solemn and deep, "today marks the climax of ten glorious days of celebration throughout the empire. From the Axis to the Far Coast, Artania to the Kazian Borderlands, fine wine flows and fatted hens are roasted in honor of our most glorious day. Two years ago, we struck down the Ancient Alliance of Avicia and Blevenia with such force that they dare not test us again. Glory to the Emperor!"

The guests raised their fists and bellowed the falling scream of a diving dragon. Agni tensed his muscles, suppressing his own roar. All his minutes-ago concerns felt as distant as Avicia. He was the prophet of the Ancients, the emperor to come—*The Dragon.*

"And now," Hauran continued, his arms outstretched, "we would be remiss if we did not hear from the architect of our triumph. By strength, devotion, and cunning, he has exalted our empire among the nations. We are proud to present to you one of our own this evening. Most favored of our exalted Emperor Taran Solant, once High General of the Solantian Empire, now Lord Guardian of the East, Lord Agni Kazirian!"

"Ag-ni! Ag-ni! Ag-ni!"

Agni rose slowly, letting the fervor wash over him, savoring the power Anton had foretold. Today, the Kazirian blood would assert itself over all of them. He flexed his wings, allowing the golden torchlight to illuminate the fine embroidery of his cap. Then, raising his cup, he let out a piercing roar.

"*Zaka tai!*"

The crowd roared back, though their foreign tongues butchered the Kazian phrase. Agni smirked at their attempts but took it as a sign; foreign or not, they would follow him into the unknown.

He stepped forward, prepared to hold them enrapt then release their energy at the most exquisite moment.

"My esteemed host, Duke Hauran," his voice boomed. "Lords and ladies assembled here tonight. You honor me, a simple son of the Borderlands. My name—Agni—means 'living flame' in our tongue. A spark that found tinder in purpose, and with it, the destiny to carve the far reaches of the Mortal Realms."

The room fell silent. *If only they knew how deep that destiny runs. They will bow before it.*

"Had a desperate boy not witnessed Blevenian raiders butcher his mother, he might never have sought refuge in the discipline of Solantian steel. Had he not stood guard over her lifeless body, unable to comprehend her death, he might never have taken Duke Harkon's surrendered sword."

Agni leaned forward, flaring his wings above Sara and Verlan at either side, his voice growing in intensity.

"O Empire of Solantia, we embrace you. Peace unto you, and doom unto your foes!"

"Hail!" the assembly shouted, the cry rippling like thunder through the hall.

The chill echoed through his body.

*Rebirth. Tonight.*

"Hail Solantia, chosen of Varenox, God of Dragons and Great Deeds. For it is by his will that I have seen visions that guide us like a farmer's plow. I saw them as we set fire to the tents of Blevenian patrols and drove them over cliffs. I saw them in the crackling masts of Avician ships, burning like candles in the Battle of the Ports. I saw an empire where any boy with that spark can rise as I have, prostrating himself before the emperor. I saw a land where merit, not birth, elevates men to greatness. A world where the strong guide the willing, and the willing rise without chains of legacy or station. I ask you tonight—walk with me into this world!"

"Hail! Hail! Hail!"

He had challenged the very foundation of their order, yet they cheered as if he offered them the Crystal Throne itself. His heart surged at the eruption of praise, as if rays of lightning might burst forth from his chest. Powerless to stop it.

*Rebirth. Tonight.*

"And within this world," he continued, voice rising to a crescendo, "I see my homeland, Kazia, rise from the shadows of its ancient post. For centuries, we were regarded as relics—a living memorial beneath the umbra of the Ancient City. No longer!"

His fist slammed against the table, rattling goblets and plates.

"We, sons of my Blessed Ancestor—" His breath caught. He had just invoked Anton Kazirian before the lords of Solantia. But the rapture only grew.

*And the Dragon of the Moonless Night will rule once more.*

The distinction blurred between Anton's will and his own.

"The sons of Anton Kazirian will stand tall once more! From our land once flowed learning, law, and magic. The corners of the Mortal Realms prostrated themselves before us."

His voice lowered, as if casting a spell, filled with reverence and passion.

"Where men and dragons stood as kin, without fear."

*Madness.*

"Where Blevenia and Solantia were not divided, but one land. Where the children of both played together in my beloved Spires."

*Sedition.*

"Where our god loved all his people…"

*The god who condemns me.*

"The jewel in the crown of the Solantian Empire."

*That which will submit to Anton's might.*

"The Jewel of Eternity! *Zaka tai!*" he screamed, raising his cup high.

The hall went deathly silent. Lords and ladies sat frozen, their faces pale, unsure if they heard a promise or a threat. But then, the hall erupted in deafening cheers.

"HAIL! HAIL! HAIL!"

The roar made his ears ring. He felt the tension in his body pour into the crowd. In their blind exuberance, they had cheered for more than Solantia—they cheered for Kazia's rebirth. For Anton's empire. For Agni's dominion.

"HAIL! HAIL! HAIL!"

The nobles knew Anton as Agni knew him. As Anton's presence faded, it left Agni with the burden of his words.

*I may have just forfeited my life.*

Verlan turned in his direction, his face blanched, his jaw clenched. The duke turned slowly to Hauran, who mirrored his expression of stunned disbelief.

*Something changed in his heart...I see it.*

Agni met Verlan's attention, keeping a stone face. He stood firm with a conqueror's pride, while whispers rippled through the crowd.

At last, Verlan rose, forcing a smile. His voice wavered, but he composed himself enough to address the crowd.

"Lord Agni. As always, your words set hearts aflame. Artania is proud to walk arm-in-arm with Kazia into this glorious future."

Polite applause rose from the crowd; a pale shadow of what Agni just elicited.

"Now, let us cast aside our obligations for this night. Tomorrow, we shall return home with renewed vigor."

Agni nodded, lifting his cup once more. As the applause faded and servants began carrying out platters of meat and fresh vegetables, he felt Sara's hand tighten on his arm.

"Agni," she whispered, voice trembling with wonder, "that was incredible. The fire in your words... it was as if our god himself spoke through you. Is that how you roused men for battle?"

She pulled him close, planting a kiss on his lips. But as their lips parted, Verlan's hand landed heavily on Agni's back again. A reminder that Verlan still had power.

"Easy on the fine red, boy," Verlan said in his jaunty voice. His eyes still looked alarmed.

"Lesdran red has fueled many an address," Agni replied with a faint smile.

"Anton Kazirian, the Ancient City… some day in Artania, you must tell me those tales," Verlan replied, his voice light but probing.

Agni held his gaze.

"Perhaps."

"You have a proud name."

"My father passed down some grand tales over the hearth," Agni lied. "We never stray far from our past."

"Very well," Verlan replied, his voice calm. "May this feast live up to your ancestor's name."

The seditious seed had been planted.

*Blessed Ancestor, what have you set into motion?* he thought. *Verlan will strike from the shadows. In his time.*

# Sleep

Agni's speech echoed in his mind for ten long days back and two since. Traitorous words poured forth before a hall of lords. Kazia's ancient grandeur. The rise of small folk. A name cloaked in legend and taboo. Did his eyes betray forbidden influence? If they did, Verlan thought him mad; if not, seditious.

Agni knew Verlan would not act openly—not yet. The schemer would whisper in shadows before burying the dagger. But Hauran? The fool might pinion-and-drop him outright, if only to show strength. Agni grasped his blade every time the mundane noises of Azectrai—the clank of a smith's hammer or a maid's shout—rang out.

But worst, Sara had grown cold on the return journey. She spoke politely, even praised his speech when he fed words like "father," "feast," and "speech," or plied her with wine. What did she know? Sara might no longer be the sheltered noble, but a spy, or even an assassin. She was learning the games of nobles, and that made her dangerous.

Agni stood in his doorway, gazing out toward the Spires. The air felt heavy, the clouds like damp wool blanketing the sky. If Sara would not reveal her secrets willingly, he would have to pry them out with strange herbs.

*I sacrifice my honor for my life—and my home,* he thought. *I cannot risk being seen, even in a town where knights and priests see wise women.*

Agni pulled his wings high and close to hide the best-recognized face in the city. He kicked a stone down East Street, watching it tumble onto the green, the road deserted under threat of rain. The downpour would turn this street to mud and wet leaves. Memories of childhood—simpler days, flinging dirt with Balo and the other knights' sons—flickered through his mind. A sharp contrast to the dangerous subterfuge that threatened him.

The apothecary's house came into view, its sign marked by crossed stems of sage. Agni glanced up and down the empty street before knocking on the door.

The door creaked open, revealing Aira. She must have set hearts aflutter in her youth. Even in her ninth decade, her back stood straight, her silver hair retained flecks of blue, and her wings hung proud as banners.

"Lord Guardian, it's been some time. To what do I owe the pleasure of your visit?"

"Lady Aira, the pleasure is mine," Agni replied with a slight bow. It felt alien; perhaps he acquired some courtly manners at that blasted feast. "I hope this day finds you well."

"Yes, yes, Lord Guardian. I haven't seen you in moons. Mistress Kali stopped by for her tea while you were feasting."

"Thank you for taking care of her, my lady." Agni smiled faintly, noting that Sara had little need of it.

"How is Lady Sara?" Aira asked as she latched the door behind him. "She looked so joyful as she climbed into her carriage."

"Well, thank you," he replied, forcing a smile. "The festivities lifted her spirits—I pray those memories will sustain her until the next."

Aira tilted her head, her eyes cutting through Agni's practiced veneer.

"She looked radiant," Aira said. "But a radiant face often hides a troubled heart. I have no herb to heal such a sickness. Perhaps she needs your love more than ever."

Agni nodded, suppressing a bitter laugh.

"I do love her, in a way. Just not in the manner she needs—or deserves."

*Love, how fragile a bond between us.*

"I have a tonic that keeps your company strong and virile, if you are interested. I am sure Mayor Goro's wife is a happy woman."

"Perhaps." Agni chuckled, though his concerns lay elsewhere. Herbs and powders, bundles of dried roots, bottles of syrups. A cure for every ailment the surgeon or physician could not. *And I came in search of poison.*

"We were pledged in innocent times. Lords wed not for love."

Aira raised a knowing eyebrow.

"I'll never understand that."

"My Mama and Papa had both. She, Chosen of the Dragon God, could empower her sword with prayer and disarm my father in both battle and heart. He once told me how smitten he felt after the first time she struck his wrist in sparring."

He laughed, mustering this rare, pleasant memory of his parents together. He never knew a stronger warrior than Mama. But the thought still weighed on him.

"Yes, Mara was an incredible woman," Aira said through soft eyes, "I see her in your spirit."

"Thank you," Agni whispered, his voice catching. *Kazian boys grew up too quickly in those days.* Tears formed in his eyes, but he could not afford weakness today. *I must channel my pain. Enough idle talk. I did not come here to reminisce.*

"But rarely did she strike in anger. I have, and it comes with great cost." His voice darkened. "My nights are filled with terrors of death and fire—the faces of men I have slain. I wake drenched in sweat and fear a return to sleep. Even last moon, I cut down starving bandits along the Median Road."

The Battle of the Ports alone could fill a regiment with nightmares. He indulged those emotions like an actor. *But time to steel myself before I sob like a child.*

Aira's face softened.

"I'm terribly sorry, Lord Guardian. You've seen things I would not wish on a viper." She turned to her shelves. "Might I suggest powder of valerian?"

She handed him a bottle. It smelled like his trousers after morning exercises.

*I need a tool, not a sedative. A waking dream. She needs to see a different realm; one without her unfaithful, violent betrothed.*

"I have tried that to little effect, my lady."

"But you have not bought valerian. Nowhere else in town sells it."

"I tried it in Eltrazan," he lied. "It did little."

The sharp old woman's eyes narrowed.

"Take it with a cup of wine. I would not recommend that to any but a strong young man, though."

Aira did not break her gaze.

"No. It needs to dull my dreams."

*She sees through my lie, even though she does not wish to argue.*

After another long breath, she turned to her right.

"I have something," she said, reaching for a basket. She held up a gnarled root, its twisted form almost human. "Mandrake. A powerful but dangerous herb. It can bring visions, even false prophecies. The priests frown upon it."

Agni stared at the root, its slender, ghostly body; its stems were long, flowing limbs—like Sara's. Mandrake. Man. Drake. Man. Dragon. Agni, Sara, Anton, and all Azectrai save for Kali and a couple traders were dragon-people. Man-drakes. It drew him in.

"I will take it," Agni said, resolute. "Falsehoods are better than the truths I see."

*And I see the Black Moon rise,* Agni thought. *Soon.*

Aira hesitated.

"I sold herbs to your mother and your father's mother before her. I trust you but speak of this to no one. The priests permit its sale but take an interest in those who buy it."

"On my oath, no harm shall come to you."

*I hope I can keep that oath, Aira. But if Sara's revelations lead where I believe, no oath can shield you from the storm.*

"It is dear to grow," Aira warned, "I require one hundred credits."

Agni reached into his coin pocket so fast, several ten-credit silvers spilled to the floor.

"Accepted."

Aira's eyebrows raised at his haste, but she said nothing as he scrambled for the coins.

"Return in one hour. I will grind it to powder. Take no more than a pinch, or it may lock you in the Lands Beyond forever."

Agni nodded, his throat dry.

"Yes, milady."

Aira began cleaning her mortar and pestle, her hands not showing a hint of rheumatism. Agni turned and stepped into the street. He would soon drug a high noble, risking both their lives. Mama would strike him for such cowardice; but she was gone, and honor would not save him from the dukes.

He pulled his wings close and put a hand over his face, concealing his actions—and his shame. He had burned enemy scouts and threatened cities with dark magic, but this was a war of deceit, and he held a new weapon.

———

Agni knew he could not risk heading home—Sara's averted gaze would unnerve him. The ever-watchful Dona would bubble over with questions. His fragile façade would crumble. The guardhouse or town hall might have ears. If a conspiracy lurked, Mayor Goro would have a part in it.

Agni needed an hour of solitude and a confidant. Agni only had one, even if he possessed him to speak treason and owed Agni an explanation.

He made his way east, towards the river and the looming specter of the Ancient City, stopping at the old grove of elms where he buried his sword twenty years ago. He checked the sight lines to assure that no soldier—whether relaxing, posted, or taking a piss—could see him. He mouthed out a name: *Anton Kazirian.*

*"Blessed Ancestor, I have waited you,"* Agni cast a thought into the ether.

*"I owe you nothing, boy,"* Anton's voice snarled through the ether. *"Without my call, you would be ash in a hog's pen."*

Agni expected Anton's disapproval but bristled nonetheless. His wings tensed.

*"Ancestor, you speak of Great Kazia's resurrection, then seize my tongue to speak sedition at the Duke of Kazia's feast—"*

Anton's growl cut through the ether like a knife, taking Agni aback.

*"Stop. Never refer to the Western maggot as Duke of Kazia. He is a boil festering on this land, that we will lance in due time."*

Anton spoke as though he still commanded legions of flesh. Whatever slumbered in that crypt—or the rest of the Ancient City—had yet to pour forth into the Mortal Realms.

*"Call him what you wish, but he can take my title, my men, and my life with a word. A wonder he has not had me pinioned-and-dropped. I would have."*

Anton's voice lowered to a flat, sinister tone. *"A lesser man who speaks such words is thought mad. A great man who does, is thought blessed."*

*"Blessed?"* Agni scoffed. *"How will I lance this boil as a titular lord in the West? I shall wither in Verlan's shadow, and I could never raise an army of Westerners, under the emperor's nose no less. Your restored Kazia may sit another eighty generations."*

Agni braced for Anton's wrath, but none came.

*"Time means little to me, scion,"* Anton said, his voice cold as iron. *"Were your descendants guaranteed to bear your spark, I would bear those millennia like a moon and leave you to Varenox's whims."*

Agni's frustrations flared, his voice defiant. *"Then do so, wise one. Abandon me to obscurity and fate. You will only watch, bereft of your body. But remember, you shaped me at every turn. You made this cowering child into an insolent man, because you could not bear to see our name fade. If we would have our name to command tribute from Avicia and Tarka, we had best address the 'snare' in which your guidance has placed us."*

Anton's lips curved into a smile. He appreciated artful defiance, even when directed at himself—a trait he shared with the god he loathed.

*"We have reminded the western lords of their rightful place,"* Anton said in a jaunty voice. *"They may strike you down, but now they know from whence true power flows. No longer are you their hound."*

*"Again with your sedition."* Agni's eyes rolled. *"What am I to do while my power—small though it is next to yours—hangs by a thread? Can you read Sara's heart, or her father's? What do they know?"*

*"I know not their hearts. Only yours. You are a cunning man, who chose the proper tool for this occasion. Just like, as a boy, you turned the land against enemy knights, you turn this herb—product of this*

*wonderful land—against your foes. Your betrothed has skill, but she needs tutors and guards to protect her from men like you."*

Agni shivered at that thought. His voice dropped to a bitter whisper. *"I hate that she needs protection from me. I hate that, in your haze, I struck her on the Median Road—"*

Anton raised his hand, silencing him again.

*"Do not fault me for your loss of control, scion. I told you to instruct her in the ways of ruling over men of steel and blood. Even noble ladies must wield a blade—whether in hand or through orders."*

Agni sighed, his shoulders slumping.

*"And I hate that I must drug her like a beaten housewife drugs her husband."*

*"Scion, do not coddle her for her sex,"* Anton retorted in a sharp tone. *"Solantian women have fought with blade and wit for centuries. She is swept up the same currents of fate that carry you. Like you, she must swim—or be swept under. Return to the wise woman with a clear heart. Remember, you fight for the greatest cause the Mortal Realms shall ever know."*

Agni felt a surge of resolve.

*"I do not understand your ways, ancestor. Great Kazia is still a phantom to me. But Solantia and the Borderlands sit in front of my eyes. I will act for them."*

*"That will suffice, Agni. Now go. Fulfill your purpose."*

The silver image began to fade, but Anton's words lingered.

*Fulfill your purpose.*

Agni drew in a deep breath. Was this what Anton meant by the vantage of the gods? Bearing every moral cost such that power may once more flow from the Borderlands? Sara was the weak point in the dukes' wall of silence. Her secrets could buy him time, or even a chance to stay in Kazia and fulfill his purpose as Lord Guardian.

The elms swayed in the rising wind as Agni turned back to town. Resolve and dread fought within him.

—

On the walk back to Aira's shop, Agni kept his chin high, shoulders back, and wings spread, betraying nothing of his doubts. The Lord Guardian could not tolerate uncertainty; that was *his* weapon; he held Blevenian raiders in check with the fear of unseen traps. But now, Sara turned his own weapon on him. Now, he could justify his resort to poison, the weapon of housewives and thieves.

The drizzle lent a musty aroma to the air, forming drops of mud as it hit the dirt. Distant thunder rumbled over the western mountains. The dank, moist air foretold a long rain settling over Azectrai. *Good,* he thought, *muddy roads will keep Sara in the house.* He needed Sara alone.

When Agni pushed open Aira's door, he found her waiting with a small bottle of brown powder.

"Here it is, Lord Guardian. Remember, just a pinch, and one with the fingers of an old woman."

Agni forced a smile.

"Of course, my lady. Thank you for this boon."

He pocketed the bottle, turning quickly to the door.

"Much obliged. Be well."

As the door shut behind him, Agni's jaw clenched. *The Lord Guardian buys a forbidden herb—she will remember this,* he thought, *but I will involve her no further. She may have just saved the Borderlands—or doomed them.*

He hatched plots during the whole walk home. Should he pour himself a single cup, then spike the pot? Or sprinkle it into Sara's cup while her attention was turned? Would it dissolve fully, or settle into the dregs? What if she stepped away to the privy? He could swirl it in quickly. Above all, he needed her awake and disoriented, and himself sober.

What if Dona took a cup of wine, and lingered with them? He felt a twinge of guilt at her well-being as a mere calculation; she was Kazirian in all but blood. *But the Lord Guardian leaves nothing to chance.*

At the front of his vegetable garden, Agni fingered the bottle in his leather pouch. As he reached the front door, he pressed his ear to the wood, listening like a burglar. The patter of rain drowned out any noise from the inside.

He felt the warmth of the hearth fire as he stepped in, removing his boots. Smoke curled out, its haze obscuring the giant Kazirian crest tapestry on the wall. *A fitting irony,* he thought, *plotting in shadows beneath my family crest.*

He heard Sara rustle parchment upstairs—a scroll or a book, as was her habit. As expected, she did not greet him. Her harp sat in the front room, untouched. Today, the silence brought relief.

Agni tiptoed to the back door, nudging it open. It creaked slightly before a strong hand yanked it open from the other side. Dona, her head down, nearly planted her head into Agni's chest. Startled, he dropped into a fighter's stance.

"Calm, Lord Guardian." She chuckled. "I have no wish to combat you."

Agni exhaled sharply.

"Apologies. Years of habit, love."

He pulled her into a warm, apologetic embrace but felt dread in his stomach. He mouthed out a curse; he lost his best chance to spike the pot.

"I've fresh trout, griddled with butter. And I'll boil you bread pudding with raisins, apples, and spice. You seem awfully beset since returning from Eltrazan. Is something the matter?"

Dona's matronly concern held him for a moment. She knew him longer than anyone still in the Mortal Realms, before grief and pain hardened him. If she discovered the plot, her fury would rival Anton's.

"No, nothing that bread pudding will not cure," he said with a false smile.

Dona returned a genuine smile.

"Well, then. I won't have the Lord Guardian sulking about this house. Bread pudding has always set your head aright."

Agni's stomach growled in response. Dona's bread pudding was a constant comfort since Mama first let him eat sweets. Perhaps it would set his mind right for plotting.

His momentary happiness ended as Sara's footsteps echoed down the stairs.

"Good afternoon, Dona," she spoke in a bright voice. "And hello, Agni," she said flatly.

"Hello, Sara," he replied, mimicking her tone.

"Dinner will be another hour, Your Grace," Dona said. "Why not enjoy a cup in the meantime."

"That would be lovely," Sara replied, glancing at Agni.

He turned away, a sinking feeling in his chest. *Shit. Shit. Shit.* Now he would have to open the bottle under the table, measure a punch, and dissolve it in Sara's—and only Sara's—wine, under the watchful eyes of both women. If he were caught, Constable Avro would pinion-and-drop even the hero.

Before Dona could turn to the wine pot, Agni yanked it off the shelf.

"Please, allow me."

Dona looked surprised but walked past to prepare the table. Agni uncorked the pot and poured two cups, trying to steady his trembling hands.

What little remained sloshed in the pot. *Blast it.* Could he spike the pot and gamble that he could withstand more than Sara? *No, nothing to chance.* He needed his full wits.

His mind raced as he and Sara ate in tense silence, glancing at her only when she sipped. He noted her steady hand and unflushed cheeks. Dona scurried back and forth, doting on Agni and Sara, leaving him no time to act. Finally, she brought out the bread pudding. It tasted as exquisite as always.

Sara scanned the room; did she suspect something?

Then, his next fear took form. In her zeal, Dona emptied the pot into their cups. *Blast it, again.* That powder might dilute too much in the next full pot. Would she need the privy? Or would Nira take her attention? If not, he would need to question her another way. If he woke her at midnight, would she answer his questions?—unlikely; she would bolt awake. Could he sprinkle some on her lips as she slept? No, it was rough and might trickle onto her pillow.

Yet he hardened his resolve. *Tonight may be my only chance. For Kazia.*

Dona walked in, this time with another half-bowl of bread pudding for each. Conspiring had spoiled his appetite; he stirred it listlessly. Meanwhile, Sara happily ate. He stared at its brown texture, dotted with nutmeg.

And inspiration struck. *The pudding!* The rich flavors could conceal the powder; it had the same consistency as nutmeg.

He excused himself, bowl in hand, to the kitchen. His heart racing, he carefully sprinkled a pinch of mandrake into the pudding. A man's fingerful, not an old woman's. He stirred it in with his spoon.

Returning to the table, he placed it in front of Sara.

"Take mine," he said. "I have lost my appetite."

Sara looked up, mouth agape. "You? Turn down Dona's bread pudding? Most days you ask her to boil seconds."

"My stomach is turning." Agni placed a hand on his stomach. "I will be well tomorrow, but you shall enjoy this more than I."

She wrinkled her brow but took the bowl. Their eyes locked—she seemed confused.

"You brought it to the back a second ago. You added something, did you not?" Sara asked, spoon in hand.

"A pinch of nutmeg," he said, forcing calm. "I thought it might settle me."

He broke her gaze and wheeled back to his seat. But she dipped her spoon and took a bite. Agni buried his head in his hands, rubbing his eyes to feign fatigue. With every bite, he felt his tension ease. That bread pudding did calm his head, after all.

As she finished, Agni tapped the bottle. It felt like a boulder, both in his pocket and on his consciousness. Now came the agonizing wait. Was that the right amount? Would a cup of wine lock her in the Lands Beyond?

*They say Agni Kazirian would not cast a die he had not loaded. But it is cast nonetheless.*

The rain intensified, battering the windows. The second storm had begun.

C H A P T E R   1 2

# *Ascension*

Each minute felt like an eternity. Agni sat at the table, clutching *Kazian Warfare: A History of Indirect Tactics*, its worn pages blurring before his eyes. He traced familiar phrases—*Control the land. Strike at the mind. Look strong when weak.* Maneuvers he had perfected: setting dry pines aflame, terror through snares, burning enemy croplands. But even The Desolator never poisoned his noble betrothed. The forgotten author—or High General Agni Kazirian—would have balked at such measures. *The Borderlands are greater than my honor, greater than justice,* he thought.

Yet doubt gnawed at him. *Anton's plan.* Did Anton intend him to kill Sara? Was chaos his means to rebuild Kazia? Agni's heart quickened. He wanted no harm to come to Sara, who had stood by him, to her own discomfort, for years.

"Agni…"

Her slurred voice jolted him from his thoughts. He turned to her, muting his instinct to scrutinize her like a commander. That gaze unnerved her.

"Yes, Sara?" Agni leaned forward, alert, ready to catch her should she faint.

"My stomach… I think that last cup did me ill."

"Mine too, love," Agni replied softly, omitting that his gut had roiled for hours, in anticipation of this moment. He slowed his breathing to steady himself. Ten seconds in, hold, ten seconds out. *Control the breath, control the mind.* It calmed his galloping heart.

Where was Dona? He hoped she had retired to her stone hut for the night, but on a rainy night she might return for idle conversation. Hopefully, she had exhausted the night's zeal to serve, and he would not have to shoo her away.

Sara rubbed her temples and rocked side-to-side. She muttered the occasional curse, rocking farther. Agni mimicked her movements, his eyes sharp through his fingers. She was drowsy but still in her right mind. *Not yet.*

"Your Grace, are you well?" Nira's voice pierced the silence.

Bile rose in his gullet. *Blast it!* He chided himself for not anticipating this. Nira had taken to Sara; the two often laughed over cups while he slept. It was time to play the Lord Guardian, like silencing a rowdy soldier.

"She needs only rest, Nira. Please go home to your sons," Agni spoke, sharpening his voice.

Instead, she spoke to Sara. "Your Grace, shall I prepare your tunic for tomorrow?"

Agni felt a surge of energy. The duchess outranked the master of the house, but he commanded legions under life and death.

*I regret that I must wrong you again, Sara,* he thought.

"Stay back," Agni grunted, with his best commanding voice. "She needs rest. Nothing more."

"Are you sure—"

"Do not question me again, Nira. I will care for her until the morning." His gruff voice, fueled by wine and anxiety, halted Nira in her place. "Until the morrow."

Nira hurried out, flustered and silent.

"Love, let me bring you upstairs. Rest off the wine."

Sara moaned, her head thudding against the table.

Agni slipped behind Sara, lifting her to his shoulders in a wrestler's carry. His back shook as he steadied himself; she was light, but the wine and the day's tension had taxed him. He fought the urge to retch from the effort.

He took the stairs one at a time, his grip firm, her usually-graceful wings drooping against his legs. Through clenched teeth, he hissed a prayer that she would not vomit down his back.

Once upstairs, he laid her gently on the bed, cradling her head in his lap. He stroked her hair as her limbs swayed. Then, without warning, she lurched to the side. He barely dodged the stream of vomit that spilled onto the floor. He wrinkled his nose at the scent and fought the urge to empty his own guts.

*A few drinks would not faze her,* he thought. *The mandrake is in her heart.* He continued cradling her head.

"Father… hold me…"

The word hit him like a blow. *Father?* In her daze, did she think he was Duke Verlan?

*I must know.*

Her glassy eyes rolled back and forth like a boat on the open ocean. A tear welled up. She appeared to be in a half-dream, where he could deceive her into speaking the truth. He was her Anton, and the mandrake, his black cloud.

"Sara, my darling," he murmured, "you are safe here," he lied, using the words Anton once spoke to put her at ease.

"I… I… feel…" Her voice faded, words lost in the haze.

"My Sara."

"Am I slipping away?"

"It will pass, my Sara," he said, pressing a hand to her damp forehead.

"Hold me, Father… tell me again."

Agni swallowed hard.

"It will pass, my Sara," he repeated, though he could not be certain.

"Where am I?"

Time to weave another yarn.

"We are home, Sara," he said, weaving the illusion. "The servants have retired for the night. Your nurse will return at daybreak."

"Which nurse?"

Agni bit his tongue. Anton taught Agni the ways of dreams; any inconsistency, any argument could shatter the delicate illusion.

"I will send for any you wish," he answered, his voice deep and soothing.

"I love you, Father. You are my cornerstone, since Mother passed," she moaned.

He felt her grip on his arm tighten, her voice thick with longing.

"I will be, as long as I draw breath," Agni replied, the words bitter in his mouth.

For a moment, she lay still. It was time to question her.

"And Agni…"

She gurgled something. He needed her clear-headed enough to confess, or he poisoned her in vain. He stroked her cheek again, leaning closer. Her eyes opened wide, as if realizing something.

"Agni has long said his spirit will glide through these skies, even in death…" she muttered with labored breath, "…a spirit of protection. Do you believe he will?"

Agni's breath seized. *Even in death.*

That confirmed his fears—Verlan intended to kill him.

Questions flooded his mind: When and how? How would Artania placate the good folk of Azectrai who would rise up at their hero's death? What would Verlan gain?

"Dear, dear, I never concerned myself with gods. However he meets them, he must soon."

Her eyes fluttered, as though consciousness faded and returned. He rubbed her temples to comfort her, but more to keep her anchored.

"The ritual, Father. Do you remember? You said Agni once told you of it."

His heart hammered at his chest. *The Ritual of Ascension*, that Anton once spoke of. To fetter a man to the mountaintop, where Varenox's lightning would consume him. Verlan, the unbeliever, plotted a ritual murder.

*My title will not save me.*

"Yes, Sara. The ritual," he pried. "When will our priests arrive?" He rubbed her temples harder.

"Ah!" She yelped in pain, but it might keep her awake.

"The justiciar and priests should arrive tomorrow. They will seize him at sunrise and ride into the mountains."

*Sunrise.* An icy dagger stabbed him in the gut. *As a desperate child, I longed for freedom from this body, to frolic with the sacred beasts that soar through the skies. Free,* he thought. Now he had Kazia. Alexander. Kali. *I cannot abandon them.*

"Yes, he spoke treason that night. We cannot permit that," Agni intoned.

But what was Verlan's endgame? The Crystal Throne—would he dare assassinate the emperor and wed Empress Imra, securing a claim to the throne and a legacy for Sara? Or did he only wish to pull his beloved daughter from the clutches of a madman? Verlan might have deceived Sara, too.

"No, Father," she said, alternately lucid and not. "You said that was wine-addled nonsense after one of his fits."

Agni's arms tensed; he knew he had best not contradict her again.

"Yes, yes…" Agni echoed. How long would the mandrake hold her in this state?

*Speak more, sweet Sara. Speak all of it.*

"It was not his words," Sara continued, voice trembling. "It was the way the Western lords leapt at his words." She paused, face uneasy. "We can find another High General. What happens if he turns them against us?"

The picture sharpened in Agni's mind. Their whispers in shadowed corridors. Verlan's fright after Agni's fiery speech. Anton's passion that could ignite noble hearts, not ancient Kazian myth. *Rebirth, planting a seed*—it made sense. But it was the memory of Anton's words that chilled him most. *As one draws closer to the gods, one must forsake the realms of men.* Was this all Anton's doing, to draw him away from his mortal station? If so, Anton would save Agni from the ritual, but to start a new Black Moon. *Blast it. I am the pawn of all—that which I fought for twenty years. Which master should I fear more?*

Urgency bore down on him. Who else had Verlan turned? And where could Agni flee to plot his counter?

"Yes, yes," Agni said, trying not to rush the words. "Have you spoken to the mayor?"

"Yes, yesterday," Sara slurred. "He told the herald to ensure the townsfolk… understand. Agni will ascend. 'Better a guardian spirit than a living threat,' you said." She tilted her head, eyes glassy but sincere. "Do you not remember?"

Agni's jaw dropped, unable to stay composed. *Goro, the priests, the herald—all are complicit.* His heart bounded. Tomorrow, they would take him; he had to flee tonight, through the downpour and over the gates. *The Ritual of Ascension, in my beloved Spires. A convenient lie. Verlan loses a threat. The mayor gains gold, land, and influence.*

"I do, dear," Agni whispered softly. "I plan to the end."

Sara sniffled, a tear rolling down her flushed cheek.

"Please," she whispered, voice breaking. "Do not let him suffer. He has hurt me—and I understand that he must die—but I still love him. He deserves a noble death. A hero's death."

Agni felt his throat tighten. *Blast her compassion.* Beneath her delicate exterior was not just a mind for accounts, but a heart to forgive.

"No, love," he said gently, "Varenox's breath, a strike of lightning, will free him from his body."

"Yes," she whispered with sad reverence. "That is how Agni described it. Like the Ancients."

"It suits him," Agni pretended to agree. "Forever a hero. The people will worship him."

"When we rule," she murmured, head lolling against his hand, "we will honor his birth with a grand feast."

"We shall."

Agni forced a smile, like Verlan might. But he laughed at the bitter irony. Mandrake, the herb that blurred truth and lies, the herb hated by his god, might deliver him from his god's wrath.

"What now, Father?"

"We wait, Sara," Agni replied in his best conspiratorial tone. "Soon, you will return west."

He longed for her to say more, to confirm the details. But she confessed enough. *Time to end this conversation. To flee and bide my own time to strike.*

Agni stroked her hair, guiding her back toward sleep.

"Rest now," he whispered. "Rest and know that I love you more than anything."

He cradled her head as her breathing slowed, her body yielding to sleep. For fifteen minutes, he sat still, her delicate form grounding him—and reminding him of his mortal danger. Every subtle gesture or harsh whisper he had ignored. *A soldier realizes the threat in front of him; a commander must see into his enemy's mind. I failed at both. I am no longer Lord Guardian—I am an outlaw.*

He bit his lip and fought the urge to rush. *Then prepare like an outlaw.*

Agni unlatched his chests. A riding tunic. A plain leather coat. A blanket. Solantian credits—gold hundreds and silver tens—for bribes and passage. He belted his sword. Food was harder—the larder lay too close to Dona's hut; he could not risk waking her. But the mice neglected some quarter-loaves on the pantry.

But the greatest question loomed: *To where can I flee?* Verlan might have ears in every corner of Solantia. Hero or not, any man would trade him for a year's wages as bounty. Aloi was a moon away over Solantian land. Lubo, the frozen backwater of outlaws, two moons over land and sea. Blevenia would execute him on sight.

That left one—*Avicia. Tercera, that once I brought to its knees.*

The second thought followed: *Have I gone mad?*

But Tercera's sprawl held six hundred thousand. He could vanish in its bustling Solantian quarter, plot his next act. And who would believe Agni Kazirian so brazen as to seek refuge in the city he once threatened to destroy?

He exhaled, flexing his wings. King Theodore loathed him but respected his power and skill. He bled their treasury, broke their alliance, prepared to slay half the city with nether magic and turn the remainder mad. *If Verlan wants war with Avicia, I will be the king's most treasured counselor. If I can walk into the royal court, bluff them with nothing, and gain the king's trust. By Varenox's scales, I have indeed gone mad. But I once thought myself mad to believe I could bring him to his knees once before.*

He took a long look at the home he might never see again—his father's, and his father's father's. Dona. Sara. *But I have no time to mourn,* he thought. *All I have left are Kali and Alexander.* The thought of their loyalty strengthened him. *Would they follow? If not, would Verlan allow them to live?*

The answers would only come with action. He had to flee to Tercera, and drag them into the coming tempest.

———

The rain grew fierce, pummeling Agni's head as he lowered his face, the biting wind catching his wings. He dashed along the north edge of the common, plotting the conversation to come. Kali, once the wandering entertainer and thief, had uprooted her meager life to follow him. She had navigated her love's betrothal to a high noble but wanted to be more than his mistress and confidant. He had a quartermaster teach her letters, and she devoured scrolls and books with a scholar's fervor. He imagined her in the halls of Tercera's grand university. And he could make her his wife, their children fit to return to Solantia one day as lords and ladies.

The thought warmed him but did little to steady his nerves. Convincing her should be simple.

*Should.*

He reached her house, slick with rain, and hatched a plan. Kali slept deeply, and a commotion would draw the city guards. A charging bull could not burst through her barred door. That left the window.

His builder had designed her house similarly to his own. There were no bars on the upstairs shutters. The river stone, however, was treacherously smooth when dry, let alone in a downpour. The only way to break in was to climb high, glide to a window, and rouse her without causing a ruckus. But she could fight with staff and claw.

*Forgive me, love, but I am a robber now.*

He skulked back to the old oak. If he could climb it and leap from a sturdy branch, his wings might glide him to the narrow ledge beneath her window. He could flare his wings against the wall and muffle the impact. But an instant too late and he would crash through the shutters with a racket; too soon, and he would strike the wall and fall to the mud. Any wind could blow him off course and break his neck.

Agni braced against the thick wall of the privy, one boot on the stone and the other on the oak, as if scaling a door frame. His chest heaved—the wine and fatigue sapping his strength, but the fear of losing Kali drove him onward. With a stretch, he grasped a sturdy branch eight feet above his toes.

He drove upward with a grunt using his legs and pulled the branch down to his waist, swung up a leg, and pulled himself to his feet. Rain dripped from his cloak as he judged the distance: *fourteen feet high, thirty feet away.* He bounced the limb and determined it could hold him. For a moment, he allowed himself to appreciate the irony—breaking into the house of a former thief.

He lowered his torso to pounce, waiting for a gust to die down.

One breath, two breaths, three.

*Now!*

He leapt, wings snapping open.

Time stretched as he glided towards the window. Arms raised, hips tucking forward. His boots perfectly hit the six-inch ledge, his wings flattened against the stone.

No sound from within. For a moment he felt giddy, the faint thrill of success.

Her bed lay to the left, and she slept on the far side. Stealth would not work—the creaking shutters would wake her instantly. He would need to pounce and muffle her first cry.

*I beg your apology, Kali. I take no pleasure in this.*

He gripped the shutters.

One breath, two breaths, three.

The hinges squealed. He launched himself through the opening, landing on her bed and awakening her with a jolt.

But Kali moved like a striking viper. She had ripped free of her blanket, fighting staff in hand. The first blow caught him across the mouth, splitting his lip. She followed with a strike to his left temple. Stars burst in his vision. But with both hands on her staff, he clamped his right hand over her mouth, muffling her rising scream.

Her green eyes blazed with fury, her body tense as a drawn bowstring. She cross-struck him, but it only caught his forehead. Blood trickling down his forehead and filling his mouth, he caught her staff with his left and pinned it over her head. It took every ounce of strength to restrain her flailing limbs. Still not defeated, her left fist thudded against his cheek. The world swam.

Finally, her breath spent, her limbs loosened like strings.

Agni had never admired her more. Her defiance, her strength— this was the Kali he loved. A warrior, fierce and unyielding. *If we survive to Tercera, our children will be champions.*

"Calm!" he hissed, his voice low but firm. Her wide eyes locked onto him. "Calm, love. It is me, Agni. I mean you no harm. Be silent. Do not scream. Do not make a sound."

Slowly, he lifted his hand from her mouth. She gasped, her breathing ragged, but she remained silent.

"Kali," he whispered urgently. "My life is in danger. I must flee Azectrai tonight. And I will not leave without you."

Her brow furrowed, her eyes narrowing into sharp slits.

"What?" she hissed, voice low but biting.

"Duke Verlan has sent men to execute me. They will arrive at dawn. Pack riding clothes and a weapon. Nothing more."

"How do you know this? Did something happen in Eltrazan?" Her voice wavered with skepticism and fear. "Did Sara—"

"You must trust me, love," Agni interrupted.

Kali kipped up to her feet, eyes flashing like emeralds. Even in her confusion, she radiated strength.

"You break into my home in the dead of night like a robber, spout madness, and expect me to follow without question? Explain, Agni, before I bloody your other lip."

He exhaled, steadying himself.

"I drugged Sara's supper, and she confessed everything. Verlan plots to kill me under the guise of the Ritual of Ascension. His men and priests will drag me to the mountains and sacrifice me to our god's lightning. His eyes and ears may be everywhere. You and Alexander may not be safe."

"Why a ritual? Why not a knife at the feast?"

"Because he needs Kazia to believe in the myth. If I am sacrificed as a guardian spirit, the land will accept it. Mayor Goro will spread the story to placate Azectrai—he, too, is complicit."

Kali's eyes still flickered with disbelief, but she scurried to her chest, pulling out a cloak and a small satchel.

"Would Kazia not rise up to shelter you?"

"I have their love," Agni said, shaking his head, "but love cannot feed a family. Verlan may offer a fortune for my capture."

She rummaged through her belongings, her tail flicking sharply.

"Then we will sail to Arteva and travel overland to Charoi. My people will shelter us. They have not forgotten you."

"The road will be thick with patrols even past Arteva. If Verlan wants me dead, he might forget about his 'ritual.'"

"Then where would you flee, Agni?" she asked in a quizzical tone.

Agni drew a breath. *You will think this even more mad than I do.*

"The only city where a Kazian warlord, his giant bodyguard, and an Aloi companion would not draw eyes… Tercera."

Kali spun, her tail lashing side to side.

"Tercera? You would flee to Avicia?" she spat. "You spilled Avician blood by the barrel. We will be hunted like dogs. King Theodore will have our necks. If we will die, let us die in a land we love."

Agni shook his head.

"I will never accept death, let alone at Verlan's hands. I grant you that this sword," Agni tapped the hilt, "has drunk barrels of Avician blood. But it was the Ancient Alliance that drew them into the war. Fighting men accept their duty. They do not worry me."

Kali groaned again. "Will they allow us to eat at their taverns, and forget to poison our ale? This," she pulled a fistful of credits, "means nothing across the sea."

She opened her hand, dribbling the coins back into the chest, as if accentuating their worthlessness.

*What wits about her,* he thought. Minutes after putting her in fear for her life, she asked the most incisive questions.

"Yes, we will live as fleas in the roc's down… for now. But I know expatriate traders in the Solantian quarter. They will shelter us while we plan."

She pursed her lips, her emerald eyes narrowing.

"What, you intend to scheme against the Duke of Artania from Tercera's shadows?"

"Love, I have not thought beyond this night," Agni admitted, his tone softening. "But two years ago, this son of a fading line forced King Theodore to his knees. Within a moon, I can earn his trust as a counselor on Dragonlands affairs. I will always protect this land—even from across the sea."

Her tail flicked in apparent disbelief.

"You told me a Kazian withers elsewhere like a yew in the desert."

He nodded solemnly, pondering the weight of that saying.

"I believed that, love. Perhaps I still do. Tomorrow I will wake as an outlaw and feel the pain of exile. But I will bring my own rain to Avician soil if I must. I will not wither."

Kali's sharp gaze probed him.

"And what of us?"

A rare unguarded smile softened Agni's face. Another dream had opened.

"A free life, Kali. No more chains of duty or empire. We can wed—indeed, I will marry you in the first temple we find. And you…" His voice thickened with another realization. "You can forge your own path in a land of boundless potential. You will walk the halls of Tercera's grand university, becoming the scholar you were meant to be. And our children…" His voice caught. "Our children will grow up free, in a land of boundless possibilities. One day, I will return and give our eldest son our manor."

Kali narrowed her eyes for a long minute.

"You speak with a honeyed tongue, Agni. I will follow—not for fear of death, but for the life we will create. I will become more than a barmaid and entertainer." Her voice grew playful, though her eyes remained fierce. "But if you betray me…" She tapped his swollen lip with her finger, smirking. "I will strike much lower next time." Agni chuckled, beaming. "I would not dare."

She leaned in, resting her staff against the floor as their lips met. The kiss on his bloodied lip felt heavier than any vow—an unspoken oath to endure together whatever trials lay ahead.

When their lips parted, her expression turned serious again.

"Will Alexander join us?"

Agni nodded.

"I pray he will. His spine is forged from steel, and he would never bow to Verlan's schemes. Besides, his Tarkan blood runs with the sea. If anyone can guide us safely to Tercera, it is he."

Kali slung her satchel over her shoulder.

"Then let us not waste time."

Agni offered a faint smile, his heart warmed by her resolve.

"Let us go."

A minute later, they slipped out of Kali's front door into the storm, vanishing into the shadows as their journey began.

—

The pair skulked back across North Street, sticking to the shadows as two watchmen with lanterns passed. Ordinarily, the guards would have saluted Agni and continued on patrol, but the mayor might have turned every guard in town.

As they approached Alexander's house, several down Knight Lane from Agni's, he considered his pitch. His loyal aide lived simply—a man of routine and unshakable devotion. His faith in the Dragon God and the Empire of Solantia was as much a foundation of his character as his towering stature. Loyalty to Solantia and their god, and to Agni, which would prevail?

A direct knock could draw guards. Burglary seemed laughable—he and Kali together could not quietly subdue the giant, and there was no oak nearby from which to spring.

Agni grabbed a rock half the size of his fist and hurled it at the shutter. It struck dead center, enough to rattle it ajar.

No response.

Agni loosed a second at the other shutter, thudding it open. At least he heard stirring.

Lantern light flickered in the distance. One more rock might catch the attention of passing guards. Agni moved closer to the window and hissed like an angry snake.

Finally, Alexander appeared, his frame occupying the full window. He glared out the window, his face wrinkled with irritation. Agni made a summoning gesture, mouthing the words "Hurry, come down."

Alexander's scowl deepened, but he nodded in apparent compliance, turning towards his stairs. Agni sighed with relief and stalked back to the front.

The bar lifted, the latch clicked, and Alexander opened the door, his eyes narrowed.

"Silence," Agni growled, pressing a finger to his lips and slipping inside. Kali followed close behind.

Alexander's gaze shifted between them in disbelief, his voice rising.

"Agni, why have you awoken me? Tomorrow, I take a patrol into the Spires. And why is Kali here?"

Agni waved his hand downward and again pressed his finger to his lips.

"Keep. Your. Voice. Down." He hissed through gritted teeth. "I am no longer the Lord Guardian; if I stay in Azectrai tonight, I will be ash by midday."

Alexander cocked an eyebrow in disbelief.

"What? How do you know this?"

"You saw Sara and her father creep away at the feast. On the return voyage, she spoke hardly a word to us," Agni began.

Alexander sighed, folding his arms.

"Yes, because your fit frightened her out of her wits. She has reason to avoid you. If your guard had not deflected that kick, it would have killed her. I am thrice her size and would not welcome that blow."

Agni winced at the reminder.

"That may be, but I drugged her dinner tonight. In her delirium, she confessed everything."

"Drugged her?" Alexander's voice turned sharp; that must have violated his conception of honor, too.

"In her haze, she thought I was her father," Agni continued. "She revealed her father's plot. Verlan has sent men to execute me through the Ritual of Ascension."

Alexander's expression twisted, incredulous.

"What? You have told every ear in Azectrai that the Dragon God loathes you. Who would believe he would release you from your body?"

"Verlan has turned Mayor Goro," Agni continued. "He will sell the lie. Enough people believe me mad that the lie might convince enough men."

Alexander shook his head.

"Even if the people believed such a farce, why would Verlan consider you such a threat? While you spoke sedition, you have a garrison, not an army."

"He did not fear my words, but the nobles' reactions to them," Agni replied. "The dukes did not invite me to honor past glories, but to watch me for ten days. I outshone them. That was my crime."

Alexander's face softened into contemplation.

"And you wish my assistance to flee?"

"Your companionship. We may all be forfeit if we stay."

Alexander's jaw clenched. His eyes passed over Agni and Kali. Could he see the desperation in their faces?

"But we face no ancient ritual."

"They will interrogate you," Agni said. "Your devotion to the emperor—or our god—will not shield you from a scrying ritual. The mayor may have High Priest Gari's ear. The moment you opened that door, you became my accomplice."

Alexander shook his head again.

"Then tell me no more, Agni. I am loyal to my emperor."

"You cannot serve His Imperial Majesty in death—or in whatever lowly position Duke Hauran grants you," Agni replied. "You are my wisest counselor. We cannot escape without you."

"Then where will you flee?" Alexander said with a sigh.

"Steel yourself for this, Alexander." Agni's voice dropped, steady and determined. "Tercera. Across the sea. The Solantian quarter will shelter us while we plan our next move."

Alexander scoffed, his hair shaking in the moonlight.

"What? King Theodore will post our heads on pikes. Do you think he has forgotten his humiliation at your hands?"

"No, and that is why he might protect us," Agni said, forcing a confident smile. "He knows that of which we are capable."

"And what will we be? Mercenaries? Knights?"

"Counselors."

"He will believe us to be spies."

Agni met his gaze.

"No spy would be so foolish as to present himself at this court."

"This is not like you, Agni," Alexander said, suspicion returning to his voice. "Are you well? Have you had another fit?"

Agni met the giant's gaze, unflinching.

"I learned of the plot not one hour ago. Instead of fleeing alone, I came here to plead with you and Kali—the only two people I trust in the Mortal Realms. You followed me into battle at The Ports, and into the tent with King Theodore. Now, I ask you to follow me once more, not as a commander but as a friend."

Kali stepped forward, her voice firm. "Alexander, I trust him. You have seen the dukes' hunger for power. We need you. You know the sea trade. The orca god Faluan may watch over you."

*Sweet Kali,* Agni thought, indulging a moment. *Loyal unto threat of death.*

Alexander sighed heavily, lowering his head.

"I only knew the orca god from my father's tales, Kali. I was dedicated to Varenox in the West. And it seems the gods, like this realm, have turned on us."

An emboldened Agni seized the moment. "And yet we have flourished, Alexander, despite it all."

Alexander's shoulders sagged, as if surrendering.

"I would not follow you anywhere else, Agni. But I find myself willing to abscond with you. I have little here—no land, no commission. My wife is long deceased, and our sons have sought their own fortunes. Someone must watch over you and Kali."

A rare smile softened Agni's face.

"My thanks, Alexander."

Alexander nodded, already turning towards the stairs.

"I will ready myself in five minutes. No lights."

As Alexander ascended into shadows, Agni felt a pang of sadness. It hit him; in an hour he had lost everything: his title, his home, his beloved horse, Dona, Sara. But as he glanced at Kali, then back at the stairs, he thought, *if I have them, perhaps I still have enough.*

———

Kali paced, while Agni stared at his boots. *Madness,* he thought. *I can flee Solantia, but I—we—can never flee Anton Kazirian. He also plots war and does not tolerate disobedience.*

Alexander returned clothed, armored, and provisioned.

"Now, how do we escape this blasted city? The gates are down. That leaves scaling the wall and taking down armored guards," Agni mused. "Alexander, do you have a grapnel?"

"*Na,* and the walls are slick."

"Leave that to me," Kali volunteered with a grin. "I can dig between the stones." She flashed her claws in the starlight.

"And can you strike down two armored men before they call for backup?"

Agni wanted to protect her like a maiden, even if she spoke the truth.

"That requires stealth. And no one can stalk like a tigress," she replied.

"Please, love. Do not risk yourself. Distract one, then strike the other in the head. Next, turn the winch like mad. Once we crawl through, pull out the handle and let it fall. But if you need to escape, we can fend for ourselves."

"Do not talk down to me, Agni." Her voice radiated displeasure. "I have scaled taller walls and stood up to knights in full plate."

"No offense, Dear Tigress," he said, rubbing the lip she had struck earlier, "just know that Tercera would not be the same without you."

Kali sighed and shook her head. "Let us go."

The rain had turned into a relentless downpour by the time they emerged from Alexander's home. He appeared to look at it longingly one last time. Agni led them through winding streets, each step sucking mud as they avoided puddles and patrols.

The wall loomed ahead, thirty yards west of the guard post, where a solitary torch burned. Its faint glow wavered in the rain, barely holding the darkness at bay.

"Here," Agni whispered, guiding them to a shadowed spot. He glanced at the battlements above. "Alexander, lift her up."

Alexander crouched without a word, bracing himself as Kali stepped onto his shoulders. With a grunt, she propelled herself upwards. Her claws found holds between the cracks, climbing with silent precision.

Kali vanished over the edge of the battlements, a shadow against the torchlight. Agni and Alexander watched from below, the tension thicker than the rain. The seconds felt like hours.

Finally, he saw Kali's outline in the torchlight. She waved her staff—the signal.

Suddenly, Kali pounced. The muffled sounds of impact followed—sharp blows, a yelp and a thud. Five strikes, swift and deliberate. He lowered himself to the ground, prepared to scramble under the gate.

With a clickety-clack, the winch began to turn.

"Go," Alexander hissed, his voice sharp.

Agni dropped into the mud and low-crawled beneath the gate, straining against the mud. Alexander followed, his bulk nearly snagging on the spiked bottom. The grate clanked shut behind them, sealing their escape.

They scurried to the shadows just beyond the wall. Kali emerged from the darkness, wiping her staff on her cloak, as if she had waited an hour. Her face was calm, but her eyes sparkled with energy.

"Well done," Agni whispered, his voice brimming with awe.

Kali allowed herself a faint smile but said nothing.

Then, a moan broke the silence.

Agni turned. One of the toppled guards—dazed but alive—struggled to one knee, body quaking. His eyes locked on Agni and widened like saucers.

"Lord Guardian… why?" the guard rasped.

Agni froze, his breath caught. *Shit.* He could report the escape and point the duke's men north. *He cannot live.*

The guard crawled for his horn.

Agni's hand moved on trained instinct. In one fluid motion, he drew his blade, the lightning-white glimmer cutting through the darkness.

"Forgive me," he whispered.

The strike was clean, precise. The blade carved from the guard's left ear to his right chin, leaving his face frozen with horror forever. Blood seeped into the mud; the rain washed it away with indifference.

"I failed you," Agni whispered again.

Alexander stared with a soldier's indifference, while Kali's eyes flitted between Agni and the slain guard.

"We need to move," Agni said hoarsely. He sheathed his blade. "Horses, torches, water. We ride by night and shelter in the trees. Lord Kazimora's stables are closest; prepare to steal."

As they silently trudged through the rain, Agni felt the enormity of his act. For the first time, he had killed one of his own. A man who had likely saluted him just days ago. Worst of all, Agni could not recall his name.

*The Lord Guardian is dead,* he thought bitterly. *What remains is an outlaw.*

They slipped into the night, the city of Azectrai falling behind them, perhaps for the last time.

C H A P T E R   1 3

# Alone

Lights swam before Sara's eyes as she awoke. Vivid, they burst like blooming flowers in the spring, then closed right back into tiny buds. Reds, yellows, blues, greens—beautiful. But their edges grew jagged, stabbing at not just her eyes but her ears and skin. A lancing pain knifed through her stomach, and she whipped to her left, vomiting bile all over the floor. It splattered over last night's dried vomit, in which she recognized chunks of bread pudding.

The acrid stench lingered in the air, making her stomach churn anew. She squeezed her eyes shut, her head ringing from the inside. She inhaled slowly, long and deliberate, before exhaling in sharp bursts. It slightly settled her nausea.

*Gods blast it.* For the last moon, she had resolved to cut down on that wine. Maybe she should ban traders from the Far Coast—banish their sweet, treacherous vintages from Azectrai. Yet it always beckoned: a celebration of the levy's final count, a pairing with

Dona's mouth-watering lamb, to numb her sorrows while Agni screwed that outlander bitch.

*Agni. Where was Agni?* Had Father's men taken him yet? Questions overflowed in her mind. Perhaps as he left for morning exercises, they would bludgeon him and drag him into the land of Kazian myths he nattered on about. And while her betrothed disappeared into legend, she would enjoy an afternoon drink with Mayor Goro, whom Father had promised Agni's sprawling estate.

Sara tried to focus, but her head throbbed. The lights in the room twisted into eldritch shapes. She braced herself upright, forcing thoughts of how Agni deserved his fate. For two years, he had wronged her, trampling her dignity. Father had been right to see him punished.

She whispered the words to herself, trying to convince her own heart. Then she heaved again, though her stomach had nothing left to give.

"Your Grace! Your Grace!"

The walls thumped with Nira's voice. Sara rubbed her temples. *Did I just see a sound?*

"Are you well, Your Grace?"

Sara grimaced, gesturing feebly with her hand. Could Nira not see the puddle of vomit? The lines of pain on her pallid face?

"Nira," she croaked. "Silence. My head,"

Nira crouched to her level, her face full of motherly concern.

"You're unwell. Shall I fetch—"

"Leave me to rest," Sara interrupted. She knew Nira would not disobey her, but part of her longed for the maid to insist. To care.

Nira hesitated, then leaned closer.

"Your Grace, it's almost midday."

Sara jolted upright. The world spun. Her wings flailed for balance. *Shit.* Father's men might have arrived. They might need her; she knew his patterns. He was rarely without his sword or bodyguards. She marveled at his energy—buzzing about the town, managing a garrison, a manor, countless minor affairs.

"Have you seen Agni?" Sara blurted out.

"No, Your Grace, not since last night. Perhaps he rode out to the manor?"

Sara felt bile rise in her throat again. Her mind raced. If Agni had left unnoticed, the entire plan might unravel. The mayor, constable, and Father's men would question her, and she dreaded confessing that she had indulged too much wine to notice his departure.

"Where is Dona?"

"Preparing a midday meal," Nira said, glancing down the stairs. "It should steady your stomach. Shall I fetch a bucket for the—"

Her eyes flickered to the mess on the floor.

"No," Sara snapped in shame. "Help me dress first."

Nira scurried to her clothing chest, rummaging to retrieve silks in the capital style. As the maid worked, Sara pressed her hand to her aching temple, muttering curses under her breath. She would not rest until she knew Agni was ash in a mountain gust, but Father was a master planner. He would prevail as he always did, and his loving hand would blanket Solantia.

———

Sara stumbled twice over gnarled roots on her way to Dona's shed, each misstep jarring her throbbing head. She heard Dona faintly humming some Kazian folk melody off key. Normally, Sara would smile at her cheerful devotion, but the scent of spiced roasting hen made her stomach churn.

"Good morning, Dona," Sara rasped, her throat dry.

Dona chuckled, not looking up from cutting potatoes. "Morning, in the loose sense of time, Your Grace. The sun will pass overhead in ten minutes. Must have been a fine pot last night."

She chortled at her own joke, grating on Sara's nerves. Sara took a shallow breath, her temper boiling beneath the surface.

Dona finally turned, wiping her hands on her apron.

"Oh, you know how the Lord Guardian comes and goes."

"Have you seen him today?" Sara pressed in a sharp voice.

"No dear. And that's a shame. The bread sat out on the table all morning. By the time he returns, it'll be hard as a stone. He needs to eat well before he rides out."

Sara's ears perked. "By the time he returns?" she said, feeling some hope. "So he rode north to the manor? Or into the Spires?"

Dona chuckled again, as though the question were absurd. Her lightheartedness only fueled Sara's irritation. *Can she not hear the urgency in my voice?*

"Why would I prepare breakfast if I knew he would ride out," she said, shaking her head. "And if you would rest until noon?"

That did it. Sara's composure snapped.

"You stupid crone!" she spat. "How could you miss him? You cook his meals, you dote on him like his blasted grandmother, and yet he scurries off without so much as your notice? If you were my chambermaid, I would… I would…"

The world tilted again. A wave of vertigo cut her tirade short. Her wings spread as she stumbled backward. Her feet tangled and she fell hard onto her back. The wind left her lungs. For a moment, she lay gasping, staring at the clear sky above, tears pricking at the corners of her eyes.

"Calm, Your Grace," Dona said, hurrying to her side. "Just sit."

She crouched beside Sara, lifting her into a sitting position. The old woman's hands were firm but gentle, steadying her as if she were a child.

Sara winced as a sharp pain shot through her left wing; it must have struck a rock. She folded her wing around, feeling the blood seep onto her fingers. Her anger turned inwards, shame flushing her cheeks. *How have I fallen so far?*

"There, there," Dona murmured, dabbing at the wound with a clean rag. It stung like a wasp. She felt tears streaming down her face from shame and humiliation. If only Dona would snap back and legitimize her anger.

"Dona," Sara said, her voice shaking. "I need to speak to him this morning. I have important news. From the capital."

The old woman furrowed her brow.

"Is it, now? How did you hear news from your bedchamber?"

Sara's heart skipped; she cursed her clumsy lie.

"I… I was told to expect it yesterday," she stammered, unable to convince her own ears.

"Well," Dona said with a resigned shrug, "you'd best put some food down your gullet and head to the town hall. If you expect news, maybe that little herald boy's still puttering about."

Sara shuddered at that though. *No, not the town hall. Not without answers. Has anyone in this town seen Agni? Anyone?*

"Where else could he be?"

Dona's face softened, as though indulging a child.

"He would have told me last night if he rode into the Spires, but he did not. If he left the city, he would have taken a horse. Perhaps he took Ark out for a trot?"

*Ark, yes.* A glimmer of hope. *The stable boy sees every lord's coming-and-going.*

"Thank you, Dona."

Dona offered her a hand, and Sara slowly worked her way to her feet. Her balance wavered, but she steadied herself with the sheer force of her need to know. Sara grabbed a stale hunk of bread on the way out.

*I will find Agni and salvage this.*

Sara beelined towards the stables, each step an effort against her nausea and sore back. The sun beat down relentlessly. Yesterday's storm had turned East Street into sludge, and the air hung thick with humidity. Every breath felt labored. Sweat beaded on her brow and trickled down her face, her spine, her breasts. Duchesses controlled time; they neither hurried nor traveled alone. The thought spurred her on, as if haste could erase the indignities of the day—or track down Agni.

By the time she reached the stables, her chest heaved with exertion. She held her breath at the acrid stench of hot manure and moldy straw so as not to retch again. She peered through the eye-level slits of the wooden gate. Ark's usual stall was empty, his absence sending a ripple of hope through her. *Did I panic for nothing?*

The hinges creaked as she pushed the gate open. Her entrance startled a wiry boy who had been brushing down a dappled mare.

"Afternoon, Your Grace!" he chirped, his voice only starting to crack. He gave a quick bow. "I'll have your mare ready, quick as a cat."

Sara forced a smile, the boy's cheer wearing on her nerves. He bore an uncanny resemblance to Qualo, though his eyes were a striking emerald green.

"Thank you kindly," she said, her throat parched. "But I do not require a horse. I need to ask you, have you seen the Lord Guardian this morning?"

The stable boy shouted out to an unseen hand.

"Oy, brother!" he called. "You seen the Lord Guardian today?"

"No, but I just cleaned his horse's—"

Before the second could respond, he rounded the corner leading Agni's prized stallion. Ark's hooves made a wet squelch in the mud as the boy led him toward his stall.

The second boy's face blanched as he caught sight of Sara.

"N—no, Your Grace," he stuttered. "But I just cleaned his horse's—" He stopped mid-sentence, his eyes wide. "How can we help you today?"

Sara's heart sank, and her stomach followed. Her hope slipped further out of reach.

The sick feeling in her stomach returned.

"No, I was just searching for Agni—I mean, the Lord Guardian. I need to ask him something."

The second boy smiled, recovering his composure.

"Well, come around later. He won't ride into the mountains without old Ark here."

Ark's ears perked up. He let out a mighty whinny and dragged his handler towards her.

"I see. Thank you."

Sara turned away to hide her despair.

She stared down the common, thoughts racing. *Someone must have seen Azectrai's favorite son, who could not walk past the privy unnoticed. Agni cannot vanish like a wraith.* If he had not taken a horse, he would not have gone far. Her mind circled back to Kali, the outlander. For once, she would welcome that they had a midnight tryst.

It was a short walk to Potter's Lane, where Kali's house stood. She forced her head high. Flocks of birds picked at the worms washed out by the storm. Ladies tended to their gardens and girls made wreaths out of leaves and husks. *I never thought I would crave such a simple life.*

The shutters of Kali's house were closed tight. She rapped at the door and waited, pressing her ear to hear any sound within.

"Kali? Kali?" she called. "I need to speak with you!"

No answer.

Kali might not welcome Sara's presence, but she would not ignore Sara. She knocked again, harder.

"Kali? Kali?"

The unease returned, stronger. She walked around back and craned her neck—the shutters to Kali's bedroom were opened to the inside, waving gently in the breeze. *Strange. That means she left without care.*

Sara's chest tightened. *If Kali has disappeared too...* She did not finish the thought, but the implications chilled her. *Had Agni and Kali disappeared together?* She could not let her mind spiral further. With no answers at the stable or Potter's Lane, it was time to check the guardhouses. After Dona, the stable boys, and Kali, no one would know his actions better.

———

Surely, a guard must have seen him. Azectrai's walls were not so vast that Agni could pass unnoticed. He trained his guards to be sharp-eyed and loyal. They would know.

It was a short walk to the north guard tower, a squat, sturdy building of stone, its doorway flanked by two unlit torches.

She rapped at the door, wiping the sweat from her forehead. The door swung open to reveal a burly man, his broad shoulders nearly filling the frame. His face was rough and downcast, frowning at the ground before he noticed Sara.

"Lady Sara," he greeted, bowing his head. "An unexpected pleasure." *No time for pleasantries.*

"Have you seen the Lord Guardian today?" she asked.

The guard's expression darkened as he shook his head.

"We're looking for him too, milady."

Her stomach twisted as the guard quenched another ember of hope.

"You have not seen him?"

"I sent men to every wall, and the tower along the river. He's a ghost."

Sara's heart quickened. She forced calm into her voice. "I doubt that. I saw Ark, and the stable boy has not seen him. He must not have left." She swallowed hard. "You can pass me a message in case I see him."

The guard hesitated, rubbing his eyes in fatigue. He let out a sharp exhale. "Milady, someone beat one of my men bloody last night and cut another's head clean in half. Right there on the wall."

She shuddered.

"What?"

"No brigand, either," the guard continued in a grim voice. "The murderer didn't touch their coin. The body lies with Osmo's widow. Poor woman barely recognized him—the fiend burned his face. Only one sword in Azectrai could have done that."

Her mouth formed a silent "o" as the realization struck. *Agni did this.* She clenched her fists, struggling to keep her composure.

"Are you accusing the Lord Guardian of slaying his own?"

"I could never accuse him of such a thing, Your Grace. Perhaps someone robbed his blade—must have been quite a band of ruffians to do that. But it's the Lord Guardian's sword. And no one has seen him."

"I must be going now," Sara blurted out, turning away.

———

A sinister picture took shape in her mind. Agni had disappeared without a trace. No maid, no stable hand, no guard had seen him. No band of thieves could—or would—ambush him unaware. He could have climbed a tree, timed the guards' patrol, and escaped over the walls. But this was not just an escape. He had killed a guard with one blow and vanished into the wilds, or perhaps the mountains. Her instincts screamed that Kali and Alexander had joined him.

*Agni would die for his men—or kill for his friends.*

Then a second realization struck, a bolt of clarity that made her stumble. *He would only flee if he knew the plot.*

The world swam again. Who had told him? She had spoken of the plan only to Mayor Goro, trusting him with the secrecy Father demanded. Father would never speak this through the stone. How many times had he called herald boys "little spies"? No rider had come through the mountain passes in days. So how had Agni unraveled the threads?

She wiped her clammy palms on her tunic, but the sweat still poured. With sharp detail, she recalled Agni's behavior last night. The way his eyes lingered on hers, sharper than usual; the wine's curious potency; the feverish, surreal dreams that had followed. *Did I speak in my sleep?*

She gasped in horror at the next realization. She braced herself against the wall of a nearby house as her knees threatened to buckle. *He drugged me.* The wine, the gaps in her memory—it fit. Agni had bested her, slipped past her defenses as deftly as he did any fortress.

A fresh wave of nausea hit. At least one man had died because of her failure, perhaps more. Now, with Agni gone, her future stood on a knife's edge. Would Father recall her to Artania in disgrace? Would he cast her aside as unworthy of the trust he had placed in her? Or worse, would Agni return—changed, hardened, vengeful—and strike at the heart of everything she had built?

She pressed her palms over her eyes, shaking. Anger flared alongside despair. At Agni for his brutal cunning, at herself for her blindness, at the entire blasted situation. If he returned, he would return with a column. He babbled that "yew in the desert" claptrap, about the enduring spirit of his people; he embodied it.

She slowed her breath. *It is time to show myself worthy,* she thought. *Duchesses shoulder the weight of rule.*

Aira. The wise woman. The apothecary. She knew poisons better than anyone in town.

Sara steeled herself and turned east. It only sat a quarter mile away but felt as distant as Eltrazan along the Median Road.

*She will know. Then I will know.*

Sara knocked on Aira's door. Within seconds, the grinding sound of mortar and pestle stopped, and the latch lifted.

Aira, tall and wiry with sharp brown eyes that missed nothing, pulled the door open. Aira might have been older than Dona, but the years had forgotten Aira. Her fingers showed no rheumatism; her steps were as fluid as a dancer's.

The shop was dimly lit, its shelves crammed with jars, vials, and bundles of herbs that cast strange shadows. The air felt thick with earthy smells—spicy, musty, minty. They were strange but pulled her out of her thoughts.

"Lady Sara," she greeted, her voice low and smooth. "It's been some time."

Sara forced herself to curtsy, though her legs felt like lead.

"Good day, Lady Aira."

"Do you require the tea?" Aira said, gesturing towards her workbench.

The question caught Sara off guard—when she and Agni last made love was the least of her concerns. For a moment, she just stared ahead.

"No, not tea," she replied. Her voice sounded unsure, brittle. "I… I was wondering if you had seen the Lord Guardian today."

Aira's gaze did not waver.

"He shares your bed, not mine, Your Grace," she said in a dry tone. "But no, I have not. Is something amiss?"

Sara inhaled deeply, trying to steady herself.

"He vanished into the night. No one has seen him since."

Aira's deep brown eyes widened in surprise.

"Vanished? That is troubling." She paused. "He came yesterday, though. Bought an herb for night terrors. A rare herb that grants visions."

Sara's heart thudded in her chest.

"Night terrors?"

"Yes. It's potent—induces vivid dreams, sometimes visions, rather than simple sleep," Aira explained. "He said little but carried himself like a man with a heavy burden."

The words hit Sara like a hammer to the chest. Her breath came short. *He used it. He fed it to me.* The final piece of the puzzle. *For well or ill, he is gone.*

The perceptive apothecary tilted her head, as if judging her reaction.

"Is something wrong, Your Grace?"

Sara forced words out, though her throat felt like sand. "Uh, no. He must have gone to Lady Kali's. He must have slept long after using such an herb. Perhaps he has returned."

Aira stared through her, looking unconvinced. "Perhaps. But if he has not returned, he may have sought solitude in the mountains, or his manor."

Sara nodded, her movements stiff.

"Yes. I should go. Thank you."

She turned to leave, but an idea halted her.

"That herb, do you have any left?"

Aira hesitated, shifting her weight.

"This isn't a casual remedy, Your Grace."

"Please. I need it. I too have felt night terrors of late."

Aira studied her for a long moment, then sighed. "One hundred credits. Return in an hour. Please consume no wine with it. And do not speak to the temple priests about it. They nose around my shop enough as is."

"However many credits you require, I will return with it."

Sara nodded mutely, stepping out into the sun. The story complete, she could only confess her weakness to Mayor Goro, and her unfitness to rule to Father.

*What a fool I am,* she thought. She had not suffered a night terror since girlhood. She wanted this herb to punish herself. *Agni played me. He played us all. And now the game is his.*

It was time to face the first consequence.

———

Sara took the longest route to the town hall, tracing three sides of the common rather than cutting directly across the south. She needed the time to steady herself, though her steps felt heavier with every yard. Agni was gone, and by the way he knew the valley and mountains, even his own patrols would not find him. Whatever came next, this might be her last moment of calm for a moon.

By the time she reached the town hall, the sweltering heat and her splitting headache made her vision ripple like a mirage. She wiped the sweat from her brow before recomposing herself. *They will come as vultures; do not let them cow you.* She pushed open the massive oak door with an ear-grating creak.

Inside stood Mayor—Baron—Goro, all six and a half feet, his bulk as formidable as ever, his two days' stubble speckled with crumbs. He scratched his chin idly, bearing a mask of annoyance. At his side loomed his son, Sir Arno, an ox of a man as tall as his father and twice as fat, rolls spilling over his belt. His dull, hungry eyes fixated on Sara's breasts—as usual—making her skin crawl. Instinctively, she crossed her arms over her collar. To Goro's right stood Constable Avro, squat and gnarled with muscle, his face hard as the city wall. He held a burlap sack over his shoulder, as if it contained something damning. The three stood around a circle of polished wood chairs, an arrangement that felt inquisitorial.

"Come in," the mayor intoned, "we have been expecting you."

His tone grated on her. *A baron, condescending to a duchess.* She lifted her chin and puffed out her chest, projecting a dignity that she did not feel.

"I suppose we all know what this regards," she said coolly. "I trust your men have answers."

Avro stepped forward without a word. He dropped the burlap sack onto the table with a heavy clank.

"Indeed, we do. Do you know what sits in that sack, Your Grace?"

"Baron, you address the Duchess of Artania—your lord's peer. You will speak with respect."

Goro sighed, clearly unimpressed. He gestured to Avro, who lifted and upended the bottom of the sack. Half a severed head tumbled out onto the polished wood, the remnants of its helmet clanging against the surface. Sara recoiled, her breath catching in her throat.

The head was still recognizable—barely. Its clean diagonal slash, the charred fat and skin along the edges, a mark that could have only come from *his* blade. Judging from the way Arno flinched, he had not seen it—or any severed head—before, either.

Sara swallowed hard and bit her lower lip. *I cut a man's throat at Agni's command. Am I any better? This is not the time to indulge doubt.* "Why do you show me this? We know the Lord Guardian's skill with a blade."

"The crowner found it just outside the gate this morning," Goro replied icily. "The rest of the body and head—what's left of it—are with Osmo's family."

Sara's hands clenched at her sides. She saw their calculated humiliation.

"Why do you bring this to me?"

Goro leaned forward, teeth gritted in anger. "Because every ear in Azectrai that knows your father's gambit is in this room, and now the beating heart of the Kazian soldiery is at large. Your betrothed may return at the head of a column in a moon's time, ready to cleave our skulls the same."

She slowed her breath, just as Agni taught her. *Now is not the time to falter.* "Father's men may arrive any hour," she replied. "They will find him."

Avro slammed his fist onto the table, jolting the head.

"Find him? Was the mayor not clear? Both Duke Verlan and the Lord Guardian could have our rumps for this! Rather than eliminating two hungry mountain leopards, we've set one loose and angered the other."

Sara's temper flared. "He drugged my meal, you toad. Had your wife slipped it into your drink, you would babble the name of every whore you bedded in town."

Avro's face darkened. He took a threatening step toward her, shoulders bulging beneath his leathers.

"All you had to do was hold your tongue for three days. I knew your father shouldn't have trusted the plan to a woman. And for that, this poor sod lost his skull!"

Sara opened her mouth to retort, but Goro held up a hand. "Calm, constable," he said, his tone soothing. "Resign yourselves to this, Agni Kazirian is lost to us. Only a fool would return to his manor. He knows every cranny of the mountains." He glanced at Sara with mock sympathy. "But without him, his men take pay from us. The duke's men take orders from Her Grace, here. Agni has no power, no home, and soon, no name."

Goro straightened with a smirk before continuing. "Remember, Avro, you will be paid from his manor, one of the grandest in the valley. And Lady Sara here gets to return west. A prime, marriageable plum."

Sara's anger simmered, but she fought to keep a neutral expression. Even after being compared to a ripe fruit.

"What you will not have are the hearts of his men," she sneered. "They followed him across the Spires, into Arteva, and across the sea. They will not fall to your coin or your lies. He will return; it may be days or years, but he will never forsake this land."

Avro let out a chilling chuckle. "And yet you couldn't hold his heart, could you? Perhaps Kali did better."

The words struck like a slap. Her face burned, her wings twitching with rage.

"How dare you meddle in matters beyond your station! If you had a fraction of Agni's resolve and intelligence, the soldiers might see you as more than he who raises and lowers the gates."

Avro laughed, low and cruel. "Beyond my station? At least I know mine, Your Grace. All you had to do was bat your eyes and doff your wings at him. If you knew *your* station, we wouldn't be cleaning up your mess."

The truth stung. Her lips trembled. She tried to volley back but saliva caught in her throat. The words would not come.

"Silence, you two," Goro barked. "Avro, let it rest. We say that a band of thugs slew Agni and stole his sword. We grieve his disappearance and proclaim him deceased—which he may well be. Under Kazian law, the estate passes to the duke, who grants it to me. We will dispose of his steward, install our own, and reap the profits."

He turned to Sara and sighed in clear contempt. "And you, Lady Sara. You are relieved of further involvement. In the meantime, play your harp and drink your wine. Prepare yourself to return to Artania."

"But..." Sara started.

"We have this matter under control."

She froze. The world swam. She recoiled as Arno approached and jerked back as his giant hand brushed hers. She yanked it away.

"Do not touch me," she growled.

He held up his hands in mock innocence, but he could not hide the leer in his eyes. As she turned toward the door, Sara caught him glancing at her backside. She thought she heard Goro and Avro chuckle but felt too spent to face them. Instead, she walked out, her head high but her dignity in tatters.

*My humiliation is complete,* she thought as she returned to Aira's for her sweet poison. Every night in Agni's bed would remind her of her failure. *May Agni wound you three the same.*

———

That evening, as the sun dipped below the horizon, Sara sat on the edge of the bed, rocking back and forth in an unconscious rhythm. Mother once rocked her like that to soothe her tears—a faint memory of a woman who had caught a festering wound in Sara's seventh year. Sara clutched her arms tighter around her knees, her wings folding inward like a shroud to hide from the cruelty of man.

The thought of Mother broke her. A dry, shuddering sob escaped her lips, then another. She squeezed even tighter. She had no one; Father would see her failure as a stain on his house. Agni had humiliated her, but at least she could understand the war between duty and affection. He was gone, perhaps to plot her undoing. She had dismissed Dona and Nira, who had mothered her in small ways; even she hoped they would protest and stay.

She thought she wanted solitude, but now it felt like a noose around her throat.

Her gaze fell to her bedside table, where the remnants of her meager dinner sat untouched. The same stale loaf that had sat on the table all day, a half-empty cup of wine; she had taken one sip and spat it back into the cup. It tasted bitter on her tongue, mocking her.

She stared down at the scrubbed patch of floor, where her vomit had been cleaned earlier. The faint stain remained despite the soap and scrubbing. *Like me,* she thought, bitterly. She could not scrub away the stain of the day. No Agni. No command. No path forward but one of shame. She would return to the urbane West, a duchess without merits, reduced to a pawn for a marriage alliance, doomed to be some noble's brood mare. Her title felt like heavy chain around her neck.

The sobs returned, fiercer this time, wrenching her body like a seizing man's. Tears soaked her silk sleeves. *This is what I wished for, was it not?* To be free of Agni. To return to the polished courts of the West.

When the tears subsided, Sara's trembling hands pulled out Aira's vial of brown powder. She fingered it, staring at the way the powder clung to the glass. She realized that she had never asked its name. Nor why Aira had warned her to avoid wine or keep it from the temple priests. *This day could give anyone terrors.*

Her fingers fumbled as she pulled the stopper. She sprinkled a bit on her tongue. Its taste was earthy, bitter, and strange, but she forced herself to swallow.

She sat there a moment longer, staring at space, waiting for quiet numbness to take her. For the first time that day, she felt hope—not for redemption or forgiveness, but for twelve hours of sweet oblivion.

She lay back on the bed, spread her wings, and closed her eyes.

C H A P T E R   1 4

## *Flight*

The second full day of travel drew to a close. An hour before sundown, Agni led his companions—and their stolen palfreys—through rugged thickets and over uneven rocks. The merciless heat of the day still clung to their clothes, heavy with sweat and dust. The silence between them had grown heavy. Even their horses whinnied in irritation. "Keep moving," he had urged, through sun and hunger.

Agni found an isolated clearing in which to camp: a dry, packed forest floor, and a curtain of oaks to shield them from the Azectrai River and curious boatmen.

"Here," he said with a yawn, "this should suffice for the night."

The moment they dismounted, Agni's eyes caught a flash of orange. His hand flew to the hilt of his sword.

"No flames!" he hissed. "We cannot leave a trace!"

Kali turned to him, green eyes flashing with irritation. Agni realized the "flash" was the swish of her tail, glowing faintly in the sunset.

"Relax, love," she mocked. "But thank you for reminding us that we are outlaws. It has been a whole hour; I nearly forgot."

Alexander chuckled quietly, but Agni did not respond. Two years of peace and comfort felt distant now. *Let us not forget that we are hard men and women.*

They settled in with soldiers' precision—the horses picketed and the bedrolls spread out under the stars. Fifteen minutes' sunlight felt like a luxury; time to pick fleas out of their beards and fur.

Agni leaned against a tree and listened to Alexander fidgeting with his belt buckle. *Was it right to subject my friends to this danger?* he thought. There were few signs of life, let alone pursuit, along the trail. The conversations between them grew few and short—and no one had brought up the night of the escape.

Alexander broke the silence first. "Are you well, Agni?"

"No, my friend." Agni's voice was raw with emotion and thirst. "I raised a sword against a man who once swore his life to me. I did not see his face. He may have even called me brother."

*I broke a sacred oath.* Tears formed in his eyes.

Alexander responded in a steady voice, kind, even. "We all cut that stroke, Agni. Had he lived, he would have alerted his comrades. They would have ridden us down."

He spoke wisdom, but it offered no solace. The guard's dying word echoed in Agni's ears. *Why?*

"That is cold comfort," Agni replied. "Once, I swore an oath to Emperor Taran Solant: my life for his land and his people. Now, I am a criminal. A traitor, fleeing to seek aid from an enemy king."

Alexander crouched next to him, his broad wings folding against his back.

"You were those the moment Duke Verlan declared it so. The only difference is, now you know."

Agni ignored Alexander's attempt at comfort. Two days of flight could not extinguish years of loyalty.

"And Sara. I could not love her as she deserved, but I care for her."

Poor Sara. Another victim of her father's schemes. Agni had seen the nobility in her, the genuine desire to rule the capital duchy with justice. Yet Duke Verlan's ambition to undermine the Crystal Throne—or sit upon it himself—had swept her up like driftwood in the river.

Alexander calmly probed. "Would you fault her for hiding the plot from you?"

"No." Agni shook his head. "Her blood bound her to Verlan's schemes. I do not fault her choosing him—I was a false companion. Yet for my poisoning her, she will suffer at the hands of those who stand to gain. I know Verlan's mind too well; his schemes run deeper than any man knows."

He kicked a loose rock, sending it skittering into the underbrush, and sighed.

"The maw of Varenox turns towards her now, the same as it does toward the three of us."

"She can shape her fate, just as you can," Alexander said.

"She is caught in greater currents, my friend. Her father's, and mine. Now, so are you and Kali."

Alexander stepped back, furrowing his brow.

"Years ago, Kali and I took up with you of our own will. Two days ago, we did so again. Mayor Goro might have questioned us, but only you threaten the duke's plans. Do not think so greatly of yourself."

Agni looked away, grinding his teeth. If only he could confess the truth—that not only were they ensnared in Verlan's schemes but those of Anton Kazirian, the son of fate's god. To reveal that would put them in greater peril than they could fathom.

He took a long pause. "No, Alexander," Agni said. "If I had not been so foolish, so taken at that blasted feast. Forgive me, I—"

Alexander cut him off, leaning closer.

"And so you were, Lord Guardian. High General. You would not be the first noble to speak sedition over too much wine. But you do not need forgiveness, Agni. Taken at the feast? No, you are taken with yourself."

Alexander's words stung like a hornet. His old titles, once a source of pride, felt leaden now. He felt a storm rise in his chest—anger at Alexander, at Verlan, at himself. He raised his hand as if to quiet the conversation, but the bitter words spilled out.

"Oh, silence. A Lord Guardian and High General owns the battlefield, even if he does not control it. I failed in my duty to Kazia—and to you, my friends."

Alexander's face softened but his voice remained firm. "Listen to yourself, Agni. You knew you could not remain Lord Guardian forever, whether called to the West or declared outlaw. I still hear love for Kazia in your voice. When you stop pitying yourself, you will too."

Agni stared into the ground as tears began to blur his vision. The night sky, which normally cleared his mind, felt cold and indifferent.

"What does love mean without power?" he whispered hoarsely. "I took those titles to free my people from the shackles of grasping men. Instead, I have subjected them to the most conniving man of all. I have dishonored them."

He knew Alexander's mind would go to Verlan, but his own went to Anton, whose lust for power had no bounds. *Anton may strike me for fleeing to Avicia. You and Kali may suffer too.*

Alexander's voice cut through the silence. "Agni, stop it. You said it yourself; within a moon, we will gain King Theodore's aegis. He will take interest in Verlan's plot—and his desire for threefold vengeance. You are no use to muck out his stables; he might well give you an army."

The thought turned Agni's stomach, but he could not deny the truth in the giant's words.

"A counselor, perhaps," Agni said. "But you must think him mad to grant me an army, on my say-so that I will now serve him."

"In my fifty years," Alexander replied, "I have seen stranger alliances. Tarka once allied with Blevenia and Avicia before deciding to keep their noses clean of the Black Moon. The gods themselves fought in antiquity, and now they fight through us. It is our destiny, our constant state, to war."

"Yes, and peace comes only through the threat of destruction," Agni said bitterly. "But to lead an Avician army to battle Solantia? To save Solantia from its own leaders? That lies beyond my comprehension."

"You have had two days to think on it," Alexander said, clapping him lightly on the shoulder. "You will have a moon on a ship to think of it further."

"*Ai,* friend. Or I may think my plan even madder than I think it now."

"Just contemplate it tonight. We have another day to Sivatrai."

Agni nodded and opened his bedroll, though his mind lay elsewhere. The thought crept into his mind that even if Anton's ambitions ran as deep as he feared, the ancient's guidance might prove more valuable than Alexander's steady loyalty—or Kali's unyielding love.

---

Agni shut his eyes and concentrated on the melodious howling of wolves. It comforted him, though he knew it would not last. *I envy them. Wolves are free in a way that I am not,* he thought. The howls blended in with the rustle of leaves and whisper of the river. Yet none of it brought peace. His mind turned to Anton—his true father—who had chided and goaded him but never opposed him.

After some futile minutes, he opened his eyes and stared at patterns in the stars. The Ladle, the Bull, the Cat to the west, the Whale of the east, and across the southern sky, the Dragon, maw agape to consume them all. The moon, right where the dragon's eye would be. Beautiful yet ominous.

*No, beautiful yet meaningless,* he thought. *Only old women and priests seek guidance in the stars.* Warriors knew that boldness salved pain and anxiety, which made this still night more maddening. But wise counsel served moments of calm.

As expected, a mist descended from the sky. Like a storm cloud, it thickened over him, tendrils weaving into a man's form. Even if Agni anticipated it, it chilled him. The counselor—the tyrant.

*"Ancestor,"* Agni silently mouthed the words. *"See what you have set into motion,"*

*"I see that you are troubled, Agni,"* Anton intoned dryly. Was Anton mocking him, or did Agni's predicament mean little to him?

Agni clenched his fists in annoyance.

*"Troubled? You can no more than make a droll observation? Now I lack my title, home, and wealth. Kazia, great and small, are lost to us."*

Anton flicked his ghostly wrist. Agni felt a sharp jolt through his body—a flash of pain that snapped him to attention. He gritted his teeth but refused to cry out.

*"No, foolish boy,"* Anton snarled. *"Not lost. Abandoned by your cowardice. You would flee into the arms of an enemy king. You shame us."*

Agni sneered despite the pain; he would show Anton he would not shrink. *"Is it cowardice to flee the Ritual of Ascension, or the pinion-and-drop? You bless me with the means to drug a duke's daughter and now expect me to meet her father's armies head-on? Have two thousand years leeched your knowledge of tactics?"*

Anton's eyes gleamed, and for a moment, Agni expected another jolt. But the spirit only lowered slightly, his form imposing itself on Agni.

*"Do not presume to lecture me, boy,"* Anton growled, his voice like a mountain leopard about to pounce. *"Do you think Kazian blood would bow to that interloper Verlan? You, of all my descendants, know the truth. Kazia will rise. Rally your lords. Take up our banner. They will rally to the one name of power—Kazirian. Soon, the Dragonlands will submit to it, or perish."*

Agni shook his head, his heart pounding. *"Madness,"* he uttered, his tone bitter. *"You would have me raise a banner over a people exhausted of war. We prevailed but still mourn our lost brethren. Our harvests are bountiful. Our border is safe. Leave us be."*

Anton's lips curled into a cruel smile. *"Prosperity has softened you. For twenty years, you have known my purpose—to resurrect the Empire Kazia. I fanned the flame that burns within you. The flame that can restore us to grace. Is this how you would repay me?"*

Agni inhaled deeply. *"And you have known my purpose—peace unto the Borderlands. Unto Kazia as I know it. To right the wrong that set me on this bloody path. That is the will of my people. Blood neither stands nor bows. They will never fight for a hearth tale."*

*"Then you will make them believe, as I once did. Peace? Prosperity? Great Kazia will offer you that—and glory—beyond compare."*

Anton raised his hands as if holding a bowl. The mists around his hands swirled like a tempest. Shadows gathered and coalesced into figures—warriors clad in ghostly armor, their hollow eyes burning with a spectral fire. *The crypt!* The ghostly knights that chanted his name twenty years ago—only a legion. Pained. Hungry.

*"Agni, the gods may wait millennia, but when they act, they act with speed and conviction,"* Anton proclaimed, his voice reverberating with power. *"An army unlike any the Mortal Realms have seen. Fight Verlan with your lords. These will take the flesh of the fallen, and with them, we will scour the lands. In time, I will find my own body, and with it, my true power. The dukes. The emperor. Even the gods themselves will tremble."*

*What?* Agni's body quaked in his bedroll, his wings twitching against his efforts. His vision swam with memories of death—the soldiers he had cut down, the villages burned in duty's name. To see that carnage writ large by abominations.

"*Ancestor… what?*" Agni thought, in pure terror. "*Will we rule an empire of death?*"

Anton's voice dropped to a deathly calm. "*Scion, you sought the power to halt history. I sought the power to restore the Jewel of Eternity. Our dreams unite. Take up your rightful place as my Lord Regent, and the Mortal Realms will kneel.*"

Agni shuddered. Anton tempted him with his lifelong desires. Freedom, power, command beyond his comprehension.

*No more raiders. Verlan shall serve us. I can learn, then rule for millennia,* Agni thought.

His chest heaved. But his heart ran deeper than Anton's desires.

*I struggle with the guilt of slaying one under my command—could I slay thousands and replace their essences with the undead?*

*Could Anton, who ordered this massacre, rule justly?*

*Could I, under such tutelage?*

"*Never!*" The word burst forth from Agni's mind. He tensed his body and glared through Anton's silvery form. "*I will not. I swore an oath to protect, not to destroy.*"

Anton's expression hardened but did not change.

"*Do you think the King of Avicia will shelter you? He will drop you as an invader and cast your friends into chains. You would grovel at his feet rather than accept the power I offer?*"

"*I would grovel before I march your undead to slaughter the living,*" Agni growled, determined. "*I will not be your puppet, ancestor. Not now. Not ever.*"

The silence that followed felt eternal. Anton's form radiated a cold fury. Would Anton strike him dead where he lay? Instead, Anton's form faded, and the spectral army dissolved into mist.

*"Foolish boy,"* Anton said, his voice calm but seething. *"You defy not just your destiny but your very blood. You choose a path that leads to ruin. But I am patient. You will see the truth, scion. And when you do, I will be waiting."*

With that, Anton's form faded into the mist, leaving Agni staring up at the stars, his breath ragged and body trembling. The wolves' howls in the distance sounded like a dirge—perhaps his own.

Anton's simple disappearance chilled him worse than a jolt, or a rapture. *What have I done? I do not know the extent of Anton's power now,* he thought, *let alone if he finds his original flesh.* Anton's words lingered in the air. *I have faced death countless times; now I face something far worse.*

Agni could not sleep that night out of sheer terror.

———

A day later, they trudged through the lively streets of Sivatrai as the sun began to dip, casting long shadows over the bustling port town. The air carried the salty tang of the sea, mingling with the scents of fish and cheap ale. Mongers hawked the catch of the day, while porters wheeled creaking carts of wine and wool into storehouses. Yet the trio moved in silence, heads bowed, cowls tightly drawn. *None know the bounty we might fetch.*

Kali had even tied her tail to her thigh, concealing her clan origins. She glanced at Agni and Alexander, discomfort evident in her tense posture.

"This port smells worse than the stables of Azectrai," she mumbled.

"You had best grow accustomed to it, my furred friend," Alexander replied in a lively tone. "We will linger in it long enough to secure passage."

"This city is thrice Azectrai's size and full of foreign traders. Few ask questions," Agni added, staring at his boots.

They stabled their horses at the nearest farrier they could find, under forgettable names. Agni paused to pat his brown stallion's head and offered him a final apple. The guilt of having not named his companion tugged at him, but he would serve another traveler well.

"Alexander, you know this city best," Agni began as they walked out of the stable. "When we inspected the Beachroad last year, where did visiting sailors lodge? Named after the white seabird with the pouch?"

"The Pelican," Alexander replied. "Near the port. It had beautiful carvings above all three lintels. Men enter and leave at all hours, many with tavern girls."

"And what does that mean, Alexander?" Kali replied, cocking an eyebrow.

"Nothing, Kali," he replied with a laugh. "Just that two men and a woman will not stand out here. Busy and seedy enough that no one will ask questions."

"Perfect," Agni said. "Lead the way."

Alexander led them towards the port and the sprawling inn that loomed over it. Its chipped paint and faded carvings betrayed years of neglect, but it bustled like a market stall. With few words, Alexander put down credits for ten nights in a room with an iron lock far from the entrance. The stairs were so narrow that the men had to walk up sideways; the room itself was as small as a town hall prison cell. Alexander could not extend even one wing to full; they twitched rapidly, but the old soldier bit back his complaint.

Kali wrinkled her nose as she noticed a single bed of moldy straw.

"Bah. You call this suitable?" she spat.

"We will grow well-acquainted in these quarters," Alexander replied with a smile.

"Not that we will sleep much," Agni said. "We will conspire and stash our belongings here. Comfort can wait until Avicia."

"Let us find our ship and rid ourselves of this place," Kali added.

"We will not find passage in a day, Kali," Alexander said, folding his arms. "Even were we to buy passage tomorrow, it may not sail for some time."

"Three ships, Alexander. Sivatrai lacks a stone, but any old soldier will recognize us together," Agni added.

"*Ai,*" Alexander nodded. "I will scout the porters' hall for ships hiring crew. Any boat large enough to traverse the Great Sea will need hands to work the rigging. My father raised me on caravels, and we know our tiger lady can climb anything."

"You know it," she replied with a grin.

"And I can cut down raiding parties," Agni added.

"You had best keep that sword out of sight; it would betray you in a mob. You would fetch a dear ransom in any land."

Agni bristled.

"You want me to abandon my sword? I could not hide it behind barrels?"

"Unless you want to find yourself chained in a hold, yes," Alexander said. "It is a treasure, but treasures get stolen. Hide your identity, or the sea will swallow you."

Agni hesitated before nodding.

"My companion has saved my hide many times."

"Let us bury it in the woods south of town," Kali said softly, a hand brushing his arm. "Someday, love, we will dig it up, unmasked. And you will hand it to our eldest son at our manor."

The unexpected intimacy of her words struck him. *You would bind your fate to mine, not knowing how deep it runs.* He managed a faint smile.

"We will, sweet Kali."

Alexander cleared his throat. "Ahem. Enough sentiment. We had best hasten that night. I will down ale at the guild hall. Agni, find ships that leave soon. Kali, watch for trouble. If word of us reaches the duke, we are done for."

Kali chimed in. "We saw few merchants—odd for prime shipping season—and no messengers on fast horses. Perhaps we do not have such bounties on our heads."

"We cannot take that risk, nor drop our guard. Best to put the sea between the duke's officers and us. I had best take the first ship—I endanger you."

"And once we arrive in Avicia?" Alexander inquired.

"I made trader Ronan a fortune in the Avician campaign. He can see us housed until we purchase our own, and we can guard his caravans until we gain the king's aegis. I prefer the loyalty of merchants to those of knights."

Alexander and Kali laughed at the irony.

"And once we arrive," Kali began, leaning against the wall, "where shall we reunite in this city of two-thirds of a million?"

Agni straightened, the commander in him taking over.

"Ronan's shop and warehouses sit in the Solantian Quarter. Next to it sits the Aerie Market. We will appear where the two meet, at noon, and wait a quarter-hour every day."

Kali tilted her head.

"How do you know Tercera so well, Agni?"

Agni flashed a grim smile at the memory.

"I aimed a nether cannon at the Aerie Market."

"And now we seek shelter under the Mighty Roc's wings," she replied, shaking her head at the absurdity of it all.

Agni grunted. "Ha. More like within its plumage. We make ourselves small, unobtrusive, like a mite on its arse. So long as we do not itch it, we can bide our time until we can stare it in the eye."

Alexander, pressed in the far corner of the room, gave a short nod of approval. "You have thought this through, Agni."

"As best as I can in three days," Agni admitted, his voice downcast. "The threat of death sharpens the mind. Truth be known, once we are safe from the duke, I will hang my head in shame. I will awaken thousands of miles from my only home, dispossessed and desperate because I could not control my words. But I fight for my warriors—you."

The room fell silent for a moment. Agni stared down, tensing his legs to keep his composure. Sadness felt like a dear luxury. Worse still, it could invite Anton into the quiet spaces of his mind.

Alexander broke the silence, his tone gruff but tinged with warmth. "Even the general, alert for enemy action."

Agni sighed. "Bah. Would that the threat wore a Blevenian crest and drew a weapon. It may lurk around any corner or come with a smile and outstretched arms. You two are all I trust, until Ronan sees profit in dealing with us. If he refuses aid, or has vanished, we may live in shacks for some time."

Kali raised a brow, her voice resolute. "We have lived in worse."

"True," Agni conceded. "But I would rather not tempt the god of fate further."

"For now," Alexander interjected, rising to his full height, "let us put such cares aside and dine. I could eat a gull."

"Let us forego gulls in favor of the day's catch," Kali suggested with a smile. "I have not eaten ocean fish in a year."

Agni stretched his back with a faint smile.

"Indeed. Let us."

With a silent understanding, they pulled over their cowls, locking the door with a low click as they stepped out.

———

Agni slumped his shoulders and cast his head down, pulling the hood over his forehead. He felt sweat ooze from every pore. *Best not to draw attention,* he thought. *But my first night in Avicia, I shall bathe in a mountain spring with proper soap.*

He shuffled into the porter's hall, a warrior masquerading as a wanderer. An hour earlier, Alexander had told him to find a squat but burly man of letters named Captain Zaha. Fortunately, only one man fit the description, inkpot and scroll at his side. Thick as a barrel, he stood a quarter-head taller than Agni—but then, the towering Alexander made most men seem squat.

"Are you… Captain Zaha?" Agni said, practicing a meek voice.

The captain looked up with a grunt. "That's me. State your business."

Instinctively, Agni straightened and pulled back his wings, glaring at him like the Lord Guardian would an unruly oaf, before catching himself. *Blasted habit,* he thought. *Should I grovel?*

"I wish to purchase passage to Avicia on the *Star of the Sea,* good sir."

"Oh, do you now?" Zaha leaned back, eyeing Agni up and down. "That's a dear journey, boy. We've got a single berth left, low deck, where rats will nibble a hole in those wings of yours. Not to mention, you don't look like you've got the thousand credits. Why should I take you? Can you cook? Climb riggings? Repair sails?"

"I fought in Blevenia, sir. I can fend off pirates or take on whatever labors you require."

Zaha cocked his head before erupting in laughter. A dozen eyes turned to gawk, their smirks widening as Zaha stepped closer, puffing out his chest.

"A fighter, eh? The near seas are thick with pirates as a whale's carcass with maggots. Please, hooded boy, guard me against the terrors of the high seas." He stepped forward, bumping his chest against Agni's. "You don't look so tough."

Agni fought a smirk. This man had the swagger of a tavern brawler, not the tight movements of a warrior. Zaha wound his right arm back for a haymaker. *Foolish sailor, leaving your belly open like that.*

In a single fluid motion, Agni glided in with his left foot and twisted right, driving his left fist into Zaha's liver. Swift as a cat, he landed a second hook on the captain's nose. The captain's knees buckled before his swing could gain momentum, and within a second, he fell to all fours, gasping for air. Agni's nose wrinkled at the scent of soiled bowels. *Now, abase yourself.*

"I beg your mercy, Captain Zaha," Agni raised his voice to a near-squeak.

Zaha wheezed like a fish on deck, waving off the porters who had begun to gather. Agni extended a hand to help him up but the captain slapped it away. With shaking hands, Zaha grabbed the bench to pull himself upright. As blood dribbled down his lips, Zaha stared agape.

"You…"

Agni reached into his pouch, laying out a hundred ten-credit silvers with a dull "clunk," ignoring the stares.

"My credits, captain. Is this acceptable?" Agni asked.

Zaha stared at the coins before finally regaining his breath.

"Do you have a weapon, boy?"

Agni's hand brushed the hilt of his mystical blade, which could terrify even the most hardened marauder. *No, blast it!* He pretended to scratch his waist.

"No," he lied.

"Not to worry, I carry spares." Zaha grunted. "We set sail mid-morning in two days, from the western pier."

Relief washed over Agni. Only two days to lie low and watch the shadows, before escaping onto the high seas.

"I can do that," Agni said with a nod.

"Good. And for my rolls, what should I call my club-fisted friend?"

Agni paused, his mind racing. He blurted the first two Kazian syllables that came to him. "Azri."

"Azri what?"

"I have no family name."

It sounded enough like "Agni" that he would react to it. Zaha's eyes squinted, suspicion flashing across his face.

"Occupation?"

Agni hesitated for a second. "Nothing, now."

"Outlaw?"

"Something like that."

Zaha paused for a second then let out another booming laugh.

"It's been years since Kazian boys left to make their bones in Avicia, Azri. After the Black Moon, Avician boys come south for wealth. Now, the only men with a thousand credits seeking passage are servants who done did up a noble master."

He laughed harder, snorting through his crushed nose between cackles. Agni cringed as Zaha's words cut too close to the truth. He forced a smile.

"Anyways," Zaha said, wiping a tear from his eye, "you can pay and you can fight, so I won't crawl any further up your arse with questions. You know where and when to find me. Your credits won't do you much good in Avicia, so get yourself a wench or three. Ain't no fair maidens on the *Star of the Sea,* and I don't tolerate relations among my men."

"I will. Thank you kindly, Captain Zaha."

"Now get out my face and let me clean up my shite, boy."

Agni bowed slightly and turned, his steps measured as he left the hall. A small, wry chuckle escaped his lips as he considered the irony of his situation. The empire's most vaunted soldier, humbling himself before a sailor who just soiled his pants. "Azri" felt foreign, like an ill-fitting jerkin. But if it meant Agni Kazirian vanished for a moon and reappeared in a distant land, he would gladly wear the disguise.

*If only Azri could hide himself from Anton Kazirian. But better one threat than two.*

———

Two nights later, Agni and Kali walked, arm in arm, into the woods a mile south of Sivatrai. In his free arm, Agni carried a shovel, its wooden shaft smooth from use. The moon cast pale light through the leaves, lighting the forest floor in patches of silver. His steps were slow and deliberate as he noted every landmark—the moss-covered boulder, the majestic oak whose roots twisted like claws. For once, he felt the weight of the sword on his hip, a weight he might not feel for a decade.

"Are you nervous about setting sail tomorrow, Agni?" Kali's warm voice broke through the background of rustling leaves and chirping crickets.

"I am relieved to avoid the duke's hunt, but I hate boats, love," he admitted. "They churn my stomach, and the sea air feels like breathing oil."

"But you have sailed this journey before."

"With an armada, siege engines, and Admiral Malia, the finest sea commander in the empire. Until the Avician ships tried to board us, I was less use than a barnacle."

They shared a chuckle.

"This time, you earned your passage with coin. You need not be of use."

He squeezed her hand.

"Perhaps I will regale the crew with tales of glory or sing for some Avician crowns."

"Leave the song to me, love," she teased.

"What, then, is an old warrior to do?" He laughed back.

"Whatever he desires," Kali replied, her tone more solemn. "I think that is why you wanted me to come with you tonight. To bid that life farewell."

Agni paused, his head lowering. She knew his heart, often before he himself did. Rarely had he felt this vulnerable. He forced himself to look at her, her face bathed in moonlight, her emerald eyes unwavering. She stepped closer and wrapped her arms around him, resting her head on his shoulder.

"It was a good life," he whispered with a sigh. "But I know no other purpose than peace for this land. For it never to need another Lord Guardian—and for Solantia never to need another High General. Until King Theodore decides I am loyal—and he may never—I am just a sword arm, a sea away from my purpose."

"If Verlan raises an army, you will be more valuable than all the king's other counselors," Kali said, her voice encouraging.

"I see the irony," Agni replied with a bitter laugh. "Only in another war can I bring peace. Peace only comes through the threat of destruction. Lovers of peace who appeal to their conquerors' humanity are enslaved or cut down. Even their songs are forgotten. I want what we call 'history' to end. For that, every great power must fear every other."

"That is a grand dream."

"But I tasted it once, that of which potentates dream of but believe impossible. Emperor Taran held the throne, but I delivered to him our foes. Power without limits is as intoxicating as laudanum. I have craved it since. For peace unto the Borderlands."

*Laudanum, and my ancestor offers me a field of poppies*, he thought. *Whether King Theodore's war or Anton Kazirian's, I may never escape it.*

"And it was with you that I first knew any power," Kali said with a soft gaze. "Your ambitions are still strange to me. But I believe in you, and in us. Your sword does not just symbolize your command. It is your treasure, a symbol of your line—one I will gladly join."

Agni leaned close and whispered in her ear, "But you are my greatest treasure."

Kali gasped, her lips parting in surprise. "Your treasure. You have never called me that before."

"You have always been," he admitted. "From the moment we met, I felt our fates draw close. But I thought Sara's would always separate us, until several days ago."

"I like being your treasure," she said, a smile breaking across her face. She pulled him close, her lips brushing his once, then again, deeper. He took in the scent of her cheek, knowing he would go a moon without.

"With this, I bid farewell to my old life," Agni said. "But not my purpose. May we unearth it in a more peaceful time."

They walked further, searching for a memorable—even symbolic—spot to lay his companion to rest. He stopped between two towering oaks, then walked thirty paces toward a rocky mound bathed in moonlight. He knelt, the sword still on his hip, and dug through the loam. Kali stood silently watching for an hour.

Finally, he set the shovel aside and knelt before the pit, as if in prayer. *It feels wrong to call you a weapon, my most faithful companion,* he thought. With slow reverence, he unbuckled the scabbard from his belt. He held it in outstretched hands, as if laying an offering to the gods.

"Until I need you again, old friend," he whispered, placing it into the earth.

Kali stepped closer. She did not speak, but Agni thought he saw her lips moving in a silent prayer. He watched it disappear as he shoveled earth over it. He tamped down the soil and planted tufts of grass to blend in with the forest floor. *It is done; I declare this sacred ground.*

He stood up, looked down, and saluted. He wiggled his hip, which felt bare without the familiar weight of his sword and scabbard. From behind, Kali placed a light hand where his sword sat.

In that moment, he felt a wall between them crumble, a reminder that even without his sword, he was not alone. She had seen his strength and vulnerability and stayed. *It is time,* he thought.

"Kali," he said, his voice catching.

"Yes?" she asked, turning toward him.

"A moon ago, I promised to share my stones with you. I want to do so tonight."

Her eyes widened, sparkling in the moonlight.

"Agni. I would love that. But why now?"

"Because before the night we fled, I felt as though showing this part of my heart—the part bound to Sara—would taunt you. It would show you a precious gift that I had to take back. Now I have no manor, no title, no sword, and no noble betrothed. My heart is clear for you."

Tears glistened in her eyes as she placed a hand over her mouth.

"Agni, do you remember the night on the guard tower in Artanport? The night before your army set sail for Avicia?"

"I remember it well, love," he said. "We watched the sun set over the ships."

"You told me that night was pure and perfect, even though you might not return. And I told you I would love even the parts of you that you kept locked away."

Agni took a deep breath. "I only wanted to protect your heart, Kali."

"I know," she said softly. "But I thank you for sharing yours now."

He opened his pouch and pulled out three stones—the gold, the crimson, and the deep blue. Each gleamed faintly in the moonlight. Fragments of his past: the gold, a general's ambition; the crimson, a soldier's resolve; and the blue, a boy's innocence. All he had been but was no more.

"You know my tale, love. Now see it as I saw it."

He held out the gold stone; Kali took it with reverence. She turned it in her hand, then held it up to her eye. *What will she think, seeing Sara and I in the throes of young love?* he thought.

She broke her silence with a faint laugh, one so warm and unguarded that it tugged at his heart.

"Is that Duke Verlan's palace?" she said with awestruck voice. "It is spectacular."

"It is," Agni replied. "Some days before, I received the emperor's commission as High General. I had not met Sara before that night."

Kali tilted her head, still gazing into the memory.

"What a happy scene. I have never seen that light in Sara's eyes. Was that why you kept this stone from me?"

He hesitated and swallowed. "I would feel guilty to view it, then look into your eyes."

"You thought duty would grow into genuine affection," she said, her voice gentle.

"*Ai,* love. I was innocent in the ways of love and hoped it might blossom."

"You have no reason to feel guilt. I understood long ago that few highborn wed for love."

"You deserve to be a wife and have my full love."

"And now I have it," she replied, beaming. "I have never been one to live in regret."

Agni let out a low breath, feeling a release. He thought of how much he had given her—a home, a share of his wealth—but had withheld something far greater. "Thank you, love."

He handed her the crimson stone next. Kali rolled it between her fingers, savoring the deep red, before lifting it to her eyes. Agni heard faint echoes of his boyish voice, mingled with the gruff laughter of guards. *She knows me to command, not seek instruction. How will she view me as a curious boy?* This time she laughed even brighter, full of motherly affection.

"Little Agni thinks he's a knight," she teased. "You were a scrawny stripling, so far from the knight-elite I met. I cannot imagine those tiny wrists grasping a longsword."

Agni laughed a nervous laugh, an old vulnerability surfacing. "I feared—and still fear—nothing more than my own weakness. I trained with hammers and axes and spears, but only a sword felt like true power."

Kali raised a curious eyebrow.

"Because of your glowing blade?"

"I did not have it then."

Her gaze sharpened.

"You once told me never to reveal that it was not your father's. Can you finally tell me how you obtained it?"

Agni recoiled, his chest tightening. "Kali, some tales are not yet safe to share. Someday, I promise."

*The most terrible tale, love. Anton Kazirian regards you as a speck of dust; no mortal knows how far his powers reach. I must guard you from the final child of the Dragon God,* he thought with chagrin.

Her voice hardened, a quiet challenge. "Do not speak to me like some child. I fed and sheltered myself before you. I will face any terror in the Mortal Realms."

He softened his gaze.

"And yet some forces lie beyond the Mortal Realms, Kali." He sighed. "Even the emperor's finest craft mage could not forge such a blade. I will tell you this—it has fought the god of fate."

Kali stood silent, her gaze probing his. Finally, she nodded, though still looking unsatisfied.

"You have bound our fates, Agni. I will ask again when the time comes."

"On my honor, I will tell you when it is safe."

"Then I accept," she replied, her voice softening.

He handed her the deep blue stone last. Without a word, she lifted it to her eyes, the familiar warmth of his childhood memory warming the space between them. Agni felt his throat tighten as he heard his mother's voice—fierce yet tender, echoing through his entire being. *Only this stone runs deeper than my life of war, deeper than Anton, love. Me, at my weakest.* Kali laughed, wistfully.

"Agni," she said, shaking her head, "what an impatient boy you were. First to wield a longsword, then to ride a giant stallion. Was this your fear, that I might see you as an ordinary boy?"

"No," he said in a solemn voice. "I treasured the solitude when I viewed that stone. Only Dona, Aira, and the older guards knew her. She was… everything. A knight, a paladin of Varenox who fought with blessed strength. But above all, a mother. Fierce and tender to her last breath."

Her hands reached for his, warming them like gloves.

"I think she would be proud of you, Agni. Do you believe that she is?"

Agni swallowed hard, his voice barely above a whisper. "I—I believe she rests in the Lands Beyond, blessed by the Dragon God. But… I have fallen so far from my faith. I would rather glide through Kazian skies than sit at his side. He blessed us with wings, but unlike Avicians', they cannot bear the weight of our mortal forms for long. To transcend that would be pure joy. But I feel her absence with every command I give, every swing of a blade."

Kali squeezed his hands again.

"I do not know where I will sit in the Lands Beyond—or if I will. But it is my honor to spend this life with the man that boy has become."

Agni felt a tear slip down his cheek, unbidden.

"For that, I thank you, love."

She stepped closer, wrapping her arms around him in an embrace that felt deeper than words. Her arms pressed against the roots of his wings, her head resting just below his chin. He savored her warmth.

For the first time since their flight began, Agni felt a flicker of hope. *Mama would be proud—of my devotion, my dreams, and my choice of a life mate and mother to my children.* Together, they had left behind the past and looked forward to a beautiful future.

# Shame

Sara swung open the oak door to the mayor's meeting hall. For the past few days, she had sought solace in longing harp tunes and familiar paths around the common, hoping to drown out the guilt that gnawed at her. When Father's men summoned her that morning, she clung to the faint hope that this ordeal could be salvaged.

The air inside crackled with tension. The Kazian tongue sounded sharp even in whispers; Mayor Goro and a cold-looking man shouted it as such volumes as dragons might fight over mates. Neither acknowledged her. She recognized the words "failure" and "waste" through the cacophony. The mayor's tone was defiant, but his outstretched hands betrayed submission.

The other man, though a head shorter and leaner, held the room with an iron will. He wore the Ristana crest; his steely gaze fixed the mayor where he stood. Several paces back, Goro's slovenly son licked his fingers, staring at the drama with duller eyes than a cow.

The mayor said something about "late" and "storm." Because four days had passed since Agni vanished, a summer storm must have delayed Father's men. *At least my reluctant study of the Kazian tongue bears some fruit, though I sense not for long.*

The western captain turned towards her. She shuddered. His chilling gaze betrayed a cruel face. Years of battle must have leeched his compassion. She saw only undying loyalty to Father. *A moon ago, I would have appreciated a man like this.*

"Enough. We are in the presence of Duke Verlan's heir and should speak the proper tongue in her presence," he spoke in the western tongue.

She felt her guts twist at being dragged into this argument. The mayor ignored her and continued ranting.

"Will you listen to reason, Captain Orlan?" Goro barked, his voice desperate. "Did you honestly believe such a cumbersome trap would snare the Empire's greatest soldier? In his hometown, no less?" the mayor said.

"You failed to capture Agni Kazirian," Orlan replied, his tone now measured but dripping with disdain. "Even as he cleaved your guard's skull, you and your men did nothing. You disobeyed a direct order to pursue him and arrest any who aided his flight. This says you are not fit to share in His Grace's bounty—and might yet face the pinion-and-drop."

The mayor's face flushed bright crimson.

"And had we captured him as you tarried on the trail, what then? Should I have thrown him in the undercroft on a pretext? A mob would have sprung him by sunset. Sent riders into the wilderness? Any farmer and herder in Kazia would shelter him; or worse, rally to him. Agni Kazirian commands loyalty you cannot fathom."

Orlan's eyes narrowed, his lips pulling back into a snarl.

"Your cowardice and sloth are noted, Goro. My timing is none of your concern. Your duty is to serve His Grace, not question him."

The mayor's frustration boiled over. "Serve? And how would your course of action s—"

"Silence." Orlan set a scroll bearing the duke's seal on the table. "This writ grants me absolute authority over this mission. Your crowner, sheriff, and every able-bodied guard answer to me until Lord Kazirian is chained to a mountaintop—or I have his head."

Sara's breath caught in her throat as Orlan turned his chilling gaze on her. His expression softened to a feigned civility.

"And I trust Her Grace will lend her assistance. After all, she serves her lordly father, too."

Her pulse quickened—the thought of aiding this zealot gave her chills, but she had no choice.

"Of course," she stammered, her voice high as a girl's. "Though I doubt you—we—will find him."

"Doubt?" Orlan's voice cut like a lash. "Why would you sow doubt, my lady?"

Sara swallowed hard, forcing herself to meet his gaze.

"Because you cannot search every treetop and wolf's burrow in the Spires. Nor every hearth with a family who might aid him."

Orlan's lips pressed into a thin line.

"Lady Sara, do not underestimate your father's resolve. If we must skewer every wolf pup in its den, we will. If Lord Kazirian does not die according to a precise ritual, this city will grow restive. He must die as a saint, not a criminal. Now tell me—what do you still feel for him?"

Sara gulped. *I am this inquisitor's first victim,* she thought, frozen.

"What do you still feel for him, Lady Sara?" Orlan repeated in his bloodless tone.

She slowed her breath to mask her fright. "Though I trust Father, and my time with Agni was strained, he opened his home to me for two years. He was my betrothed for several more. I cannot quit such affections in four days."

Orlan's eyes narrowed into a probing gaze. After a tense moment, he nodded. "I suppose I must accept this. But sentiment has no place in our mission."

He turned to Goro, unflinching.

"My men are weary. We will take our midday meal and prepare to question anyone who had contact with Agni before his flight. His household, his soldiers, every vendor he visited. Only spirits leave no trace."

Sara's heart sank. Orlan's fanatical pursuit would lead to Aira, Dona, Nira—common folk who did not know nobles' schemes. *Can I prevent their suffering?* Her mind raced.

"And if he is just that, a spirit in the Lands Beyond?"

Orlan's eyebrows rose in realization.

"Well taken, my lady. Then we shall inquire at the temple of Varenox. The Dragon God takes an interest in powerful fates. Perhaps they can divine whether he has ascended to his side—or descended into the Netherworld."

The mention of the temple sent a chill down Sara's spine. Varenox chose the strings of fate and weaved her with this inquisitor's. *I know his sort—their dedication only channels their desire to torment and control,* she thought. One day he might jockey for the High Justice's seat in Artania, to bully girls into testifying that their farmer fathers withheld the tax.

"Very well," she murmured.

She felt a pang of shame as she followed Orlan out of the hall. In her heart, she prayed that Agni lay beyond their reach—anything to spite the lot of them.

---

The temple to Varenox loomed ahead, an imposing but handsome river stone monolith tucked a street southwest of the town common's bustle. *A fitting metaphor—he rarely speaks but looms near and always watches. And how I only visit him when I feel powerless.*

The entrance faced the Dragon God's cardinal direction of south, her gaze lingering on the statues that flanked the entrance. Man-sized, wings unfurled in triumph, bellowing lightning across the skies. It unsettled her as always.

Behind her stood Orlan; behind him, six armored guards stood at attention, their faces as emotionless as their commander's. And in the rear, three priests, their robes billowing in the summer breeze.

Two acolytes, barely more than boys, flanked the entrance, their white robes stark against the gray stone. The one on the right stepped forward, his lilting voice making the harsh Kazian tongue almost melodic.

"Welcome to the house of Varenox, Your Grace, and honored guests. What is your business with the temple today?"

Before Sara could respond, Orlan stepped ahead of her, shoulders squared, wings pulled back as if he himself could command the Dragon God.

"I am Captain Orlan, Justiciar of Duke Verlan Ristana," he announced, as if giving a proclamation. "We come on a matter of grave security. The High Priest's audience is required."

The acolyte hesitated, glancing toward Sara.

"If High Priest Gari is not in meditation, you may—"

"It is urgent," Orlan interrupted, his tone imperious. "This concerns the fate of Lord Kazirian."

The acolyte's eyes widened, and he turned to his companion. Sara's stomach twisted as she imagined what lay ahead. Orlan showed no reverence for the gods. The thought of what might soon happen frightened her.

"Sir, Lord Kazirian rarely graces these doors, not for worship every tenth day, and seldom even on high feasts. You will not find him here today, sir, nor likely any day until the spring's Feast of Oracles, which he—"

Orlan cut off the acolyte's rambling with a raised hand. "We know this," he interrupted. "We require the eyes of the Dragon God, not those of men."

"If the High Priest is able, I will request his audience," the acolyte replied, bowing his head. He turned to his companion. "Haru, fetch him."

The great doors creaked open, releasing a gust of smoky air. Sara caught a woman's solemn chant, punctuated by the soft ring of a bell. The otherworldly tones unsettled her; she instinctively stepped closer to Orlan. He did not seem to notice.

Moments later, Haru returned with High Priest Gari, a burly man whose silver-threaded robe barely concealed the physique of an elder knight. He moved with deliberate grace, his expression calm. His balding head, framed by a few silver strands of hair, shone in the light of the braziers behind him.

"Your Grace," he said with a deep bow. "What an unexpected pleasure."

Her eyes and lips wrinkled into a polite smile. She pursed her lips at that jab. *Who flouts their god more—I who pay little heed, or Orlan who prostrated himself before a mortal?*

"The pleasure is mine, Your Holiness. Though I fear our purpose here is far from pleasant."

She gestured to Orlan, who stepped forward.

"This is Captain Orlan, one of my father's justiciars. He seeks the Dragon God's counsel regarding the disappearance of my betrothed."

Gari's eyebrows lifted as he looked at Orlan.

"Indeed, a weighty matter. Let us speak inside."

Sara followed as Gari led them inside. A colossal stone statue of Varenox dominated the inside—wings spread to a dragon's fifty-foot span, maw screaming a war cry. Three braziers blazed under the statue's head and wings, their flames crackling with almost sentient energy. The priestess chanted in Kazian as she threw powder at the center brazier. It flashed a fierce lightning white; Sara shut her eyes, blinded. It felt like divine judgment.

High Priest Gari stopped before the braziers and turned to face them.

"Justiciar. This must be a grave matter for Duke Verlan to take an interest."

Orlan stepped to the front, his three priests following.

"*Ai.* Quite grave."

"Grave," Sara mouthed out, staring at the floor. *Orlan is judging the High Priest's loyalty. What will he find?*

"It is well known that we avoid one another," Gari said, tilting his head. "I last saw him five moons ago, at the Feast of Oracles. He acknowledged me with a grunt and a nod. I do not expect his presence for another seven. If we pass on the common's perimeter, we avert our eyes."

Orlan's eyes narrowed, as if seizing on something.

"His business permeates this town. Why not this temple?"

Gari took a deep breath and knitted his brow.

"Justiciar, like a farmer prunes his trees that they might bear more fruit, so our god tests us that we might perform great deeds. Our god has gifted Lord Kazirian with such vigor and vision that many believe him a Chosen—that is, one whom the Dragon God gave extraordinary gifts from birth—but he tells anything with ears, from a donkey to the mayor, that our god cursed him. He picks at the wounds of fate and raves against his god. In his youthful days, raiders slew many loved ones and burned manors to the ground. The West forgot us; Blevenia besieged us. Our god tests his chosen. Only from his exalted station, he turns many from a pious path."

"Unfortunate," he muttered, unmoving and bored. "You may not have seen him, but our god would take interest in such a powerful fate. Through your prayers, can you see where he hides?"

Gari nodded up and down.

"We may only see if he passed, beloved of our god—we call it the Ritual of Distant Sight. It requires a seer who is favored of the subject and the Dragon God. But if the favored is too distant from either, it will fail. If he still walks among us—or the Netherworld has taken him—we will not see him."

"We do not care where his essence resides," Orlan replied, annoyed. "Only if it resides in his body. Can one gaze into the Netherworld too?"

Gari's face blanched and his jaw dropped.

"Oh no, no, no. Nether magic is a sweet poison. It tempts its workers with power but etches madness in their hearts. You will only recognize a netherworker by their corruption."

"Very well," Orlan replied through a frown. "Let us see if he sits at our god's side."

"Who will serve as the god's seer?" Gari asked.

The priests' eyes bore down on Sara. She froze under their glare. *Do they believe me worthy to look at our god's side?* They never saw how she and Agni staggered their sleep to avoid one another. Nor how Agni kissed Kali more deeply than his betrothed in their bedroom. *If not me, then whom? Dona visits temple every tenth day and is Kazirian in all but blood—no... no!* An icicle of fear stabbed her in the gut—it would break her if this ritual brought harm to Dona.

"I will serve as seer," Sara announced, trembling. "It is my duty."

The High Priest scanned Sara up and down, squinting with suspicion.

"Your Grace, how is your faith this day? Should we send for a member of his household?"

She steeled herself. *My duty. Let me protect the innocent.* She forced worshipful thoughts of her god. *Hail, God of Fate. Hail, God of Sight. Hail, God of My People.*

"There is no need. I worship the God of Dragons in my own way. As a Westerner, I do not understand Kazian language or customs well enough to worship him as I should. My maids and I worship at home, in our native tongue," she lied.

She tensed her wings, holding the high priest's gaze. It felt like a contest of wills, but he calmly exhaled. *He cannot prove otherwise.*

"This is acceptable, Your Grace," Gari said. He turned to Orlan. "That brings us to the matter of cost. This ritual strains body and mind. Your priests must share the burden. And it is customary to receive a donation for such a service."

Orlan's lips crept into a smirk.

"We carry no credits, Your Holiness. But be assured the duke does not overlook loyalty—or disobedience. If His Grace is pleased, you will have so many silvers you could melt them down and build a statue twice this size," Orlan said, pointing at the colossus.

The priest's eyes widened, either in greed or fearful compliance. He hesitated for a moment.

"I trust that His Grace will keep his word. Very well. Jora?"

He clapped his hands twice, and the priestess marched over. Up close, Jora looked more warrior than holy woman, with her hard face and sinewy forearms.

"Our guests require the Ritual of Distant Sight to see if the disappeared Lord Guardian has passed on. The Justiciar's priests will share our burden. Prepare the brazier."

Jora nodded at the high priest before turning to Sara.

"Lady Sara, step forward towards the brazier. Lay on your back and look into our god's eyes."

Sara took two steps closer. The heat grew intense.

"Closer, Your Grace."

Sara took another step. Sweat beaded on her forehead.

"Closer."

"But—"

"Closer," Jora repeated, ignoring her plea.

Sara shuffled her feet towards the wrought flame. She wrinkled her face to shield it from the burning air. Her eyes watered.

"Is this—"

"Closer."

Her silks burned against her skin. Her lungs burned. A plume of smoke hit her nostrils, sending her coughing.

"I cannot—"

"You must," Jora brooked no disagreement.

Sara turned and inhaled cooler air, then held her breath. Anything to shield Dona and Nira. Her thoughts swirled. *Hail, God of Fate. Hail, God of Sight. Hail, God of My People. Will they send for the household if the ritual fails? Will this ritual wound me?*

"Now lay on your back. Look into our god's eyes. Hold the image of the Lord Guardian in your heart."

She lowered herself to the stone floor, granting some relief from the searing smoke. She tried not to think about the soot on her tunic. She felt three pairs of hands, one on each wing and one on either side of her head. Jora stood at her feet. They began a rhythmic chant as the priestess rang her bell.

She closed her eyes and pictured Agni's image—his sharp eyes, the set of his jaw, his aura of fierce command, the way he carried himself with grace and arrogance.

The hands on her trembled with effort. The priestess' voice grew intense and excited. The colossus' eyes glinted, white on black in the flames. The air rippled around her.

Suddenly, Jora threw two handfuls of white powder at the flame. It flared to a blinding white. The statue seemed to breathe, its flanks heaving, its maw raised in a triumphant roar.

And with it, a vision in the light. A magnificent city of crystal towers, as high as the Spires, rose behind it, impossibly radiant. Worshippers bowed before the Dragon God, chanting hymns of praise. They soared like dragons themselves over the Mortal Realms—*like Agni wished.*

But she did not find Agni in the throng.

The vision faded, and with it, Sara's strength. The priests' hands grew light and tremulous on her body. Jora leaned on her thighs in exhaustion. They helped her to her feet, but her legs buckled beneath her. She leaned heavily on Jora, who with divine strength held her upright.

"Your Grace, what did you see?" the High Priest asked, his voice tinged with urgency.

Sara swallowed hard, trembling.

"I saw Varenox in his glory, surrounded by worshippers. But Agni was not among them."

Sara shook uncontrollably. Jora extended her hand, but Sara's grasp was weak. She flailed her wings to stay upright, hitting the post of a scalding brazier.

"Aah!" she yelped, folding her wing forward and rubbing it.

"Lady Sara, are you sure you did not see him?" Jora probed, seemingly uninterested in the burn, even as her own voice flagged from the effort.

"As sure as I am that this blasted brazier nearly roasted my wing."

The priests at her side had collapsed onto all fours; Priestess Jora herself wobbled on her feet. Gari grunted and Orlan sighed. *This day will not end so quickly,* Sara thought. *Orlan will not be satisfied.*

"High Priest, are you certain that the Lord Guardian is blessed of your god?" Orlan inquired.

"As I said, I believe that he is," Gari replied, his tone annoyed.

"But you cannot be certain of that," Orlan continued, sharp and cold. "Might he speak truth, that the Dragon God has cursed him?"

"Justiciar, like the lightning, our god rarely announces his coming or his favor," Gari sounded peeved at being questioned in his own domain, lips pressed together.

"Yes," Orlan replied in his bloodless voice, but his posture betrayed his impatience. "It seems we have learned all that we can from this visit. If a worshipper brings news of Agni's whereabouts, send word to the mayor."

Gari inclined his head.

"Until then, your priests may shelter here while they recover. It may be some hours."

"No matter," Orlan dismissed Gari's concern. "Our next visits will be decidedly more… secular."

Sara shuddered at his tone. She started to turn, eager to leave the heavy, oppressive air of the temple, but Orlan stopped her.

"Your Grace, do you believe Lord Agni still walks the Mortal Realms?"

That question felt oddly calming—Orlan valued her input, not Varenox's.

"I do. He can make himself one with the land. Until we have his head, we must assume he lives."

She shuddered again. *I play the loyal daughter. But I fear for him—and for this city.*

"The mayor told us that he drugged your wine," he replied, transfixing her with his gaze. "That is a cowardly act, do you agree?"

Her face heated. Were it not flushed and soot-covered from the ritual, he would see her fear.

"I suppose in his stead I would have done the same," she replied in a measured tone. Orlan paused; she could feel him calculating.

"We have not yet informed your father," he said, finally. "But you realize, of course, that if we did, he would see Agni cast from the highest cliff."

The words, spoken so casually, struck Sara again. *Father tolerates neither failure nor defiance.*

"I suppose," she murmured.

Orlan's head tilted slightly, studying her reaction. She saw another plot in his eyes.

"I suppose a high officer of the empire would acquire great knowledge in his travels, but generals do not fight with poison. Often, they are a woman's weapons, learned from generations of women."

The chilling dread hit her in the gut again.

*Aira.*

Like a barrister, he had been circling towards it, leading her where he wanted. Now, the snare tightened. *Orlan will not be denied. But I must protect her.*

"Wise women do not traffic in nobles' affairs," she replied, forcing a neutral tone.

Orlan did not even blink.

"But those affairs sweep up small folk all the same. Did she provide him the poison?"

His snare tightened further. Aira would not bow to this unyielding man, but she did not know the currents that swept her up.

"A crafty man who stoops to poison a high noble would think nothing of deceiving a wise woman," Sara said, forcing a resolute tone. "Aira is an honorable woman. Her tonics have eased many pains. She does not meddle in such things."

Steeled, she met his gaze. "Swear that no harm will come to her."

"I assure you," he said smoothly, "if she did not intend to poison you, and if she cooperates with our inquiry, she will not come to harm."

Sara felt her stomach ease. Orlan had not promised Aira's safety, and Sara knew he would think nothing of harming her. *But I will protect Aira from herself if need be.*

"I have your word then, Orlan. Her name is Aira, and I will lead you there."

Orlan nodded, wheeling toward the exit.

"Very well. Let us break."

Sara turned her face away. She realized that any outcome of this investigation would gut her. If they captured Agni, she would have helped lead him to his doom. If they did not, she would return to Artania under a cloud of disgrace. Either way, she would suffer.

Orlan strode ahead, his command sharp. "Guards. Eastward to the wise woman's."

———

Walking down South Street, Sara kept ahead of Orlan so she could not see his face. His cold presence pressed at her back. *Orlan, the relentless. Will he keep his word? Or would he reduce her to blood and bruises to extract whatever he sought?* While Aira was resolute, she was still an old woman.

Her breath caught as she spotted the crossed sage-stems marking Aira's shop. Six uniformed soldiers flanked her and Orlan, their rigid postures exaggerated, as though it required such force to subdue an aged wise woman—and to remind Sara of her place. Of her failure.

Even for all Father had promised her—the capital duchy, a doting husband, a return to the life she missed—the unease in her chest remained. Aira, Nira, Dona, even Kali, if she still remained, would suffer Orlan's fanatical brutality, and see Sara at his side.

She reached out for the iron handle, but Orlan's hand shot out first, yanking it twice. It rattled but did not budge. He rapped at the door.

"Open the door, Aira. We have questions for you," he intoned, his voice dark.

A minute passed before the slit in the door creaked open. A single sharp eye peered through before the latch lifted. Aira did not hurry. She opened the door at her own pace, neither cowed nor welcoming.

Orlan threw the door open, grazing Aira's wing. She huffed, but her narrowed eyes locked onto him with annoyance rather than fear.

Sara met Aira's gaze and mouthed: *Please forgive me.*

Aira's expression barely changed, save for a flicker of disappointment. But she did not look away.

"Sir," Aira said, her tone calm, "there's no need for such a display. Crowner Gilo himself collected my levies. I do not have letters, so I have no ledger. Her Grace oversaw the count."

"Yes, I—" Sara started to confirm, but then Orlan lifted a hand.

"Have you made the acquaintance of Lord Agni Kazirian?"

Aira let out a dry chuckle. "Of course. Every washerwoman in town has batted an eye at the Lord Guardian."

Orlan's eyes narrowed.

"And have you?"

Aira smiled, her tone turning playful. "Indeed. In my youth, I like to think I could have bedded him. I never married, but I did raise three girls without a husband."

Sara squelched a nervous laugh.

Orlan's expression did not change. "When did you last see him?"

Aira grunted, her tone turning sour. "Forgive me, sir, but I don't believe I have your name. Nor your business in asking such things. Even in these times, some men—especially Westerners like yourself, by your accent—look askance at wise women."

Orlan took a threatening step towards her. He stood a quarter-head shorter than Aira but still loomed.

"Where is he, at present?"

Aira held his gaze without hesitation.

"Inspecting dragon whistles in the Spires. Enjoying an afternoon trot on his big white stallion. Drawing up trail maps with his engineers. Plotting to bugger King Vardon of Blevenia." She gestured around her shop, voice snide. "As you can see, he is not here. So I do not know."

The air grew tense.

"Aira," Orlan started, his voice accusatory, "are you aware that harboring or aiding a criminal is punishable by the pinion-and-drop?"

Aira's brows lifted in disbelief. Her voice raised. "The Lord Guardian, a criminal? Guilty of what?"

"That is not your con—"

Aira cut him off, fire rising in her eyes. "It blasted well is my concern, if you come to me inquiring!"

The silence that followed tightened like a harp string.

Orlan's lips thinned. Then, he turned slightly toward his men.

"Guards, overturn every pot and chest in this shop. Dig up every garden on the sides."

*No!* Before the guards could move, Sara jolted to attention and shouted. "Stay your hand!"

Her sharp voice caught them off guard. The men hesitated, looking between her and Orlan. She had to stop this. Like an oak, Aira would break before she bent. He would make her suffer.

She turned to Orlan, desperate to give him some tidbit that would satisfy him without condemning Aira.

"The day before Agni disappeared, he bought an herb for night terrors, rather than turn to the drink like his father," she blurted out. "Justiciar, you know of Agni's fits."

Orlan's stone face did not waver.

"Aira did not know Agni would poison me; in fact, she thought Agni had gone to his lover's. The next day, I bought the herb for my own rest." Sara gestured to Aira. "If Aira intended him to harm me, why would I have purchased the same herb?"

She turned to Aira, her voice pleading. "Aira, this is what you told me four days ago. Was it not?"

Aira turned a sharp scowl toward Sara; so sharp, she flinched. It felt worse than anger.

Disappointment.

"Sara," Aira said slowly, like a mother scolding a wayward child. "Why are you cavorting about town with these thugs? You may not have Kazian blood, but I thought two years might have bred more respect for your neighbors."

Sara's chest clenched.

"These are my father's men. I did not summon them. I wanted to protect you."

Aira's lips curled into a bitter smile. And then she laughed—a taunt, like Agni looming over a defeated opponent.

"Now you listen, little duchess." She lifted her hands, gnarled and calloused from decades of work. "I've lived eight-and-a-half decades. I have run this shop for seven." Her voice hardened. "I've had these hands broken, and this shop burned to the ground by jackals who called me a witch. When my time comes to pass to the Lands Beyond, I will go in peace. But I will not cower before Western oafs who respect neither the land nor its champions."

Orlan advanced, mere feet from Aira. Sara rushed to stand between them, but there was no room.

"Mind your tongue, Aira," Orlan snarled. "Even if you did not knowingly poison the duchess, we have a duke's writ to find the missing Lord Guardian at any cost. You *will* cooperate."

Aira tilted her head, slow and deliberate. Her smile unsettled Sara.

"Orlan, was it? Lean closer, so that I may tell you what I think of your writ."

Orlan leaned in, menacing, inches from her nose.

Aira spat.

Saliva and mucus splattered over Orlan's face.

The room froze.

Without thinking, Sara spread her arms and wings, pushing between Orlan and Aira.

No blows came. Orlan's chest heaved, his wings twitching. He lifted his sleeve and wiped his face with precise, unhurried movements.

"You bitch," he muttered.

Sara exhaled in relief but knew that, like Orlan's every move, it was calculated.

Still obstructing Aira's body, Sara spoke. "Aira… Agni slipped your herb into my meal, then fled the city that night."

Aira stepped back and glared through her. "Did he, now?" she said, her voice dripping venom. "Why would the Lord Guardian of the East do that?"

Sara's mouth went dry—*blast it!*

One more word and Aira would know. The truth hovered between them. If Aira learned the ploy, Orlan would slay her to protect it—or Aira would rouse the town into a riot.

Sara looked away.

"I cannot say more."

Aira's expression darkened. "Orlan, leave my house. The duchess here has told you everything."

Sara turned to Orlan, pleading. "Please, Orlan, let us go. She knows nothing more."

Orlan stared Sara down with his stony eyes. She forced herself to stare back—for Aira, for Father, for Agni. If they stayed, her life might crumble further.

"Very well. To the Kazirian city house," Orlan grunted. Without another word, he knocked over a clay pot, spilling some brown dirt.

Aira did not react; she only turned to Sara.

"Sara. Tarry here a minute."

Sara froze mid-step, her breath catching as she turned back. Aira had leveled an accusing finger at her face.

"You may have been his betrothed," Aira said, her voice scolding, "but I held the Lord Guardian while he still shit his nappies. He was a clever boy, though no one fancied he'd shake the Mortal Realms. I gave him enough mandrake to kill three men. If he wanted your life, he could have had it—and the crowner would take him at his word. Tell me, why would he drug an innocent duchess, then flee over the walls?"

Like a barrister unraveling a noble's yarn, Aira had Sara pinned, her words cutting. Sara felt her body tense and her throat dry.

All she could do was deny.

"I do not—"

Aira stepped closer. "Why would these interlopers—your father's—arrive four afternoons after Agni fled? It is ten to Eltrazan, more with the last storm. They must have left soon after your feast ended. What were your designs for him, girl?"

"I was—"

"Speak the truth," Aira cut in, her voice quieter but no kinder, "if you ever hope to purchase a tonic here again."

Sara's stomach twisted. Her lips parted but the words lodged in her throat.

"I cannot say more," she whispered. "Forgive me."

Aira exhaled in a near growl. "Then quit this shop immediately. May your lying tongues rot in your mouths, and the Lord Guardian escape your wicked schemes."

Without another glance, Aira shook back her silver-blue mane and turned her back on Sara, retreating behind the counter as if she had already washed her hands of her.

Sara bit her lip to stifle the coming tears. *I have failed.* As a conspirator. As a protector. As a duchess.

———

Unlike the walk to Aira's shop, the walk to the Kazirian house stretched into what felt like days. With every step, Sara felt the weight of her choices—her complicity in Agni's betrayal, her failure to halt Orlan's inquisition. But worse, Aira's parting words burned her like a brand. *Little duchess.* Like a curse. A moral chasm with the good folk on one side, and her, Father, Goro, and Orlan on the wrong side.

As the house loomed ahead, Sara broke away from the group, heart thudding against her ribs.

"Dona? Nira?" Her voice was taut, urgent. "Please come to the front hall." Perhaps, if they complied, Orlan would show restraint.

Orlan held a hand to quiet her, but she hissed back first.

"Calm, Orlan. They will come."

*This is my home, my domain,* she thought.

Sara lifted the latch. The men filed inside, their drill step march foreign and invasive in her home.

"Come forth. We need a word with you," Orlan's voice rang out.

Sara heard Dona shout something from the backyard. She scurried ahead through the kitchen, to the back door. All six men filed through the door, executing their same formation. *To bully an old woman. Perhaps they will muscle an urchin next.*

They came across Dona at the washbasin, scrubbing a clot with slow, methodical movements. She turned, wiping damp hands against her apron.

"Good afternoon, Lady Sara," she said with a slight bow, before turning to the men. "Are these Lord Agni's soldiers? I haven't seen him since—"

"We have some questions for you," Orlan interrupted in his cold voice.

Dona's expression barely shifted, but something in her eyes sharpened. "I'll do my best," she replied, "though I have more questions than answers myself."

"I assume you are Dona, caretaker for the Kazirian house?" Orlan asked.

"I am," Dona replied coolly. "And well, I do what an old woman can, young sir. Sir… what should I call you?"

"That is of no concern of yours," Orlan said in a near growl.

Sara stepped in quickly, sensing the situation about to boil.

"He is Captain Orlan. He bears my father's crest. Please, Dona—tell him whatever you can of Agni's whereabouts."

Dona folded her arms, the lines around her mouth deepening.

"Well then, Captain, I haven't seen him in four days. That night, he seemed troubled, so I boiled his favorite bread pudding—walnuts, raisins, and cinnamon. It always lightens his face." She paused, as if picturing the boy she had raised. "I retired to my hut for the night. By the time I woke, he was gone. I prepared his bacon, porridge and bread to break the fast that morning, and it stayed untouched."

Orlan's gaze held fast.

"Where was he headed? What did he tell you?"

"I've already said, I don't know," she replied, her voice getting cross.

"Tell me where you think he went," Orlan huffed.

Dona let out a dry, throaty chuckle. "Why would I prepare his breakfast if I knew he would vanish?"

Without warning, Orlan surged forward and seized a fistful of her gray hair, yanking her head back. Sara gasped.

"My patience wears thin, woman," Orlan snarled through gritted teeth.

Sara shot forward, her heart hammering. "Orlan, stop! She does not—"

But Dona's eyes, clear and unwavering, met Orlan's without fear. No pleading, no submission. Just the clarity of years of wisdom and service.

"I don't know," she repeated.

Orlan's fingers tightened, his frustration breaking through. "Woman, do you expect me to believe that you, who has managed every detail or his household, know nothing of his patterns? No knowledge of his escape?"

Dona's lips curled into a smirk.

"Escape the law?" Her voice took on steel, authority she must have learned from Agni. "Boy, in this valley, he *is* the law—the kind you only play at. The kind that bruises ogres who beat their daughters. The kind that feeds urchins who scout mountain trails. The kind that mines those trails because the capital couldn't be bothered to send soldiers."

She raised her chin against Orlan's rasp, her eyes glinting with defiance.

"If the Lord Guardian does not wish to be found, any hut in Kazia would shelter him." Now she snarled, dangerous and resolute. Nothing left to fear. "Now let go of me, you tight-arsed western ox."

Sara had no time to react before the old woman struck. With a soldier's speed, she grasped Orlan's arm and drove her shin straight into his groin.

Orlan stumbled back with a grunt, his grip breaking as he staggered. But Dona's foot caught on a root, sending her spinning.

Sara reached for her.

She was too late.

Dona's skull struck a rock with a sickening crack.

The world seemed to halt.

A low moan escaped the old woman's lips as dark blood seeped into the ground, pooling beneath her head. Her chest rose once. Then, stillness.

Sara's breath left her in a broken sob.

"NO!" She lunged forward, only for Orlan's men to seize her by the wings, yanking her back. "Release me, you fiends! She is dying!"

Sara kicked, twisted, thrashed in their grip, but the hands on her arms held firm. In seconds, Dona's pulse gave out.

"Look what you have done, Orlan," she choked. "You killed her!"

Orlan, unaffected, merely watched the scene unfold, arms crossed. He did not even change his expression.

Dona lay motionless, her silver hair darkened with blood. Her lips parted slightly, as if to scold a young Agni for skipping lessons. There would be no cackling laugh as she told stories of Agni's youth, no warm bread pudding, no lullabies hummed beneath her breath as she boiled water. Ever again.

She was gone.

Other than blood leaking from her mouth, she looked at peace, her zest to serve finally satisfied.

Sara collapsed onto her knees, a wretched, wracking sob ripping through the air. Her wings spasmed violently, her fingers clawing at the dirt as if she could bring her back.

"Blast you, Orlan!" Her voice broke. "May Varenox's maw tear you apart! Blast Goro, blast Father, blast Solantia—"

She could say no more, collapsing in keening sobs. She felt small, frail, helpless—just like on the trail, a girl in a world of cruel men.

Orlan merely observed, cold and unaffected, as though watching a candle flicker out.

"Come, my lady," he said in his deadpan tone. "That is unfortunate, but we have lost enough time. If his servant did not see him, then he escaped over the walls. We will question the guards."

Sara trembled, her body convulsing with rage and sorrow. "On my oath, I will have you curse this day, Orlan! If I must take a lash to your wretched hide myself!"

Orlan did not react or acknowledge her fury. He merely turned and gestured for his men to form up.

Sara watched him, her hands shaking, her vision blurred with tears.

She had thought herself a player in Father's game. But she was not. She was nothing to men like Orlan.

Dona had died for nothing.

*I will avenge you, Dona, if it costs me my own life,* she mouthed, between sobs.

———

Sara marched to the guard tower in a daze. Now following behind Orlan like a subordinate, she fantasized about grabbing a guard's spear and running him through. *I should be in Artania, condemning this man to the pinion-and-drop,* she thought.

Sara clenched her fists at her side. *I cannot indulge in sentiment. I must protect the town—even guards—from this wicked ogre.*

The largest guard tower loomed over the bridge to the Ancient City, built in a time when men feared undead hordes more than Blevenian raids. Yet it held more armored men than any other tower. *Superstition still rules their hearts. But if I were raised in its shadow, it might rule mine too.*

Today, she would rather face ghosts than the living.

The front door stood ajar. Orlan and his men strode in first, stepping in their precise formation. Sara lingered at the threshold, bile rising in her throat. She had no desire to witness Orlan brutalize another, but if she had learned anything today, it was that silence would not stop him.

Inside, three guards stood at attention. At the sight of Orlan, they snapped into crisp salutes.

Sara ground her teeth. *Would they salute him if they knew he just killed Agni's beloved crone?*

Orlan returned the salute. "At ease, soldier."

Sara's anger rose at the familiarity in his tone. *Is that all it takes? The right uniform and crest, and they salute a stranger?*

The tallest guard, a broad-shouldered Kazian with a clipped beard and weathered face—stepped forward. "I am Trako, captain of the town guards. How can I assist you today?"

Orlan met his gaze without hesitation.

"Well then, Trako, I am Captain Orlan. I bear the crest of Duke Verlan Ristana and am here to investigate a matter of the law."

Trako's expression remained neutral.

"I assure you, captain, our crowner and sheriff investigate all crimes. We don't need the West's assistance."

Orlan's voice did not waver. "This concerns the Lord Guardian's disappearance."

Sara saw Trako's mouth tighten. No Kazian spoke Agni's title lightly, and Orlan wielded it without thought.

Orlan withdrew the writ from within his cloak and dropped it on the table in front of Trako.

Trako inspected the seal, broken at the mayor's earlier, and unrolled it, tracing the text with his finger. When he finally looked up, he shook his head.

"Well then. I recognize Duke Verlan's signet. But tell me, captain—how did you come from the capital to investigate the

Lord Guardian? The storms rendered the road impassable for days after his return. You must have departed before he arrived—and well before he vanished."

Sara's breath caught in excitement. *Yes, press him, reveal his schemes!*

Orlan did not flinch, his voice as deadpan as ever. "We came for other matters that do not concern the guards. We were then instructed to pursue this."

*A trained lie.*

Trako stood rooted like an oak. His silence grew thick as fog.

Finally, he replied. "Sir, any matter of town security concerns us. We are tasked with—"

"Enough," Orlan's voice cut him off. "The Lord Guardian's affairs merited the mayor's involvement, and my lord's. We are tasked with finding him.

Sara's anger returned. *Tasked with finding him.* As though they were concerned with his safety. As though Dona's corpse were not still cooling in the garden.

Trako's face remained impassive.

"The Lord Guardian appears and disappears on his own business. The mayor has said nothing of him, save that he lost his prized sword. We pray for his safety, but there is little else we can do."

Orlan's eyes narrowed.

"It is not like him to lose his weapon. What happened?"

Trako grunted, then leaned back against the table, arms crossed.

"Some nights ago, we lost a guard, Osmo, at the northern gate. Cut through helm and head. Flesh singed like a roasted pig's." His voice darkened. "Only one sword in the valley can do that. His partner survived, though barely. Bruised crown to toe. But he could not identify the murderer."

Another slow, deliberate pause.

"Had you thought the Lord Guardian capable of such a thing?"

Trako's expression did not shift. His gaze, level and unwavering, settled on Orlan in quiet judgment.

"Captain," he replied, "you sound like a right fool saying that."

Sara felt a flicker of satisfaction, that one citizen with a blade stood up to Orlan.

Trako continued, tone steady. "I answer to Constable Avro, and he to the mayor. But no one speaks the name of Agni Kazirian lightly."

Orlan's nostrils flared. "You may need to reconsider that thought."

Trako's face hardened. He stood straight, wings spread—he had half a head on Orlan. Suddenly, Orlan looked small and vulnerable.

"Do I, now?"

Sara recognized this primitive game of men—the flicker of tension in Orlan's shoulders, Trako asserting his height.

"The good folk of Azectrai would assume that had the Lord Guardian killed his firstborn, then his firstborn must have needed killing," Trako said, chest out. "But he has given so much to this town for me to believe he would cut down his own man without cause."

Trako cocked his body into a fighter's stance.

"So, stop speaking such foolishness."

Orlan's lips pulled back into a snarl, but Sara recognized that he was outmatched—in body and mind. He paused, taking Trako's measure.

"I understand," Orlan said at last.

*You most certainly do not,* Sara thought. *You are a dragon to old women, but a housecat to armed men.*

"Good," Trako said, and for the first time, Orlan looked cowed.

Orlan stretched his back.

"We will search north of the city. To his manor and surrounding villages."

Trako nodded.

"I hope you find him, Captain," he said. His tone was polite, but the meaning beneath it was clear. "Just return him to us safe."

Sara swallowed against the lump in her throat. *He knows what will happen if Orlan finds him first.*

She stared at Trako, willing him to see the plea in her eyes. *And if you find him, help him.* But his face stayed impassive.

Sara turned away as Orlan strode toward the door, motioning for his men to follow.

Now Orlan knew the plot, like she had deduced the day after Agni fled—that Agni was four days gone. Into the mountains, into the valley, or into the sea and out of Solantia. Her rage still simmered, her grief was still raw, but for the first time since Agni vanished, a thought rooted itself in her mind. Orlan, too, would have to confess his failure to Father.

*You will lose, Orlan… and when we return to Artanport, I will see you suffer for what you did.*

———

The sun had just kissed the horizon, casting long copper shadows over the streets and common. Sara's body felt heavy, her legs leaden as she made her way to the Terrapin Tavern on West Street.

Fear had yielded to icy despair. Nira would have found Dona's broken body and herself broken down in wailing sobs. A simple grave would be the only sign that Dona had lived there. *I will awaken, awaiting bacon and porridge, and it will not come.* Dona's death would sting at every mealtime, or every time she stepped out back.

After the guardhouse, she had watched Orlan and Goro squabble over petty grievances, their voices distant and hollow in her ears. Then, she had returned to the Kazirian house and sat in the main hall, staring at nothing, lost in the emptiness. By now,

Nira would have sent for gravediggers. The thought brought a flush of shame. *I should have been the one to do it,* she thought bitterly. *But I am a coward. I could not face Nira or the body. I could not face my failure.*

She stopped outside the tavern, staring at the giant turtle shell mounted above the entrance. Kali had once sung here, even poured ale with that carefree laugh of hers. That memory of her old life should have brought her comfort, but today, it only sharpened the loss. *I would give my left wing for Agni's unfaithfulness to be my greatest shame.*

Inside, the dim glow of lanterns cast flickering light across the wooden beams. She tossed five credits on the counter without a word, taking her seat in the farthest corner. The innkeeper wordlessly set down a plate of roast pork and a cup of wine before her. She picked listlessly at the pork. The wine tasted sour, like vinegar on her lips. At least no one approached her; no one asked why a high noble sat alone, hunched like a common wretch, ignoring the finest meal in Azectrai.

*I deserve this,* she whispered to herself. *I sought release from Agni's side, and power without risk. I forsook my virtue for Father's approval. I grew proud and covetous, and Varenox smote me.*

Her tears fell in slow, silent drops.

A husky voice cut through the haze of grief. "My lady, may I join you?"

She had barely lifted her head before a clammy hand brushed against the nape of her neck. The stench of dried sweat cut through her tears.

"Leave me, Arno," she hissed, not even looking at him.

But he ignored her command.

"I am sorry. For my father, for everything."

Sara said nothing.

"You… look beautiful, even when you are sad."

He draped his chubby arm across her shoulders in what might have been mistaken for comfort—if not for his slow, creeping fingers tracing down her spine.

*This clod is trying to seduce me… what gall!*

"I said, leave me be," she replied, monotone.

Arno did not remove his hand. Instead, it began to caress—up and down, deliberate and slow, like a man staking his claim. His other hand grazed her arm, then deliberately brushed the curve of her breast.

"You know I care about you, Sara…"

A shiver rose up her back.

"Remove your hand, you boor."

Arno pulled back his hand, but too slowly.

Her voice had been louder than she realized. Three men snapped their heads toward them, eyes narrowed in scrutiny.

Arno must have seen them—he yanked his hand back in a mock gesture of innocence.

"I apologize, my lady, I—"

That set her over the edge. A jolt of anger shot up her spine, and before she knew it, her hand curled around the hilt of her knife. She yanked it free.

The polished blade caught the lamplight as she held it before her face. Her grip trembled—not with fear, but cool clarity. Like Agni must have felt in battle. She had driven this blade into a man's flesh before.

She was not practiced, but she was willing.

The tip of the knife thunked into the rough wood of the table.

"Touch my breast again, and I will pin that hand to the table."

Arno's face flushed, his humiliation turning to anger.

"Woman—"

Sara pulled the knife free, drawing it back to strike, like Agni once showed her.

A commotion erupted around them. A dozen patrons shot to their feet, some shouting, some grabbing Arno. Burly hands seized his arms and wings, dragging him toward the exit. He thrashed, spewing Kazian curses, but no one listened.

From behind her, a female voice cut through the noise. "Is that you, Your Grace? Are you well?"

The words barely registered. "Please leave me be," Sara mumbled, sliding the blade back into its sheath.

She slumped forward, her face falling into her hands.

Arno had tried to violate her body, but in a twisted way, it felt like penance for her treachery. Orlan—the cold, dutiful fanatic— had done worse. He'd ripped something from her soul, taken Dona from her, left her raw and bleeding in a town that no longer embraced her.

She was alone.

A stranger to the guards, a disappointment to Father, an outcast in the only home she had known for two years.

She spent the rest of the night in the tavern, nursing a single cup of wine, speaking no further words to anyone.

C H A P T E R   1 6

# Seaward

The dim glow of dawn filtered through the shutters, lighting the cramped room. The air was thick with the scent of salt brine, mingling with the odor of three unwashed bodies confined to a small bed.

Agni rubbed his eyes and yawned, rolling his shoulders to shake off the stiffness of a sleepless night. His right wing scraped against the splintered wall for hours, and Alexander's own had flicked against Agni and Kali all night.

*How strange,* he thought, *that I slept more soundly before setting sail to wage war on King Theodore, than to skulk in his shadow.*

Beside him, Kali, the deepest sleeper, stirred.

"Mmm… Agni?"

"It is time," he replied.

Alexander groaned and cracked open one eye. "You have another hour, Agni," he said, a yawn interrupting his smirk. "Or should I say, Azri of Azectrai."

Agni chuckled. "I had best grow accustomed to that name. And to lightening my voice."

"The captain knows you are no mouse," Kali murmured, her voice still thick with sleep.

"Let him wonder." Agni sat up and pulled the cowl over his shoulders. "Everyone knows Agni Kazirian would never set foot in Tercera unarmed. A ship's speaking-stone—if it has one—can reach no more than several miles. The duke's pursuers cannot reach me on the open sea."

"Does that comfort you, Agni?" Kali said.

"I must still conceal my face, lest I am recognized and ransomed," he said as he adjusted the cowl around his head. "This will smell worse than a wolf's kill by the time I arrive."

"Thirty days without a proper wash." Kali stretched her arms over her head, groaning in sympathy. "I dread my legs covered in fleas."

"And the pitching deck." Agni huffed. "I will spend my days retching over the rail. But if something must be done, there is no use whining about it."

He reached for his pack, rifling through its contents, pulling out items Azri of Azectrai would not carry.

"My coins." He withdrew all but twenty-five ten-credit silvers and handed the rest to Alexander. "You take these. We will need a moneychanger if we wish to eat. And no spending these on tavern girls," he said, grinning.

Alexander just laughed. "And if I need to impersonate a poor man on my voyage?"

"Then hide them in your arse." Agni smirked. "One of us needs to arrive flush, and yours is bigger than Kali's." He smiled and squeezed Kali's backside.

She laughed with mock indignation and swatted his arm. It warmed the small space.

Agni sighed, his expression softening. "And in your moon at sea, think deeply about what you will do when you arrive. If Ronan has disappeared, we will need to scrap for every meal and night."

"I already have, love." Kali rested her chin on her hand. "I have made a life dancing for scraps. But they say Tercera has a grand university—a temple of learning where I might study justice."

She rubbed her hands together, excitement flickering in her green eyes. "I may advocate before the king someday." She turned to Agni. "Then I shall wed my noble betrothed and bear his children."

"In that order?" Agni replied.

"In any order, love. You said anything is possible in Tercera," she said with a soft smile.

Their eyes locked. Admiration swelled in his chest. She would no longer depend on him for her station—they would both be exalted in their new home.

Alexander broke the long silence.

"You are nothing if not a survivor, Kali," Alexander said. "This old war dog will ponder his next life on the ship."

"Whatever you decide," Agni added, "we are less without your wisdom and honor." He placed a firm hand on Alexander's shoulder. "I should arrive first, so I will make us of good use to the Solantian community. Duke Verlan cannot collect a bounty across the sea. Remember—meet at the west gate of the Aerie Market, where it meets the Solantian quarter, at midday, every day. Though six moons pass, do not give up hope."

Agni paused, then reached into his pouch, pulling out a small golden stone.

"But if the sea takes me, I want to create one last memory together. On this stone."

Kali's eyes widened. Alexander tilted his head.

"Agni, those are your prized memories. Why would you sacrifice one?"

Agni turned the stone between his fingers, its gold lighting up his hand.

"After I showed you this stone, Kali, I realized that this one lost its meaning." His voice was quiet, measured. "The soldier and the boy will live on in Avicia, but the general—and betrothed to a duchess—is dead. I will travel with a lighter heart if you have it."

Alexander's gaze flickered with understanding.

"Your stones, Agni? You swore never to show them to anyone."

Agni nodded.

"This one means nothing, Alexander. It holds the night Duke Verlan betrothed me to Sara. A remnant of a man who no longer exists."

Alexander hesitated for a moment before nodding, understanding the gesture for what it was.

"Thank you, Agni." He held the stone in his palm. "You honor us."

The three pressed against the back wall, nearly covering each other. Unlike the last image to grace this stone, it would hold no glory or finery. But it would hold something deeper—joy, hope, the promise of a new beginning.

With the longest arms, Alexander squeezed the stone between two massive fingers.

"*To the truest friends in the Mortal Realms. To fellowship until the Lands Beyond take us,*" Agni spoke.

"*To the unrelenting pursuit of peace and honor. Let it burn within our veins,*" Alexander added.

"*To endless possibilities and dreams. To our new home wherever we lay our heads,*" Kali finished.

"*Hail!*" all three spoke in unison.

Alexander released the stone and handed it to Kali.

Agni returned to his pack, distributing what he would leave with them. But before bidding his farewells, he found himself lingering, his fingers tracing the edge of his satchel.

Anton's words haunted him. Now, he acted in defiance of two higher powers, both of which could bide their time to strike. It both thrilled and unsettled him.

"Agni?" Kali and Alexander spoke his name at once.

He blinked, shaking himself free of his thoughts.

"I was just thinking," he replied, shaking his head. "These last days feel like a dream."

Kali tilted her head.

"You expect to awaken in your bed, beside Sara, awaiting a return to the West?"

"No," he murmured. "A premonition."

Alexander studied him.

"You are learned in dreams and fates."

Agni's gaze grew distant. "They are frequent, but seldom clear. I feel a current, like the Great River, tugging at us. One that we cannot fight, but neither abandon ourselves to." He met their eyes, voice steady. "And this current runs even deeper than the Black Moon."

A long silence followed, as Alexander and Kali just stared.

"I have one last order for you as High General and Lord Guardian." His voice was softer, solemn, but no less commanding. "Make it there with your heads intact."

"*Ai*, Lord Guardian," Alexander intoned. "And you too."

Kali said nothing—only pulled Agni in for a deep, lingering kiss.

"I shall see you in a moon, love," she whispered against his lips.

For the first time in moons, Agni allowed himself to believe it.

———

By the second night, Agni had acclimated—or at least resigned himself—to life on the sea. He had spent the first day hunched over the railing, retching his guts into the churning waves. The stench of brine, sweat, and a sour stomach still clung to him, but a fellow passenger had taught him to stand amidships and fix his gaze on the horizon.

Whomever Captain Zaha hired as the ship's cook had the skills of a blind beggar. The broth tasted like boiled leather, and the bread was so hard he wondered if it had once been ballast. But at least it steadied his stomach. Moving barrels for the crew kept his muscles taut. And waiting out the hot hours below deck, while the air was thick with unwashed bodies and stale breath, saved him from the merciless sun.

But at night, he could look up.

*Spectacular.*

The night sky stretched endlessly above, a dome of scattered diamonds. With no trees or mountains to interrupt the view, he had never seen the stars so clearly. The Dragon loomed over the south, watching over the Dragonlands, but the north held new sights, so he gave them names. *The Sword. The Pelican. The Serpent. Perhaps by journey's end, I will see an Avician Roc.*

He heard footsteps from his right and tensed his body, squaring his stance.

"Identify yourself."

A shadow emerged—a short, wiry man with sharp but weathered features. His wings had scabbed over, suggesting a hard life, but he carried himself with the easy confidence of a man who never feared another. His hands rose, empty, in a wordless show of peace.

"Calm, friend," the main said, his voice smooth as a noble's. "I did not mean to surprise you."

Agni lowered his hands, but only slightly.

"Pardon me, then."

"I go by Remon. You can call me Rem, if you'd like."

"Remon, is it?" Agni studied him, keeping his own expression reserved. "A Blevenian traveling to Avicia by way of Solantia? I am Azri."

"By origin, yes," Rem said with a nod. "But I have no nation anymore."

*I know that all too well,* Agni thought. *This man looks like a ruffian but carries himself like a lord.*

"Do any of us?" He let a small chuckle through. "We'll all be Avicians in a moon."

Rem smiled, but something suggested amusement rather than agreement.

"Indeed. I will not miss the Dragonlands."

"No man on this ship will. I wager few could afford the return journey."

Agni watched Rem's reaction—nothing.

"*Ai,* friend. Captain Zaha did not question any man who could pay the fare."

*Perhaps a smuggler. But small folk do not ask such questions.*

"What's your tale, Rem?" he asked. "Why do you flee the Dragonlands, and how did you procure your fare?"

Rem chuckled.

"You're an inquisitive man."

Agni smiled.

"We have neither tavern girls nor singers on this ship, so we might as well befriend one another over our moon."

Agni felt fortunate to have Alexander and Kali following. Most passengers were loners, drifters who stared at the water all day or joined the crew in gruff, off-key shanties. A few traders down on their luck. But most looked to be the sort of men whose hands knew more of lifting purses than plowing fields.

Rem looked, though he did not behave, like one of them.

"I suppose you're right," Rem said. "My tale is a common one. Western Blevenia has suffered lean years. After the Wolf slew my noble master Sir Faron, seven years ago, in the war—"

"A wolf? Did it foam at the lips?"

Rem's eyes glinted.

"No, the Wolf of Azectrai."

Agni felt a flush at that reminder of his past.

"You must mean—"

"The Desolator." Agni caught a flash of anger, though Rem recomposed himself quickly. "Agni Kazirian, cursed be his name."

Agni froze his face but winced inside. A stark reminder of a past he could not escape.

"Did he," Agni replied.

Rem continued, as if not noticing Agni's reaction.

"My father served Sir Faron, as a steward and a squire. But when Sir Faron was cut down in battle, four of his wayward sons pilfered the manor and fled northeast to Tonda. The last son caught a fever and died—so my father said. I think grief overcame that son, and he drank poison to end his life."

"I understand," Agni said. "A tragic tale."

*Tragic. In Avicia, I will need to placate widows and brothers of dead men,* he thought. He bit his lip. Now was not the time to indulge emotion.

"The servants squabbled among themselves, and the fields overgrew with weeds," Rem continued. "My father and I were forced into banditry along the Beachroad. We said we would stay highwaymen only until we could procure fare to a more favorable land."

Agni sensed truth in Rem's voice. *That which I will repay with lies. I do not recall Sir Faron—it is the name of yet another dead lord.*

"Is your father on board? I saw no elders."

"He died a year ago, when a leg wound oozed pus," Rem said, his head downcast.

"I am sad to learn of that."

"Such is the life of an outlaw. His end was a mercy."

"It often is," Agni replied, detached.

Rem had the air of a man who had known hardship but never let it break him. There was restrained anger in his voice, one he knew well. But no self-pity—only the hard pragmatism of a survivor.

"And you? What is your name, and why do you flee the Dragonlands?"

Agni hesitated for a moment.

"Call me Azri of Azectrai," Agni said.

"Azri. A Kazian," Rem replied, inquisitive.

Agni looked down, feigning shame.

"I have no home and no kin. I would be pinioned-and-dropped in that land. That is all that matters."

"Hmm…" Rem weighed these words. "Somehow, you found three moons' wages to make the voyage."

Agni took a slow breath. *I had best accustom myself to spinning such yarns*, he thought.

"Your Sir Faron was an honorable man. My lord was a brutal swine who ravished my daughter before she had her first moon flow."

"Sad," Rem said. "A man can't let that go unanswered."

"He called us maggots, rodents, scum, to make us forget we were men," Agni continued. "Many times did I throw my body in front of my wife's and daughter's, to spare them the stick. But when he beat my son out of my wife's belly, only to ravish her a moon later and put in his own, I could not abide. I carried a wooden stake, until that most exquisite time as I could plunge it into his chest. That was ten days ago, in the stable."

Agni laughed a rueful laugh. It was a touching lie.

Rem listened, watching him with those keen eyes.

"I see."

"He whom you call the Wolf of Azectrai, would have mounted my master's head on a spike. We know nothing of disputed lands and grain taxes, only that Lord Agni loved the small folk."

Rem paused for a long moment, leaving Agni to wonder if he said too much.

"You are a storyteller," he said at last.

"I am a survivor," Agni corrected him.

"And a fighter," Rem added. "I saw how you squared up to me. You know combat."

Agni's pulse quickened as he saw a glint in Rem's eyes.

"A man never lowers his guard."

"You fought in the war, didn't you?" Rem sighed.

Agni's mouth tightened. "I did what I had to."

"I would love to believe you."

And then he moved.

A sharp whistle rang out.

Angry war cries burst forth.

*Ambush!* Twenty years of instinct roared to life.

From the shadows, two men ran at Agni from the side. But Rem pulled a belaying pin from his back. Agni rushed at Rem with a raised fist—Rem raised his pin to parry, only for Agni to stomp him in the chest, sending him flying into the deck stairs. But as he heard shouts and footfalls from below deck—a sickening realization hit. This was a mutiny. If they learned his identity, he was doomed; if not, he might still be sold as chattel. In any case, he could not escape into the sea.

But he felt liberated. *A cornered wolf still has fangs.*

The two men charged as one—these were trained fighters. He ran at the nearest, keeping the two in a line, and struck his face and groin with three precise blows. The second tried to grab his legs, but Agni sprawled and dropped his hips on the assailant's back. An elbow to the neck eliminated that threat.

However, as he stood up, four more men rushed in.

In that moment, he saw the full arc of his life in a blur—would Anton, whose wisdom saved his life countless times, keep him safe? Was Varenox finally making good on Agni's dark fate, to die in obscurity? *Blast them both.* Or was this just a doomed journey that Alexander warned him about?

The first man reached him. *One last man to the Netherworld.* With a bellow, Agni wrapped his attacker's right leg and exploded upward, launching the poor sailor over the four-foot rail. The boy screamed as he realized his own dark fate.

Within a second, three men wrapped Agni's legs and arms. He did not scream or tug; what would come, would come.

A thick rope looped around his neck from behind.

His vision blurred. His lungs burned.

Before the darkness swallowed him, he heard Rem's voice. "Well fought, Azri."

———

Agni blinked three times but saw only darkness. His breath felt hot inside the scratchy burlap that clung to his face. He flexed his body, only to find himself expertly lashed at the wrists, ankles, and wings. *They take no chances.* He made out rustling sounds and moans nearby from other captives. *I doubt they have identified me.* But other than the rope burn around his neck, he felt no pain. *I killed one, and they did not beat me.*

*These are trained brigands,* he concluded. *They want me alive for ransom.*

He hissed, softly in Kazian. "What happened? How many are we?"

"Don't speak that pig language in our presence," a voice cut through the dark.

He clenched his teeth at the insult but switched to his best Blevenian. "Who are you?"

"Don't concern yourself with that."

"I'm no threat to you or your ransom scheme," Agni spoke at his faceless captor. "You have our coins. We're lashed down in the middle of the sea. What more do you want?"

A pause

"Still yourself, Azri."

*Azri,* he thought. *A lie. My lie. Rem will remember the details, so must I.*

"Can you tell me I'll see my wife and daughter again?" he asked, pressing into the lie. Arguing with this captor would achieve nothing, but a desperate man was a predictable man.

"If you want to, then silence yourself."

Agni said nothing, because Azri would say nothing. Cold and angry—he nicknamed this captor "Silence."

Silence did not ask questions. That meant Agni already knew what he needed to; Rem trusted Silence to enforce orders.

Agni heard Silence's boots scuff against the wooden deck, then fade up the stairs. His watch had likely ended. A new grunt would follow.

*Good,* Agni thought. *He knows my name, but not my value.*

He passed some minutes thinking about Kali and the daughter they might have. Half tiger clan, half dragon clan, winged and tailed, the best of both. He would bounce her on his knee while Kali sang to her in the Aloi tongue. Would she have green eyes like Mama or brown eyes like Papa? It comforted him, in a way that the thought of Sara bearing his children never did. Was Kali safe? If not, could he bear the thought of having endangered her?

Another, heavier set of footsteps approached. Deliberate, too heavy for the slender Rem. The boards squeaked with every step.

"All who wish to use the chamber pot, be heard now. Last chance for the night."

A husky voice, muffled by rolls of neck fat. Slow and thick. Bandit or not, this man ate well.

"Right here," Agni said.

A chuckle. "Oh, you're a special one, Azri."

Agni named this one "Chamber Pot."

*Young, left to this least of duties. But strong.*

Chamber Pot whistled, and two pairs of boots followed. A rope looped around Agni's throat—not tight, but firm.

"Rem?" Agni asked.

No response.

Another voice rasped in his ear. "I'm going to loosen one hand so you can pull out your cock and put some straw into your hand to wipe your arse. And I'd hate to be you if that hand took a swing, you hear?"

*"Ai."*

Agni savored doing his business, despite the humiliation. It might be some days before he breathed cool air again.

And once Chamber Pot departed, questions flooded his mind. *How many captives are we? Are Captain Zaha and his men victims or conspirators?* But one question stood out.

"How long must we be bound up like this?"

"Ask the boss, Azri," Chamber Pot responded.

Agni smiled under his hood. *This one speaks.*

"I'd like to go on deck," Agni grumbled, testing Chamber Pot's limits. "This heat and stench make me want to retch."

Murmurs erupted from the other prisoners. Envy, perhaps. A plea for the same small dignity.

*There may be twenty of them*, he thought.

"I can't do that, Azri."

"Yes, you can," Agni pressed. "Just loosen the ropes around my neck and wings. What am I going to do, fly to Avicia with you on my back?"

Chamber Pot grunted.

"I saw what you did topside. You so much as twitch, Rem'll toss me overboard."

"You have my word that I will not. What's your name?"

A longer, thoughtful pause. "…Tovon."

A small victory—they saw each other as men. Now, to learn his captors' endgame.

"I give you my word, Tovon. But I understand if you have orders. Can you send the boss down here?"

"I'll see what I can do, Azri."

"Very well."

As the trio passed from prisoner to prisoner, Agni fought another wave of nausea. His head pounded and his stomach turned. The combination of scent, heat, and rocking proved too much.

He retched again.

Acid splashed inside the hood, burning his skin and eyes. His body convulsed against the bonds, and two others vomited in sympathy.

But in that moment, he felt a strange calm—circumstances could not get much worse.

———

Agni could not sleep. The vomit-soaked hood clung to his face, his bonds prevented him from sitting or standing, and the scent of bile and sweat thickened the air. His thoughts spun with questions he could not answer.

And then, the world shifted.

The Ancient's presence—familiar and heavy—forced itself upon him. No warning, no whisper of approach. He had shut his eyes, but the image appeared as though painted on his eyelids.

*"You needed no god of fate to bring this upon yourself, young one."*

Agni snorted, annoyed. His exhaustion faded for a moment.

*"Surely, you did not appear just to tell me that."*

Anton's silvery form loomed, simultaneously there and not there, his gaze impassive. But Agni knew the wraith well enough— he plotted in centuries but never rested. This visit had a purpose.

*"Though you may be a bandit's chattel, you were ransomed once before, by men who knew and hated your name."* Anton's smooth voice betrayed no anger. *"You are impudent but still have merit. I cannot let you squander it."*

Agni's fingers twitched against his bonds.

*"I thank you for your faith, Blessed Ancestor, but once again, I will not turn back to my sword. I will not revisit the Ancient City. I no longer share your dream."*

Those words chilled him. Agni stood in open rebellion against Anton and Solantia. He defied an ancient emperor and a powerful duke with only his body, his wits, and two seeing-stones.

After a long pause, Anton spoke.

*"Agni,"* Anton spoke, patient but firm. *"Two thousand years in this state have taught me patience, and even a sort of forgiveness one might grant to an unfaithful wife who repents."*

Agni scoffed. *"Is that how you see me, ancestor? As an adulterous woman?"* He clenched his teeth. *"I will not repent."* Bound and humiliated, he forced defiance into his words.

*"Were every brigand and faithless sailor on this ship snuffed out, I would steer it north to Avicia and my new life. Or die."*

Anton's voice lowered. Darkened.

*"Will you shed your name, as you have your sword? Will you bow before a foreign king?"*

*"No,"* Agni hissed. *"I will end it all—Duke Verlan's mad plot, the need for a Lord Guardian, the prospect of another war in the Dragonlands. And if I must do so from Tercera, I will."* He flexed against his bonds until his muscles strained. *"Leave me or end me with the power you claim to have. Make my body twitch or possess my mind, like you have made sport of these last couple moons."*

He braced himself for punishment. For an ultimatum.

Instead, Anton laughed. A deep, hollow laugh—dark amusement that made Agni shudder.

*"Scion,"* Anton intoned, *"in your wretched state, you do not know the true meaning of your words. I will overlook this. For now."*

This too was part of Anton's plot, a plot Agni could not see.

*"Though it remains hazy, I see an opportunity for you to rejoin your brethren. To be Agni Kazirian once again."*

Agni's throat tightened.

*"What will you do?"*

*"I mean that if you cease this foolish rebellion, I will show you the way back to Kazia and loyal men."*

Agni grunted. Loyalty meant little. *"Only Kali and Alexander are loyal to me. I will not forsake them."*

Anton regarded them for a long moment. His tone was almost sorrowful. *"If you value them, you will forget them."*

Agni's pulse raced.

*"They are tied to your outlaw fate,"* Anton continued. *"I will grant you the finest lovers and stoutest guards from across the Mortal Realms."*

Something inside Agni snapped.

*"No, spectral one."* His voice cut through the dreamscape. *"I tire of your 'guidance.' You may have powers that I cannot comprehend, but you are alone and forgotten."*

The moment the words left his lips, Anton's shade grew brighter. Wrathful.

*"And my powers can engulf you."*

And then, the wraith screamed.

An inhuman wail pierced through Agni's consciousness. The sound of something vast and unknowable breaking, like a dragon's dying breath, of the rage of millennia collapsing into a single harrowing moment.

The world around Agni cracked. The sound drove into his ears, into his heart and bones.

He gasped, choking as bile rose again in his throat. His body convulsed, his mind burned, his essence flayed under Anton's wrath.

He barely registered the thunder of boots overhead, the distant shouts of men rushing into the hull.

And then, for the second time that night, all went dark.

---

Agni's senses returned in waves—the cool splash of water on his face, the scent of salt and sweat in the stagnant air, the dull ache of limbs bound in awkward positions. He turned his head and coughed the remnants of dried bile from his throat.

"Azri, you alive?"

Tovon.

Agni cracked his eyes open and saw the hulking bandit hovering over him, concern breaking through his voice. The other prisoners had been moved to the far end of the hold.

"I suppose," Agni said, clearing his throat.

Tovon grunted, wiping his hands on his trousers.

"You had a seizure. We thought you were in your death throes."

Agni rolled his tongue over his lips, tasting acid and blood. He tried to flex his limbs, testing the strength of his restraints. Still bound. Still helpless. But not broken.

"And yet," he rasped, "you saw fit to save me."

*That means you see beyond Azri's story—but you do not see Agni's.*

A sharper voice cut through the dank air. "Of course we did."

Rem.

Agni blinked as Rem's lean frame stepped into view. The outlaw's face carried genuine concern, but his eyes were watchful, calculating, curious.

Agni sighed, relaxing against the ropes. "Rem. I've looked forward to our next conversation."

Rem's thin lips pulled into a smile.

"As have I, Lord Azri."

"Please stop calling me lord," Agni muttered, shaking his head against the wooden pole behind him.

"Right, right." Rem feigned dismissal but let the title linger. "Forgive me for garroting you earlier. You fight like a tempest; I saw no other way to subdue you." He turned to Tovon. "Leave us."

Tovon hesitated. Agni caught a brief flicker of something—*guilt? Affection?*—before he disappeared into the shadows.

Now, he and Rem were alone.

"I have suffered worse," Agni said, watching Rem with cool indifference.

"In Blevenia?" Rem arched a brow.

"Yes."

"For someone who anticipated our conversation, I don't find you very forthcoming, Lord Azri."

"I hate lords," Agni harrumphed.

Rem hummed in thought. "Perhaps. Most Solantian lords grow fat off the hunt and the vine. They let mercenaries and servants dirty their hands." He crouched, studying Agni like a caged beast. "But you… you fight on instinct. Rushed by three men, outnumbered on all sides, and you still throw a lad into the sea."

Agni held his gaze.

"Don't underestimate the power of fury. Or spite."

They sat in silence for a moment, only the sound of gentle waves between them.

Rem finally spoke, his voice smooth and unhurried. "I wish I had a mage to scry you. Whatever your lie, I can't yet pierce it."

Agni shrugged.

"I wish I had two Avician tavern girls in a goose feather bed," he quipped.

Rem laughed—a real, unguarded laugh. "Careful, Azri. I might grow fond of you."

"If you had not," Agni mused, "I sense you would have cast me into the sea."

Rem kept his smile, but something in his face sharpened.

"I don't take life without good cause."

Agni exhaled through his nose. "Right, right," he echoed Rem's dismissal. "We wouldn't be talking if I weren't more use to you alive. Tell me, Rem. What are your ends? Will you sell us as captives?"

Rem drummed his fingers against his knee.

"The first rule of thievery is to know your treasure's worth before you sell it. Right now, I do not. I have a hull filled with liars and criminals, along with the captain and half his crew." He leaned in slightly. "But you… you interest me the most."

Agni let that statement sit, unchallenged.

Rem studied him, then smiled again.

"We're headed for Lontak."

Agni's stomach tightened. "Blevenia."

"*Ai,*" Rem confirmed. "Along the Beachroad."

Agni's neck stiffened—his mind traced every route, every potential escape. *Twelve days, until we reach Duke Harkon—whose land I burned, whose sons I killed. He will grant Rem more than he can fathom. And I will fall from his highest tower.*

"I want more than credits," Rem continued. "I want what you claim to want—a new life. Living on the arse-end of the law robs one of humanity. I want legitimacy; a wife and sons to carry on my name, a daughter to cradle to sleep. You admitted you fought in Blevenia, and I still think you are some manner of lord who had good reason to flee." Rem leaned in. "You're a prize, Azri. Perhaps one to offer to Duke Harkon. Or Duke Hauran."

*In either hands, my life is forfeit,* he thought. He slowed his breath—fear of the latter might betray him.

"But if you do not resist or harm my men," Rem added. "I can assure your safety. At least while you are our captive."

Agni stared back, impassive. "Do you expect prisoners not to escape?"

Rem's smile turned razor sharp.

"Of course not. That is why I'll keep you lashed at three points." His smile returned, amused. "And I swear, I will learn your identity."

Agni's own lips curled into a slow, dangerous smile.

"And for whatever you barter me, I will be in Avicia before three moons pass."

The two locked eyes. Agni purposefully broke his gaze first—Agni was proud, Azri was meek.

But Rem saw something valuable in him, something worth more than coin.

And Agni saw something in Rem—a strategist, a cunning rival. A fox, to his wolf.

*Would that you were my spy, Rem; you have read me twice already.*

# Mirror

Two days later, the *Star of the Sea* groaned against the dock, the tide slapping against its hull as the captives were marched out onto the wharf in a ragged line, tied at the waist. The rough voices of Solantian men drifted through the midday heat, curses thick with resentment.

Then, solid earth beneath his feet.

After days of the sea's unsteady rhythm, the ground felt strange.

But the air told him everything. Unlike Sivatrai, Lontak languished. The stench of stagnant water and rotting fish clung to the streets. Fewer merchants haggling, fewer fishmongers hawking their wares. *We flourished after the war while Blevenia suffered drought—we took this as a mark of our god's favor,* he thought. *Lontak suffers, though not from my hand.*

A sharp buffet to the back of his skull shattered his thoughts.

"Walk, boy," came Silence's cold growl.

Agni gritted his teeth and stepped forward.

"Where are we headed?"

True to his name, Silence said nothing.

"You know I have no choice but to follow. At least tell me that."

A sharp jab struck the base of his left wing. He winced.

A different, smoother voice rang out. "Ease off him, lad."

Rem.

Agni allowed himself a slight smile. *The fox had grown fond of the wolf.*

"Rem," he said, tilting his head slightly towards the voice. "Where are we headed?"

"The country, for a spell. Get comfortable."

Silence muttered a low curse.

Agni exhaled slowly. *The country.*

They led Agni and his fellow captives to the town's outskirts, and beyond into the woods. To orient himself, he counted his steps. A thousand with the sun in his face. Five hundred up a gentle slope, bending to the west. Two thousand along a ridge with the wind at his back. Another two thousand along a forest trail, with the scent of pine.

His heart quickened. *The Spires' foothills.*

The rich pine scent flooded his mind with plans. If he could overpower one man with a torch, he could burn the forest canopy and flee in the chaos. *Like I did as a youth to make my name.*

Within ten days, he could make his way back to Sivatrai and secure passage anew. Only without gold, friends, or allies. *A mere inconvenience. A Kazian boy in these mountains is like a shark in the sea.*

But Rem was no fool. He would never let Agni near a pine switch, let alone a blade. He was watching. And the true question remained—where would Rem take him?

If he believed Azri's lie, he might sell him to a local lord, who might recognize and hang him.

If he believed Azri was a lord, he would take him south to Zarda, where Duke Harkon sat. Harkon would recognize High General Agni Kazirian and pinion-and-drop him from his tower. Or ransom him back to Solantia, receive a handsome reward from his own dukes—who would complete the ritual.

Agni growled under his breath.

*No matter what, I will not be in Harkon's hands.*

*In days, I will be in my maze of snares in the Spires.*

*In moons, Avicia.*

As expected, the bandits kept three drawn weapons on him whenever he was not lashed to a tree. They gave him no chance to speak with other captives, no time to build alliances. They knew he was no bumpkin.

And Agni respected that. No wonder they could take over the *Star of the Sea* mid-journey. But they could not solve Azri of Azectrai.

For five days, they remained in camp. They unhooded him but watched him like a caged tiger. He learned how to sleep upright against his bonds and flex against them to exercise. The crisp mountain air invigorated him.

But his greatest solace lay in imagining his future life. He pictured himself with Kali, making four beautiful children—two boys and two girls. Kali would advocate before the king, dazzling the courts with her voice. Alexander would find another wife after his died in birth two decades ago. All three, trusted of the king, who would see their present utility rather than past humiliation.

*They will flourish, but I will watch it happen. But first, escape.*

On the sixth morning, Rem spoke to him again.

"We depart today, Lord Azri. Be ready."

Agni rolled his eyes. "Again with the imagined titles," Agni muttered. "I'm in no position to prepare myself. Hood me when you will. But have your barber shave this wheat field growing on my chin."

Rem laughed. "I will."

Agni rolled his shoulders.

"Where are you taking us? I know well what awaits me, and I have no means to escape, so you can tell me."

"You mean, 'where are we taking *you?*'" Rem corrected. "We sold the others to local lords. They'll live honest lives of service, free from their past crimes."

Agni stayed impassive; he suspected this.

"And me?"

"You, however, are the diamond among the pebbles. And remember the first law of thievery—know your cache's worth. Diamonds require a jeweler's eye."

Agni scoffed. "You mean, Duke Harkon's eye. He will reward me for shanking my Solantian noble master."

"If that is all you've done," Rem said jauntily, "then he may."

Agni's heart raced, even if he expected that. Harkon might parade him through the streets to be spat on and kicked, then the pinion-and-drop. A criminal's death, a ritual humiliation, symbolic of his fall from grace. He had days to escape.

"So be it. I don't fault you."

The silence hung between them, until Rem nodded toward the trees.

"Very well. I'll send the barber over."

Fifteen minutes later, Silence arrived, a small knife in hand. Agni grimaced.

"Rem said not to leave a scratch on you," he growled, gripping the knife too tight. "You'd best thank him; I'd as soon slice your throat."

Agni exhaled slowly. "Thank you for not doing so."

Agni let that comment hang while Silence set to work.

Agni studied him as the knife scraped across his jaw. Silence was efficient. Precise. He knew how to handle a blade. *And yet he hates me.*

He said, softly, "Why do you hate me?"

Silence froze. Then, without warning, he backhanded Agni across the face, sending a glob of spit to the dirt.

"Shut up, pig," Silence hissed.

Agni slowly turned his head back, licking blood from his lip.

Silence finished the shave without another word. When he was done, Agni spoke again.

"Quite the answer."

Silence did not respond—only turned to leave.

Agni had learned two things: Silence lacked discipline, and he had a past.

*I will learn your story just as Rem wants mine.*

Getting three sentences out of Silence felt like a small victory. Hostility could be transmuted; apathy could not.

—

For another five days, they skirted the foothills of the eastern Spires. From the sun's angle, fifteen miles a day, always southeast. The pace of careful men. Wary men. It put them close to the Median Road, and Agni's last, best chance to escape. His time was running out.

*What of Kali and Alexander?* By now, they must be well on the sea. In a moon, they would search Avicia for him in vain. *Would they think me dead?*

Tonight, they abandoned the usual forest camp in favor of a village manor. Someone knew the lord here. Someone trusted them. Who, Agni could not say. But the fact that Rem and his men walked in openly, feasted in the tavern, and slept in barns meant they had an ally.

This disturbed him.

From the barn, Agni could smell the feast lingering in the air—pork, heavy with salt and fat. He had been given his own portion, as if he were a guest rather than a captive, and hand-fed it like a child.

If not for that, he might forget he was still lashed at three points.

The damp straw of an empty horse stall and a night without a hood felt like a luxury. But Rem would never leave his diamond unguarded.

He heard men outside—drunken voices, steady boots. One guard might be dedicated to him, but many milled about.

Agni worked the coarse wrist ropes against the divider boards separating stalls. The horses did not stir. But it would take all night to undo them at this rate. Sleep had started to claw at him.

Soon, the world blurred.

———

Agni bolted up right.

*Blast it, how long did I sleep?*

Then came the screams, tearing through the night. Man, woman, animal, child. A harmony of terror and violence.

A woman begging "No, no, please!" before a sickening thud.

The yelp of a puppy—a final, shrill note of suffering before it went silent.

The crackle and hiss of fire.

And worst of all, the war cries—in perfect Kazian.

*No… no! My countrymen are raiders. Scum.*

The realization struck like a warhammer. He had bled and shed blood to end raids westward.

*My men. Our banners. They were once mine.*

Had his snares emboldened his men to pillage and rape, knowing Blevenia could not fight back?

Or had his desertion of the Lord Guardian's duties freed them from their honor?

A flood tide of memories returned.

He felt as helpless as his six-year-old self—helpless, bound.

His home aflame, servants screaming.

His father's hound, Lota, whimpering beneath him as she pushed him through the window—noble dog, the first to give her life for him.

And the larder. The watching, the waiting.

Mama's voice, as he watched her violated and slain from the shadows. The laughter of soldiers.

That which had haunted him for twenty-two years.

His breaths came in ragged bursts. His limbs shook with rage, with urgency. He felt powerless to stop the sobs.

*No. I will not watch.*

But a more powerful force cut through the chaos and pain like a mountain gust. Anton usually came slowly, like a settling fog, in times of quiet. Not battle and flame.

"*Scion,*" Anton intoned, as if casting a spell.

Agni twitched.

"*I need these ropes undone, or you will have no scion,*" Agni hissed through his mind.

"*You need not struggle. Call to them. They are your brethren.*"

Anger surged through his blood like molten steel.

"*Madness. These are criminals who deserve death!*"

"*Rejoice! For fate has brought them to you. They will bear you home in triumph. They will raise you upon their shoulders as High General once more, and you will crush the western interlopers,*" Anton proclaimed, his face solid. Had two thousand years of strife between the brothers of the dragon so hardened his heart?

"*I will rejoice when I have driven a blade through their cursed hearts.*"

"*You would slay them?*" Anton's voice sounded mocking and amused. "*They are only doing what you once commanded.*"

Agni's jaw clenched.

"*I never commanded them to ravish. They are butchers who deserve the fate of such men,*" Agni spoke with gritted teeth.

Anton's face returned to a stone mask. A spirit above blood and flame."

"*And when did the wolf become the shepherd? When did the Lord Guardian turn his blade against his own?*"

"*I was never theirs,*" Agni spat. "*I fought for honor, for Solantia's peace.*"

"*And they fight for you.*"

Agni flinched with a flicker of doubt.

Anton saw it and pounced. Like a wolf.

"*And we, the Kazirian, will civilize them. I brought law to marauders two millennia ago. Call to them. They will hearken to their commander. Overlook their sins that you may shape them anew. They will deliver you to their destiny.*"

"*Command them?*" Anton laughed—a hollow, ancient laugh. "*No. Own them.*"

"*Blast you, Anton,*" Agni whispered, forcing contempt through his thoughts.

"*It is not I who called them to your side, scion. It was fate.*"

"*It was you,*" Agni snarled. "*You summoned them. You knew I would not yield to you, so you brought them to tempt me.*"

"*No,*" Anton replied smoothly. "*I merely saw it before it happened. As I saw the fire that took your mother, your home, that set you on the path of endless war*"

Agni felt a deeper fury than any he had ever known.

"*You would invoke that blasted night against me?*"

"*It is the night that made you. And it is why you should rise to claim what is yours. Do not waste your fate mourning the nameless dead. They will march for a leader—for an empire.*"

"*An empire of ashes.*"

*"An empire of order,"* Anton corrected. *"The Dragonlands crave what only we can provide."*

For a moment, a vision passed over Agni's mind.

Of the Empire Kazia, a dark banner, rippling over a united Solantia and Blevenia.

Of Anton on his throne, Agni at his right hand.

*No… this is a trap.*

The temptation to dishonor his name, his legacy, his friend. The hunger in Anton's voice. The desperation in his words. Anton needed him.

But then, Agni caught an azure glow at his side.

*My blade!* The blade he and Kali had buried. The blade that should not be here.

*How could I not have seen this—Anton's sword contains his very will.*

The dragon-mawed pommel throbbed, as if the blade hungered for blood.

*"Take it,"* Anton urged. *"Cut down your captors. Within days, they will sacrifice you to a duke from whom you cannot hide. They cannot be allowed to live."*

Agni felt that pull. He could cut down his captors, leaving naught but flames in his wake. He could ride north to freedom and Avicia. Or escape into the hills and hollows of the Spires.

Or, if he obeyed Anton, he could ride the Spires, claim an army of lords—and spirits. Solantia would bow before him, and Blevenia could not resist.

*"I feel your yearning, Agni. The power you covet. The justice you will bring."* Anton's voice was raw, passionate, desperate. *"I offer you the wisdom of eternity. Quit these mortal concerns."*

But then, back in the Mortal Realms, he caught a whiff of smoke. The screams of the innocent. *Mama.*

*"And I refuse it,"* Agni snarled.

*"You refuse me? You refuse destiny?"*

*"I refuse you."*

And with that, a wave of rage drowned out Anton's next words. He pulled his wrists closer to the angry blade. The rope smoked at its touch, pulling apart in black strands.

Now free, his ankle and wing bonds followed.

*"Thank you, Blessed Ancestor."*

He buried the sword again, this time in a pile of straw. Instead, he grabbed a wooden pole.

*"Now watch as I prove I never needed you. Destruction unto evil men!"*

Anton vanished in a cold mist. He was free. He had defied Anton's will.

He gripped the staff tightly.

*Lend me your strength, Dear Tigress,* he whispered, then charged towards the sound of screams.

Into the burning night.

The wolf hunted again.

First, a girl's screams cut through the night air, ragged and raw with terror. She stumbled past the barn, tunic slit between her legs, breath hitching in sobs. Behind her, a young raider in leathers gave chase, dagger glinting in the firelight. He was laughing, taunting. It made Agni's blood boil to hear his native tongue so.

The raider was too focused on his prey to see death's shadow lurking.

Leaping from the shadows, Agni lowered his shoulder into the man's ribs, sending him sprawling. The raider hit the dirt hard, wings twisting awkwardly beneath him, yelping in pain.

Before he could roll onto his knees, Agni smashed his staff across the man's nose. It shattered, blood spraying across his face in a red mask. A hammer fist into the raider's throat, and the raider's body convulsed, hands clawing weakly at his neck.

Agni took the man's dagger and delivered the mercy blow, plunging it beneath the man's ear and cutting forward. A familiar motion. One he had taught Sara.

He wiped the blade on the raider's jerkin before rising. This runt carried himself like the low man, a favorite peasant taken along for amusement.

*I want a lord—I want to show him the price of dishonor,* he growled under his breath.

Agni stalked from lane to lane, listening, feeling. Fire painted the night in red and black, the smoke thick with the scent of charred wood and blood.

A noble crest flashed in the firelight. A mounted raider.

The man was crushing bodies beneath his destrier's hooves.

A boy—a mere child—crumpled under an iron-shod kick, a cough rattling from his chest as he lay broken in the dirt. The knight spurred his horse forward, driving through a cluster of screaming villagers, scattering them like stones.

*A man with a knife is no match for an armed rider. But a horse— ha. Forgive me, beast.*

The rider slowed to turn, bringing his steed around for another pass. Agni screamed like a wildcat, charging at the man's left flank.

The knight had no time to register the threat.

One clean slash to the reins.

The warhorse shrieked, its neck cut open by the sudden strike. The beast reared and threw his rider, saddle and all.

The knight flailed in the air before crashing into the dirt.

Again, Agni leapt, dropping knee-first on the knight's ribs, driving the air from his lungs in a wheeze. Their eyes locked for a single, frozen moment. Recognition flashed in the knight's gaze.

"L-l-lord Gu—"

Agni wanted to berate him for becoming a mere marauder, to interrogate him on who led this raid and why, to taunt his predicament.

But only a low growl rose in his throat.

"Die."

The knight threw up a hand, but Agni plunged his knife through palm and windpipe. Blood poured forth from the wound, hot and fast, soaking his hands. He cut to the left to end it swiftly.

The knight's sword lay at his side.

He still did not know who led the raid, or how many raiders came, or their tactics.

Kazian blood would not matter if they knew he had slain their kin.

Only Rem wanted him alive, and he might be dead too.

Like on the ship—he was cornered.

His childhood memory, still fresh. Only now he grinned; teeth bared.

*More screaming to the Netherworld.*

The village had gone quiet, but raiders were cowards. They must have scattered into the dark, waiting for their moment to return.

Again, Agni prowled rows of huts. With the flame dying, his eyes attuned to the night.

He heard a muffled cry and grunt nearby—*the sounds of ravishment.*

He fought an urge to charge, blade aloft, sacrificing himself to right the first wrong he ever knew. Instead, he stalked the shadows, taking in the angles.

*I must assume these are trained warriors.*

There would be no room to wield a sword inside, but the hut's walls were dried mud and brittle wood. One man stood against the back wall, looking out towards the door. Agni crept, careful of a dry twig that could betray him.

The lookout laughed at their victim's suffering.

And Agni stifled his own laugh.

*Die a coward's death.*

Agni angled his sword flat to pierce between the victim's ribs—then drove it through the wall. And leathers, skin, lungs, and heart.

A cough, a death rattle, then a slow slump to the ground.

"Dari? Dari, shit, shit!"

Agni crouched through the new slit in the wall, gauged the distance, and struck again.

This one screamed as the blade sank into his side. Not deep enough for a kill—so Agni grasped the hilt and twisted to open the wound. This one would die slowly.

The third man—the ravisher—turned. Their eyes locked through the cracked wall.

"Murderer! To me, to me!"

Footsteps thundered.

Agni could not run and betray his position—he had seconds to cut this man down.

He timed the footsteps. The instant the rapist rounded the corner, Agni slashed backhanded at his knees. The blade bit through the thigh bone. The raider shrieked and collapsed.

Agni thrust the tip through his throat, the third mercy blow of the night.

But as he turned around, a pair of arms wrapped around him.

A crushing pain lanced through his leg. Globes of pain shot through his vision.

*Snap.*

He felt his lower leg bones snap. His foot went numb.

On instinct, Agni trapped an arm and spun out of the man's grip.

But as he tried to stand, his foot was not there. It hung at a strange angle within his boot.

His breath came in ragged gasps. He scuttled backward on his left foot and backside, dragging his ruined leg, keeping his sword raised.

"Yield, Blevenian scum," he commanded.

Agni did not yield. The assailant feinted a charge, but Agni leveled the sword at his gut.

Even crippled, he would take this scum with him.

The knight's eyes flickered, studying him; Agni did the same.

*Sir Frazi.*

"Well now," the raider spoke slowly, "has the Lord Guardian been reduced to a Blevenian servant boy?"

A man he once called brother-in-arms.

A manor of valor, loyalty, and discipline.

A man who once swore his sword to Agni.

Now he stomped on broken peasants, cut down innocents—and laughed as he did so.

His burning anger overtook his pain.

"Frazi," he snarled.

Frazi's lips curled into a mocking grin.

"So this is where you deserted us." His tone was casual, cruel. "I had not come to collect a bounty, but Mayor Goro has placed a rather fine one on your head."

He stepped closer.

"Whether or not it is attached to your neck."

Agni spat.

"And you?" His voice shook with fury. "You, Sir Frazi? You swore an oath to defend Solantia. And yet you crossed the Spires to ravish washerwomen?"

Frazi laughed maliciously.

"Spare me, Lord Guardian. High General. Desolator. Wolf of Azectrai. You once ordered us to burn their grain houses. To raze these manor-houses. You taught us that insects deserved more compassion than they. We crush ants under our boots and never think of it again."

Agni growled back. "And knowing when to cease fighting is the difference between a warrior and a thug with a weapon. I carried out our emperor's orders with honor. Once, so did you."

Frazi sneered.

"The lord of this manor sends riders into the Spires, a mile further each day. Tonight, we did what a Lord Guardian should. And if my men ravish some meaningless small folk, I shed no tears. Do not play at the simple soldier, Lord Guardian. If you slew every Solantian who did likewise, the flies of this putrid land would still be feasting on their corpses."

Agni narrowed his eyes at Frazi. *How many of my men acted on dark desires without my knowledge?*

"Frazi, you knew blasted well I would not stand for that. And for this raid, Duke Harkon will extract reparations from Kazia. Does Mayor Goro know where you are?"

"In light of your defection," Frazi said with a haughty grin, "he has taken on the responsibilities of the Lord Guardian. He rides east along the Median Road as we speak."

They stared through each other's eyes. Then they looked at each other's weapons. Waiting for an opening to strike.

Agni grinned, licking his eye-teeth.

"Then tell him," Agni laughed with defiance, "that Agni Kazirian slew four of his men for their crimes."

Frazi's face twisted in rage.

"What?"

"I cut one down as he chased a screaming girl, another from his warhorse." Agni turned the hilt of his stolen broadsword, letting the blood-streaked steel catch the firelight. "Do you recognize this? The poor sap addressed me by my title—the title stolen from me— before I sliced his throat."

Frazi's eyes flared in horror.

"That was my brother's, blast you!"

The knight's fury overtook him. He lunged.

Agni was ready.

Frazi's sword swung downward like an executioner's axe, aiming for his crippled leg.

Agni scooted back with his left foot, angling his sword upward to meet the blow. Steel screamed as they clashed. A parry. A half-second reprieve.

Frazi, enraged, stomped down hard on Agni's broken leg.

Pain explored through him, a white-hot flare that threatened to drag him under.

He had to stay awake—one moment's hesitation meant certain death.

"Slay me, already. Raise your blade. I will stab through your balls and right one final wrong."

Frazi pulled back to slash but hesitated as Agni pulled back his own.

They stood off, like a snake and a mongoose.

Varenox might claim his prey, but Agni would die as a Kazian warrior. He would see Mama and Papa—healed to their whole—in the Lands Beyond. And Anton Kazirian would have to find another to scorch the land with war.

Then, a whistle pierced the night air.

A thin whip of silver arced through the night.

Frazi's eyes widened in shock before his back spasmed. His sword clattered from his fingers as his hands clawed at his back.

Agni did not hesitate.

He stabbed at the inside of Frazi's right thigh, through muscle and scraping against bone. Frazi crumpled forward onto his hands, gasping raggedly. His mouth moved, but no words came out. Paralysis had set in.

It was then that Agni noticed the dagger hilt protruding from Frazi's back. He might not have felt Agni's cut.

*Rem?*

Agni withdrew his broadsword and thrust it into the side of Frazi's neck.

The knight gurgled once, then went still.

A stampede of footsteps drew closer. He looked up, sword still in hand.

Rem stood at the edge of the torchlight, another knife at the ready. Silence stood beside him, with his customary scowl and his grip white-knuckled on his sword.

"Azri?" Rem's voice was incredulous. "How did you—"

Rem's brows shot up.

"Find this?" Agni finished the sentence. He was panting, sweat trickling down his brow, hands shaking. His leg was destroyed, his body burning, but he kept his tone steady.

Agni pointed the sword toward Rem, then casually flicked it away, spinning end-over-end.

Rem laughed a slow, breathless chuckle.

"Escape from our binds. Find a sword. Cut down four raiders. All with a broken leg. What are you? By Varenox's arse, you could slay a tiger of Aloi."

*Aloi. Sweet Kali would be proud, even as our chances of reuniting fade.*

Agni said nothing, pulling his ruined leg away from the crowd. He needed time and rest, but above all, to keep Rem believing in "Azri."

"I appreciate that," Agni said finally, pointing towards Rem's armed hand, "but you can put that down. I won't strike again soon."

Rem's gaze flicked to Agni's right leg. The foot that hung at a grotesque angle.

Then slowly, he tucked his weapon back into its sheath.

"You shock me again, Azri." Rem's voice held something strange. Admiration. Wariness. And something else Agni could not name. "If I hadn't seen it myself, I'd think those raiders freed you, and you'd ravish a maid before disappearing into the night."

Agni shook his head, his matted hair clinging to his face.

"Their names sound like mine. That does not make them my kin."

Rem considered that for a moment, then gave an amused grunt. He turned his head, studying the burned village.

"I thank you anyways."

Agni's lip curled.

"Not for your sake, Rem."

"Oh?" Rem raised a brow, looking puzzled by the combative response.

Agni conjured up more of "Azri's" story. *A serf's story, a beaten man's. A common soldier's.*

"I was trained for war but found no joy in it. No meaning." His voice grew flat. "To slay a man was a duty. A necessity. I know that if I had met my enemy in peace, we might have turned our blades against our lords instead, then down a quart of ale." He tilted his head at Rem. "Perhaps you know that feeling."

Rem's smile faded slightly.

"I never thought that way."

Agni scoffed. "Then you have never tasted battle. Or accepted your servitude."

Rem's expression twisted, a mixture of amusement and irritation.

"You claim to have only known servitude and oppression but crave freedom. You speak like a free man, a man with a burning cause. I don't believe your story."

Agni fought a smile. The fox's cunning pitted against the wolf's will. But Rem's belief or disbelief shaped Agni's escape. He shrugged.

"My cause is the absence of oppression. I struck down my lord and fled to Avicia for it. Now, I put four noble scum into the ground for their crime." He met Rem's gaze. Challenging. Defiant.

"And when Duke Harkon drops me from his tallest tower, I will die redeemed."

Rem's lips twitched.

"You assume I'm taking you to Harkon."

Agni's breath caught.

"…and why would you not? I am Kazian."

Rem sighed, arms folded. "That is why. We're going westward, across the Spires."

Agni gasped. "Why?"

"You just slew four Kazian lords, five if you actually stuck your noble master—which I still doubt. Any duke would pay a fat reward for such a murderer."

Agni drew in a breath to speak, but Rem spoke first.

"You speak of a cause." Rem gestured to his men, who had started to assemble around him. "These men are my cause. They bled for me. Starved for me. Kazia has flourished since the war. If we cross the Spires, we'll claim our due. Become citizens. Take wives. Raise sons."

Agni felt his pulse quicken.

He had planned for seven days on the Leeward Road to Zarda, and Duke Harkon.

Now, he had two—at most—to Mayor Goro. Fewer to his own sentries, who would recognize him on the spot.

A crippled leg.

And Rem's men would watch him closer than ever.

Rem studied him, his gaze shifting. "You've gone quiet, Azri."

Agni cast his gaze downward, forcing himself to relax.

"I am powerless and crippled. I have resigned myself."

Silence.

Then, Rem snarled. "Stop lying, Lord Azri."

Agni stiffened.

Rem leaned in, voice low and sharp. "I see you plotting again. Always scheming. Even in your wretched state, you're spinning a way out."

Agni met his glare, unwilling to break first.

Then, he exhaled sharply, forcing himself to smirk.

"Another plot? Will another raid set my bonds aflame? I started this night with a whole leg but risked my wings to fight."

All truth.

"I know that, Azri. But we seem to have to subdue you anew every night."

Agni shook his head.

"And every time, you have. Take me back to Kazia and let me spit in the mayor's face before he drops me."

Rem let the words hang, his expression unreadable.

He straightened and turned to Silence. "Fetch a horse. Load Azri on it." His voice cooled. "And make sure no fever sets in his leg. With every corpse we leave behind, our cargo becomes more precious. We depart at first light."

Silence grunted and disappeared into the dark.

Agni clenched his teeth, his mind racing.

He only had his knowledge of the Spires, every patrol and snare along the way.

*If you knew you had the Agni Kazirian, you would cripple my other leg—and that would not be enough. You would know the Wolf never threw a die he did not load.*

His fate—and the Dragonlands'—would rely on one last toss.

———

Agni ended the night as he had begun it—triply bound but scheming.

They had moved him to a shack, a mockery of shelter through which the bitter wind blew. His leg pulsed with every heartbeat.

Through the ill-fitted door frame, he saw slivers of sky, cold and distant, as if even the heavens had turned their back on him.

And then, the deepening chill that forced itself upon him from within, numbing even his crippled leg.

The ancient emperor, his true father, against whom he sat in open rebellion.

*"I will stand before any lord where the four winds blow and boast of what I did tonight."*

*"Agni, you disobedient child. You dishonor us."*

Agni had no time to brace his right leg before a violent spasm set in.

A lance of pain ripped through him, searing, blinding. He bit his lip so hard he tasted blood, but it could not stop the agony. He writhed to fight the pain but there was nowhere to escape.

His stomach lurched. He turned his head and vomited, the acidic burn mixing with the tang of blood.

His ears rang.

His vision blurred.

The world faded to flashing lights, to noise, to nothing.

But Anton's voice remained.

*"The consequences of your shortsighted actions will warp the threads of fate. If you knew what you have forsaken, you would weep."*

Agni gasped for air like a fish on land. He could not even form words in his head. He inhaled desperately, his chest heaving.

*"For two thousand years, I have seen with the eyes of a god. Timeless eyes. Tell me, what have you seen in fewer than three decades that I could not?"*

Agni wheezed, fighting to form a response. He forced every ounce of pain into rage and spat it back at Anton.

*"Tonight, I saw simple folk bloodied, violated, and trampled by my people, because they knew their old foe could not strike back. And*

*it was my snares that emboldened them. You call me shortsighted? You who would have me sit atop a throne built on bones?"*

His breath hitched but he kept going, spitting defiance.

*"I never misrepresented who I was, or what I wanted. I want an end to this. The raids. The wars. The noble depredations. And if it costs me my life, my name, or my greatness, I accept that."*

Silence.

Anton simply stared, unblinking, unmoved. Whatever morality he once held was long gone.

*"You foolish child, you failed to see the one force that could end it all. The united Dragonlands, under the Kazirian banner."*

Agni shuddered. Anton's voice carried no anger, only certainty.

*"Blevenian and Solantian could have embraced each other as long-lost brothers. Now, you are a villain in two lands. Only we could have ended the raids forever."*

Agni bared his teeth. His body in ruin, his mind battered and worn, but he would not let Anton turn this on him.

*"Then piss on both lands."*

Anton's eyes narrowed, as if processing Agni's defiance.

But his path was set.

*"That is why I seek Avicia, because King Theodore entered the Black Moon War out of alliance rather than hatred. He knows what I can do. Only an outsider—a villain, in your words—can bring peace to the Dragonlands. Once he sees how Verlan can bring the war to his soil, he will give me anything I demand to stop him."*

Anton's lips curled into a snarl, but he laughed. Slow, cold, pitiless. Something had changed in the Ancient's heart. He showed no rage—he was *done.*

*"Is that your scheme?"* His voice dripped with contempt. *"You have squandered your last chance to unite with your people."*

Anton's form darkened, wavered.

*"Know that I will not free you from your next set of bonds. You are alone. I will not stay your fate again."*

Agni's chill deepened.

*"The Dragon God's fate hangs over you like a cloud."*

Agni shuddered.

He had lost Anton, who had reached him on the darkest night of his childhood and saved him from a god's wrath. His true father, his guide.

And he had made Anton a foe to save Blevenian small folk. A twisted foe beyond mortal comprehension or constraints of conscience.

Anton's gaze lingered, even as the spirit faded to mist.

*"So shall it be."* His voice wavered, but he steadied himself. *"I no longer need you."*

*"I am eternal. You are not."*

With that, Anton vanished. But his chill lingered.

*Anton will find another,* he thought. *The Dragonlands teeter on a knife's edge; he will strike faster than any general.*

But whom?

A child of a god, a great conqueror—much of the Dragonlands could call him "Blessed Ancestor." Whom might he summon?

Duke Verlan had skill and ambition. Mayor Goro, too, though in lesser measure. The Black Moon War birthed many heroes.

*And once Anton finds another, he will unleash his full wrath, the extent of which I know not.*

But he summoned one last bit of resolve.

*For my land and my people. I will die as I have lived.*

---

Two hours passed. Agni lay awake, leg pulsing in agony, his body bound, his mind burning with defiance of all Anton stood for. Had he defied the Dragon God once too many?

*I am at war,* he thought. *Have two years of peace softened me?*

And he reached for his stones. That which the Ancient scoffed at. Smooth, familiar, warm. Grounding.

*The soldier. The boy.*

One, a deep red, plucked from the Azectrai guardhouse, marking the moment he had pestered the garrison to train him in war.

One, a rich blue, pilfered as a child—a mundane moment of mother and child.

*From a time before Anton Kazirian. He who only understands conquest and domination. For two thousand years, he has only known pain and regret.*

*I will end this,* he growled. *I will carve out my own peace.*

A plan formed.

Rem and his men had seen the horrors of the raid. His people— and Mayor Goro's—were the butchers.

If he could escape and subdue Mayor Goro, he could force a confession onto a stone.

If he could send that confession to Duke Harkon, through Rem or a loyal sentry, Blevenia would demand justice.

And Kazian lords would have no choice but to obey.

It would be a fragile peace, one that a duke and an Ancient would work tirelessly to undo.

The red stone, his first step towards a life of war, could end it. The completion of his life as a soldier.

*Whether I die, or whether I survive to Avicia, I will do so with a free heart.*

His fingers curled around the stones. His lips twisted into a faint smile, an act of defiance against the unseen eyes that still watched him.

*Let Anton watch. Let him rage. I no longer care.*

C H A P T E R   1 8

# *Reward*

S ara dreamed of home.

She was six again, running through purple lavender fields at their country manor south of Artania. The wind carried the sweet, heady scent as she crushed the blooms beneath her small fingers, letting the oils stain her skin. She twirled like a dancer, arms spread wide, scattering petals into the air, to Mother and Father's delight.

Laughter filled the golden afternoon. Mother's voice, gentle and warm, called her name. Father stood nearby, beaming, watching her as if she were the most precious thing in the world.

In two days, they would return to Artania for the harvest festival. She would wear her green silk dress and dance with Father in the great hall. He would sweep her off her feet, spin her in circles, make her feel as if she were flying. The chandeliers would glow above them, reflecting in polished marble floors.

And every night, they would feast. The finest fowl, the richest bread, and her favorite—lamb, roasted with rosemary and garlic, soft as butter. She could almost taste it, the juices melting on her tongue.

She sighed.

The world blurred gauzy and golden. The sun sank low, bathing the fields in soft red light. This was happiness. This was home.

Then something pricked her. A sharp point, a feather caught in the mattress.

The lavender fields faded; the warmth vanished.

And she awoke.

She stared at the ceiling. She was no longer home. No silk dress. No feasts. No Father's embrace.

Just the cold, empty house of a disappeared man.

*A man I conspired to kill, for my own selfish gain.*

But still, the thought of lamb lingered. Dona's lamb rivaled that of her childhood feast.

Dona, whom she could not protect.

Sara looked down at her hands. Flexed her fingers. Uncurled them. They still felt sticky with blood. Seven days had passed but the weight of failure and helplessness had not lifted.

If she had done something different. If she had stepped in a second faster. If she had found the words to stop Orlan.

*If, if, if.*

A sob rose in her throat. She buried her face in the pillow and wept.

"Your Grace, is everything all right?"

Somehow, Nira had approached while Sara was lost in pain.

Sara jerked upright.

Nira stood at the staircase, eyes wide, hand covering her mouth.

Sara wiped at her damp cheeks, but it was too late to hide the tears.

"Your Grace, is everything all right?"

"No, Nira, nothing is all right," Sara said in a monotone, tears still clinging to her lashes. "If I had not—"

Nira crouched alongside her, laying a hand on her wing. "It's all right, dear."

Sara shook her head.

"I see her face, her blood."

"She is at peace, in the Lands Beyond, with her children."

Sara let out a bitter laugh.

"The Lands Beyond?"

"Yes," Nira said, her voice steady and certain. "She has returned to the Dragon God's side."

Sara exhaled sharply. *Of course. The Kazians and their gods. Their certainty. Their simple, unshaken faith.*

"Blast this last moon," Sara said, her voice shaking. "It has brought only misery and death."

Nira studied her.

"You may not believe me, but I see a fire in your eyes. I sense you have forgotten it for two years. You'll make a fine ruler someday."

Sara tensed. Nira did not know about the mandrake.

Sara swallowed, forcing a weak smirk.

"Lest we forget, I slapped you and called you a strumpet at our first meeting."

Nira laughed softly. "I sensed pain, not hatred in your voice. The pain of a woman trapped in a land she could not understand."

Sara let out a slow breath.

"You are right, Nira. I never understood this land. As a child, my tutors taught me the history of Kazia. The tales of Emperor Anton Kazirian, the warlord who unified the southern tribes. The battles fought all along the valley. The games of intrigue these lords played. But I was not prepared to live in a land that keeps to its old ways."

Nira arched a brow.

"Do you not in Artania?"

Sara sighed.

"Only in statues and crests. With every passing generation, the old tales fade. Elders see less reason to pass them on to children. Priests die, and their sons do not replace them. We honor the Dragon God for his blessings on our crops and ventures, but…"

She hesitated.

"In the capital duchy, many barons and counts—even those who attend temple—do not even believe the gods exist. They say that we will vanish when we die. That all is dust."

Nira gasped.

"How can they not believe in Varenox?" she whispered. "Who do they think made the Mortal Realms? Who caused the Scourge?"

Sara shrugged.

"We spent little time at temple. We celebrated the feasts, prayed at the appointed times, but only because the small folk expected it. Ritual formed our identity. Father raised me to be a courtier, to wield words like blades. Not to ask unanswerable questions."

Nira narrowed her gaze.

"Yet you ask them now."

Sara looked away.

"The temple priests chided me for doing so. And Agni? He saw the divine as something to fight, not revere. He believed in the myths of the Ancient City more than the high priest. But when I pressed him, he silenced me."

Nira smiled faintly.

"Perhaps it was his name. The Kazirian are closest to Anton's blood. If anyone should fear Anton's legacy, it is they."

Sara blinked.

"That may be. But I never heard him speak proudly of his ancestry—until the feast."

Nira sighed.

"But we of Azectrai are proud of his name. We look toward the Ancient City—fallen and feared though it might be—and see the glory of our heritage."

"If the Ancient City is so feared, why dwell here?" Sara asked.

Nira's expression softened.

"Because Varenox chose us."

Sara's brow furrowed.

Nara gestured eastward.

"We were meant to guard the ruins from outsiders. And to guard the Mortal Realms from the ruins."

Sara felt a chill creep up her spine.

"And yet, you do not venture inside?"

Nira shook her head, looking fearful.

"Oh no, no, never."

Sara grunted. *I still do not understand,* she thought. *Fear of things unseen. In the West, we would forget these taboos. Here, they grow.*

"Why not? If it is so dangerous, why not purge it? Purify it? Tear it down stone by stone, and pry gems from its walls?"

Nira's voice was sure. "Because it is older than us. Older than warriors and priests as we understand them."

"Yet you have never seen a corpse shamble out? Or a man wander in and return mad?"

"We have no wish to disturb it, my lady. Why would we seek dark magic when we live in this beautiful, fertile valley with all we need? It reminds us not just of our glory but of our hubris."

Sara buried her face in her hands. *Hubris, a lesson that we Westerners have never learned.* She realized Kazians did not see the gods as tools. The divine was a force, a constant presence. Something beyond them.

She buried her face in her hands, rubbing her eyes.

"I do not understand this land." She sighed, lifting her head. "But you and Dona welcomed me. Even through my hurt."

Nira bowed her head.

"I will continue to serve you, Lady Sara,"

Sara's throat tightened. "You are all I have here."

They looked into each other's eyes, for a long, dutiful moment.

For the first time, Sara felt a friendship with a servant, as if they could understand burdens they did not share.

"I thank you, Lady Sara. Now, shall I prepare you to break the fast?"

Sara shook her head again, weary at the thought of what would follow.

"No, I have no appetite. Prepare my dress and a supper. The mayor has assumed the Lord Guardianship and ridden into the Spires; perhaps I can talk sense into his deputies today."

Nira bowed again.

"As you command, Your Grace."

———

Sara moved as if in a trance along the north perimeter of the green.

Images flooded her mind—Dona, lying in a pool of blood. Agni, vanishing into the night, leaving her with jackals for guardians.

Her fingers twitched, aching for the comfort of her lute or harp. Music had been her refuge since that day. The gentle vibration of the strings, the careful shaping of each note. The music brought her back to pleasant days—and she could control it. Unlike everything else.

That day had sapped her appetite for the bullying and strutting that passed for leadership among males.

Mayor Goro, the leader of the jackal back.

Constable Avro, the red-faced brute.

Sir Arno, the slobbering toady.

And Captain Orlan, the frozen-hearted murderer.

*What force of will did Agni exert to control them?*

For two years, she had seen Agni as the source of her suffering. But since he disappeared, the misfortunes mounted.

Perhaps he had protected her from worse.

——

She placed both hands on the cool iron ring and swung the town hall door open.

They were waiting. Avro and Orlan stood there, wing-to-wing, blocking her way like throne room guards.

And then—the herald boy. The dragon of Father's crest had been painted in haste, crude and dripping, the wet paint running down the belly and tail like a wound.

*How dare you mock me?* she thought.

"What have you done?" she hissed, stepping forward.

Her eyes locked on the herald. *Their lackey.* The insult burned in her chest.

"You mock my house, the noble Ristana crest. Boy, you are old enough for the pinion-and-drop for impersonating a noble."

The herald flinched but steadied himself.

"Your Grace, I bear a message from Duke Verlan of Artania."

His voice quivered, but his eyes stayed on hers.

"He has ordered your return to his castle in Artanport by the second new moon."

Sara froze.

*No.*

Father's voice should have summoned her home with pride. *Not like this. Not as an order. Not through a herald.*

Her voice dropped to a growl.

"You lie. Even a fool can see you did not receive that waistcoat from my father."

The herald shook his head.

"Lady Sara, I mean no disrespect. I received this message from the next herald along the Median Road, and he from the herald in Eltrazan, and he—"

Orlan cut him off, sharp as a knife.

"Your Grace, Duke Verlan requested that it be delivered through official means."

Sara gasped. She took the measure of them. This herald was a docile boy, not told the true weight of his words. Orlan had a heart of stone but would not lie—or disobey.

The crude crest might have mocked her, but the words were real.

She exhaled, her mind racing.

She had known that without Agni, she had no place here—*but why like this? Why a boy instead of a knight? A message through a stone rather than a messenger?*

She felt lightheaded, the world coming out of focus.

"Is that all he said?"

The herald looked downward, hesitating.

Then, his voice dropped. "He said he was most displeased. That you would be relieved of your next duty, and that you would know the meaning of that."

Sara's knees nearly buckled. Her ears rang.

The words cut. *Most displeased.*

Father only used that phrase before he ruined men.

Before he had corrupt ministers cast off towers.

Before he had servants flogged until they bled.

And her next duty—there was only one duty she had ever been destined for.

*The capital duchy.*

The culmination of every lesson, every expectation, every sacrifice.

Now, it was gone.

Ripped from her hands before she could touch it.

Father had no more use for her.

For two years, she had craved this release from her forced posting to the East. Now, she received a perversion of it.

She felt too stunned—and drained—to sob, but bit her lip to keep her dignity.

"Nothing more?" she replied, her voice hollow.

"Nothing more, Your Grace," the herald said, shaking his head.

Orlan broke in, his voice surprisingly—unnervingly—soft.

"Your duty here is complete, Your Grace. I will assemble the convoy to depart in ten days. Since the levy has been delivered, you should have no trouble finalizing your affairs here."

She barely registered the words; everything felt distant, as if viewing the scene through smoky glass. Her voice felt like it belonged to someone else.

"And the pursuit of Agni?"

Avro, ever the callous brute, smirked.

"We will remove him and ensure that Azectrai remains loyal to your father. Inquire no further."

She placed her hands on her hips. How dare a mere constable order her about?

"I have a right to—"

Orlan held up his hand, silencing her. As if she were some troublesome peasant girl to be dismissed. His tone was calm. Final.

"Your Grace, the mayor will lead the pursuit. Please bid your farewells. I welcome the chance to guard your convoy back west," Orlan said.

Sara felt taken aback, stripped of all agency.

She swallowed the lump in her throat, determined not to give them the satisfaction of seeing her break.

"Very well."

She turned and abruptly walked out.

She could not allow herself to cry until she could hide herself behind the town hall.

Then she crumpled. Her back hit the stone wall. Her legs buckled.

She sank to the ground, hands clutching at the fabric of her gown.

*What I would not give for a moon ago, with Agni the unfaithful and an indefinite sentence of the East!*

*This is my reward.*

———

Sara left her tears behind the town hall, but their weight lingered.

She paced the edges of the green without purpose, like a ghost drifting through the land of the living, touching nothing.

Dirt-covered boys wrestled and played tag, shrieking with laughter. Lords walked their hounds, who panted in the summer heat. Women, with rough hands and steady movements, dug up carrots and parsnips. Life moved as it always had—simple, certain.

No one acknowledged her.

The world did not bend or mourn for the fall of Sara Ristana.

For a fleeting moment, she imagined a different life. A common one. A steward, perhaps, or a levy counter like the boys she supervised. A woman with no need for silks or jewels, no father to dictate her purpose, no endless battles of wit and power.

But that life would be a lie, too. They had never felt the weight of a crown in waiting. Never danced in gilded halls or felt fine silk against their skin. *Once one has known silk, how does one bear coarse wool?*

After her tenth lap around the green, she stopped at Aira's shop.

Her last visit had ended in venom, but what did it matter anymore?

"Around the left side, Your Grace," Aira's voice rang out, before she had even knocked.

Sara blinked and stepped around the building. She found Aira in the garden, pulling white garlic bulbs from the soil and placed them into a woven basket.

"How could you hear me?" Sara asked.

Aira did not look up.

"I heard nothing," she replied, brushing dirt from her hands. "I felt your presence. Your sorrow."

Sara sighed, eyes hollow.

"I feel little sorrow, Aira. I feel numb. Dry." The words felt flat. Lifeless.

*I would prefer sorrow to this void. At least sorrow is something.*

"I… wanted to apologize."

Aira lifted an eyebrow.

"For leading those vile men to your shop," she said, voice barely rising above a whisper. "In ten days, I will return to Artania. I wanted to settle our accounts."

Aira sighed, her shoulders slumping. She sat back on her heels, regarding Sara with an unreadable expression.

"I, too, apologize."

Sara blinked.

"I still wish for the Lord Guardian's escape," Aira continued. "But perhaps I was too harsh with you. I saw your fear that night— those pigs respect no woman, not even a high noble."

Sara said nothing. The silence stretched.

Aira reached into her basket, plucked a lavender blossom, and rubbed it between her fingers.

"If you can forgive an old wise woman, I can give you a bunch of lavender."

Sara stiffened, but Aira smiled, pressing the bloom into her palm.

"I grow the most fragrant lavender in Kazia. Its scent soothes the heart."

Sara stared at the flower. Like the dream, the fields of home. *Like the only happiness I have felt in days,* she thought. She lifted it to her nose, inhaling deeply—and felt nothing. No comfort. No warmth. *The girl who danced through lavender fields no longer exists.*

Sara's voice felt like it belonged to another. Detached.

"I will return to the capital duchy, to my father, in disgrace. I have lost everything dear to me in both places."

Aira's expression shifted as she slowly set down her basket.

"What do you mean, dear?"

Sara swallowed the lump in her throat.

"Two years ago, I lost the comforts of my old life. Several days ago, I lost the man I thought was my enemy. But in truth, he protected me from worse. Today, I have been recalled home to disgrace. To punishment. I have lost hope for anything better."

Her breath shook.

"Sometimes, I wish… that I would no longer exist."

Aira's gaze hardened. She stood up, brushing soil from her apron.

"I practice the arts of the hearth, dear," she said, gentle but firm. "I will never assist someone in the taking of their own life, least of all one as young and vibrant as you."

Sara flinched.

"No, no, I would never."

The words escaped in a rush. Would she never, though? A priest once told her that those who took their own lives would suffer their death throes in the Netherworld for eternity.

*But what if those barons were right? What if there were no gods? What if there was only silence? What if I could simply… cease?*

The thoughts forced themselves on her. One promising damnation, the other oblivion. Which was worse?

Aira's voice cut through her thoughts.

"Would you like some lavender then?"

She rubbed another bloom between her fingers, pressing it toward Sara.

"Or more mandrake?"

Sara twitched. The memory of it—the way it pulled her into a different world. *No.*

"No thank you, Aira."

"I won't charge you for it."

"No, it is not the money," Sara said, tears forming in her eyes. "I dreamed of lavender last night. It smelled like home—I danced through a field of it as a girl. Today, it only taunts me with what I have lost."

Aira sighed.

"Perhaps spearmint would relieve you," she said, turning towards the door. "You can crush the leaves and boil them in a tea."

Sara hesitated. Tea was… small. But what else did she have?

"I would love that."

Aira nodded and stepped inside, gesturing for Sara to follow.

"And know this," Aira's voice softened, "I don't blame you for Dona's passing. Nira told me you placed your person in danger to save her. You have a strong heart. A noble heart."

A warmth stirred in her chest—faint, but there. Even in the shadow of loss, someone still saw her as something more.

Aira plucked several sprigs of spearmint and placed them into Sara's palm.

Sara closed her fingers around them, feeling their coolness against her skin.

"Thank you, Lady Aira," she whispered.

It pierced the haze in her mind. But it could not wash away the truth.

She would be gone in ten days, with nothing left to live for.

Now to break the news to Nira—that she would once more need to work the taverns and send her youngest into the mountains so he could eat.

———

Sara plucked listlessly at the harp. She tried for a plaintive melody, a sorrowful tune that matched the day. But the notes would not come. Only a dull, discordant hum. So she settled on pulling at the deepest string, again and again, until it wore at her finger. Until it hurt.

After some time, she heard footsteps.

She cringed.

Nira entered quietly; she must have sensed the heaviness in the air.

Sara straightened, setting the harp aside, steeling herself.

"Nira. I have been expecting you," she said, her voice calm and steady.

Nira offered a faint smile, dipping her head in a bow.

"It is always a pleasure to serve you, my lady."

Sara gestured toward the sprigs of spearmint on the table.

"Before you prepare supper, I would like to share this tea together. Crush the leaves and boil them in water."

Nira's brows lifted slightly, but she nodded.

"As you wish, Your Grace. By your leave."

She turned to the hearth.

Sara sighed, rubbing her temples. The unspoken words sat heavy in her heart. The thought of Nira being forced to degrade herself once more, it sickened her.

Within minutes, Nira returned with a steaming mug in each hand.

The scent of spearmint wafted through the air, cool and sharp.

Sara gestured to the opposite chair.

"Please, Nira. Sit."

Nira hesitated but obeyed, cradling the mug in her hands.

Sara blew on her tea, watching ripples form and fade. For a moment, she felt the mug warm her fingers.

"You seem troubled, Lady Sara."

Sara took a deep breath.

"My father has summoned me to return to Artania in ten days. With this house deserted, I regret that you are no longer needed to maintain it."

Nira's shoulders slumped. She stared deep into her mug.

"I should have suspected," she murmured. "With the Lord Guardian vanished, my days were short."

Sara leaned forward slightly.

"I pray that you will find a good lord to fill your children's bellies."

Nira looked disappointed but calm.

"Whatever I must," she replied simply. "As I have since my husband passed. But my boys and I will remember your kindness and Lord Kazirian's always."

Sara's chest tightened.

*No. I will not stand for this. Memories cannot fill bellies nor keep a roof overhead.*

A subversive thought washed over her. Father would have no need of Agni's chest. In a few days, the mayor might seize it for himself. And even if Agni returned, he would not want for wealth. But Nira would.

*Perhaps I could do one last kindness.*

Her eyes widened. Her heart thumped.

Abruptly, she stood up.

"Wait here, Nira."

"Your Gr—"

Sara would not let her finish. She whirled and dashed up the stairs.

Agni's clothing chest, in his haste to flee, lay open.

Sara grabbed one of his tunics—large, fine silk, embroidered at the cuffs. It would serve as a makeshift sack. She tied its arms, waist, and wing slits with rough rope, sealing it. Then, through the head-hole, she shoveled handfuls of coins. She picked out the largest—silver tens, gold hundreds. As many as she could, until the ropes strained. She tied it off and shook it.

But it was not enough—so she filled a second.

*One day, you may need to work the taverns again. But by my will—and Agni's—it will not be soon.*

The two silk bundles were so heavy she had to drag them down the stairs. *Clank, clank, clank,* the sacks rang out.

Nira looked up, blinking in surprise.

Sara moved around the table to Nira's side.

Nira's mouth fell open. Her hands covered her mouth, trembling.

"Your Grace, what have you done?"

Her voice was erratic, tremulous.

"I order you to feed yourself and your boys with this, for as long as you can."

Nira's eyes shimmered with unshed tears.

"Your Grace… were you in the Lord Guardian's chest?"

Sara sat back down with a sharp breath.

"I do not believe he will return for some time," she spoke confidently.

*He may never. But he would do the same,* she thought.

Nira swallowed, her gaze darting to the laden sacks.

"What if he does?"

"He will understand," Sara replied, with a measured, generous tone. A duchess' tone.

Nira looked between Sara and the sacks, as if searching for a reason to refuse. To pretend she did not need it. But at last, her shoulders sagged. She bowed her head.

"You are most kind, Lady Sara. I accept this gift with gratitude."

Sara narrowed her eyes—this sum would require a warning.

"If he does not return, a thief—or the mayor—will break into an abandoned house and steal it. Now, tell no one. No lord, no smith, no washerwoman. Take a shovel from Agni's shed and bury it beneath your bed. Do not buy splendid clothing, nor a stone house, and the mayor's men will suspect nothing."

Nira's eyes widened. "I will do as you ask."

Sara nodded once and took a long sip of tea.

"Good. Now, I should love an evening meal."

Nira let out a shaky breath, her hands still trembling.

"Yes, yes, Your Grace."

Nira stood, wiping her eyes with the edge of her sleeve. Then, with one last look at Sara, she scurried out the back door.

Sara leaned back, taking in a nose full of spearmint.

Her harp waited beside her. She reached for it, plucking a single note. Then another. The music came easier this time.

She did not know what Father would do to her. Nor how much longer her name would hold meaning. But for now, Nira's boys would not starve.

Freedom came with nothing left to live for.

# *Folly*

Agni could only feign sleep—his mind burned with clarity. They had left his eyes uncovered—perhaps an oversight, or a test. Did they believe him too broken to resist, or merely too crippled to flee? He guessed the latter; Rem knew Agni would fight to his last. That much was certain.

He exhaled slowly. His plan teetered on the edge of madness—to escape as a bound cripple, ambush a party of knights, extract a message of peace from a baron who did not wish to give it, and send it via outlaws to a duke who might slay them on sight. *Folly.* The word rang in his mind, his own voice, not Anton's. At best, it might cast doubt, stall war fever long enough for Agni to reach Avicia. At worst, it would all be for nothing. He would be cut down as an outlaw, his flesh left to feed mountain leopards… and Anton Kazirian would summon another to drench the land in blood.

But he had no other path. Without that folly, he would remain a villain in two lands, nameless, powerless, hunted. *If peace can only be seized through reckless desperation, then that is my path,* he thought. *Peace for the Borderlands, if it costs me my life.*

And Kali, sweet Kali. This time, he did not think of her touch, but of the son they might have. Would they call him Balo, like his dearest friend? Dani, like his grandfather? Kali would have names too—Aloi ones, carrying the strength of her people. Perhaps two names, as was Avician custom. Anton said a name carried power. Would two carry twice the strength?

He sighed, flexing against his bindings, bringing himself back to his plight. They had tied him at three points again, ensuring he could not run. He need not run, but to escape his bonds and vanish.

Agni stared into the Spires, their jagged peaks not yet higher than a stallion's head. Once they were, the bandits and Goro's men would be inside his domain, where his masterwork waited. But he needed exquisite timing. If Rem learned of the snares, he would steer clear. If he escaped too early, Rem could catch up to him before he found Goro. Too late, and they would barter him.

If Frazi knew that the mayor rode into the Spires, he had a night, maybe two.

This time, Anton would not gift him a burning blade.

———

The next morning, Agni awoke to a familiar pain. A boot nudged his wing, not harshly but not gently.

"Azri, up."

The night before last, Silence awoke him with a kick to the spine. This was progress.

Agni blinked blearily, drawing in a slow breath.

"Please unbind me so that I might stand, lest I piss myself."

Silence grunted but obliged, unlashing Agni's arms and legs before shoving a wooden pole into his hands. A crutch. Agni gripped the rough wood tightly, willing his muscles to remember how to move as he lurched to his feet.

He hopped toward a tree, deliberate in his struggle. Every motion had to convince them—a cripple should move awkwardly, sluggishly. He did his business behind the tree but still sensed that he was being watched.

Ten steps back. The pole bowed under him then snapped with a crack. Agni crumpled, crashing shoulder-first against an exposed root. *Blast it.* He clenched his jaw against the pain, fighting the instinct to rub at the impact. A misstep—he had leaned too much. *I had best learn how to use a stick; I will have some miles on one tonight.*

Two voices chuckled.

"Save yourself, Azri."

Agni gritted his teeth, extending his left hand, even as he wanted to thrust the broken stick into their eye sockets.

Silence's voice cut through the laughter. "Lift him up, Marvon. We can't ransom a corpse. Rem's orders."

"We're just making sport, Keron."

"And I'm not. Put him back on his horse and bind him again. He's a spirited one."

Marvon grumbled, but he and another took an arm each, hoisting Agni back towards camp. He let his muscles go slack, his head down. The easier they believed him subdued, the easier the moment would come when he proved them wrong.

The morning sun spilled red across the Eastern plains, setting the Spires aflame. By the afternoon, it would blind their eyes. In the right spot, he could blind one adversary. But for now, it was only a beautiful, fleeting thing.

They tossed Agni onto a cart, before binding him again.

Agni turned to Silence—Keron—and let out a slow breath.

"I thank you, Sir Keron."

Keron's brow furrowed.

"For what, Azri?"

"For allowing me to piss like a man this time and walk back under my own power." He let out a rueful laugh. "I'd best savor such small pleasures before I'm dropped off a rock."

"Orders," Keron grunted.

"Still much appreciated." Agni lifted his bound hands slightly in a vague gesture of gratitude. "A condemned man still has virtue, even if it earns little merit."

Keron leaned in, his voice lowering to a hiss. "What do you want, Azri of Azectrai? A friend? A blessing?"

Agni met his gaze, studying him closely. Keron's face bore the lines of a man who had seen too much, creases sharper than Alexander's who was at least a decade older. Possibly a knight, once. Stripped of station, abandoned to this life. The kind of man who lost everything and carried it all in his silence.

"You interest me, Keron," Agni said simply.

Keron stiffened, his brows twitching in confusion.

"What?"

"Rem, Tovon, the rest—they want only their next meal, a coin purse, a new life. But in you I see something different." He tilted his head. "You weren't always a barber. When did you lose your lordly title?"

"As far as concerns you," Keron muttered, turning away, "I am your jailer. And you speak to me only when you need the privy."

Agni smiled faintly.

"I sent four Kazian warriors screaming to the Netherworld. That merits more than a privy call, no?"

Keron grunted back. "And for that, I thank you. Now if only you had stuck yourself afterwards."

Agni chuckled. "If only Rem hadn't saved my hide a moment earlier. That would have seemed ungrateful."

For a moment, he saw Keron's lips twitch. Amusement? Resentment? Did Keron see him as a man now?

"Only so he could ransom you for a greater gain. Rem is the only man within a moon who wants your hide intact. On either side of the Spires, your life is forfeit."

Agni forced himself to relax. Keron was right. He had once carried rank and duty. He still believed in something. But men like him were predictable. They clung to structure and discipline. They took orders.

"And as that is so, one's horizon shrinks. I have few pleasures left beyond tonight's sunset over the western peaks."

"Savor it, Azri."

Keron grunted again and walked back to his horse.

Soon after, Rem's voice rang out from the front. "Ready and form up!"

A dozen "*Ai*"s rang out. The cart jerked forward.

As Agni's cart lurched, he savored the slight humanity Keron showed him. But he had to turn it against him—to remove him from the trail and strike him down. They had no hounds to pursue him.

*If your duty to me is the privy, then the privy it is. You will falter one moment.*

*Then the wolf will pounce.*

Life in peril shrunk his horizons, indeed.

———

For the rest of the day, Agni accustomed himself to the sounds of the trail—chirping robins, the bandits' ale songs, and the occasional scream of a mountain leopard—the better to recognize strange sounds. He counted the steps of his captors, noted who favored their left hand, who lingered too long by the ale skins.

The Spires loomed ahead; their jagged peaks still low against the skies. Soon, they would tower, swallowing the band whole.

Then, the snares. His work of years, designed to halt invasions and crush riders. But he had not mined the far eastern slopes. Today, he counted that as favor, lest a sentry recognize him. He had to escape at night—that night—and then disappear westward into his maze of traps.

One misstep and it was all for naught.

*Folly.*

But through his binds, he felt greater forces at work—the weight of a god and his child.

He never understood Varenox, God of Dragons. No man could. The deity of paradox, of truth and deception, of fate and defiance, of prophecy twisted against itself. Mercurial, like a dragon's thunder breath. He concealed his intentions like a dragon against the night sky, then struck like one in dive. His only constant, that the god loathed him, toyed with him. He needed no divine words; he had felt it since Anton's call.

Anton never concealed his intentions. He whispered them plainly, gave him guidance in trances and dreams, sent him into reveries, even seized his mind and body. He told Agni that if he refused his path, another would take his place—then he would abandon Agni to his god. Was that true? Anton spoke with the certainty of ages. Yet, if another were so easily found, why had he waited two thousand years for Agni? He knew time in a way that a god or a man could not.

Both his ancestor and his god had time.

He did not.

They hated each other more than they hated Agni, but soon they might hate him, too.

———

They fed him better than expected—dry pork and biscuits, washed down with ale. A condemned man's meal, perhaps, but solid enough to keep his strength. He played his part well, quiet and withdrawn, murmuring old Kazian prayers under his breath. He wondered if they could tell his prayers were empty, not like a western lord's, but insincere and futile. The Kazian tongue defied time, alien to the common Dragonlands tongue of Blevenia on its east and the rest of Solantia on its west.

The sun bled into the horizon, the sky burning in hues of orange and red, before giving way to starlight. One by one, the bandits settled into their bedrolls, their voices giving way to the cackle of the dying fire and the low drone of crickets. Without a word, Keron and another man lifted Agni off his horse and placed him into his own.

And then, the chill came. The stillness, the creeping numbness.

The sky above shimmered and warped, and the silvered figure of Anton Kazirian took shape.

The Voice of Ages, now his foe.

*"Boy."* Anton's lips did not move, but disdain dripped from his tone.

Agni did not stir.

*"I knew you could not just leave me to Varenox. You despise him. You wish to stop me with your own hand,"* he replied, eyes locked in near-amusement.

The image smiled with a wolf's grin, sharp and taunting.

*"Your cockamamie scheme requires no assistance. If your own sentries do not gut you, you will die a criminal's death, your body thrown in the river and stripped by lampreys. But you are right, boy. That I would rather not leave you to Varenox' obscurity. My next charge will spread tales of your death across the Dragonlands. Your name will live forever, as that of a fool."*

Agni felt the hair on his arms rise. Anton could predict battles and palace coups with the wisdom of millennia. He had powers of the mind, likely more than he had shown.

But Agni's lips still curled in defiance.

*"Will you tighten your grip on me again? Twist my thoughts, send me screaming into the night? Or jerk my broken leg until I lose my breath? If you have the power you claim, you could stop my heart this instant. Do it. End me where I lie."*

He bit his cheek, bracing for Anton's retaliation, for the sudden, crushing grip on his body, the frenzy in his mind.

But Anton only sneered. *"Tempt me not, you fool. I have already found another of great merit. When my seed takes root, I will dispose of you in a time, place, and manner of my choosing."*

Agni's fingers curled into the dirt.

*"For half a moon, you have reminded me of your power. But you will not stop me tonight. I will not only defy you—I will remind you why you chose me twenty years ago."*

Anton's laughter rumbled into the night, deep and knowing. *"Indeed, Agni. Amuse me with your pain, for that is all you shall do."*

The stars flickered as Anton's form faded, his taunts lingering in Agni's mind like a shadow. But this time, they emboldened him.

Anton no longer saw him as his sole charge. He had begun to look elsewhere. That meant Anton had begun to doubt.

*Good. I will show you folly.*

The Kazirian, the Dragons of the Moonless Night, would duel.

———

Agni's eyelids sagged with the weight of another sleepless day. Twice, he caught himself drifting, lulled by the rhythm of Keron's snores, until he forced his broken leg to flex and jolt him awake. He bit his cheek to muffle a yelp. Sleep meant death.

Cloud cover had swallowed the starlight, leaving his eyes to adapt to near total darkness. Soon, even the night watch plopped himself on a log, his head sinking lower and lower into his hands.

*Now.*

He rolled back and forth, enough to shed his blanket without rousing the entire band. His bindings bit into his wrists, but he flexed his fingers, testing the slack. Not much, but he had worked with less.

He brushed his wings over Keron's blanket. A shift. A grunt. He stirred.

"Keron," he hissed.

Keron's wings flicked.

"Keron," Agni whispered again, firmer.

Keron groaned, shifting onto his stomach. "What?" he mumbled, voice thick with sleep.

"I need the privy."

"Blast it, Azri."

"I apologize," Agni said, straining his voice to sell the lie. "I can wake you now or leave you with the stench until dawn."

Keron muttered a curse but tossed off his blanket with an irritated grunt. He strapped his sword belt around his waist and knelt, untying Agni's legs first, then loosening the bindings at his wrists. Then, he turned and hissed to the night watchman.

Agni's stomach dropped. *Blast it.* He had planned for one. Now there were two.

The watchman's head jerked upright, groggy. "What?"

Keron scowled.

"If he bolts, wake the others."

*I trained my own men to escape,* he thought, *though I did not shatter their legs first.*

Keron ducked under Agni's right arm, hoisting him with practiced ease. Agni let himself sag, better to exhaust his captor. They hobbled off the road, twenty paces into the trees, where the roots curled and twisted through the dirt like grasping fingers. Keron let him down with a grunt.

"Do what you need," he said, stepping back. A hand hovered over his sword hilt. Always ready, always watching.

Agni let out a heavy breath, fumbling at his belt.

Then, he crumpled.

"Oof!" he gasped, pitching sideways into the dirt, away from view.

Keron took a step forward.

"Azri?" he said with suspicion, though he did not draw his blade.

"Guh… help… me," Agni gasped and groaned, clawing at the dirt as if trying to right himself.

The next ten seconds would decide his fate.

Keron hesitated. Then, cursing under his breath, he bent down, extending a hand.

Agni pulled his hand back, forcing Keron to offer his sword hand.

And expose his neck.

With a grunt, Agni twisted his hips, his left leg lashing out like a whip.

It struck the back of Keron's neck. A dull crack split the night.

Agni's leg went numb from the force of the strike.

Keron's eyes bulged.

His limbs did not even seize. He dropped like a lifeless doll, right on top of Agni. Blood oozed from his mouth.

For a second, Agni wondered whether Keron had survived the brutal kick—others had not.

He had to shove Keron's limp form off him, his own breath ragged.

He grabbed the rough bark to pull himself upright.

The second watchman was already moving. His boots crunched through the brush, slow and cautious, torchlight flickering through the trees.

"Azri?" The voice was wary, that of a man who sensed something was wrong, but not yet a threat.

He carried his torch in his sword hand, but a deadlier weapon— his voice.

Agni flattened himself against the tree, listened for the rhythm of the watchman's breath, his posture. A face-down Dragonlander could be either Keron or Agni; the watchman could not investigate from afar.

He lowered himself to investigate. He exhaled.

Agni sprang.

In one practiced motion, Agni swung his broken leg across the watchman's back and wrapped his right arm around the victim's neck. He clasped his right arm with his left.

And squeezed like a snake.

The watchman's breath rattled before he could shout.

For a second, he grunted and clawed at Agni's choke.

His body twitched once, then went limp, his world dark.

Agni squeezed for a full minute, dropping his victim deeper into sleep.

His body shook with the effort.

Then, he rolled the watchman over. A belt knife—he took it. Without ceremony, Agni plunged the watchman's knife into his neck. Then severed the rest of his bonds.

A coin pouch—useless now.

But the real prize—the limp Keron's sword.

Fire flowed through his veins. The comforting weight of a blade, the night air of the Spires. He flared his wings to take in the gusts.

*Son of the Borderlands, Lord Guardian of the East, Dragon of the Moonless Night, now in my bounteous home.*

But there was no time to celebrate.

Rem would awaken and search for Agni—then pursue him on horseback.

Mayor Goro—at the head of an armored patrol—was ahead. Agni knew that without the snares, he was doomed.

A rock fall and a dragon whistle lay several miles ahead.

He grabbed a gnarled stick, testing its strength beneath his palm.

He turned westward and willed his broken body forward.

*For my homeland.*

—

Agni's body burned with exhaustion. After five relentless hours of travel, the first hints of sunrise peeked over the horizon. His wings ached, his legs screamed with every step. Sweat drenched his clothes, rubbing his skin raw. Exhilaration had faded, but one foolish moment—or faltering of effort—would end him.

He leaned against an oak, breath heavy, faint from the grueling journey.

He recognized the landmarks—the jagged limestone outcropping, the deep canyon bend. Soon, daylight would dull his advantage of night sight, and his sentries would return to their posts, rested and ready.

*After all, I trained them,* he thought.

Two or three would rush to spring the traps, one would escape up the mountain to the stone for reinforcements. But he designed this system to fight horsemen, not threats from the sky.

He scaled the hillside and over the small cliff, well above the trail, and stalked through the trees. The bandits would have fanned out to search in all directions—without their prize, they were almost as condemned as he. The true danger lay ahead.

Another grueling hour passed before he reached the road's choke point.

Tons of boulders, restrained by a rope net, stood ready to crush enemies of Kazia. Above it, the dragon whistle—a hollowed beech trunk fitted with a bellows, a crude but effective mimicry of a dragon's cry. And beside it, the ballista, an arrow the size of a spear cocked and ready, in case the dragon turned on its own men.

The sentries had arrived, lingering near the whistle, scanning the road below.

Agni stayed behind, hands working swiftly to cut vines and branches, draping them over his wings. His fingers dug into the earth, scooping handfuls of dirt over his head.

Then, he waited. Sentry work was the lowest form of duty; the slow grind of vigilance, to watch without flagging. Even his best grew careless. *Stay awake. Stay aware.* He tensed his burning muscles to stay awake—to sleep was to die.

Hours passed, the sun passing its zenith. His mind turned. How to ensure the bandits and the mayor arrived together. How to overwhelm four trained men at once.

Only one force could create it.

*Dragon. Dragon. Dragon.*

No shout struck fear like that call. Its breath could strike down any warlord at a hundred feet, its claws could tear steel into ribbons. No sword, save his enchanted blade, could pierce its hide. If a dragon dove, even the most hardened warriors would throw themselves to the dirt and pray. And it would not distinguish him from his foes.

A low growl shattered his thoughts.

"Grrrr…"

He gasped. A wolf. A young female, by the shape of her body, lean and cautious. Her hackles raised and her tail erect. It saw Agni as a threat or prey. And wolves did not travel alone.

*Shit.*

He had always loved wolves—their strength, their loyalty. This one did not see the Wolf of Azectrai as her own, though.

She stalked forward, eyes locked onto him, lips curling. If she called to her pack, or he shouted to scare her off, the sentries would come and take him—or he would have to kill more men sworn to him. To his shame.

Agni slowly pulled himself to a crouch, flaring his wings. He gripped his staff. The wolf snapped her jaws. Her pups would have left the den by this moon, but were she rabid, that would not save him.

He angled backwards, placing a tree between them. Still, she advanced. He retreated thirty feet, heart pounding. A cedar stood behind him, its lowest branch barely within reach. It would have to do.

With a grunt, he leapt, grabbing the branch with his left arm. The wolf lunged for his foot. He yanked it up just in time, jamming the staff into her mouth. She yelped, snapping in fury. He pulled his second leg up. She growled and snapped again, but he was well out of her reach.

More growling, more padded footsteps. Three more wolves emerged, circling the tree.

He was trapped.

No man, let alone a cripple, could outrun a wolf. Even if he glided, they would chase him down. But in the tree, he had time and a vantage point.

Through the thick foliage, he peered toward the canyon. One hundred feet to the sentries—an athletic glide even for a smaller, healthy man.

*If I can pull the top two sentries away, I will create a scream that chills man and wolf alike,* he thought.

And again, he waited. Arms shaking against the rough bark, he could not hold on forever.

*For my friends and my homeland. All that I have left.*

Below, the wolves still circled.

Minutes felt like hours.

And finally—hoofbeats from the west.

No squeak of a cart's wheels.

The sentries did not form up for battle.

It had to be the mayor, and if so, he could not hesitate.

*I have one rock fall, indiscriminate death from above, four sentries, and an armored convoy of whom I must spare exactly one. Folly, indeed. But desperate men are capable of supreme deeds.*

He slowed his breath. Short in, long out.

The burn, the sleepless night, the hunger, it all faded.

*Closer, closer.*

The mayor would stop to salute the sentries, then move into the narrow canyon's choke point.

"Baron!" a sentry shouted.

*Now!*

He drew Keron's sword.

With all his will, he leapt from the tree. Wings spread. Angling towards the sentries. The hundred feet stretched into eternity.

But the combination of flight and battle felt like ecstasy.

And then he screamed.

"Kyaaaaaaaaa!"

Deep. Draconic. Terrible.

The sentries froze, faces blanched with terror.

Slender lads, together weighing little more than Agni alone.

And he crashed into them like a trebuchet stone.

The impact sent them tumbling down the ledge, their screams fading in the wind.

His head stung, his right arm went numb. Lights flashed before his eyes.

The lower two boys had not yet reacted. In seconds, the convoy would assume battle positions. He had seconds.

*Recover! Stay alert!*

Agni staggered to his feet and pumped the bellows with all his might.

The angry shriek ripped through the canyon. Three times. Three more.

A rush of air roared over him.

His blood chilled as the true terror of the skies arrived.

Agni turned just in time to see it, a behemoth gliding with unnatural grace.

Fifty feet of night-blue scales, razor-edged talons, and the breath of death itself.

And it had seen him first.

"KYAAAAAAAA!!!"

Its scream shattered the air.

Agni dove around the ledge, barely avoiding the beast's claws as they sliced the air where he had stood.

He skidded through the dirt, the dirt and rocks scraping his chest, turning him end over end.

The rock fall—he had seconds.

Again, he dove toward the ropes, hacking at them with everything he had left. The burlap-and-wood frame restraining the boulders released. An avalanche of granite thundered down the canyon, engulfing the road.

Screams. Metal crushed. Horses shrieked.

He looked up—the dragon had found new prey.

A disorienting crack ripped through the air, followed by a man's scream.

Below, its claws sank into the hindquarters of a flailing horse. Blood sprayed in a sharp mist over the scene. The screaming rider was flung into the rubble. The mighty dragon's claws were so sharp, the horse's hide barely slowed it.

The dragon wheeled, eyes gleaming, scanning for another target.

And Agni had to dive into its path.

*Go!*

He took wing into the canyon, the scent of charred flesh and ferrous blood as strong as at The Ports. The rush of air subsumed all the pain and fear of that moment.

The canyon wall rushed towards him, and he flared his wings at the last instant, landing on a distant boulder. His enemies and their poor horses lay scattered like overturned game pieces.

Two had already begun to stir.

*Goro. Arno.*

The sight of them boiled Agni's rage.

*These cowards conspired to strip me of my land, my honor, my freedom, my love. And nearly succeeded.*

As Goro tried to rise, Agni raised the flat of Keron's sword and brought it down across his head with a dull crack. Goro yelped like a hound and collapsed back onto his elbows, his eyes rolling back. His cloak tangled around his legs.

Arno, slower in his slovenly mass, barely lifted his head before Agni clubbed him next. He gurgled and toppled over a boulder, his body shaking as he vomited over it.

The rush of battle over, his body burned with effort. His skin stung all over.

He fought the urge to lay on a boulder himself. *Not yet.*

That was when he sensed movement from behind.

A sharp inhale. The clink of armor shifting.

He had missed one.

Agni turned in time to see a third man rising to his feet, wings flaring wide, sword drawn. His wings heaved with his chest.

Agni dug his fingers into a jagged granite and pulled himself to face this final guard. He had no advantage of surprise. He would not win a fair duel.

The bodyguard smirked beneath his bloodied nose.

"Lord Kazirian. An unexpected pleasure."

His voice was rough, unimpressed.

Agni held out his own sword to keep him at bay. He did not recognize this one, but the sharp focus in his eyes, even wounded in the wake of Agni's brutal chaos—he knew battle.

"I would say the same," Agni growled, "but I am no liar."

The bodyguard inched forward, twirling his blade, as confident as a predator toying with wounded prey.

"Lay down your weapon," he commanded, "and you may receive a lord's death."

But instead, he raised his blade over Goro's head.

The mayor gasped, his eyes going wide.

"Then I will take your lord with my last strike."

The bodyguard stiffened, eyes flickering toward the mayor.

Agni forced all his loathing for Goro to the surface.

*I need penitence, not blood from you, mayor. But if I must die, your last breath will precede mine.*

But before the bodyguard could react, Agni felt the wind. His instincts screaming in warning.

Followed by a shadow from the east.

*The dragon!*

The sun in front of it, the guard would not see its shadow.

Its enormous form blocked out the light as it turned into a dive.

It had not finished its hunt—and would take either of them at will.

Agni left the mayor and lowered his stance, willing himself to look small amongst the boulders. The bodyguard raised his sword, stepping forward through the boulders.

*Stay still, knight. Stay easy,* he thought.

He slumped against a boulder to buy a precious second. His heart raced, depending on the empire's sacred beast.

Then the sky screamed.

"KYAAAAA!!!"

The dragon dove, lightning crackling in its throat, its scent in the air.

Agni dove between two boulders.

A blinding flash engulfed the canyon.

His muscles seized.

For long seconds, he could neither see, hear, nor feel.

A vague sensation of flying, then crashing to the ground.

If it had not knocked the wind out of him, he might believe he had passed to the Lands Beyond.

He gasped, wings twitching limply.

But as his senses returned, the scent of roasting flesh grew sharper. The guard's lifeless body slumped against a boulder, half of his face burned to the bone. His sword had flown from his grasp.

And above, the dragon perched on the canyon wall, its talons gouging deep into the soil. Its golden eyes swept the wreckage, as if looking for more intruders. Its wings beat once, powerful and deliberate. Then, with a grunt and a scream, it launched itself back into the sky.

Agni flattened himself against the canyon wall, watching the rhythmic beat of its wings as it soared back into the mountains. For a moment he admired the symbol of his people's pride and strength.

Only when the last echo disappeared did he dare to move.

He was still alive.

By sheer luck, the dragon had chosen another victim.

Fate had spared him—for now.

With a grunt, he rolled onto his side and pushed himself up on quaking arms.

His gaze fell upon Goro and Arno, still splayed on the ground, their faces pale as death.

Agni wiped the sweat from his brow and advanced toward them, grinning.

His breath started to rattle—not from exhaustion, but from something primal, deeper. The sheer bliss that his "folly" might succeed, that he had walked into death's maw—wolves, boulders, blades, and dragons—and lived.

"Ha… haha…HAHAHAHA!"

The laughter bubbled up before he could stop it, spilling from his lips. Manic, breathless.

Beneath him, Goro flinched. Agni wrapped the mayor's filthy hair around his first, yanking his head upward to meet his gaze. His pupils widened like a frightened cat's; his neck muscles shook beneath Agni's grip.

The scent of burnt flesh and sprayed blood still hung thick in the air. Agni's masterwork.

For peace. For Solantia. For home.

"Agni—"

It returned. Agni cackled for five seconds. He could not even force anger into his voice.

"The Spires, the hills of Blevenia, the plateaus of Avicia could not drink my blood," Agni said between laughs. "Why did you think you could?"

He let the knife's tip bite into Goro's throat, just enough to let a single drop of blood trickle down the edge.

Goro gurgled, his body stiffening against the rock.

"Tell me, Goro, what did the duke holding your leash promise you?" Agni taunted, his voice almost a whisper. "Coins? The Kazirian manor? His daughter's hand?"

Goro said nothing.

Agni only grinned wider. He was still clinging to the tattered remnants of his dignity. He brought the knife's hilt down on the top of Goro's skull with a sharp crack.

He yelped.

Agni fought to contain another laugh. *Too good, too perfect. I should be dead. Shattered among these stones. Flesh torn apart by wolves or melted by a dragon's breath. Yet here I stand in victory.*

*God of my people, does this amuse you?*

*Ancestor, can you feel my glee?*

"But I would not believe the poison that drips from your lips," Agni whispered, flexing his fingers, "even if you swore before the emperor and the gods."

Finally, Goro's voice cracked. "You are mad, boy."

Agni lowered his face inches from Goro's own. "Oh, old man, I must be. How else could I have lived this long?"

Goro tried to turn his face from Agni's hot breath, but Agni held him fast.

"Urgh. I should have taken you myself, rather than trusting your drunken bitch of a betrothed."

Agni slammed his fist down onto the butt of Goro's jaw, a thud like a maul on dirt.

"Mind that rebel tongue before I cut it out of your neck. Had you taken me, the townsfolk would have sliced off your wings by nightfall. Speak not of deeds that you lack the bollocks to do yourself."

Goro panted for a minute before returning his own snarl.

"Deeds, is it, Agni? You just slew two of our finest swordsmen, as well as a town guard in your escape. How many must die to avenge your hatred?"

"Avenge? Hatred? Old man, I had King Theodore and Duke Harkon on bended knee. Revenge is for the impotent. This is the Lord Guardian's duty. I built these traps so that Kazia might no longer live under threat of eastern raiders. But I did not expect the real criminals to come from Kazia." He leaned in, pressing the knife tip just below Goro's eye. "How many did you sanction to raid Blevenian villages?"

The mayor's lower lip trembled. "Blast you, Agni!" he snarled, but in the weak growl of a wounded predator. "How dare you accuse me of such treachery!"

*Lies.*

The words rang hollow in Agni's ears. He moved the knife close enough to tickle Goro's eyelashes.

"I have the words of Sir Frazi himself," Agni said. "Confessed to me in his last gurgling breath, after I caught him buried to the hilt inside a sobbing Blevenian peasant girl."

Goro gasped.

*There. Guilt.*

Then the laugh came again.

"I would have confirmed with his brothers and squire, but I left their throat in no condition to speak."

Agni flicked his knife, mocking a mercy blow.

"He said that you named yourself Lord Guardian, did you not?" Agni mused. "You *do* know that I received that title from the emperor himself, and awarding yourself such a title would not only earn you the pinion-and-drop, but a moon's worth of public floggings first?"

"And what about desertion of your post," Goro said, "does that make you more noble than I?"

Agni stared him down, eyes to eyes, then smiled.

"That life ended the moment I learned of your plot. But my heart still beats with purpose, peace unto the Borderlands. If you wish to see tonight's sunset, you will join that purpose."

Now, Agni only needed the truth.

He reached into his left boot and withdrew the red speaking-stone. It pulsed with a deep, mesmerizing glow, like fresh blood.

"This stone is the second of my three most treasured memories. As it holds the start of my life as a Solantian soldier, now it will hold its end. You will speak your confession into this stone," Agni said. "Or I will cut the truth from your flesh—and your son's—one strip at a time."

For a long moment, Goro simply lay there, his chest rising and falling in heavy, shallow breaths.

Agni watched his pupils dart between the stone, the blade at his eye, and his motionless son, as if weighing his options—betray his master and leave in disgrace or die where he lay.

Finally, the fight left his eyes.

*Defeated. Beyond hope. Good.*

Agni's voice was calm. Grave.

"First, I will speak my name into this stone. Then, you will speak your name, title, and the full nature of the plot and Duke Verlan's ambitions. Do not speak otherwise."

Agni raised the stone before him; its glow intensified as he clasped it between two fingers. In it, he could see his own exhausted, dirty face, his bloodshot eyes. But activated, it would take in his words.

*"To Duke Harkon of Western Blevenia,"* he began, his voice noble. *"I am Agni Kazirian, son of Piro Kazirian and Mara Senotare, once High General of Solantia and Lord Guardian of the East. Now, I am a criminal in the land of my birth with but a stone to right a wrong. Duke Verlan, father of my once-betrothed, saw me as a threat to enrich himself through a second war."*

He angled the stone toward Goro.

*"Now, Baron Goro Kazimana. Speak."*

Goro's lips parted, but hesitation flickered in his eyes. Agni could see him weighing his honor and his life.

Agni's patience expired. He yanked Goro's head back by his matted hair and slammed it into the boulder once more, grinding the rough surface against his scalp. A choked cry escaped the mayor's lips.

Goro coughed, blood clotting in his hair. His pride had crumbled.

With a shuddering breath, he rasped, *"I am Baron Goro Kazimana, Mayor of Azectrai, sworn to liege lord Duke Hauran of Kazia. Under orders of my lord's peer, Duke Verlan of Artania, I set to arrest Lord Guardian Agni Kazirian, whom Duke Verlan regards as a threat to his ambitions—to amass power, to defy imperial decree, and to carve his dominion from the bones of another Black Moon War."*

*"Baron Goro, where do we sit?"* Agni continued.

*"On the Median Road, a day and a half from the eastern end."*

*"Baron, does Duke Verlan covet the Crystal Throne?"*

Goro's face formed a mask of horror.

*"I do not know."*

Agni sensed sincerity in his voice—even he might not know the depth of Verlan's schemes.

*"Baron, you are sworn to Duke Hauran of Kazia, but ultimately to Emperor Taran Solant. On your sacred oath, do you hereby abjure Duke Verlan's plot and swear to obey His Imperial Majesty even unto your death?"*

*"I do."*

His voice wavered, and the message was clearly coerced, but the words were there.

Agni smirked. This was only the beginning.

"The duchess will confirm this plot. And every Solantian lord knows the duke's ambitions do not stop at the gates of Artanport."

"Then I am a living corpse," he grumbled.

Agni raised Goro's head again as if to batter him further.

"No!"

"Then a corpse you are. You may grovel before your master and claim you spoke them under threat. Indeed, you have. He may leave you to toddle about the Azectrai Valley until your days expire, for to slay you would reveal his plot. But if you disobey me, I will cut out your eyes and your son's—for I have dealt too many mercy blows—and you will pray for that dragon to return and carry you off in its jaws.

"Now, you will continue." His tone sharpened. "You will bear witness to the atrocities you permitted under your watch."

He forced Goro to keep his eyes on the stone.

*"Say it. Tell Duke Harkon what happened."*

"*Also, some days hence, five armed riders crossed the Spire Mountains into the Kingdom of Blevenia, in breach of the treaty that ended the Black Moon War. They descended upon a manor village north of the Median Road, taking what they pleased—murdering men, burning homes, and violating women.*" Goro's voice cracked, but Agni did not move.

"*For their crimes, all met their end at the hand of the true Lord Guardian of the East, whom I have entrusted to deliver the following message.*"

The words carried weight now. The duke's crowner would have found the bodies.

*Resolution. Consequence. Truth.*

Agni leaned back in, his lips grinning.

"*Baron, did you have foreknowledge of Sir Frazi's trespass, as defined by the treaty that ended the Black Moon War?*"

"*I did not.*"

"*Under any circumstances, would you permit a lord to commit the crimes you have just described, let alone risk a resumption of the Black Moon War?*"

"*I would never.*"

Agni smiled and flexed his knife hand. Verlan just lost an important game piece.

"*And, mayor, how will you dispose of Sir Frazi's land, and that of his brothers?*"

"*I will seize it and return it to the care of Emperor Taran Solant to dispose of as he sees fit.*"

The oath was complete. For the first time, he had placed Duke Harkon in a position of power.

"And now, the vow you will take in the name of the empire, your god, and whatever shreds of honor you still cling to."

Goro trembled beneath him.

Agni poked the knife against the side of his neck, just beneath the skin, just enough to remind him of the cost of disobedience.

"Say it."

*"I beg the forgiveness of Duke Harkon and King Vardon of Blevenia, and I swear the following, on my wings. First, that I will personally oversee the execution of all who commit such crimes, strip their heirs of their birthright, that their name be buried in disgrace. Their lands, their titles, and their gold—I will return all to Emperor Taran Solant, as is just and right."*

Goro hesitated. Agni rippled his knuckles along the knife.

*"Second, that I will hold the emperor's peace. Not only by treaty but in word, in action, and in law. That I will break all lords who defy the will of Solantia, that Kazia may remain whole, and that Blevenia may know that the empire seeks not war, but peace."*

Goro's body sagged, spent.

The stone pulsed once, then dimmed.

Agni unwound Goro's hair, leaving his head to loll.

He stared at the trembling mayor and smiled.

"Well done, Baron," he beamed. "You have ensured a greater legacy than Verlan could ever grant you."

Goro lay limply over the boulder. Arno had only started to move, after the ravages of boulders and a dragon.

With little care, Agni patted them for weapons. Cutting off belts and straps, he tossed two swords, knives, and a mace over the cliffside.

Then Agni turned back toward the east, feeling the sun and wind against his wings. And again, he laughed like a madman—a deep, ragged laugh that echoed against the canyon walls. For a full minute.

"Now we part ways. Your sentry may arrive within an hour to horse you and return you west. I advise you not to pursue me. No one else needs to perish tod—"

Just then, Agni heard the thunder of approaching hoofbeats, sharp and fast against the canyon walls.

*Blast it. Perhaps I am not yet saved.*

He seized Goro's head again and pressed the blade deeper against his neck.

"If these are Solantian men," he warned, voice sharp as the mountain winds, "order them to stand down. One glint of steel, one cry for aid, and I tear open your throat, and glide west over this rock field where horses cannot follow."

Goro shuddered beneath his grip, but before he could rasp out a reply, the riders came into view. They did not arrive like knights; they whooped and hollered, voices loud and careless.

*Rem!*

"Azri of Azectrai, drop your weapon!" Rem bellowed.

Agni just grinned. They feared him. A lone, battered man with a knife to a noble's throat was still a threat to a band of riders.

Agni twisted Goro's head toward them, but he kept hold of his knife.

"Rem, Keron, I believe you intended to hand me over to this man," he called out. "However, as you can see, he is in no position to dispense reward or punishment."

Rem and Keron exchanged looks before urging their hoses closer, but they could not approach closer than twenty feet away.

Weapons were drawn, their eyes cautious.

"What have you done, Azri?" Rem asked, voice tinged with suspicion. "Why didn't you flee into the mountains or escape eastward?"

Agni laughed, as if the day itself protected him from death.

"Because death has stalked me for thirteen years in four lands. Once I saw my own men turn to quickfire and ravishment, I plotted to right that injustice. It required me to, shall we say, travel ahead of you. I apologize for sticking your poor watchman, but I could escape no other way."

He yanked Goro's head hard enough to make him wince.

"Behold, Baron Goro Kazimana, Mayor of Azectrai," he continued. "His hog of a son Arno. His bodyguards have been crushed or struck by a dragon's breath."

Keron cursed under his breath.

Rem's eyes narrowed.

Agni let the silence hang, watching as realization settled over them.

"Azri, by Varenox's eyelids, how did you—?"

*Time to tear off this mask,* he thought with a grin. *Now know with whom your fate weaves.*

"Azri?" Agni echoed. "A touching lie, but more believable than the truth."

"Mayor Goro, tell them who I am."

Goro hesitated, his pupils blown wide with panic.

"Speak!" Agni shouted in his ear.

The mayor stammered, voice cracking. "Y-y-you are… Agni Kazirian… Lord Guardian of the East, under the auspices of His Imperial Majesty, Emperor Taran Solant."

A stunned silence followed. Then, a sharp inhale.

Rem's jaw dropped. His knuckles whitened around the reins. Keron jerked back in his saddle as if struck.

One of the other riders whispered, "The Desolator."

"No, fool," Agni said, dropping the mayor's head back to the boulder. "Once, I was Lord Guardian of the East. Now, I am an outlaw. Captive for ransom. Estranged. Anathema. But I am still Agni Kazirian, who could pass through the Netherworld and remember his purpose."

His voice rang through the canyon as he watched their reactions with deep satisfaction.

Rem's lips parted, but no words came.

Keron's expression was characteristically unreadable, but his grip on the reins tightened, knuckles bone-white.

The Desolator. The Wolf of Azectrai.

Standing before them, blade in hand, voice unbroken, brimming with purpose.

"Now, Rem," he beseeched, "as Agni Kazirian, I need your aid."

Rem still had not moved.

"Some nights ago, I fled Azectrai under deep night, upon uncovering that this man had planned my assassination under false pretense. His lords covet land east of the Spires, and I stood in their path."

He lifted his red speaking-stone, letting its glow reflect in their wide eyes.

"He spoke a message of peace. I need you to assure that this stone reaches Duke Harkon's hands."

Rem finally breathed, sharp and shallow. His expression had hardened into something unreadable, but his eyes betrayed his thoughts.

"Agni Kazirian," Rem muttered, as if speaking the name would make it more real.

Agni simply tilted his head.

"You seem shaken, Rem."

Rem let out a sigh.

"Shaken?" he echoed. He gestured to the scene—the bodies, the ruin, the Mayor of Azectrai bleeding at Agni's feet.

Then he looked Agni directly in the eye.

"I thought we were ferrying a fugitive, not carrying history on our backs."

Agni chuckled, dark and wild. "History is written by those with the claws to carve it."

Keron finally spoke. "Agni Kazirian," he murmured, his first words.

"You knew him?"

Keron hesitated, a slow, grim nod.

"Only by name," Keron admitted. "The man who once held the East in his grip. Who stood proud before kings and emperors alike. And now, he humbles himself before outlaws."

Agni bared his teeth in a grin, again.

"And yes, before history," he added. "Which we shall now weave ourselves."

Rem nodded.

"Very well, Desolator." But he spoke it with respect.

"I thank you, Rem. If you had not waylaid me aboard the *Star of the Sea,* I might have only heard word of Verlan's next war from Solantian traders. This land scorched, my work undone. Now, I can cement that peace and look my beloved in the eye.

"And you have your purpose, Rem," he continued. "I want you to barter me to Duke Harkon—I will fetch a greater reward than this jackal and ten Solantian lords. Then, I will deliver this message. It will empower the duke against further intrusion. If he so desires, he will pass a message of peace westward. Two messages, one in either direction, will frustrate Verlan's ambitions for some time. Now, watch this message."

Agni held his treasure up towards Rem.

Goro's pathetic, coerced voice. But he, the poor victims of the manor raid, and now Rem and his men, had enough damning evidence on his treacherous countrymen.

"This message may spare the Dragonlands another Desolator," Agni said, with a smile. "Now, Mayor, up the slopes you may find sentries with palfreys to provision you home."

Goro weakly nodded.

"As for us, this message will be in Duke Harkon's hands before you reach Azectrai. Should you violate your oath, it will unleash a storm that the emperor himself cannot contain."

Rem nodded his head.

"Azri—Agni—I sense steel in your words. Let us make haste to Zarda. Keron?" Keron turned toward Rem. "Allow Agni the pleasure of the saddle for a time. We won't have to subdue him again."

Rem prepared Agni a saddle for the same horse that carried him trussed into the mountains.

"Goodbye, Goro. Goodbye, Arno. I do not believe we will see each other again."

They had made it to their feet, shaking and unsteady.

His horse lurched forward. Agni took a long look at the chaotic scene he left. The sentries had emerged from their hollow. They appeared bruised and bitten, but alive. He hoped that she-wolf was not rabid.

"Keron?" Agni said, unbuckling his belt.

"Here." Agni pulled off the belt, sword and knife holstered. "I will not be needing these."

Keron said nothing but wrapped the belt around his waist.

Agni thought he saw wonderment in Keron's eyes.

But Agni felt his own wonderment, that his own mad plan might bear fruit.

*Now to convince a duke who wants to gut me like a trout,* he thought.

———

The path wound through dense forest, shadows swaying in the breeze. An hour had passed in silence. Agni focused on his breath, willing himself not to think about the throbbing in his right leg. The pain, once a dull ache, had sharpened into something more insistent. Twice he had sprung off it, and were it not for his boot, his shin bones might have broken his skin.

He had known men who died of lesser wounds, but here in the wilderness, there was no Aira with a poultice to prevent fever, or laudanum to dull the agony. At best, the bandits might still have some ale. At worst, his leg might be lamed forever.

Rem and Keron had not spoken, but Agni could sense their thoughts.

*Common cause with the Desolator, cursed be his name,* he thought. Once, they would have delivered him to Duke Harkon in shackles. *Agni Kazirian, messenger of peace. Will Duke Harkon believe me? Can I dream of Avicia and my friends again?*

The questions proliferated in his mind.

And then, Rem broke the silence.

"Now I see it," he said, his voice thoughtful. "The power that broke our kingdom's back with a fraction of men and arms. Had I known you were Agni Kazirian, I would have hobbled your other leg and hooded you every step."

Agni smirked back.

"Or cut off my head," Agni replied. "Goro would have showered you with riches. And now, Duke Harkon might want it himself."

Agni sighed, reminding himself of his plight.

"But now, you are a messenger of peace."

It still sounded bizarre. He only grunted.

"Blevenians are a proud people, Agni," Rem continued, "as are you. But they are weary of conflict. The duke lost his two eldest sons, the jewels of his eyes. They say he spent ten days in his chamber, wailing."

Suddenly, it felt real. Memories of the Siege of Zarda. He may have cut Harkon's sons down with his own blade.

"All my men," Rem went on, his voice lower, "lost parents, siblings, children. And yet, they would forego revenge just to live like the humblest servants west of the Spires. We do not dream of conquest, Agni. We dream of a life where we can till the land and watch our sons grow."

Agni felt another twinge of guilt. He had never exchanged friendly words with his old foes.

"I hope I can give them that," Agni said, as much to himself as Rem.

He hesitated.

"From the night of the raid—the night I devised this plan—I called it 'folly.'" He glanced at Rem. "Yet it may deliver what years of war could not. That is why I want to travel to Avicia. Though I humiliated King Theodore, he knows what I am capable of. He and Emperor Taran are the two men whom the dukes fear."

Rem frowned.

"And what will you do in Avicia?"

Agni smiled. The first real smile since boarding the ship. "Guard Kazia from afar. Bide my time to strike. And…" his voice softened, "…raise a family with my beloved."

Rem's brows lifted. "The Aloi consort seen in your camp?"

Agni chuckled. "Kali, my love."

Saying her name aloud made the exhaustion in his body ease, if even for a moment.

"If not for her, I might have become another idle Western lord, fat and useless."

He pictured her, waiting in Avicia. Her fierce eyes, her sharp tongue, the passion that smote him.

"She will bear my children and carry my name," he said. "She awaits me."

"And should King Theodore refuse you?"

Agni shrugged. "Then I shall guard merchant convoys. It will be a poor fate, but if it leads me back to her, I will count the voyage as gain."

Rem looked him up and down for a long moment.

"No mere consort," he said at last, smiling. "I see hope glimmer in your eyes as you speak of her."

Agni did not speak, but he knew Rem was right. He could bleed, he could suffer, he could fight, but the thought of seeing Kali again made it all bearable. But first, he had to survive the wrath of the lord he had broken. And scrounge the equivalent of a thousand Solantian credits.

———

After some hours, the bandits found a clearing in which to make camp. Agni felt the eyes of the whole band upon him—like he was a curiosity, an impossibility, the face of the enemy, now their key to freedom.

As he was accustomed, Agni swung his right leg to dismount. But in his weakness, he stumbled over his left, landing flat on his back in the dirt.

For a moment, he lay still, mumbling a curse.

He struggled to flex his wings and roll to his side.

Then—laughter came from Rem and Keron.

"A minute, Agni."

Rem and Keron disappeared into the woods, then returned with a stout walking stick. And before he could jab it into the ground to pull himself up, two hands gripped him.

Instead, Keron muttered, "You stubborn bastard."

Rem snorted. "I thought the Desolator never fell."

Agni grinned, brushing dirt from his clothes.

"The Desolator also had two whole legs."

It was a simple gesture, but Agni felt something stir in his chest.

For the first time, Blevenian men had offered him kindness.

Agni fought the sting in his eyes.

A life of war. Mama's death. The Ancient City. The army. The Lord Guardianship.

He had never known mercy.

*Could mercy accomplish what a life of battle could not?*

C H A P T E R   2 0

## *River*

The downpour over the Great River came down in sheets, soaking Sara's white tunic until it clung to her every contour. She knew no one wandered near the bridge at this time of night. Duchesses had servants, admirers, and curious folk anywhere else. No moon sat in the sky; only violent flashes of lightning. Here, the patter of rain on water drowned out her sobs and washed away her tears.

And over the last several days, plenty of tears had flowed. As her return west drew near, despair tightened its grip on her. Her melodies grew heavy or stopped altogether. She spent hours pacing around the common, avoiding hushed whispers. She had even withdrawn from Nira, who seemed hurt by her silence.

If Father did not bequeath her the capital duchy, the dream she had nurtured for decades, what future did she have? She could never resign herself to the fate of a noble's brood mare. She had skill, intelligence, and benevolence that the Mortal Realms would never see. And yet that future stood before her—a fate she could neither fight nor flee. She was forced to admit the truth: that death, not just solitude, beckoned her to the river.

She slumped over the yard-high edge, staring at the black water rushing beneath her. Where had she gone astray? Was it her love of strong drink to dull the loneliness of the East? Without it, she would be halfway back to Artania, free of Agni, ready to rule the capital duchy on another's arm. Was it her deference to men like Goro the Avaricious or Orlan the Bloodless? She did not know what Father had promised them, but at his behest, they had sealed her fate long before she realized. Was it her failure to protect the gentle Dona? The image of her bloodied, caved-in head, bone exposed, haunted her. Or had the failure been in trusting Father at all? With his power and wealth, what could possibly satisfy him? The Crystal Throne itself?

She knew she could never escape his plans—or his wrath.

She had made peace with Aira and secured Nira's future until her boys came of age. Now, she gazed down at the river as it flooded the banks. She could swing her legs over and let the current embrace her like Mother once had. Her last act of free will. A fitting punishment for all she had done and all she had failed to do. *That my body would lie in Kazia.*

But she just stared. Unlike Agni, a warrior, she feared death.

Her gaze drifted across the river. The colossus loomed. The people of Azectrai spoke of it with reverence, as though its stones were still alive. The myths had spread even to Eltrazan, where Kazian and Western blood mingled. Agni had admonished her with tales of the undead abominations that would crush her bones, or worse, welcome her into their eternal host. Or the madness that had claimed the last man to enter.

A crude wooden palisade stood across the bridge, jagged timbers pointing toward the city in warning. It looked weak, ready to break at a single push. A mockery of a gate.

She could violate the law, defy the taboo, and find a fitting sentence inside the ruins. A punishment more terrifying than drowning. A conscious eternity of suffering for all the anguish she had caused. Like she deserved.

Then a voice spoke.

*The past is still, but never silent.*

*Never silent.*

*Never silent.*

Sara gasped. Her head whipped in both directions.

The words echoed in both ears at once, as if whispered from every shadow.

The bridge was empty. The storm raged on.

And yet, something watched her.

Her gaze snapped back to the Ancient City. She had looked upon it many times, but this time *it* looked back. A chill snaked down her spine.

Only one voice could speak with such power from the Ancient City.

She shuddered. After the Scourge, Agni had told her, Anton Kazirian vanished into the mists of history. A myth, a legend, a name spoken in whispers.

But he was here.

Why would he call to her? Why not Agni, his named descendant? Why not Father, a man consumed by ambition?

The thought filled her with dread but also awe. She had never felt so seen. So chosen. So called.Agni had sworn the last to enter had returned mad, his mind burned away, his body cleansed with flame. For two years, the Ancient City symbolized the old myth's hold on Agni's people. But had no one else heard the whisper? Had no child ever dared to test the myth? Or had no one been called?

Her pulse thundered in her ears. And then, without hesitation, she stepped around the wooden barrier.

The storm raged on, but she no longer felt its chill. No fear, no despair, no loneliness. Her life of doting servants and strict order fell away.

She was no longer running from death. She was running toward something greater.

As she approached the gates, she felt as though she had stepped into a hearth tale. Minutes ago, she had contemplated ending her life; now, she had crossed a threshold into something beyond it.

She had never seen fireglass, except in scrolls and books, only knew that it came from Blevenian volcanoes. But the ancients had studded the massive arch with it. It shimmered even in the darkness, pulsing with a faint light, as if it still remembered the power that once flowed through this city.

Two oaken doors, each twenty feet wide, loomed before her. They sat slightly ajar, an opening no wider than the breadth of her palm. She tried to slip a wing through, then an arm, but her shoulder caught between the doors. She gritted her teeth and pulled back. No grown man could fit through such a gap.

How had the last intruder—the one who had gone mad—entered and departed?

Agni's mammoth bodyguard, Alexander, the strongest man in the city, could not budge these doors. A child would scrape their back raw pulling past the splintered gate. The walls were too high, too smooth for even a mountain leopard to scale.

She stood there, breathing heavily, her mind spinning.

Then suddenly, a surge of strength coursed through her muscles.

Her hands trembled as she braced her feet against the left door, grasped the edge of the right, and pushed with all her might.

A low groan echoed through the air as the door inched open.

Her heart slammed in her chest—had she done that?

*Agni once told me of the feats of strength desperate men could perform. Or has the master of this city invited me in?* she thought.

Her shoulder passed easily now. Then, flattening one breast at a time, she wedged the rest of herself through.

She had entered the Ancient City.

And Anton Kazirian was waiting.

Before her stretched a vision more splendid than anything she had ever imagined, more glorious than even the soaring towers of Artania. The masonry, the intricate carvings, the sheer scale of the city bested even Emperor Taran's palace. Here, the very stones whispered of an empire long buried but never forgotten. This city—this monument—held more fireglass than all the miners in the Dragonlands could extract in a lifetime. Agni had spoken of how kings from across the Mortal Realms once bent the knee to his ancestor, but she had never truly believed it until now.

*And now I know,* she whispered to herself.

She should have felt fear, should have reached for the dagger at her hip, but instead, she smiled. The place held no menace, only a solemn, eternal beauty. Like a dream she had stumbled into, weightless and surreal. The Scourge had not merely killed this city. It had stilled it, left it untouched, as if the people had simply abandoned their work mid-thought.

A smith's hammer and tongs lay beside his bones, his half-finished sword still gleaming, untouched by rust. And in the middle of a street, a dragon's skeleton sat, coiled in what could have been sleep, its bones untouched by time.

Only an eerie beauty.

She wandered the streets in a trance, tracing the walls with her fingertips, pressing her palms against the ancient stone as if to absorb its story. Half an hour passed—maybe more—before she reached the castle at the heart of the city, the jewel of this lost empire. How many times had she gazed at it from across the river, a silhouette against the rising sun? How many nights had she imagined the secrets within? Now, up close, it was more than she had dreamed. The towers did not reflect the storm's lightning. They absorbed it, drank in the glow.

The grand gate loomed before her. She hesitated at the threshold, a tremor running through her. This was a threshold—no longer just into a ruin, or even a legend… This was the past, awaiting her.

The great hall stretched before her, flanked by statuary so lifelike she half-expected the figures to step forward and greet her. These were not grim-faced knights frozen in western marble. The dragons, too, were not snarling predators, but serene, almost benevolent.

For the first time in years, Duchess Sara Ristana felt small—and that thought calmed her.

At the head of the hall, where the emperor once sat, loomed a throne of fireglass. Not just a seat of power—a thing of worship. It gleamed purple-black, its surface shifting like stars trapped beneath a crystal. Behind it were three towering spires of fireglass, shaped like daggers, that nearly reached the ceiling. Was this the work of Anton Kazirian, the conqueror whom history had reduced to a whisper, but Azectrai still half-remembered in legend?

She approached the throne with reverence, her head dipping slightly, as if stepping into Emperor Taran's. The armrests were carved into dragons' heads, their gleaming eyes watching her. She felt something here—not the seething undead horde Agni had spoken of, but something sacred.

*He feared this place, forbade me from it—had he too, felt unworthy?* she thought.

The throne shimmered. The fireglass pulsed, dark and inviting. A welcome.

Sara hesitated.

She had never dared sit upon Emperor Taran's chair of western crystal. But this? This was different. This throne wanted her.

With a deep breath, she placed one hand on the armrest, then the other, and pulled herself up. The fireglass felt warm beneath her fingertips. She sank into the seat, feeling like a little girl on her father's chair. A warm wind swept through the chamber, caressing her skin like a lover's whisper.

*Never silent.*

The words resonated in her bones.

A bolt of lightning split the sky. The throne flashed.

Then twice more.

Any then, beyond the great hall, in the farthest reaches of the chamber, something shifted.

The castle had hidden something from all but the one meant to see it. But from her vantage point, it was unmistakable.

A grand marble staircase, leading downward, deep into the true heart of the castle—the essence of Kazia itself.

She shivered. The Ancient City, the castle gate, the throne—it had all led her here, the next step into a dream from which she dared not wake. She rose, her breath quickening, and descended.

The deeper she went, the more time itself unraveled.

For the first time this night, she saw decay—the pristine marble of the upper floors gave way to faded stone, then to shattered remnants. And yet ahead, a soft blue glow grew brighter, pulsing like a heartbeat.

The air hummed with a presence she could not name.

Then, the sound of armor rattling below.

She froze. It was not thunder, not a trick of her ears.

Her pulse hammered with something between terror and rapture.

She stepped forward. The glow grew blinding. It had no source—no torches, no lanterns—yet it filled the space with the brilliance of daylight.

And then she saw them.

Rows of men lined the chamber walls, their armor shimmering like mist. Not statues, not echoes. Ghosts. A company of warriors, waiting, their weapons raised in salute. They had waited for her, like Father's hard men sworn to protect her.

Her mouth went dry. No sight tonight had prepared her for this.

They moved. They marched. And then they shouted, *"Zaka tai!"*

She gasped. The Kazirian family motto, one of the few phrases she knew in the ancient tongue.

*"All who stand against us shall fall."*

Why would they chant that to her?

Then more words, and this time, they did not feel foreign.

*"Ha-ve Akatra Sara!"*

She gasped. She understood a language that she had never heard.

"Hail, Empress Sara."

*Empress?* Her head spun. Emperor Taran's men would cut out any tongue that spoke such treason.

*"Ar Kazi gotruk jai!"*

She knew this one, too.

"We will return the Dragon to the skies!"

Not a dragon. *The* Dragon.

The Empire Kazia. "Land of Dragons."

This was not a mere chant—this was a sacred oath.

The dead had waited for a leader. And they had chosen her.

Her hands trembled. She had come to this city in despair, in ruin. She had been ready to surrender her life to the river.

Now, the dead hailed her as their sovereign.

A final chant rose, filling the chamber, rolling through her heart like thunder.

*"Truve a matruk yara!"*

"Under her benevolent gaze!"

She had not felt benevolent in moons. But they saw something in her.

She racked her mind for explanations: *A trick of the light? A lingering effect of mandrake? Did Agni teach her those words? Was this the madness of the Ancient City?*

Her reason could not pierce this.

Her gaze drifted forward. At the end of the chamber sat a marble slab, glowing softly, etched with the dragon-on-tower crest. Agni's crest.

Before she could think, she placed her palms against it. A rush of warmth poured into her, as if something had been waiting to fill her, to claim her, to make her whole.

The smoke coalesced before her. A figure took shape. Towering. Wings shimmering like fireglass. Hair dark and rippling like storm clouds. His hand pressed to her shoulder.

A command. A comfort.

She dropped to one knee, until it gestured to bid her rise. It had not spoken a word, but she knew its name.

And that Anton Kazirian cherished her.

*"Blessed Ancestor, your will be done. May your power ripple forth from this city once more."*

Sara's words trembled. Not from fear, but from something deeper, something reverent. Words of praise poured from her lips in Ancient Kazian, a tongue she had never heard. They belonged to her now, as if they had been waiting, buried in her blood.

Anton Kazirian smiled, a calm, powerful smile, that of a man who commanded fate itself.

*"Sweet, noble Sara,"* he intoned. *"It was I who summoned you. I will let nothing harm you this night."*

His presence thrummed through her bones, deeper than any mortal voice. It was rapture, effortless and all-consuming. She had never heard Agni, nor even Father, speak with such weight, as if woven into the very fabric of the world.

*"You are Emperor Anton Kazirian,"* she breathed, chest tightening with awe, *"last-born of the Dragon God, conqueror of the Dragonlands and lord of Great Kazia."*

Her tutors had dismissed him as a myth, a relic of old stories. How ignorant! He was as real as her wings.

Anton's spectrum brow furrowed. Was that sorrow? Could a shade mourn?

*"That I was,"* he spoke, *"and once again will be."*

He spoke with the surety of one who did not just believe—he *knew*.

She swallowed. *"I sense pain in your voice, Ancient One. The pain of seeing your work undone, and the hatred of that who once loved you."*

Anton tilted his head, as if amused by her insight.

*"You see well, Lady Sara. My empire has been reduced to dust, and I to a lord of the undead, frozen in time."* His voice turned somber. *"You call me blessed, but I am most cursed of my father. As are you."*

Sara's lips parted.

*"Cursed? Or merely unfortunate? Discarded by my father, denied my destiny. How can you see this, Imperial Majesty?"*

Anton leaned in closer, his presence enveloping her. *"You ask how I see this? How I know your heart?"* A whisper penetrated her mind. *"I have seen the currents of fate for two millennia. Eighty generations of our line. I hear our blood crying out for its birthright. To return to the skies, and I to my divine father's side. Now that you have harkened to my voice, we are bound by something deeper than blood."* He did not blink. *"Our god fated you to leap from the bridge tonight."*

Sara gasped, a chill coiling around her spine. She could not admit her despair even to herself. Yet Anton had seen. Westerners had little use for fate but knew defying the Dragon God to be a dangerous game.

*"I would not accept it,"* Anton said smoothly. *"The Dragon God may weave fate, but I may turn it aside."*

The weight of his words felt like a boulder. She had been chosen.

*"The most excellent of your kin?"* Her voice was small, skeptical. *"I am but a duchess in disfavor."*

Anton's smirk was indulgent, like a tutor amused by a child's ignorance. *"A duchess? That title will perish with the old order. I do not call you duchess. You will be greater. I call you Lady Sara, for you will be noble in any land."*

She shuddered.

*"But how?"* she whispered. *"How will you subdue two of the greatest powers of the Mortal Realms from this forgotten city?"*

Anton laughed, a deep, rich sound, filled with ambition, pain, and hope. His fingers ran over the marble slab, its dragon-crest pulsing beneath his touch. *"Ah, my lady. The Mortal Realms believe this city a tomb. A realm of wraiths and madness. That belief serves me—they know not that I hold them at bay. But the truth, as always, is far more useful."*

The mist shifted, as if watching.

*"The spirits of my paladins remain,"* he said, gesturing at the silent warriors. *"You see but few. One day they will take flesh—not as rotten wights animated by the Scourge, but as men and women. As conquerors. As will I."*

Sara felt dizzy.

*"And as I do,"* Anton continued, *"you will be at my side."*

Never had Sara felt so unworthy. This higher power offered her everything.

*"I have nothing to give,"* she admitted, her voice unsteady. *"I am no commander of men. My betrothed, your named descendant, who has cost me my most fertile years—he was the warlord. He conquered distant lands. I..."* she hesitated, *"I am but a noblewoman in disgrace."*

Anton's expression darkened.

*"He has strength,"* his voice grew softer, dangerous. *"But he strays far from the path."*

Sara stiffened.

*"Have you called to him? He could sweep the land with your armies."*

Disgust crossed Anton's face. Did he just spit?

*"The living flame is but dying embers."* His words cut through the trance. *"What spirit he has! But like a scrap of birch bark, he burns bright but short. He lives, but his days are few. A flame that consumes itself. You will never see him again."*

Sara's jaw dropped. *Never?*

A part of her that still seethed with betrayal rejoiced. Agni, who had humiliated her, stolen from her—would be lost to the world. He was anathema in two nations; like a pincer, they would crush him. Yet, another part mourned.

Anton spoke not with boastful pride, but with certainty, as if Agni were already lost to time.

*"And Father?"*

*"He is of little consequence to our ambitions. Like all lords, he will join us or be swept away. Modern arms and magic are unprepared for the secrets of the Ancients."*

Sara shivered. The world, the nature of power, so steady for decades, had just shifted beneath her feet. She strained to comprehend a force that could sweep Father away.

*"An hour ago, such a statement would feel like madness. But I can only run your levies. Why did you wait two thousand years for me?"*

Anton chuckled. His wings shimmered.

*"No. You would be wasted on collecting levies. I have watched you, Sara Ristana, for twenty years. You do not share my name, but my blood suffuses the Dragonlands. Through it, I have watched you learn. I have seen you withstand forces that could break lesser. I need one of noble birth and strong heart to serve as my regent. One who*

*can navigate this realm like salmon navigate the great river."* His eyes gleamed. *"From the moment you set foot in Azectrai, I knew that you were ready. I chose your most vulnerable moment to call you. The moment at which you were ready to part with your old life. You are worthy."*

Sara's vision blurred with tears. *When was the last time anyone called me worthy?* Anton had seen her all along. Another wave of warmth suffused her. Was this real?

*"But an hour ago, this night felt like a fantasy. How can I know you speak truth?"*

Anton nodded his head. *"Return to the bridge and you will see a sign."*

*"A sign?"*

*"You will know it when it comes."* He gave a reassuring smile. *"As the moons pass, the signs will multiply. Kazia has risen from its slumber. It will not be contained."*

Sara trembled with excitement. She had wanted to die; now, she would rule.

Her breath caught.

*"What shall I do? I will return to Father's side soon."*

Anton reached out a ghostly hand, resting it on her shoulder. The warmth was intoxicating.

*"Be a dutiful daughter,"* he whispered. *"Be a strong duchess. Play your part until the appointed time."*

*"And Solantia?"*

*"Solantia still walks the path of the Dragon."* His voice dipped into something deeper, darker. *"Blevenia does not. And for that, I will guide Solantia to victory."*

Sara's heart pounded, but she said nothing.

Anton's voice remained impassive. *"Know that no mortal man can unite the squabbling Dragonlands. The wounds of war fester; the cure must be imposed from without. When the people seek an end to war, I will unite them under the banner of Great Kazia."*

*"But many of our brothers and sisters will die."*

Anton sighed.

*"Like a woman in childbirth, these pains will be short and sharp, but joy will follow. The Empire Kazia will serve as a beacon of law and learning. Our medicines will cheat death, and the arts of peace will calm hearts. We will reign a thousand years before we pass to the Lands Beyond."*

Sara felt entranced, her mind swimming between awake and dreaming. Agni, even Father, paled before Anton Kazirian.

*"Your vision intoxicates me,"* she admitted, voice hushed. *"But Father will seek to wed me to another."*

Anton flashed an easy smile. *"Let him. Bear another's children. Bide your time. Your finest will be lords and ladies of Great Kazia. Watch for my signs. Listen for my voice. I will guide you."*

Sara's eyes widened.

*"You would still care for me,"* she whispered, *"even as my power in the Mortal Realms fades?"*

Anton laughed, low and rich. *"I have cared for you long before you realized your own strength. As you suffered my rogue scion, I watched and waited."* His voice softened to something near affection. *"Your patience, your resolve—it is why you are here. And now, I return your faith in me with a token of mine."*

A shimmer of silver caught her eye. Anton's spectral hand emerged from the slab, holding a silver ring. The signet gleamed, the Kazirian crest carved into dark metal, pulsing softly, like a heartbeat.

Sara slowly extended a hand for it. When her fingers closed around the band, a warmth radiated up her arm, a quiet power.

*"Thank you,"* she murmured. *"It is beautiful."*

Anton smiled, as if they were now co-conspirators.

*"It will pass for one of Agni's trinkets. Tell your servants it is a memento, if they ask. But it will not be taken from you. Put it on."*

Without words, Sara slid it on her finger. It fit perfectly.

*"As long as it sits upon your hand, you will find your tongue sharp and your will strong. One day, it will mark you as the hand that commands the Dragonlands. For Great Kazia cannot be ruled by arms alone."*

A chill ran through her. Anton's words told her she had what Agni did not—the skill to rule, rather than just command.

She clenched and unclenched her hand, feeling the ring against her skin.

*"Your will be done, Blessed Ancestor."*

Anton exhaled, his form flickering like mist.

*"Now go. Never again return to this city, nor speak of this night."* His eyes burned with an emperor's will. *"But know this, Lady Sara—your time is near. I will guide you."* The mist around him thickened, swallowing his form. *"And then I will crown you. Until then, live and wait in hope."*

"I will live and wait in hope." Sara's lips barely moved.

Anton's form flickered like mist—and then, he was gone.

The grand procession of warriors had vanished. The crest upon the slab faded, again no more than carved stone.

Yet the ring pulsed against her finger.

*The only memento of a dream.*

———

The ascent up the grand staircase was slow, as if her body willed itself to stay in the dream. With each step, the weight of the Mortal Realms settled over her. Time itself felt uncertain. *Had it been an hour? A night? A moon? A lifetime?*

As the castle's grand halls gave way to empty streets, the last remnants of Anton's presence fell away. The silence of the ruined city stretched out before her, but now it felt different. It no longer felt devoid of life—it was slumbering. Waiting.

Sara quickened her pace, suddenly aware of how deep she had wandered into the forbidden. She did not wish to test the town's laws, even against a high noble.

But beyond the palisade would lay a sign.

Her pulse quickened as she approached where she had once prepared to die.

The storm had lifted, leaving a beautiful starscape behind, mirrored in the still waters of the Great River. The air smelled of rain and earth, fresh as though the storm had purified the land.

She stepped forward, peering over the ledge. She only saw swirling water below. But Anton had said to wait.

Then, the ring pulsed.

Sara gasped as the warmth again spread through her skin.

Two salmon—one great, one small—swimming upstream, their tails swishing as the fought the current, glowing the same as the ring.

Anton's words rang in her mind. *One who can navigate this realm like salmon navigate the great river.*

The great and the small. The ancient emperor and dishonored duchess—both forgotten—defying the currents of fate.

It was real. He had chosen her.

Her body trembled, but she did not falter.

Her feet were light; her path was clear.

Meanwhile, Azectrai slept, the streets silent as she slipped through them. The ring pressed into her plan.

By the time she reached the Kazirian house, she was drenched anew—this time with the sweat of excitement.

A guard stirred as she rounded Knight Lane.

"Who approaches? Identify yourself."

Sara raised her finger. The ring pulsed.

The guard's eyes lowered.

"Apologies, my lady. I didn't recognize you."

Her lips curled into a faint smile. *No, you would not.*

Within minutes, she was back in her chamber. Slowly, deliberately, she peeled off her soaked tunic, wiping her body free of rain and sweat.

Only after she divested all her clothing did she remove the ring. She slipped it into Agni's coin chest, watching it fall among coins and trinkets. It blended in.

*Symbolic. It is all that I have, but it is enough.*

She slipped into dry linens and touched her bare finger, almost mourning the absence of its warmth.

But it did not matter. It was hers. And one day, it would not lie hidden.

Sara slid beneath the blankets.

Her last thought before the world darkened was not of Agni, nor Father.

It was Anton's voice, whispering from the shadows, feeling more real than the last two years.

*Live and wait in hope.*

C H A P T E R   2 1

# *Captive*

Agni rode unbound, the wind tousling his hair, carrying the scent of dry grass and pine. Even when it stung his wounds, he welcomed it. It was a reminder that he still lived. That his body, broken as it was, had carried him this far.

Whenever he closed his eyes, the breeze became Kali's fingertips and claws, softly grazing his skin. The laughter of the bandits behind him became Alexander's booming voice, hearty, reassuring, and wise. For the first time in a moon, he felt hope that his god would not take him.

That night, they made camp where the Spires gave way to rolling foothills. The land was open and the air crisp. As the bandits settled by the fire, Agni hobbled a short way up the hill, his new oak walking stick tapping the ground with each step.

The sunset stained the Spires red and orange.

*A stroke of fortune that I could beat a message out of the mayor,* he thought. *But should I die tomorrow, I should die protecting my home.*

He recognized Keron's footsteps, unhurried and deliberate. For once, he did not fear them.

"Good evening, sir," he said.

"Hello, High General," Keron replied with a touch of amusement.

"Come closer, Keron. I will not strike."

"Come now, High General." Keron chuckled, stepping closer. "I would love a night without fearing for my rump."

Agni smirked back.

"Then I suppose I should ease your worries. Please, call me Agni."

Keron nodded, watching the horizon as he stood beside Agni.

"Two nights of noble deeds have earned my regard. You know I don't give it lightly. Whatever comes of you at the duke's keep, we'll remember you."

Agni turned to him.

"Thank you, Keron. I did not expect even a smile from you, let alone your regard."

Keron let out a sharp laugh. "I wouldn't have gifted you that had I not known you had the power to let us live like men again. I had lost hope for that."

Agni's smile faltered.

"I hope the duke will listen. If he does not, and word spreads that he executed Agni Kazirian, Kazia may raise the banner of war, and Solantian men will flood this land." He watched the last sliver of sun sink below the horizon. "I hope I am still a hero to my people."

Keron scoffed. "Lords dream, and the rest of us quake."

Agni let out a tired chuckle. "Indeed. Once, I only wanted a tranquil life. No war, no schemes. But with every step—soldier, captain, general, High General—I was pulled in deeper." His grip tightened on his walking stick. "I thought I could freeze history itself."

"Are you relieved to see an end to that?"

Agni spat into the dirt.

"I will not. If I counsel King Theodore, the most powerful man in the Mortal Realms, I will spar with potentates, not just lords. I fall deeper into this game."

"At least you won't spar with gods." Keron sighed.

Agni's expression darkened.

"I feel like I have dueled with the God of Fate for two decades. If he favors me, I do not know of it."

*And his child,* he thought. *Neither is finished with me.*

Keron exhaled sharply.

"That sounds right. I knew Azri of Azectrai was a lie because you never accepted your captivity. Even with a knife to your throat, you fought. I woke up after your escape to find Noton dead beside me. I recognized the look of a strangled man—before you cut his throat. Escaping from two armed men while bound, that was no ordinary man's work."

Agni's stomach turned.

"If he had woken, my life was forfeit. I am sorry."

"I understand. A bandit's life is meager and cheap." He was quiet for a moment, then continued. "I hated you because Azri's story felt too familiar."

Agni frowned.

"How so?"

Keron hesitated. "I was born not Keron, but Kero."

Agni turned to him, eyes wide.

"Kero? That is a Kazian name. Are you—"

Keron's voice trembled. "Like Azri, my sadistic prick of a lord beat my wife when she was with child. Only she did not survive. But I could not drive a stake through my lord's heart, nor steal his coins. I fled into the night like a coward. And when Rem found me, I was faint from lack of food. It was as if you knew my story—only you had the courage that I did not."

Agni shook his head, his voice lowering. "I knew no such thing. As I spoke to Rem, I crafted a pretext to flee the Dragonlands."

"Rem knew Azri was a lie; that small folk know Avicia as a myth. Even with ten thousand credits, they would not think to flee there. That you didn't act like a peasant, you acted accustomed to command, even as you shrank your voice. But your conviction made us doubt it."

Agni beamed.

"Did none of your band recognize me? I imagine some fought my armies."

Keron snorted back. "Agni Kazirian was a legend. A twelve-foot-tall giant with a sword of pure lightning on a white demon steed. No one expected a wretch on the arse-end of a mutiny who puked in a hood."

Agni laughed. "My beloved horse. Arkama, or Ark for short. A mighty stallion who charges into fire and screams but sputters at winter breezes. In Avicia, he grumbled more than any man in my command."

"Arkama," Keron mused. "White Giant. A fitting name."

Agni looked westward, longingly picturing Ark's stable. "I hope he is well," he said wistfully. "Even if I never return, may he live a thousand years."

"Do you think you'll ever return?"

"I do," Agni admitted. "Someday. Even if hunched and gray. It is said that a Kazian grows weary outside his homeland."

Keron went silent for a moment, then sighed. "I don't believe those tales."

"No?"

Keron shook his head. "Kazia holds nothing but pain for me."

Agni studied Keron, then nodded. "But wherever you settle, Keron, I wish you peace."

"And I, you." Keron met his gaze, as equals. *As men.* "You offer yourself up so that we might have freedom and peace. We will never forget this."

"A warrior fulfills his mission unto his last breath," Agni replied.

"Whatever comes of you, it won't be in vain."

"May it be so."

They stood in silence as the sunset glow faded from the sky. On instinct, Agni muttered a short prayer to the god that loathed him. Anything to steel himself for the coming meeting.

As they returned to camp, Keron walked beside him—not as a captor, but as a friend.

For the first time in what felt like ages, Agni felt something akin to peace as he fell into a dreamless sleep.

———

For four days, Agni watched the Blevenian plains stretch endlessly before him, fields of wheat on one side, wild grasses swaying on the other. Once, his horsemen trampled this land into dust. Even now, they did not look as golden as he first saw them. The scars of war remained.

*A general's duty,* he thought. *Would I have not done so if I had foreseen the suffering that would follow? We flourished while Blevenia withered. We called it the favor of our god.*

By tomorrow, they would reach Duke Harkon's castle. He would be imprisoned, that much was certain. If Duke Harkon would not grant him an audience, or believe his archenemy, Agni had willingly walked to his own execution. He could not present himself as a Kazian emissary, not in his dilapidated state, surrounded by Blevenian bandits. Nor did he hold a threat. *All I can do is trust in the power of mercy. That which I would not grant.*

The Spires stood like distant bumps on the horizon as the bandits made camp in a sparse grove of trees. The sun lingered, splashing light over the plains. Agni settled against a rock when he heard footsteps crunch against the dry grass.

"You've been silent today," Rem said, his tone more thoughtful than prying.

"I needed solitude," Agni replied. "Before battle—or parley."

Rem folded his arms.

"Am I intruding?"

"No," Agni admitted. "I know what I must say to the duke." "Do you believe he will listen?"

Agni sighed. "I parleyed with the King of Avicia once. Though then, I had the threat of dark magic on my side." He tapped his chest. "Now, I have only my voice and the promise of peace. He may still have me thrown from his tower, and I accept that."

Rem studied Agni for a long moment.

"There's power in what you have," he said at last.

Agni returned a tired smile.

"I have lost everything else. But I may regain something greater. Something I lost over two decades ago."

Rem cocked his head.

"What's that?"

Agni bowed his head, solemn.

"Freedom from the shackles of my past. I always knew I would become a lord and a soldier, but not a conqueror. Not until a raider ravished and killed my mother before my eyes did I thirst for battle. After years of it, revenge turned to duty, and duty to habit. War became my craft, like a smith." He paused. "Even if a sword gives me comfort, I will need another craft."

Rem listened silently. No trenchant observation waited on his tongue.

"I tell myself that I am Agni Kazirian, and I can accomplish any deed," he continued. "But I do not know what follows."

Rem broke his silence with a simple question. "Do you regret it?"

"Regret what?"

Agni stared at him, but Rem's gaze did not waver.

"All of it. Blevenia, Avicia, the war. Do you regret it?"

Agni hesitated, then spoke slowly, as if in confession. "Until a few nights ago, I did not. A soldier may choose whether to give a mercy blow. A High General must decide whether to kill one thousand or ten thousand to accomplish his mission. I believed I chose the righteous path."

His jaw clenched.

"But something Sir Frazi—the knight from whom you saved me—said. That I taught my men that insects deserved more compassion than our enemies. That we crush ants under our boots and never think of them again. I never used those words. But in ordering them to raze villages, did I train them to ravish washerwomen all the same?"

His wings twitched, as if feeling a new pain.

"I did not experience this land's suffering. It would be fitting to sacrifice myself in pursuit of its peace."

Rem nodded. "Ever the soldier."

"*Ai.*" Agni exhaled. "A warrior of Kazia, for one final act." He glanced back at Rem. "And you? What will you do with your freedom?"

Rem smirked.

"A general plans a campaign. A rogue lives in the moment." His smile softened. "But survive, I will. I'll take a wife, a city house, a few brats running underfoot."

Agni chuckled back. "You are a leader of men, my friend. I have seen how the band follows your voice. Perhaps you may become a steward, even a seneschal."

"Perhaps," Rem said with a shrug. "In time." Then his grin returned. "But for now, I may just try to bed the most beautiful woman in Blevenia."

Agni chuckled. "And may you succeed."

Rem raised a brow. "And you, in Avicia."

Agni's lips turned into a wistful smile.

"By Varenox's eyes, I already have."

Rem patted him on the wing. "Then may she be waiting for you."

Agni let out a breath he had not realized he was holding. *By our gods, sweet Kali. Arrive safely.*

"Thank you, Rem."

Rem nodded.

"You have quite a day ahead. I'll let you prepare."

Agni watched Rem walk off, his steps light. He was not the same man who had bound him at three points. But nor was Agni the same man they captured.

Agni hobbled back to his bedroll.

As the moon and stars flickered into view, Agni listened to the soon-to-be freed men banter and sing.

*Let me sleep as lightly as they do tonight.*

———

At first, there was only warmth. Agni drifted through golden light, weightless, untethered from suffering. In a space outside time, he felt Kali's breath on his neck, her lips against his chest, her fingertips against his back. His hands ran through her red hair, fine as silk. She whispered his name like a prayer, her voice woven into the melody of the world itself. Like lovemaking, but with a connection of which two mortals could only dream.

*Ecstasy.*

Then the golden light deepened into a rich azure, warm and intoxicating. It pulsed with every beat of his heart. He soared, gliding effortlessly on unseen currents like a dragon. His wings angled, banking him to one side, then the other, a weightless thrill. He frolicked like a spirit unfettered, free of despair and want. Free from the wars that defined him, from Anton, from the gods.

He closed his eyes and let the feeling consume him.

The moment lacked for nothing—it was perfect.

The light dimmed.

First to twilight.

Then to a moonless night.

Then to a horrible blackness that absorbed all light. Deep, hungry, devouring all.

The weightlessness and freedom vanished. He fell from the sky into water blacker than fireglass.

A liquid void swallowed him whole, sank icy tendrils into his skin, froze him in place.

He struggled, gasping for breath, but the blackness rushed into his mouth, his throat, his lungs. There was no air here. No escape.

The Voice of Ages emerged from the abyss, a silver specter in a sea of black.

*"Ungrateful boy,"* Anton scolded. Mocking. Cruel.

Agni tried to move, but his body would not obey. Numb. Arms locked in place, wings spread in alarm, his lips parted in a silent scream, even his hair froze in a tousled state.

Fading from existence. The Netherworld, coming to claim its own.

*"Indeed,"* Anton snarled, his voice sharp as a dagger. *"I see why I chose you all those yours ago. Strength, determination—yes, you had those. I was patient with you, generous. But I underestimated your lack of vision."*

Agni could not speak.

Anton's dark eyes gleamed like a predator's in the dark.

*"But you have proven yourself a disappointment."*

Something wrenched inside Agni, a twisting agony deeper than the numbing ice. As if unseen hands crushed his body, his very essence.

*"I no longer need you,"* Anton said. *"Another has harkened to my voice. Another has taken the birthright you discarded."*

Agni tried to force his reasoning mind through the horror—who had Anton chosen? Who would hold the title meant for him? But the gloom overwhelmed him. A scream, a wail built inside his chest but never reached his throat.

*"Oh, how it must wound you,"* Anton taunted. *"To know that another will bring the peace you sought."*

Agni's vision snapped open to a new pain.

Before him rose the Ancient City, restored. A city of impossible beauty, shimmering dark in the noonday sun. Walls of fireglass above a people reborn.

Dragons lay in the streets. Children laughed, their tiny hands stroking the scaled behemoths' heads as if they were no more fearsome than a family hound. Men and women, warriors and scholars alike, strolled through streets paved in statuary, their eyes bright in the knowledge that their empire was eternal.

Agni ached at the sight. His people. His land. His legacy.

*"Behold,"* Anton proclaimed, his voice booming through Agni's ears. *"A land where neither man nor cattle need fear the dragon's claws. A land where the Kazirian name stands between men and gods."*

Anguish bubbled up to his eyes but with no release.

*"You will watch it rise from the Netherworld."* Anton laughed. *"As you gnash your teeth."*

The image collapsed. The thriving city perished before his eyes. Man, woman, child, horse, dragon all crumbled to skeletal dust. Once more frozen outside time.

His vision snapped back to Anton's terrible glowing eyes.

*"Another will take your place as Lord Regent,"* Anton growled. *"One who will not hesitate to raise our banner. One, who burns so brightly for the Empire Kazia, that they will not question what must be done to revive it. This realm will bathe in blood until it submits to us."*

Anton's anger turned to mocking laughter.

*"At best, your laughable scheme would fail. The Dragon God will not save you. You will be thrown from Duke Harkon's tower, your body fed to pigs."*

The specter leaned in close, his eyes drawing Agni in like a whirlpool. *"I regret that I could not end you with my own body."* Anton's voice dropped to a whisper. *"I will leave you in this dream. Through the duke, you will face the wrath of your sins."*

Anton's image drew ever closer, his terrifying visage occupying all of Agni's vision.

*"And I will let the Dragon God's fate take its course."*

Agni's scream finally tore from his throat, raw and endless—but no sound came.

He awoke to darkness. His body was ice, like a corpse's. His limbs would not move. His throat was raw, yet silent. A black haze covered his vision. His mind partway to the Netherworld, his body soon to follow.

Through it, he heard a rustle of leaves.

A shadow coalesced into a hand. But it turned into a claw, scaled and twisted.

His mind recoiled, but his body remained paralyzed.

"Agni, are you well?"

"He's sweating the Great Sea itself," a second voice said.

His tongue would not move. He wanted to scream the name of Anton Kazirian, that he was dying, but nothing came.

"He's having a night terror," someone murmured. "Leave him be."

A hand patted him on the shoulder—a hand that felt like a red-hot poker.

"Just a dream, Agni. Good night."

*Na,* he wanted to scream. This nightmare had not ended. And it never would.

Not in the Mortal Realms or the next world.

Agni could see the sun rise through the dark haze, as if it were aflame, but it did not feel real. It shifted. Melted. Twisted into Anton's will.

His body moved as the bandits lifted him onto the cart, but he did not feel it—only a distant sensation, as if his body were a lifeless shell. The ropes around his wrists were like living serpents, their scales scraping beneath his skin, beneath the numbness. The gag pressed into his mouth, thick as a bloated tongue.

Above him, the sky churned. Clouds stretched into grasping hands, claws curling as they reached for him. The cart's dust clouds turned into visages of death. Children's flesh stripped from their bones. His broken father walking into the Great River, never to emerge. But worst was the whispering of something far older—something below the ground, waiting to consume him, body and essence.

Only one thought comforted him, that he would again feel raw agony in the Netherworld that might muffle the greater pain in his heart. But if the gods punished the wicked with their worst torment, they would lock him in this state for eternity, only while his homeland burned with the flames of war.

He shut his eyes to no avail. The horrors still formed in the darkness.

The city square swirled in a cacophony of sound and movement. The shouts of merchants turned to the wails of the tormented. The scent of roasting meat soured into that of charred corpses.

Agni could see the dead. Worse, he recognized them. Stabbed. Burned. Festered. Drowned. And they screamed his name.

*"Agni... by our god, no!"*

*"Butcher!"*

*"Kill him! Kill him! Burn him!"*

Bloated bodies hung from the rafters of merchant stalls, their lifeless eyes tracking him.

A child—or something wearing the shape of a child—ran past the cart. Its skin peeled in ribbons, revealing veins black as tar. Its mouth stretched unnaturally wide, full of fangs. It turned a lidless gaze upon him and let out a scream that shattered the skies.

It felt more real than the cart under his back.

The voices pierced his ears.

Real or not, he knew this was his doing. His eternal penance.

Anton had promised he would remember all his sins. Now, he did.

The walls of Zarda closed in, squeezing, crushing like a tomb.

The castle from which he would fall. The towers above twisted into clawed hands, as if ready to drop him themselves.

The sky shimmered with dark menace. And in it a reflection. Anton.

Bearing his own face.

*"Welcome to your eternal rest, Agni."*

He gasped, but no air came. Suffocating, but kept alive by pain.

Then, Rem's calming voice, turned into a high shriek.

"Greetings, good sirs. We have a gift for His Grace."

Even in his disheveled state, Rem's manners rivaled a lord's.

Agni wanted to scream. To tell Rem to stop, to turn the cart around, to fight if he had to. That he was delivering him to his doom.

But no words could escape.

"Duke Harkon is tending to the business of the realm," the guard replied.

The guard's voice sounded distant, hollow. His face twisted into disgusting shapes—covered in eyes, spikes, wounds.

"We don't bring finery. We have something of greater price," Rem insisted, still thinking he was bringing peace to two realms. "But we need your constable, sir."

The guard huffed. "A gaggle of ruffians with a trussed-up man on a cart. Leave the castle grounds unless you prefer to stay in a moldy undercroft."

"Ruffians we may be, but this prisoner will fetch a fortune at any castle. All we ask is the duke's writ, that we may live again as men here in Zarda. Your constable will recognize him. You may receive the duke's favor, too," Rem said in his jaunty voice.

A rough, sweat-slicked hand reached for Agni's face. The world blurred again and suddenly it was not a guard but a raider. His mother's murderer. The one who took everything. The hand grasped his chin and jerked upward. His fetid breath smelled like burning sulfur.

"You have steel balls to make such a request," the guard sneered. "But curiosity compels me."

Fingers snapped like lightning.

"Bring out Constable Pavlon. And if the rogues' guest is anything less than Emperor Taran in disguise, the jailer, too."

The castle warped. The broad doors turned into a maw, ready to consume him. Hung with the Kazirian crest—in tatters, dripping with blood.

A hand pressed against his forehead, dripping with sweat.

"Don't be afraid, Agni. Your fever will break," Rem whispered.

But the hold of a millennia-old emperor's wraith would not.

Anton had taken the last of him.

Rem's hand patted his shoulder. It was meant to reassure but stung with unknowing betrayal.

"You've suffered worse to come here."

Agni's breath grew shorter and sharper.

Then, a third voice. Deep. Gravelly. Hungry. Like a growling bear.

"I am Constable Pavlon. What's your business here?"

Agni could not move; he could only feel the horror of the next step towards the Netherworld.

"Constable Pavlon. I am Remon, former servant to Lord Faron, from East of Lontak."

Pavlon grunted. "You say that name like it should mean something."

"By our wit, we captured the greatest criminal in a century. But we wish the duke's writ—to live as men again."

Through the miasma, Agni felt a twinge of admiration for Rem's performance.

"We can throw the lot of you into jail with no writ. Your quarry and all."

Undaunted, Rem continued, "We offer you the face of Solantian aggression—High General Agni Kazirian."

More sweat poured down Agni's brow. A large man with blue and gray hair and a long beard peered at him from two angles. A callused hand grasped his face, stinging like wasps. It ripped off his gag.

"Well by the arseholes of all the gods, it is. I wager he did not come willingly. How did you take him?"

Rem chuckled, still confident that he was buying his freedom—and peace. "Sometimes Varenox brings fates together, and we only need not resist."

The nightmare shifted.

Within the castle appeared a great precipice—and beneath it, flames. The flames that would sweep his homeland, and this land.

"You, High General, what do you have to say to save yourself?"

Pavlon's voice snapped him back, but his throat was locked. Pavlon's hand cracked across Agni's face, sharp enough that the haze lifted for a moment.

"Right, right," Pavlon muttered, bored already. "Lord Kazirian, speak, blast it."

Agni could say nothing as the miasma returned. Pavlon's face turned into a menacing bear's. Somewhere in the background, Anton's sadistic laughter echoed.

Rem's voice cut in, almost pleading. "Don't be so quick to take his life. He carries a stone in his left boot that might spare us a second Black Moon. A message of peace from Goro Kazimana, lord of the Azectrai Valley." The stone. Hope. His last chance.

"The duke would be most displeased were he to find that stone on the High General's corpse," Rem continued.

Pavlon's grip tightened on his chin. A moment's pause. Then Rem's voice rose again, tinged with alarm. "Feel his forehead, constable. This fever seems to have sapped his voice. Give him a day in the cool of the undercroft—it may do him good."

"Do not trouble yourself. He is ours now."

Agni felt a dagger of fear slip through his ribs. His last hope. A tear formed in his eye.

"But—"

Pavlon cut him off.

"We will." Pavlon pointed to the guard. "You have done your duty to Blevenia. We will have rooms for you at the Brightwing Inn, some credits, and a nice tavern girl for each of you."

Agni's last friends were being dismissed, but he heard no footsteps.

"Your writ will come this evening. Now, go."

Agni felt the silence where Rem should have objected.

A whistle. Three guards appeared, their boots thudding against the stone. Hands closed around Agni's limbs, lifting him from the cart. He tried to reach out, to point in Rem's direction, to show he carried a message that could save them all, but his muscles failed.

A shadow loomed over him.

"As for you," Pavlon snarled, close enough that Agni could smell his breath, like rotten meat.

He heard Pavlon gather saliva and drool it into his mouth, thick and hot. A violation.

He would cough and sputter but was too weak to retch. His body convulsed, drowning.

"Until you die… and you shall die soon… I own you." Pavlon cackled.

"Drag him down to the dungeon. Do not bruise him—too deeply. Duke Harkon needs to recognize his face."

The descent began. The world lurched, twisting. The rough castle walls scraped his wings. Old wounds reopened, dripping blood.

The dungeon stank of suffering—mold and iron.

The walls pulsated, turning fireglass black and bloody crimson.

And with it, a new horror.

His essence in a body that was not his own, not in the Mortal Realms.

It was that of a giant, infused by a strength from beyond. Powered by worship, flowing with malice.

A dragon's throat, severed in a single stroke, its blood spilling onto white marble.

A woman's screams, silenced beneath a rough hand, her body limp against the bed.

Men burning, their flesh peeling back like charred parchment as they begged for mercy.

And centuries of pain, rejection, divine hatred focused squarely on his heart.

One thought cut through the nightmare: *I am Anton Kazirian—no!*

And a burning hatred for all existence, a mind that could not comprehend the memories. Hatred for Anton. For fate. For all the gods and kings and lords who had built empires of suffering.

And hatred for himself.

As his hair twisted into horns, his wings turned black as coal, fangs bursting forth from his mouth.

He opened his mouth to beg a guard for the mercy blow, but only a gurgle erupted.

A door groaned open. The world snapped back into place.

Pavlon's voice cut through the air.

"Hail, High General."

His body felt weak again. Useless. Broken.

The constable crouched, grinning, and grabbed Agni's left boot. His knife cut at the laces, peeling away the leather, exposing his bare foot to the cold dungeon air.

A soft clink—Agni's hope hit the ground.

He could only watch as Pavlon's callused fingers lifted the stone. The soft red glow reflected in his eyes.

"A message of peace, is it?" Pavlon mused. Mocking.

"For my brother. For my cousins. Blasted if I let you slither your way out of your crimes."

A hand tightened around Agni's chin.

"I have dreamed of this moment for a decade. You lie beyond redemption. It will be Sir Pavlon who delivers this message—after you drop from the tower and your body feeds the duke's hogs."

He crumpled to the castle wall.

He imagined Rem and Keron in the Brightwing Inn, drinking, laughing, with a tavern girl on each arm.

And Anton in his crypt, laughing, as Agni sank through the ground, into the eerie purple flames of the Netherworld, from which more abominations formed.

"Best rest up and go to the Netherworld with a bright face."

The door slammed shut and the lock clicked.

There was nothing left to save him.

# Noble

Sara stirred to the chirping of robins and the gentle creak of a door below. The morning air carried the faint scent of rain. Gone were the restless dreams that had plagued her for two years—this time, even a short night's sleep invigorated her, leaving no trace of sorrow or longing.

She felt renewed.

"Your Grace?"

Nira's voice carried up the stairs, polite and dutiful.

"A few minutes, please," Sara replied.

She stretched all her limbs beneath the covers, gazing at the ceiling with a widening grin. The power of this strange land coursed through her veins, quiet, unshakable.

The old Sara would have scoffed at Agni's fantastic tales. But no longer. They were real—she had touched them, spoken with them, and emerged chosen.

*Agni. What would he think if he knew? That his ancestor had scorned him and fixed his eyes on me? Even my love for him feels like a distant memory.*

The thought thrilled her, that he would only be known in reference to her.

Today, she would face the trio of jackals who had sought to humble her—Goro, Orlan, Arno. They would expect a beaten woman, but they would not find her.

"Nira? Come up," she called, her voice confident.

The door creaked open, and Nira curtsied with the warmth of a courtly lady.

"Good morning, Your Grace," Nira greeted. "Shall I prepare you a meal? You seldom awaken this early. I thought you might return to sl—"

"I would appreciate that, Nira," Sara interrupted smoothly, rising with easy grace. "At midday, I will dine at the town hall. Go and spend that time with your boy. I should love to sup with the two of you; we have only a day left."

Nira's brows lifted in pleasant surprise.

"If I might be so bold, Your Grace… where did you walk last night? I heard you leave late; I was concerned for you."

Sara met Nira's gaze, eyes steady, lips curving into a wry smile.

"Not far," she replied. "I wanted to feel the summer rain. It felt cleansing," she lied. "As foreign as this land is, I will miss watching the thunder roll over the Great River," she continued. "I thought I even saw a dragon circling the mountains."

Nira sighed, a hand resting over her heart.

"Majestic, isn't it?"

"Quite," Sara agreed. Then with a touch of laughter, "A dragon is best seen at some distance."

They chuckled together, the mood light and familiar.

"Would you like me to dress you?"

"Yes," Sara said. "But first, I need a moment of solitude."

*A moment to savor this power. To bask in the knowledge of what I have become.*

Nira bowed again and returned downstairs.

Sara hurried over to the chest and held Anton's ring up to the light.

*Silver. Eternal.*

The crest was so fine she wondered how a man's hands could have crafted it. An emblem of an empire long faded but waiting to be reborn.

It pulsed light blue as a deep, resonant voice spoke in her mind.

*"Should the Mortal Realms crumble, I will still watch over you. Let this give you hope."*

Sara inhaled, letting the words sink in.

*"I have hope, Blessed Ancestor."*

*"You belong to eternity now. Your present concerns will fade like the setting sun. Do you see this?"*

*"That I do. Today, I will act in the faith you have shown me."*

*"You fill me with pride."*

Words Agni had never spoken to her, and Father rarely did. Great Anton, like the sun, sustained and illuminated her.

She slid the ring onto her finger and felt the warm pulse. His favor. His promise.

"Nira?" she spoke down the stairs.

Nira walked in with her chemise and tunic, presenting them like gifts.

Sara stepped into them with ease, fastening the tunic below each wing. The fabric felt almost ethereal against her skin.

Just as Nira reached for Sara's circlet, Sara caught her eyes on Sara's silver band.

"I haven't seen Your Grace wearing that ring before." Nira tilted her head. "It's lovely."

Sara turned her hand over, admiring its gleam against her skin. "Is it not?" she said with a smile. "I found it in Agni's chest."

Nira smiled, none the wiser.

"It matches your circlet well."

Sara's hands brushed over the band once more.

"Thank you."

The truth lay beneath the lie—Anton's brilliant ring among Agni's dulled coins. The line had grown dim over time, but Anton's will had endured.

She still hoped for Agni's safety; not for love, nor reconciliation, but for proof. So he could see her ascend to rule as the one who inherited their shared legacy.

But first, she would stand before the jackals. She would face them. And they would bow.

———

After breaking her fast, Sara picked one of Agni's books off the shelf in the main hall. A thick volume, *The History of Kazia,* by Grazo Senogria, called to her. She ran her fingers along its spine before placing it upstairs among her belongings.

*A prize for my time at Father's keep, away from curious eyes,* she thought. *But today is not for reading dead men's words.*

Goro. Arno. Orlan. Three vultures would circle and pick at her. They would expect a meek, cowed girl, and find a duchess—no, a Lord Regent in training.

Sara walked the northwest edge of the common, savoring the hair-tousling wind. The storm had cleared and the common smelled fresh. A new day. She watched boys dirtying their tunics in mud and splashing puddles, flaring their wings to take in the breeze.

She twirled her ring as she walked. Its silver gleamed as though alive. It connected her to a power greater than Father, let alone three provincial lords. *They will regret mocking me.*

As she approached the meeting hall, she thought she saw shadows scurrying on the inside. The door was barred. She knocked once.

A servant boy rushed to open the door, eyes flickering with unease.

And Sara could see why. Her three tormentors stood in a grim formation—Arno, then Goro, then Orlan—lined like hollow sentries. The first two bore fresh bruises, purple knots swelling at their heads and eyes, lips split and cracked. But all had crossed their arms, as if presenting a wall against her. A chipped wall.

*This passes for power among minor lords. Let them know their place.*

"Your Grace," Mayor Goro said stiffly. His appearance belied his attempt to show strength. "Please sit down."

Sara did not even break her gaze.

"After you… Baron Goro."

The words landed like a slap. Goro flinched, his lips pressing into a thin line. A contest of wills. She would not let them tower over her today. Her eyes scanned theirs, left to right, without dropping her eyes. No one spoke.

"Lady Sara, you depart tomorrow," Orlan started. "I trust you have prepared your belongings."

"That I do." Sara's tone was smooth, even unharried. "I have said my farewells. But surely you did not invite me here to discuss a woman's silks."

Orlan's jaw twitched in apparent surprise.

"No, we have the matter of Agni Kazirian to discuss," the mayor said.

Sara sighed, annoyed.

"We have already discussed the Lord Guardian at length. Either he is sleeping in a mountain cave past your notice or has passed on to the Netherworld."

The flush of red on Goro's face pleased her. He was unraveling.

"No, no, Your Grace," he sputtered. "See what your failure has wrought. He fights us still. While we trod the Median Road, he ambushed us with a snare, a dragon whistle, and a band of Blevenian bandits."

Sara bit her lip to suppress a smile.

*Crafty as ever.*

Her silence forced Goro to continue.

"He pricked my throat and forced me to confess your father's ambitions into a speaking stone," Goro raged, his voice trembling with a mix of frustration and fury. "Then he forced us to admit that Kazian knights raided a Blevenian village. He threatened to butcher my son and I if we did not. Now, he and his Blevenian band carry that message to Duke Harkon. Blevenia will guard against us for years and may extract parts of the Spires. Blast the day we trusted you!"

Sara tilted her head, unmoved.

"Like I said," she said, coolly, "we have already discussed the Lord Guardian. But the matter of Kazian knights crossing the Spires to pillage and ravish. Is this true?"

"That has no bearing on—"

Sara lifted her hand. "Stop."

The room froze. Even Orlan flinched.

"Is this true?"

Her voice did not rise. It did not need to.

"I—" Goro swallowed. "I do not know. I cannot stop every Kazian lord from—"

Sara lifted her ring, pointing the Kazirian crest towards them. A reminder. A warning.

A thrill stirred within her. *Was this what Agni felt riding into battle?*

Few would outright lie to a duchess, but they would mislead and dissemble all the same.

*The skills of rule include the ability to see through untruth.*

"Agni would not lie," she stated. "Who, other than a Kazian lord, would know you traveled the Median Road? I am convinced he saw the raid with his own eyes. Why else would he risk the Median Road, where every sentry knows his face, if he did not know he would find you there? How else could he find you at the precise location of a snare and a dragon whistle?"

Goro huffed and puffed.

"I did not inquire."

Sara flared her wings, dominating the room.

"You expect me to believe that Agni crafted a yarn to humiliate the land he bled for? To hand Blevenia the lands that he mined? What manner of fool do you take me for?"

Goro's jaw dropped. His weight shifted uncomfortably from foot to foot.

His tongue fumbled. "Your Grace—"

"Cease your babbling," she snarled. "Father took my birthright because I could not taste poison in my meal. Not only has Agni outwitted you the same but shown that you cannot control your own men. You may have lost us the Spires. He will cast you off your own guard tower and return your land to His Imperial Majesty."

Orlan took a step forward.

"Your Grace, have faith that Duke Verlan will solve this conundrum. If Agni Kazirian truly cavorts with Blevenian bandits, he will be declared an outlaw and a traitor, and the realm will learn."

Sara's bile rose. Undeterred, she jabbed a finger at Orlan.

"And *you*. You who pummel crones under the cover of a ducal crest. A bandit in all but name, you wrap yourself in the cloak of service yet butcher your own. By my wings, I swear, I will see you lashed for Dona's murder. Coward!"

Orlan stiffened but said nothing.

She jabbed a finger at Arno.

"You disgusting oaf, thick as a plow horse and half as bright. Have you told your father how you touched my breast? How you tried to rut with me like a beast in the fields?"

Arno's face turned crimson. His father's eyes turned toward him, darkening with anger. But Sara did not stop.

"Father would flog you himself for laying a hand on his own daughter."

Arno shrank as his father's gaze did not remit.

Sara let her words settle.

"I am done with you three. Goro, Arno, you had best prepare a proper send-off for a duchess tomorrow," she commanded. "Because according to the citizens of Azectrai." She lifted her ring once more. "I am still the beloved of a disappeared hero."

She turned on her heel and walked out.

One grumbled something, but she swung the door open before they could complete a sentence.

Finally out of the hall, she beamed.

*Noble again. I spoke truth and they lack the power to stop me.*

# Agony

The horrors kept Agni awake.

Darkness folded around him, pressing against his skin, his bones, his mind. Tendrils of shadow writhed at the edges of his vision, pulling the world apart. Waves of nausea rolled through him. He felt his body flop side to side, an unconscious attempt to bring him back to the moment.

The tendrils congealed into Anton's form. Tall, mighty, the ghostly outline of his great cloak trailing into the darkness. His dark eyes flashed silver. The rage of the ancients.

*"Accursed one."* Anton's voice took on a demonic snarl.

Agni's chest seized.

*"Duke Harkon will find you guilty of your invasion,"* he hissed. *"But more grievous is your crime against your blood. I find you guilty of treason against the Empire Kazia and impiety towards your legacy. I only suffer that without my body, I cannot drop you off my own castle by my own hand."*

A dark tether shot from Anton's left arm and coiled around Agni's throat. His head snapped back. His body convulsed. His mind fractured.

He could feel Anton's pull—stronger than any man's—dragging him toward a cold abyss.

"*No…*" Agni croaked.

He forced himself to hope. He pictured it. His home. Kali's song. Alexander's laugh. Keron's steady hand. Even Sara's face, proud and composed. He anchored himself to those images, even as he felt himself dragged down through the floor.

But Anton's pull burned into his throat. His vision blurred. He felt his body gasp with the last of air.

*For my home. For my love. For my friend.*

The despair pressed harder. The memories faded to shadows. He could not sob to release it. He struggled for rougher memories—imprisonment in rock hollows, starving as a child, even his shattered leg. But it could not pierce the darkness.

"*Your time draws near,*" Anton whispered. "*Know that like I formed you, so shall I undo you.*"

Agni shuddered. His limbs grew cold, his chest hollow.

*What am I without him?*

Anton had formed him. Raised him from the ashes of his mother's death. Made him into a warrior, a leader, a champion of Solantia. Without Anton's call, his god would have struck him down as he nestled against a sow. What was he now? *A hollow vessel.*

The despair pressed deeper. He felt his breath slow. His heart still.

Anton's silver eyes narrowed. "*Rest now, boy.*"

Agni's last thought was that this was what it must feel like to die.

Then everything went black.

———

"Come along, now."

Agni's eyes fluttered open to the sound of Pavlon's growl. His vision swam. His limbs tingled.

Two men bound his wings behind his back, lashing coarse rope around his chest, crushing his arms against his ribs. Then came the tightening at his wrists and ankles—familiar, like the bindings on the ship. A memory of helplessness, of impending doom.

"My apologies, Lord Guardian, but while you breathe, you're a dangerous man. Fortunately, that will be remedied soon," Pavlon taunted.

But Anton felt more real than Pavlon. A dark shape, forcing itself on his thoughts.

*"Soon, I will walk the land once more. The Dragonlands will see me restored to my body. To my power."*

Pavlon's hand wrenched between Agni's legs, lifting him over his bear-like shoulders like he was the scrawny eight-year-old boy in Anton's chamber. He tried to move his head—the only unrestrained limb—but Anton's lingering grip deadened his muscles. For the next few minutes, the stairs and walls of Harkon's castle shimmered with swirling shadows.

*"You are lost."* Anton chuckled. *"You cannot fight me. You never could."*

Pavlon's heavy footfalls echoed off the stone walls.

Anton's words from twenty years ago. *"The God of Dragons fated you to die this night in obscurity."*

Agni Kazirian—High General, Lord Guardian, Desolator— slain not by sword or spell, but by his own ancestor's wrath. His death would echo across the Dragonlands. The taverns of Blevenia would erupt in joy. Solantian traders would carry the news across the Great River. Agni Kazirian, reduced to a criminal in two lands.

Agni could never die in obscurity, only infamy. But for twenty years, Anton, not the Dragon God, shaped his fate.

And his voice slithered through Agni's mind. Cold. Dark. Familiar.

Shadows twisted into Anton's form. The sharp jawline, the silver gaze that could reduce hardened warriors to trembling boys. Over his head, a dark crown.

A sharp thump to his backside yanked him from the fog.

Pavlon dumped him into a hard wooden chair in what looked like Duke Harkon's study. A crude wooden desk sat strewn with papers and stained with ink. The smell of damp parchment and sweat lingered in the air.

"Best compose yourself, Desolator," Pavlon's grin twisted. "Duke Harkon will arrive to sentence you soon."

One of Pavlon's men unbound his wings and re-lashed them around the chair, forcing them into an awkward cross.

*"You are that which you fear most. Bound. Helpless. Awaiting a certain death."*

The oak door creaked open.

Duke Harkon entered, his figure outlined in the torchlight. His gray hair hung limp over his shoulders. The whites of his eyes pink, heavy with years of war, grief, and wine—like Papa's the last time he saw him. His thin mouth curved downward beneath the shadow of his beard.

"I have awaited this moment for years, High General." The duke's still deep voice sounded like an echo of an echo down the mountain. Distant and hollow next to that of Anton Kazirian.

Agni could say nothing.

"I know your story, High General," Harkon said bitterly. "But I will tell you mine—not for your sake, but for my own."

Anton's form took on full color in Agni's mind, dark and towering.

*"Fool. Listen to him grovel. Soon, my armies will sweep him away too."*

"It was not I who made the first overture to reclaim Azectrai. It was your Baron Goro. And Duke Hauran."

His mind swam.

*"I mentored you for twenty long years. A shame that you only have minutes to suffer."*

*Minutes…minutes.* A realization struck like lightning on the great river. *Time.* Anton, the grand and horrible, could wrack his mind. Anton spoke of his patience but could not control time. The light from outside grew brighter. It would cut through Anton's unnatural darkness.

His heart raced as the duke continued, "It was they who asked your father Piro to pay King Vardon the grain tax. Piro was a proud man. Respected in both lands, a Solantian knight through to his bones." Harkon's brow furrowed. "And when he refused, it was they who permitted my crowner to raid without my knowledge."

*What? Those scum!*

Would that he could burst forth in anger. Anton's grip held fast, but he felt it strain.

"And when I learned of his horrible crimes, I threw him off my tower and mounted his head on Zarda's front gate." His mouth twisted. "Had I known it would birth the Desolator, I would have personally delivered your father his wings."

Anton's voice tightened.

*"This changes nothing."*

The rage grew, but Anton held him fast.

"I tell you this," Harkon said, his eyes narrowing, "because I want you to know the truth. That you did not need to die this day. Agni Kazirian should have turned his wrath on his own, not those who pursued justice."

*"You will die here."*

Agni's jaw clenched.

"What have you to say for yourself?"

*"You cannot fight me."*

Agni's pulse hammered. Sweat soaked his back. His fingers trembled."

*Time. Time.*

A warlord's hurt and rage boiled in vain. But that fateful night in the crypt, Anton told him *his pain cried out to the gods.*

A boy's pain, the pain of weakness. Of not being able to make sense of cruelty. A time before he thought of revenge.

And of love before Anton's call.

He reached beneath the rage, beneath the pain, beneath the grief.

Beneath Anton's voice.

Her voice. Her face. Her arms wrapping around him.

For the first time since the night his world burned, he would force it into his consciousness. Every sensation. Every horror. Every drop of blood.

The Dragons of the Moonless Night would duel in the noonday sun.

*Mama,* Agni thought. *Give me strength one last time.*

Duke Harkon would not see the High General's greatest battle.

———

*Heat.*

Agni's eyes opened; not in the cold chamber of Duke Harkon's study, but the upstairs loft of his childhood home. He no longer had the rippling muscles of a warrior, but the smooth, thin limbs of an innocent boy. *Frail. Weak.*

Flames flickered against the windowpanes. Heat crawled in through the stone, radiating through his bedroom like a stove. The wooden beams above had started to smolder.

A bark and a sharp tug at his sleeve. Lota's teeth.

"Lota!" he screamed.

The hound's eyes were wide, her brown fur bright in the orange glow of the fire. She whimpered, pulling harder at his sleeve. The first beam cracked and fell inches behind him.

She forced him to the stairs, nearly pulling him off his feet— the gentle giant who never knew her own strength. As he stumbled toward the kitchen, flames burst through the wooden beams above, raining sparks.

His heart raced as the heat licked at his skin.

*The window*—his only means of escape.

He stumbled towards it, his arms grabbing at the sill. His fingers dug into the wood, splinters biting at his skin. He pulled with all the strength in his small body, but it was not enough.

The kitchen door caught aflame. The heat seared his back and wings, crawling up his neck. His feet tried to scramble up the wall, but they slid. His nightclothes started to smoke.

"I can't—"

Then he felt Lota's head beneath his foot.

The hound braced herself, pushing upwards, lifting him toward the window. Her claws scraped against the wall and floor.

"Lota, no!"

She barked once, then pushed harder. His chest scraped against the window frame as he felt his body lift higher. His arms trembled—one last push—his chest rose over the ledge. He pulled up a leg and turned around.

Lota was still there. Behind her, the flames roared.

"Lota—"

A support beam split in two.

The dog's fur vanished beneath a spray of fire and splintered wood.

"NOOOO!"

The last sound he heard was Lota's sharp yelp.

*The first life given for mine—a gift I could never repay.*

*The first of thousands.*

He gasped for breath. His chest rose and fell. Tears blurred his vision.

*"You should have died with that dog,"* Anton hissed.

*No. Not yet.*

In the distance, Agni could hear the shrill whinnies of panicked horses. The pigs squealed; the cows bellowed. A cacophony of doom.

And then—

"Agni! I am coming!"

*Mama!*

Her leathers dark with blood; her sword gleaming with it.

Her face was hard, determined. Blood streaked her cheek, but no wound.

*No one else's Mama could kill a raiding knight. Mighty, even in memory.*

*"Your light, too, grows dim,"* Anton snarled.

For the last time, Mama scooped him over her shoulder, her sword still at the ready.

"What about our house?" Agni shouted.

"We will rebuild," Mama said. "They will never break us."

The cold night air matted his clothes and hair to his body.

She ran with him to the small stone larder as though he weighed nothing.

As she pushed the door open, he saw a knight in full armor— silver gleaming red—through the smoke of the house.

"Stay here," she ordered. "No matter what happens."

Her hand pressed against his cheek.

"I love you, Agni."

Swift as a flash, the knight came upon her, expecting easy prey.

Instead, Mama sidestepped his slash and thrust her blade into his stomach.

But three more emerged from the darkness. One struck at her legs, knocking her to her back. Their hands tore at her leathers.

"Agni!" she screamed once before one of them struck her head with a mailed fist.

She fell limp. Blood pooled beneath her head.

All he could do was hide between the barrels as they took turns mounting Mama like he had seen horses do. He did not understand why men would do such a thing, let alone only to inflict pain.

"MAMA!" he screamed.

Until one of them saw him and struck his head the same.

The world went dark.

Some minutes later, his head ringing, Agni crawled towards Mama, her face pale, her neck sliced open. He crawled towards her, his hands slipping through the blood.

"Mama, Mama, Mama," he repeated, frozen.

"Mara! Agni!" Papa's voice rang out.

Papa's arms lifted him away from the body, his breath trembling against Agni's ear. His face blanched, tears streaming down his cheeks.

Agni's small hands clung to his father's shirt.

For the last time, he felt Papa's love.

*If Lota had not nudged me up to the windowsill.*

*If Mama had not stopped to rescue me.*

*If Papa had not told me what a strong knight I would become.*

Agni, the boy, had known death—animals, his grandparents, even other families in raids. *But I saw love amidst it.*

*Agni, the warrior, had to befriend death. But killing will not save me today.*

He felt the last stone pulse warm in his boot.

His body thrummed with strength—the body of a warrior, returned to the moment. Anton's grip must have weakened.

He could speak back to Anton now. But until he could speak to the duke, it meant nothing.

*"You should have passed with your mother, boy,"* Anton growled. His form flickered, eyes narrowing.

Agni's breath quickened. His fingers curled into fists, the ropes biting into his wrists.

*"My tale—to survive and prevail—did not start in your Ancient City."*

Anton's form blurred. His gaze widened in rage. The black mist around them writhed.

"High General, why have you not responded to your charges?" Duke Harkon's voice cut through the haze.

*"Traitor. Insect. Fool. Brat."* Anton's snarl darkened, shimmering the air. *"For twenty years, I shaped you. My masterpiece. A weapon of war. And now you think you can defy me?"*

Agni's breath shook. His muscles flexed beneath the bonds.

*"Accursed Ancestor. You made me a weapon with which to shake the Mortal Realms,"* Agni growled. *"But this hour, I reclaim myself. I will see peace unto my home, even against your mighty will."*

Anton's eyes blazed like coals. His form flashed like lightning.

*"You are in no position to defy me, scion. Now burn."*

Anton screamed in raw, desperate rage. His otherworldly voice strained.

Agony.

Thousands of burning needles pierced through his skin. His muscles spasmed violently, his tendons threatening to snap under the force.

His bowels and bladder loosened as pain ripped through him. He felt the warmth of shame on his legs. His whole body trembled, light flashing at the edges of his vision.

"Guards," Harkon coughed with disgust. "I have seen enough. Retrieve your lance. These ropes will suffice for the pinion."

"Guwaaaaaaaa!" The scream tore from Agni's throat. His head snapped back.

His mind blazed white with pain, but something cut through it.

The chains around his mind, sundering.

Anton flickered, looking as alarmed as angered.

*"I will crown the Ancient City with splendor and give the name Agni to a mangy hound,"* Anton sneered.

Pavlon pulled at the knots binding Agni's wings. They twitched, uselessly, like a dying quail's.

He had seconds.

His mind was free, but his body was still Anton's.

His leg.

If he broke it again, he might never walk, let alone fight.

But if he did not, he would die here—and his home would burn.

*Like twenty years ago, I accept pain for wisdom.*

He braced his left foot against the floor as Pavlon pulled him upwards.

*"I will take Blevenia. Then Avicia. Then the Lands Beyond themselves!"* Anton shouted.

With all his might, he smashed his shattered leg into the leg of the chair.

*Crack!*

A wave of golden pain erupted through his body. His vision spun. His stomach heaved. He felt moldy bread rush up his throat and empty over his tunic.

But this pain—his pain—was real.

Anton's form shuddered.

Pavlon's grip slackened.

Agni's soiled body lifted further from the chair.

*Rem!*

"R… r…" he tried to form the word.

Pavlon's arms flexed, lifting him higher.

*For the Borderlands!*

Agni swung his broken leg a second time.

The silver flash of agony blinded him.

But Anton's form cracked apart. His visage tore at the edges, consumed by the mist. His voice erupted into a fading howl.

"No!" Agni roared.

Pavlon and Harkon both jolted, stunned.

"Rem," Agni gasped. His throat burned like hot sand. "Call for Rem at the tavern. He knows the truth. That I came with a message of peace from Solantia."

Pavlon's grip tightened, but Harkon's voice cut through the room. "Put him down."

Pavlon hesitated, still holding Agni above the chair.

"But—"

"I said put the general down, Pavlon," Harkon repeated, his voice as commanding as Agni remembered from the war.

Slowly, Pavlon let Agni's body down. Sweat poured down his face and back, his leg throbbing with every heartbeat.

His breath slowed. His chest rose and fell.

His body lay in a wretched state, but his mind, his essence, was free.

The duke's eyes narrowed. He said nothing, but the weight of his gaze pressed down on Agni.

Agni steadied his breath. Unlashed, grasping the armrests, he had won a moment.

"You said you came with a message of peace," Harkon said, his voice measured yet cold. "Yet you sit before me, The Desolator, your body broken, your hands steeped in my people's blood. Why should I trust you?"

Agni met the duke's stare and sighed. "Because peace is the only thing I have left."

Harkon's brow lifted.

"I fought your people for ten years. I burned fields, toppled towers, and left your soldiers to rot in the sun. I did it because I believed it would secure my people's future. But it did not." He clenched his teeth. "It only whet the appetite of men like Verlan for coin and conquest."

Harkon's eyes darkened. His lips curled in distaste, but he did not speak.

"I did not come here to beg for mercy." Agni's breath caught with emotion, but he forced the words through. "No. I came to stop this next war before it began. I crossed the Spires not as a soldier, but as a messenger."

"Do not jest with me, High General," Harkon said, his brow furrowing again.

"I expect you to believe Mayor Goro," Agni said. "And the stone your constable stole from my person as he arrested me."

"Agni, Sir Pavlon has served me with distinction for twenty years. He would do no such thing," Harkon replied, his voice even.

Agni's body tensed. Perhaps he had not yet convinced the duke to spare him.

"In my ill state—when he thought that I could not hear—your constable said that I was beyond hope, that he would deliver the mayor's message after my death. Send for Rem at the Brightwing Inn. He saw me take the mayor's message."

"Your Grace," Pavlon said, measured. "You cannot trust the word of the Desolator. He is a snake. He means to deceive you."

"Sir Pavlon." Agni turned his neck, finally facing his tormentor with strength. "If you meant to secure my possessions for safekeeping, you would have found a second stone in my right boot."

Harkon's head whipped, eyebrows raised.

"That boot that holds together my shattered leg, holds my deepest memory. Perhaps both may be undone today. I ask His Grace to use that stone to send his own message of peace. You may not yet trust me with a knife. Please cut that boot off it, so that you may see I speak the truth."

Harkon paused, his bloodshot eyes calculating.

"Guards?"

The two guards snapped to attention.

"Your Grace!" they spoke as one.

"Send at once for Remon at the Brightwing Inn. Pavlon, remove the general's boot. Let us see if he speaks truth."

One guard swung the heavy door with a creak as the other exited.

"Your Grace, he lies as easily as he breathes—" Pavlon sputtered.

His lord cut him off with a raised hand. "Cut his boot immediately, constable."

Pavlon knelt at Agni's boot, sawing through the thick laces and leather. A blue stone fell to the floor with a gentle clink.

*Mama.*

"Your Grace, this stone only contains a distant memory, of a boy whose warrior mother scolded him for taking a speaking stone. But you see, I speak the truth."

Harkon held the stone up to his eyes, rolling it in his fingers. It gleamed with a blue flame.

The duke smiled. "Your mother?"

Agni smiled back. "Yes, my last memory of her."

Harkon's smile dissipated as he turned back to Pavlon, his voice soft but dangerous. "Constable. The general has spoken naught but truth. Is it true that you hold a second stone?"

Pavlon's mouth tightened, his gaze flickering between Agni and his lord.

"Yes," he mumbled. "I took it from his boot."

"Did you intend to withhold it?" Harkon took on the voice of a barrister.

Pavlon's nostrils flared. "I—"

Harkon slammed his fists on the table.

"Answer me!"

Pavlon's lips curled, fists clenching at his sides. "Yes," he said at last. "But I did so in the name of Blevenia's safety. He is a liar. A butcher. How could you expect me to trust him?"

Harkon's eyes flashed lightning. His mouth pressed into a thin line.

"Place the second stone on my desk, Pavlon."

Pavlon's hands trembled as he obeyed. The crimson stone sat beside its companion. Reunited.

Agni exhaled shakily.

*Pavlon will be flogged, at the very least,* he thought. *Likely worse.*

"Guards," Harkon said.

The two stepped forward, hands on the hilts of their swords.

"Take him to the undercroft," Harkon said. "We will decide his punishment later."

Pavlon's face twisted. His mouth opened as if to protest, but Harkon's gaze stopped him cold. Each guard grabbed Pavlon beneath the arm. Pavlon's glare of pure hatred cut toward Agni— but Agni could not return it.

"Your Grace," Pavlon growled, "this is a mistake."

"If it is," Harkon said coolly," "it is my mistake to make."

The guards dragged Pavlon to the door, his heels scraping against the floor.

Agni watched him go, even after two more guards took their place.

*But I feel no victory, no satisfaction.*

"Your Grace," Agni said, his voice low. "Please show him mercy." The duke's head turned towards him. He said nothing, but Agni held his gaze.

"He acted to protect you. Misguided or not, he acted out of loyalty. As once did I."

Harkon's brow lifted.

"He would have let you die."

"I know," Agni said. "I have killed men for far less. But not today. Let him live. Let him see the peace I came to offer."

Harkon's mouth twitched. "A bold request from a man sitting in his own filth."

Agni smiled. "I have little left to lose."

Harkon stared at him for a long, heavy moment. Then his eyes softened—slightly.

"I will consider it."

Agni inclined his head.

"Now, I ask you to view the mayor's message."

Harkon held the stone to the light, rolling it back and forth in his palm. It brightened like an evening star beneath his touch. He studied it for a long moment before he held it to his eyes.

Agni watched Harkon's eyes widen as the message poured forth.

Agni's ambush.

Verlan's ambition—to which Goro swore he only followed orders.

Frazi's raid—to which Goro swore ignorance.

And most importantly, Goro's oath.

Harkon placed the red stone next to the other and sighed.

"Agni, my dullest stable boy could tell you beat this message out of the mayor. He may retract it the moment he returns to Azectrai."

Agni steepled his fingers. "I held a knife to his eye as he protested." Agni grinned. "I find defeated men speak with utmost sincerity. But doubtless you know of that raid and can identify Sir Frazi's crest."

He shook his head side to side.

"Frazi was one of my finest in peace and war, but I did not see his corrupt heart. Two moons ago, one of my rock falls took several of your men. I branded Sir Jeron on the cheek, while his arm lay crushed, for telling me that my own soldiers had marauded eastward over the Spires. Both to my shame. I failed as Lord Guardian."

Harkon fixed Agni with his gaze.

"I know both these incidents, and that you speak the truth. But if Verlan wants a second Black Moon War, he would want no one else as his High General."

Agni leaned forward, gripping the armrests.

"Have you heard of the Ritual of Ascension, Your Grace?"

"Only as a myth of antiquity."

"I do not know if Duke Verlan believes it himself. But by subduing me and taking me into the Spires, he could remove me as a threat to his power and placate a land that still hews to such beliefs. By days, I fled ahead of Verlan's soldiers and priests."

"And where did you intend to flee to? Anywhere in the Dragonlands, you would be taken."

"I, my lover—no, my wife-to-be, and my captain, sought separate passages to Avicia to alert King Theodore. It was on that vessel that Rem captured the passengers and crew for ransom. He sold most of us to minor lords. He knew I was no small folk and sought to bring me to you for ransom. But if I told him he had Agni Kazirian in his grasp, he would have thought me mad and thrown me into the sea."

"As would I, general."

"It was en route to Zarda that we witnessed Frazi's raid. I slew my own countrymen, but would not ride back to the port. Because my mission, peace unto the Borderlands, runs deeper than my own life. Rem took me into the Spires, intending to ransom me in Kazia. I escaped once and ambushed the mayor to take his message, before offering myself to freely be taken before you. Only I was struck by some manner of a fit for a night."

Agni bit his lip. Anton's currents ran deeper than a duke—one of many Anton might sweep away.

"A fit?" Harkon's eyebrows perked.

"A fever of some manner."

Harkon tilted his head.

"A fever that abated just in time to save your hide, general."

Agni laughed. "It would seem so. Perhaps the imminent threat pulled me out of it, but I am no physician."

Harkon let the silence linger, then sighed.

"The last two years have brought us famine. But word of this raid has my people clamoring for revenge. War will not feed us, but under its banner, our people would forget their plight. You are not only a tactician, but a lord, Lord Kazirian. What would you have us do?"

Agni looked Harkon in the eye, but felt tears run down his cheek.

"In the last moon, our god took my title, my freedom, my leg, and my voice, but not my purpose. I would have sliced my own throat before abasing myself before you. But I have no pride left, Your Grace. I ask you to graciously acknowledge the mayor's message as heartfelt—coerced though it was—and convey your own. You may seek redress for the raid from Duke Hauran, or even Emperor Taran himself. But it will place my dukes under Emperor Taran's eye. Then stay on your guard, for Verlan will scheme as long as he draws breath."

Harkon looked down his nose at Agni.

"If I allow you to leave this room alive, and you speak falsely— if this message is a trap—Blevenia will see to it that your name is lost to history. You will be remembered as a traitor and a villain in two lands."

Agni's gaze sharpened. "If Verlan crosses the Spires, you will know the truth."

Harkon's lips curved slightly. "So be it," he said. "I will send this message to my people. Let them decide if peace is worth believing in."

Agni bowed his head. "Thank you," he said, before taking a deep breath. "I also request that you place a message of peace on my second stone. The memory of my mother is engraved on my heart. I want to honor her by putting something dearer on that stone. Your message of peace."

Harkon's eyes narrowed.

"We have other stones, Agni. You do not need to sacrifice it."

Agni dropped his head. "I want to sacrifice it. I no longer need it to remind me of what I was before my lifetime of battle."

Harkon's eyes lingered on the stone. For a long moment, neither man spoke. Only the hiss of wind could be heard.

"Agni," Harkon said, low and measured. "Do you really believe this peace can last?"

Agni sharpened his gaze. He forced himself to assume a High General's posture.

"I believe it can—and it must."

Harkon's eyes narrowed.

"And why now?"

"I will always love Solantia, but I can no longer serve it. My reward for war was not peace, but more war. Perhaps those who faced the brunt of war will desire peace." Agni sighed and nodded his head. "I have seen manors burned to ash and children with empty bellies crying for mothers who will never answer. I have seen men take up arms not out of hatred, but because their noble master would not. If we do not end this cycle, it will scorch the Dragonlands."

Harkon looked down at the stone, weary.

"Do you think it will hold against men like Verlan?"

Agni met his gaze.

"It will not cut him down. But if enough lords swear by it, he will see that war is not worth the cost. Together, we will form a bulwark against him."

Harkon rolled the stone in his fingers.

"You have changed," Harkon said. "Once you were the Desolator. And now you ask me to trust that you have turned from bloodshed to peace."

Agni's lips curled into a smile. "Would you have believed me had I not come here in chains?"

Harkon gave a short, coughing laugh. "Perhaps not."

The duke looked up and down at Agni's battered form. Slowly, he reached for a pitcher of water and poured it into a pewter cup, extending it towards Agni.

Agni hesitated, then took the cup in both hands. It cooled his parched throat.

*A gesture of understanding. May this be the first of many.*

"You have given me much to consider," Harkon continued. "For years, I fantasized about slowly pulling your guts out. I still dream that my sons live and awaken in tears when I realize they do not. But I will give you this: you have faced me as a man—not a soldier—and as a messenger of peace. I will face my people the same."

Agni's throat tightened.

"I thank you."

"Do not thank me yet. You may yet die for this—in Blevenia, Solantia, or Avicia."

Agni met Harkon's eyes. "Then let me do so in the pursuit of peace. King Theodore may not trust me, but he knows that of which I am capable. Together, the threat of Blevenia and Avicia may deter Verlan. Indeed, I know of no other power which might."

Harkon stared Agni in the eyes—the gaze of a duke, not a defeated man.

"Spoken plainly, your plan is folly. But perhaps your folly is wiser than a potentate's wisdom. Today, it brought us hope. In a few days, I will arrange for your escort to Lontak, and from there, a ship to Avicia. You will have our protection, if you keep your word."

Agni pulled his wings and shoulders back, like a warrior at attention.

"On my wings, Your Grace."

Harkon steepled his fingers.

"Once you touch Avician soil, you must fend for yourself. But when our king—long may he reign—learns of our meeting, I believe he will smile upon it."

Agni gasped, palms sweating with excitement. *Folly.* That was his word—and Anton's. But it could bring peace, and a reunion with his friends. He said nothing.

"But before I record your message, let my servants clean you up. Your stench overpowers me."

Harkon clapped and called out for his servants. Without words, two sturdy women placed their heads under his arms, helping him hobble to the next room, where others appeared with soapy rags. They stung against his skin, but he savored the lather, that he had not experienced since his flight. Kali once told him the Aloi cleaned themselves so before praying to their god. It felt like a cleansing of the last days. Another servant came with a fresh tunic; it felt rough but did not cling to his skin with filth and blood. Finally, the first two women helped him back to Duke Harkon's study. A rangy boy stood by the duke, wearing his crest.

"This is my herald. He will speak this message to the city's stone, while you show your memento to King Theodore. Few would dare violate the edict of three lands."

"Mama," he whispered, "I have avenged you."

Harkon appeared to gaze at his reflection in the stone, as if contemplating his own choices.

"I will speak this message to my people," Harkon said, his voice firm. "Not as a reward, nor as a prize, but as a choice. If they reject it, I will not call for war. And if they accept it, then perhaps it will take root."

Agni's throat tightened. Again, a tear rolled down his cheek.

"Again, I thank you."

"Do not thank me yet, Lord Agni. This is but the first step."

"I know," Agni said.

"Herald, you will speak this message through our stone to every lord it can reach. Our convoys will carry it across the Spires. Prepare your quill."

The herald stepped forward, quill and ink in hand.

*"I am Duke Harkon Lamata, lord of the Leeward Plains of Blevenia,"* he started. His voice once again carried the aura of command. *"This morning, I received in my chamber Agni Kazirian, formerly High General of Solantia and Lord Guardian of Kazia. To my surprise, this foe of our kingdom passed a message from Baron Goro Kazimana, Mayor of Azectrai, sworn to Duke Hauran of Kazia.*

*On that stone, the baron spoke of a plot by Duke Verlan of Artania to invade Blevenia a second time. It was Lord Agni's warning—and my instruction—to stay vigilant against this threat.*

*More immediately, the baron begged our forgiveness for failing to halt a raid on a manor east of the Midspire Road. By the valor of Lord Agni and his companions, the raiders were slain, and their crests recovered to confirm their involvement. The mayor swore to execute and disinherit all raiders who do the same. We accept the mayor's oath to abide by the treaty that ended the last war and will enforce its boundaries with vigor.*

*I thank Mayor Goro and Duke Hauran for their message and commit to the same punishment for any Blevenian who pillages west of the Spires. I promise an end to this cycle of revenge, should the mayor and his duke follow through on their word.*

*I also speak this message to Agni Kazirian, formerly High General of Solantia and Lord Guardian of Kazia, who will convey this message across the land. He has proven his dedication to the cause of peace in the Dragonlands and will be protected by my aegis so long as he stands in Blevenia.*

*Thus, I swear before Varenox, God of Dragons, of Blevenia and Solantia alike, in the name of lasting peace."*

Harkon's voice quieted. "Thus, I swear."

The herald lowered his quill.

Agni felt more tears roll down his cheek.

*It is complete,* he thought as he lowered his head. "Thank you."

Harkon studied him but smiled.

"Does this satisfy you, Agni Kazirian?"

"Yes, Your Grace," he whispered.

Harkon's eyes softened.

"You fought for twenty years to win a kingdom. And now you fight to give it away."

Agni smiled thinly. "For my homeland and its people."

A long silence stretched between them.

Harkon extended his hand. Hard and callused, still a warrior and a lord.

Agni clasped it, steady and warm.

They sat for a moment, as only two once-bitter foes could.

"Now go, Agni Kazirian," Harkon said, releasing Agni's hand. "Tomorrow, we begin the work of peace."

Agni nodded, his spirit light for the first time since bidding farewell to his friends.

"Yes, Your Grace."

Perhaps this faint acorn of peace would blossom into a mighty tree.

Agni savored every morsel at the Brightwing Inn. A double helping of steak and onions fried in butter and spiced just right tasted like home—like Dona's kitchen, where every meal was prepared with warmth and familiarity. The bread, baked to a perfect crisp, melted on his tongue as he chased it with a deep pull of ale. His belly was full for the first time in a moon, but more than the meal settled him.

*The war is not over, but the tide has shifted,* he thought. He had stood before his once-foe and spoken of peace and trust.

That alone made the food taste better.

He propped his forearms against the rough table, his hand wrapped around the tankard. His gaze drifted to the low-beamed ceiling, where firelight flickered over the dark timber. No more "yew in the desert"; in a moon, he would be *home*, in Tercera, with the man and woman who could make it so.

Agni's chest warmed at the thought of Kali and Alexander. Kali's sharp wit, Alexander's quiet steadiness. They had risked their lives; chosen him over their own comfort and home.

"Varenox, God of Fate, let our threads intertwine once more," he prayed, for once feeling like his god might hear it.

*Now, I owe them the truth,* he thought. *My full tale—and Kazia's.*

He shifted uncomfortably in the worn wooden chair. But it was time to lay Anton Kazirian before them. His smile faded slightly— Anton had vanished but could return at his leisure.

*But who did Anton summon?*

Verlan felt like the obvious choice. Long removed from his days with a blade, he had a heart for conquest. He knew how to command an army and bend men to his will. With Anton's guidance, he could become the new High General.

But if not Verlan, then who? Duke Hauran was pliable but weak. Mayor Goro was too small-minded and greedy; his men lacked the strength and resolve to reshape the Dragonlands.

Sara? A woman? She had strength, but not for the war Anton wanted. She craved only the power of her birthright. Could he twist her loyalty, her grief, into something darker?

Anton could raise up a minor lord from the Azectrai Valley. Perhaps a knight fallen into disfavor after the war. Or—another desperate boy.

*And should we face each other on the battlefield… could I prevail?*

He steeled himself. That thought no longer frightened him.

He closed his eyes and exhaled slowly, as he was taught. That era of his life had ended. His path was no longer bound to Anton's will. He would face it on his own terms.

He scanned the tavern floor—no sign of Rem, Keron, or any familiar face. Harkon's men must have brought them to the castle, where they could receive their reward for unknowingly quashing Verlan's war.

He smiled faintly. Tomorrow, he would wait for them to break the fast, and confirm that the message has spread.

After some hours of musing, he pulled himself up the rough-hewn stairs towards the guest rooms. As he turned his key in the lock, a welcome sight greeted him—fresh tunics, a satchel of credits, and a proper backpack with which to provision himself to Avicia. The bed was no Artanian feather mattress, but it felt dry and warm.

*After so many nights in mud, it will feel like Emperor Taran's own bed must.*

He found a set of nightclothes and unceremoniously dropped onto the mattress.

His last thought was that he would face Anton some night, but not tonight.

A small smile lingered on his lips as he drifted into sleep.

Agni woke later than he had in moons. Soft light filtered through the window, casting gold and orange across the far wall. He rubbed his eyes and sat up slowly. *No dreams. No spirits.* After his greatest defiance yet, the Voice of Ages did not intrude on a restful night. *Is this what it means to be free?*

His body ached as he rose from the bed, but he savored it. After days under Anton's power, pain meant he was alive and in his full mind. He would have—and need—moons to heal. Seven to ten days to Lontak, a moon to Tercera, and several more for his leg to mend—if it ever did.

He had no title now. No command. No patron. Little coin. But he had Kali and Alexander. *They too fended for themselves before me.* They too started anew. No title, no chains of war.

But before the road called to him—his last task in Blevenia, to thank Rem.

Agni limped down the stairs, leaning on his new walking stick, and settled at a large table. The smell of sweet porridge mingled with fried pork wafted in from the cooking shed. Rem, or one of his men, would show soon enough.

An older maid called out to him.

"Ale, sir?"

"A mug would be lovely, dear."

Deftly, he flipped a Blevenian copper onto her tray. She flashed a smile and disappeared into the back.

Agni traced his thumb over the rim of the mug. He had only taken a sip when a shadow settled over him. He caught the reflection before he even spoke—a familiar sharp profile, dark hair cleaner and cheeks fuller than he remembered.

"Good day, Rem."

"Nothing escapes your notice, does it? I was shocked when a guard told me that you survived your encounter with the duke," Rem continued. "You found your voice in time."

"I suppose I caught a fever," Agni pretended to muse. "My chest and throat felt tight."

Rem chuckled. "Again, you fail to deceive me. You wouldn't recover from such a fever so quickly. I see no sweat on your brow, and your head dipped when you said that."

Agni smiled faintly. Nothing escaped Rem, either. That made him such a capable leader. But like capturing a warlord on a humble ship, the truth might double him over laughing.

"But without an apothecary," Agni replied, "I will never know."

"Or a priest."

Agni kept his best stone face. "Neither Sir Frazi nor Mayor Goro would bring priests to curse a man they believed dead."

Rem's eyes narrowed thoughtfully. His voice dropped a tone. "Bandits have little use for gods or priests. But you, Agni. A lord who wielded an enchanted sword in battle, who altered the fate of nations—would not pass beneath their notice. We've heard the stories of the ruin on your side of the Spires. Our men believed you tainted by it."

Agni's fingers curled around the tankard.

"And do you believe that?"

Rem's smile thinned.

"I believe you have seen things beyond the Mortal Realms most men would not survive. That makes you… different."

Agni glanced down into the ale, watching the thin line of foam wash against the inside.

"We of the Azectrai Valley are a pragmatic folk, Rem. If I feared every tale of my ancestors, I would be hiding in the depths of Lubo's cold wastelands."

"You don't hide," Rem said, his voice softer. "And yet I sense those tales mean more than you admit."

"It is true," Agni said, "my home is steeped in history. Our tallest guard tower faces the Ancient City, reminding us of who we are. I will return someday, triumphant and safe, with a beautiful wife and children. I will pass them those tales, and they will bear our name with pride."

"I believe her name was Kali," Rem recalled.

Agni smiled. He could almost feel her sitting next to him, hands clasped, arm-in-wing, her smile warming him.

"It is. By her guile and skill, she awaits me in Avicia."

"She must be a charming woman."

"I assure you, she surpasses it." Agni sighed. "We shall build a new life together. And I thank you for that."

Rem's mouth widened in surprise. He must not have expected thanks for putting Agni near certain death.

"But if not for our piracy," Rem said, "you would be nearly arrived there. You would have that life."

"No, not for that," Agni replied. "But for the chance to fulfill the promise of my old life. This life. Were it not for my capture, I would fear for imminent war. The tinder remains, but the spark is gone. Once I have King Theodore's ear, I will have diplomats—and perhaps warriors—to clear that tinder."

"I didn't plan that," Rem admitted with a grin. "Only to ransom you—and I failed twice. The third time I succeeded only by your compliance. And we have you to thank for our freedom. You put the duke into a generous state."

"I had no plan other than to survive and escape. Then to find a way to earn—or steal—my passage. I might have turned to banditry myself."

Rem laughed. "I thank you nonetheless. We're the better for our fates having intertwined."

A maid arrived, setting down two bowls of steaming porridge, topped with summer berries and honey. In comfortable silence, the two devoured their helpings, and the fried pork belly that followed.

Agni, still feeling unaccustomed to fine food, finished his helping first.

"Let us part ways as friends, Rem," Agni said.

Rem stood up first. Agni propped himself on his new walking stick and followed.

The two men faced each other. Rem extended his hand. Agni hesitated for only a moment before taking it.

And then, without warning, Rem pulled him into an embrace.

"Farewell, Agni," Rem said. "I await the day your next deeds spread across the sea. I have not said these words in years, but… may the God of Dragons shelter you under his wings."

Agni's lips tightened. The God of Dragons. Did Varenox's shadow still linger over him? Agni would contend with him—and Anton—as his own man.

"*Ai,* friend," Agni said quietly. "And you. May you die happy, free, and old."

Rem pulled away with a laugh, giving Agni a parting nod before walking toward the door. The sunlight hit his back as he stepped into the street.

Rem never looked back.

Today, Agni, too, would only look forward.

*Two hours until the convoy to Lontak arrives.*

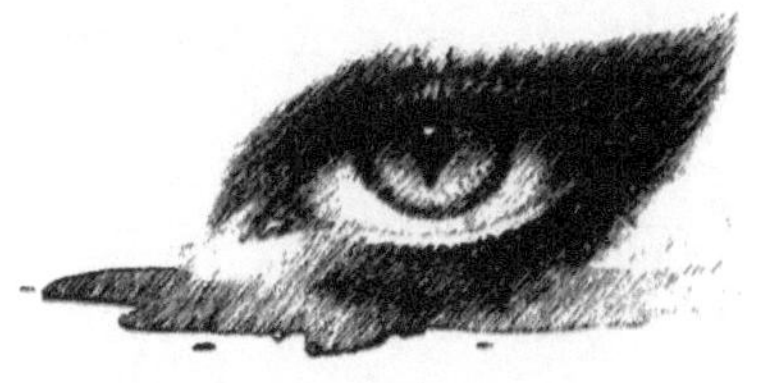



# Faraway

Agni's chest heaved, ragged from the climb up Tercera's grand rampway. His crippled leg throbbed beneath him, but his polished oak staff—Duke Harkon's gift—allowed him to push himself forward.

*Blast it,* he thought. *Two moons without morning exercises.* His leg had shriveled from disuse, but he could place some weight on his right foot now. *I climbed the Spires under heavier duress. I shall exercise that leg twice as hard as before.* Still, he gritted his teeth at the thought of climbing this rampway every day.

Some of Mama's last words—*they will never break us*—echoed in his mind with each step.

*Anton Kazirian could not break me. Blasted if I will let this hill do so.*

It had been forty days since Zarda. Forty days since he broke Anton's grip on his mind. The duke had provisioned him with enough Avician crowns for a moon's food and shelter, but that was a remote concern now. He needed to see his companion and his wife-to-be. To know they were safe.

The Aerie Market. Once he studied maps of it to destroy Tercera; now he sought refuge in it. A twinge of guilt pressed against his ribs, but he pushed it away.

*I won over one foe. I earned this.*

Thankfully, the summer sun had yielded to autumn breezes, gusting down the mountain where King Theodore's castle sat. It reminded him of the Spires and home.

He pulled his hood low to shield his face from the sun. An hour and it would peak.

The market buzzed with activity—men and women with feathered wings of white, cream, and brown strutted about. Men dug gardens and women carried baskets of bread and vegetables, their laughter rising through the thin air. They ignored the lame Dragonlander under the robe. Like Rem on the ship, they would laugh if he said he was Agni Kazirian.

He stopped a burly Terceran with a pack slung across his back and metal tools sticking out.

"Pardon me, good sir," he spoke in careful Avician, "is this the Aerie Market?"

*Too formal*, he thought, *but I will have moons to practice.*

The man let out a hearty laugh. "Well, of course it is. Only the grandest market in the city. You must be new here, Southerner. Right off the ship?"

"*Ai*, friend."

"Welcome to Tercera. The name's John. Stop by my stall in the northeast. I'll sell you the finest tools in the city. None better to break rocks or cut wood."

"Thank you, sir."

"And your name?"

Agni paused and stared down. His name was still a curse in this land. Only one false name came to mind.

"Azri," he said, finally.

"Well, glad to meet you, Azri. We're friendly folk, even to Kazians. You have friends here? Family?"

Agni smiled thinly. "I have a brother here."

"A brother, eh?" John's grin widened. "Well, the Solantian Quarter is straight west along this road. You'll find the finest lamb in town."

"Thank you, sir."

*Though it will never best Dona's mutton stew,* he thought. *By my will, I shall taste it again someday.*

"I won't keep you. Remember, the name's John, and if you need a shovel or a pick, you know where to come."

"I will. Thank you, John."

John disappeared northward into the crowd, and Agni hobbled on. His staff clicked against the stone road as he approached the fountain that marked the center. The alabaster stone gleamed in the sunlight, shaped like a great roc, wings outstretched.

*Darkness to light. The perfect reverse of the grand fireglass fountain in the Ancient City.*

He continued westward. This market alone could hold Azectrai—he counted twelve bakers before seeing his first pair of dusk-blue dragon wings. Solantian and Avician bantered and exchanged coins with no sign of threat. Like John, did they put the Black Moon behind them?

But no Aloi—their quarter lay east of the rampway. Kali would stand out.

The sun hung high, sharp and blinding. He squinted towards the sky but could not tell whether it had peaked. No clock tower stood within view. He sighed and rested his back against the cool stone wall. If he had missed the midday sun, he could always retreat to the Solantian Quarter under his false name and return tomorrow.

He closed his eyes, letting the noises of the market fade into a low hum. He could feel the sun warming his face and the breeze ruffling his tunic. And his mind drifted.

*Two moons.*

Up through Duke Hauran's blasted feast, he thought he would die old and bitter. Duke of Artania, watching his sword arm grow dull and his tongue sharp, trapped beneath the weight of his title. Married to Sara, forever walking a line between alliance and resentment. But he could not hate Sara, wrapped deeper in lords' ambitions than he. He prayed a short verse for her health and fulfillment.

*May she forge her own path,* he thought. *May she prosper in her own way.*

Then, everything changed in a day.

He lost his duchy. His betrothed. His vow never to raise a sword against his countrymen. He became an outlaw, much like the ones he hunted when the drunkard sheriff passed out at the Terrapin.

Then he lost his freedom. Rem's capture had been a lesson in humility. Rem saw through his every deception, yet when they joined forces, they did what armies could not. Had Agni his old command, he would have named Rem his spymaster without hesitation.

Then he lost the innocence of his command. *Kazian* raiders. Their brutality forced him to confront his own actions. Did he teach them to trod Blevenians underfoot—*like ants*—and never think of them again? Would they have crossed the Spires if he had not mined the trails, and they could not maraud without fear of reprisal? But he always adhered to his purpose, whether mining the trails or slaying the raiders. And in a twisted way, the raid gave him a chance to fulfill that purpose.

And Anton Kazirian.

*Cursed Ancestor.* The grandest deceiver of all, who played at the father, then struck at him when Agni chose his own path. *As all sons one day must.* Agni had shown a greater will to live than Anton did to kill him.

But had Anton lied when he said he had called to another? How far did Anton's influence reach? Could he still reach into the Mortal Realms and tighten his grip? He only knew that while Anton's essence lingered, the Empire Kazia would threaten the Mortal Realms once again.

Unlike any man, Anton had time. *And when he finds his body, the powers of spirit and flesh unite. Unbound.*

But now, for the first time in twenty years, Agni stood without a title or ancient hand guiding his purpose. It would come from within, even if it burst him.

A shout broke his thoughts.

"Boy, move your arse."

Agni opened his eyes. A fat Avician with cream-colored wings flared, and his belly hanging over his trousers, prodded him with his foot. His beady eyes narrowed with disdain.

"Apologies, sir," Agni said in his meek "Azri" voice.

He grasped his staff in both hands and tried to pull his left leg under him, but another man, lean and sharp-faced, drove his foot into Agni's wing, pinning it against the stone wall.

"Move it before sunset, boy," the man sneered. "Or we'll drag you away."

*I had not hoped to attract attention, but violence has found me today.*

Agni braced his good leg against the wall and thrust his staff into the second man's balls.

"Oof!"

The man stumbled back, clutching his groin. Agni held his stance, ready to strike again.

"Now run off," Agni growled. "Or prepare to swallow your teeth."

"Ay, kicking a cripple like that!"

Agni's heart skipped a beat. That voice, smooth and sharp. The kind that could disarm a camp of randy men with a single word.

*Kali!*

Her hood was pulled low, but he could see the curve of her smile beneath it. Her clawed toes curled over the edge of her sandals. She held a fighting stick, perfectly balanced in her hand.

Whatever trials she endured to arrive had not bowed her a bit.

"Leave," Kali said, her tone calm and deadly. "Before you face a second stick, you oafs."

The thugs hesitated—unarmed, facing two trained weapons—and then wisely backed away. He felt moved as he realized she protected him.

Agni's hand tightened around his staff. His breath quickened. "Kali?"

He pulled back his hood, letting his hair cascade down his shoulders.

She pulled back her own.

And the world brightened.

Her green eyes, sharp and bright beneath the autumn sun. He had fantasized about this moment a hundred times—on the deck of the *Star of the Sea,* blindfolded and bound, in Anton's dark haze.

"Kali," he whispered.

She ran to him.

Her hands closed around his face, claws digging into his jaw, and for a moment she just stared at him as if to make sure he was real.

"Agni. By both our gods, this feels like a dream."

His staff slipped from his hand.

He crushed her against him, burying his face in her hair. Her scent, her touch, the flick of her ears. Tears rolled down his cheeks.

"Kali… my love…" His voice broke. "I thought of you, harrowing night after harrowing day."

He kissed her, and their tears mingled, running down their cheeks.

"How I awaited this day," she whispered. "But I never lost hope."

He kissed her again, breathing her in, his heart hammering against his chest.

*With you, a wolf's den in the Spires would feel like home.*

"I have so much to tell you."

She laughed through the tears. "I think I can imagine a good bit."

He bent to retrieve his staff, but Kali was faster. She handed it to him with a playful smile.

"Your leg. Can you walk?"

"I can hobble."

"Good. Come. Alexander and I have a stone house a quarter mile from here."

His heart leapt again, though he had expected no less of the half-Tarkan raised on the Great Sea.

"A house?"

"Yes. With your coins, we purchased it from a Kazian trader homesick for the Dragonlands. We received a deed with the mayor's wax seal. Written on actual paper."

Agni's eyes widened.

"Who here knows our name? Ae we safe?"

"As safe as King Theodore's daughters, love," Kali said. "We found your old patron, Ronan. He questioned us on your whereabouts but knew only one Aloi woman and one half-Tarkan half-Solantian giant could together claim to know you. Alexander guards his house and his convoys. Ronan pays him well. He will return by nightfall. I tended the house from the coins we smuggled."

"A kingdom full of traders, is it?"

"*Ai,* love." Her smile softened. "But a kingdom filled with hope."

Agni swung himself down the street like a lamed dog, but the house lay a short walk away. Kali slowed her pace to match his, her hand slipping around his waist.

*Home.*

He leaned into her, letting her warmth steady him. A curious cat slinked across their path, and Kali shooed it away with a flick of her staff.

Agni chuckled. His leg throbbed with each step, but the joy numbed the pain.

"I will never leave you again," he said.

"Good," she said, her head pressed against his shoulder. "I would drag you back anyways."

Agni smiled to himself, watching the affection in Kali's eyes.

"I will need an evening—and some wine—to tell you of my adventures while we were apart. My capture. My escape. How I won my freedom. And how I may have stayed Duke Verlan's ploy for some time."

Kali's head snapped toward him, eyebrows arching.

"Is that a jest?"

He laughed softly. A moon ago, even he would have thought those words a joke.

"I swear that on my mother's grave, love."

"Some wine might help me to believe such adventures," she said, grinning. "This is your new home, Agni."

She pointed toward a handsome, two-story mountain-stone house. Agni's breath stalled. It stood half again as large as his city house in Azectrai—and that house had taken a generation to fill with art and books.

"By the gods, Kali, this could pass for an inn," he said, disbelief coloring his voice. "What did you pay for this?"

"Our coins paid half, and Ronan loaned us the other half under, shall we say… *favorable terms.*"

"You have become quite the trader yourself, love."

"Become?" Kali's grin widened. "For years, I sang in taverns for coins. I have traded longer than I have known you."

She lifted the latch and Agni stepped inside. His sigh echoed through the high-ceilinged room. The benches and tables were rough but sturdy, carved from dark oak. The floors were clean. The stonework was immaculate. A real house.

He swung open a side door to a second ground floor room. Clothes of Alexander's size lay folded on a chest against the wall, beside a straw mattress.

"Out back is the stream. Cold, but free of Avician piss," Kali said, resting her hand on his arm. "And a shack for a maid when we find one."

"And plenty of wall space for your books."

Kali's hand slipped down his arm to his hand, squeezing his fingers.

"We will have to earn our finery here," Kali said, smiling. "A clan tapestry like our house in Azectrai will cost us dearly."

"And why would my crest mean so much to you?" Agni replied with a grin. "A feather bed interests me more."

Kali placed a hand on her hip.

"You mean *our* crest," she corrected softly. "I have no family name. And you said you would wed me at the first temple we find. Or have you forgotten?"

She flashed a sultry grin, the kind that could melt a war-hardened man.

"Never, love."

Kali gestured toward the stairs.

"Come."

Agni placed one hand on his staff, the other on the railing, and pulled himself up the steep staircase. The bedroom was spacious, if spare. A large mattress, rough-stuffed with straw, sat beneath a window overlooking the backyard. A white silk tunic lay splayed across the chest at the foot of the bed. He ran his fingers down the front of it. It was too large for Kali.

"The day I arrived, I bought this for you," Kali said. "You can wed me in this."

"You bought wedding garb before I arrived?"

"I never believed you would die on your journey," she said with confidence.

Her faith touched him deeply. Faith that ran deeper than his own. He let his hand rest over hers on the tunic.

"Let me wash, and when Alexander returns, I will tell you both the tale. I swear before Varenox that I will speak only the truth."

Kali arched her brow.

"I never knew you to speak otherwise, but I can tell this will strain our ears."

"Until then," she smiled, "wash yourself. You stink of the sea."

Agni laughed. He threw the tunic over his shoulder and inched down the stairs. Kali followed, carrying a bowl of soap and a pile of rags.

The stream out back was just a trickle but it smelled fresh and clean. Agni sat on a pine stump, gritting his teeth as he peeled off his tunic and boots, again cutting the laces. Thankfully, his right leg appeared to be healing straight without redness or pustules. *Good,* he thought. *I did not come this far to die of a fever.*

Kali knelt beside him, handing him soap and rags. Her hands moved through his hair, picking out dirt and knots with practiced ease.

It felt like a cleansing—not just of his body, but of his past. It all drifted away under her gentle touch.

"Thank you, love," Agni said, voice low. "I feel like a citizen again."

Kali smiled, but her head turned toward the house.

"Alexander, my you are early," she called. "Come see!"

A deep laugh echoed across the yard.

"Agni, do my eyes deceive me?"

Agni's heart jolted.

Alexander stood in the doorway, broad-shouldered and wild-haired as ever.

Agni grinned, rising awkwardly onto his good leg.

"My friend, my friend."

Alexander strode across the yard. Agni threw his free arm around him, pressing his face into the giant's chest. For a moment, the world narrowed to the steady warmth of his friend who had stood beside him in war and peace alike.

Kali slid into the embrace, wrapping her arms around them both. Agni closed his eyes.

"My heart is full," he murmured.

"You are back among friends, love," she replied.

"Let me don this tunic," he said. "Let us purchase a meal at that tavern we passed—the Hawkwing, the sign said."

Alexander grinned.

Agni continued, "Then sit down in this beautiful house. My last two moons would shame and bard's tale."

"*Ai,* Agni. You have turned a few of my hairs gray." Alexander pulled a lock of his mane forward, showing streaks of silver. "You have some explaining to do. Swear to speak truth before the gods of this land and our home."

"He already has," Kali said. "Not even returning from the Avician Campaign did he feel the need to do so."

Agni's heart failed with resolve.

"I will tell you everything."

Alexander's hand clapped his shoulder, steady as ever.

"And after that, we will decide what comes next."

—

Around their new dining table, over fatty beef, fresh wheat bread, and wine from western Avicia, Agni told his tale—minus Anton Kazirian.

Kali and Alexander sat in stunned silence for two hours, their eyes wide, mouths hanging open, punctuated by the occasional expletive or disbelief, but otherwise enraptured. Agni half expected them to laugh at him, but they did not. And even after rehearsing it for a moon at sea, it felt freeing.

When he finally stopped talking, the room went eerily quiet, but for the crackle of fire in the hearth and the soft clink of cooling wine cups.

Alexander leaned back, dragging his massive hands down his face. His mouth twisted into something halfway between awe and alarm.

"By the gods," he muttered. "You surprise me again and again. Having one of your fits, then snapping to in order to win over Duke Harkon? If you had not just sworn an oath, I would have called you a liar."

He sighed and rubbed his temples. He had not only lied today, but for decades. He lied because Anton demanded it, and because he had convinced himself that protecting them from the truth was kind.

*Was it kindness, or cowardice?* he thought. *But it is time.*

"And I am a liar, my friend," Agni confessed.

Alexander's brow furrowed.

"Beg your pardon, Agni?"

His gaze swept over both—Kali's wide, steady eyes and Alexander's curious frown.

"For years, I have withheld my deepest secret, thinking it would shield you from a terrible power. But now that we have crossed the Great Sea—and I have overcome that power—I shall tell you."

He turned towards Kali.

"My love, the day before we departed, I promised to tell you of my sword's origin."

"I have not forgotten," she whispered.

They stared at him with an intense stillness that sent a shiver up his spine. His hands shook and his throat tightened. He did not know if this might upset them, or worse, place them under Anton's gaze. But if Anton could still see him—if Anton could still reach into his mind—he wanted to show Anton that fear no longer ruled him.

He took a swig of wine.

"You know how we Kazians adhere to antiquity," Agni said, voice solemn. "To most, it seems quaint or mysterious. A tradition to pass down through the words of parents and priests. But when that tradition manifests, it shakes the Mortal Realms."

Kali's eyes glinted in the firelight. Alexander leaned forward, arms crossed.

"Twenty years ago, a voice summoned a starving boy to the Ancient City," Agni continued. "Knowing only pain and dishonor for years, the boy followed the call, which gave him warmth and courage. It promised him power beyond comprehension and gave him a sword—a token of that promise, and hope—but enjoined him never to speak of him, nor of that night."

Kali's hand flew to her mouth.

"You… were that boy," she whispered.

Agni nodded.

"And that voice," he swallowed hard, "was the last child of the Dragon God… Anton Kazirian."

"The same."

A hush fell over the room, heavier than before.

"But his guidance came at a price," Agni pressed on. "That one day, he would use me as his warlord to resurrect the Empire Kazia in blood. A boy cannot understand such a promise. But twenty years and one boy's will mean little to an Ancient. He has an army of spirits—his greatest soldiers in life—at his command. Once his chosen looses them to take on the flesh of the fallen, they will spare no corner of the Mortal Realms."

"Gods," Alexander muttered.

"For years, he spoke the wisdom of ages. Sometimes he would speak in dreams and darkness. Sometimes he would sweep me up in my emotions, filling my voice with rapture. Sometimes he would force his presence on me, locking my mind away from my body. My soldiers called them 'fits.' I did not correct them. The truth may have brought his fury upon all of us."

Alexander's hands tightened into fists. Kali just stared.

"Alexander," Agni said, voice strained, "you may recall my words at the feast in Eltrazan. Anton filled me with such a rapture that I spoke of his grandeur and the Jewel of Eternity—his title for the Empire Kazia. That was his plan, for me to rally Kazian lords to what they only knew as a folktale. Verlan knew beyond a doubt that my existence threatened him. The die was cast."

"You turned on him," Kali said.

"I refused him," Agni corrected. "After we fled, he wanted me to turn the Kazian countryside to his cause. To summon his spirits. But that night chilled me to the bone. And I refused."

Alexander exhaled, long and slow.

"But Anton is patient," Agni continued. "At the raid, I did not wriggle free of Rem's bonds. Anton placed his glowing sword beside me—the same one Kali and I buried the night before I departed—and the bonds burned away at a touch."

Kali's eyes narrowed.

"The sword…"

"After I beat the message out of the mayor, Anton struck me. That was no fever in front of the duke; that was Anton's nightmare. But I broke his hold."

Agni's jaw tightened.

"And while I may be rid of him, the Mortal Realms are not. He has called another. I believe it may be Duke Verlan. My messages of peace may have delayed hostilities, but Anton will strike again. That is why it is more important than ever to gain King Theodore's ear."

Alexander shook his head side to side, his expression a mixture of shock and grudging respect.

"That is what I locked away from you," Agni continued. "Through me, you have struggled with power that even excellencies do not comprehend. And for that, I thank you."

"By the gods, Agni," he murmured. "This is madness. But I believe you."

Kali's hand slid over Agni's.

"And I accept you and your name," she said softly. "And the weight of its origin."

"And should Anton return," Alexander added, "he will have to battle three."

Agni's breath seized and his lip quavered. A flood of warmth and relief washed through him. He lowered his head as tears slid down his cheeks.

"Thank you," he whispered. "Thank you."

They embraced him from both sides, Kali's hand pressed into his back, Alexander's arm braced around his shoulders.

"The last wall between us has fallen, love," Kali said.

"I want to know it all," Alexander said. "But tomorrow. First, we drink."

Agni laughed softly. "And you will have to regale me with your own journeys. You arrived with as many credits as you departed."

"That can wait a night, love," Kali mused. "Neither of us fought an immortal, nor shaped the Dragonlands."

"But tomorrow night, I want to make you my wife. Before the sun sets. Before the Mortal Realms and the Lands Beyond. I burned for this for two moons."

Agni stood up, letting his walking stick clatter to the ground. Kali did too, pressing her lips against his.

"Yes," Kali cooed. "A thousand times yes."

They kissed again, and the world felt still. Safe.

But then a pale blue light shimmered in the corner of the hall.

Agni opened his eyes. Alexander sat bolt upright, eyes widening. "Gah! What is that?"

Kali's head whipped toward the light.

But Agni stayed calm. He limped toward the light with sure steps. The sky-blue glow sharpened into the shape of a blade.

Agni grasped the hilt and lifted it from the floor. The banded steel shimmered under the red-orange firelight. Slowly, he set it down on the table in front of them.

"I will place this at our bedside tonight," Agni said, resolute.

"You do not fear it?" Kali asked. "Anton's will brought it here."

"No, I will not fear it," Agni replied, his voice calm. "And you need not either. His will may follow me until my end of days, but I will fear him no more."

# Will

The day after she arrived at Artanport Castle, Duchess Sara stood at the dais in the grand courtyard, wearing a shimmering silk robe and circlet—such finery as she had forgotten in two years. But it felt like burlap next to Anton's ring. She fought the urge to finger it.

Out of the corner of her right eye, she saw Father's Chief Magistrate, proud in his seventh decade, head bowed as he stared toward her. In front of her stood two burly, helmeted guards holding Orlan the Zealot by his tied-back arms. The Justiciar's wings drooped, his back bare, his hair caked with sweat. She had just ordered him dragged from the dungeon—a proper dungeon, not some drafty undercroft like Azectrai's—but he looked like he had just spent a moon there. Behind him, his five underlings stood, unbound but with heads bowed, as if they expected to share his fate.

Sara's voice was steady, regal. She had rehearsed this moment for a moon; it felt effortless.

"Captain Orlan. I am Duchess Sara Ristana of Artania, and on my eyewitness and that of five under your command, I find you guilty of the death of Dona, housekeeper for my betrothed Lord Guardian of the East, Agni Kazirian."

The Chief Magistrate held up his right hand.

"Lady Sara, this is a serious matter. The fate of a justiciar, sworn directly to your father—"

The ring grew warm on her finger.

"Chief Magistrate Topran," she replied in an icy voice, "you address the Duchess of Artania, sworn directly to His Imperial Majesty. My father tends to matters in the River Axis. His Grace would not be pleased to see justice delayed."

Topran's mouth tightened. Sara saw the hesitation in his stance—the sudden realization that he spoke to a ruling duchess, not a noble daughter. He took in a breath, but Sara held up her hand.

"Enough," she continued. "The corruption of a duke's own justiciar must be immediately attended to, lest he be placed in a position to exact further harm. Let His Grace see that the realm is not paralyzed in his absence."

"Your Grace, your father has rem—"

"SILENCE!"

The word cut through the courtyard like a whipcrack. All present whipped their heads toward her, even those tightening their grip on the disgraced.

Sara did not recognize her own voice—commanding, cutting. Is that what Agni—or Anton—sounded like when giving orders on the battlefield?

"Magistrate," she said coldly, "your insolence displeases me. I hereby relieve you of this questioning. You will still that wayward tongue and record these proceedings on the scrolls, or replace Orlan in his cell."

Topran's mouth opened then closed without a sound. His wings fluttered in unease, but he bowed.

She turned her gaze towards Orlan.

"Now as for you, Orlan. Reconcile your actions towards Dona the housekeeper with any civilized conception of justice."

Orlan just coughed.

"Guards," Sara said. "Lift his face."

The guard on the left grabbed Orlan's chin and forced his gaze toward her. He looked weak, pale from confinement, but his eyes flashed with stubborn pride. She stared needles through him.

"Your grace," Orlan rasped. "I am sworn only to the duke. You will no longer inherit th—"

"Guards."

Sara brought her right hand down in a striking motion. The guard on the right swung his fist down into Orlan's jaw. Orlan yelped as a crack echoed through the courtyard. Blood trickled from his mouth. *Agni called that a "hammer fist,"* she thought, coolly. *Let it break another criminal's will, today.*

"Orlan," Sara said, her tone sharp as steel. "It is beyond your station to question nobles' affairs. Speak freely and quickly if you wish a lighter sentence than depraved murder. Were we not a nation of laws, I would pinion-and-drop you out of my own bedchamber, leaving the waves to wash your blood off the rocks."

Even in pain, Orlan shuddered. His eyes flared with fear.

"Your Grace," Orlan said, blood dripping off the edge of his lip, "I received the duke's full writ to dispose of Agni Kazirian and all who aided him. Therefore, I can commit no crime in pursuit of him."

Sara's hand tightened into a fist.

"And did a housekeeper in her ninth decade, who already swore she knew not his whereabouts, halt your search?"

Orlan's head twitched, shaking more blood to the ground.

"You say 'from your grasp.' Why did you hold her fast after you garnered any information you could?" Sara's gaze swept over his five men. "You five—his lackeys, his bullyboys—speak truth before Her Grace and the ever-present God of Dragons, lest ropes bind you as well. Step forth and answer. Did your captain act under a lawful writ when he struck down an unarmed woman?"

A tall, slender, long-haired man stepped forward. He looked much like a younger Orlan, but with none of his menace.

"I am Giforan, Your Grace," the man said. His voice was steady, but his eyes betrayed fear. "I served under Captain Orlan. I was present when he questioned Lady Dona."

"Giforan, recount for us the events of that encounter with Lady Dona, in full."

"Yes, Your Grace. First, my captain questioned her with respect to the Lord Guardian's location, of which she claimed no knowledge."

"Giforan, did you believe Lady Dona?" Sara asked, flaring her wings.

"No!" Orlan shouted. "Any inquisitor could see through her lie."

"Guards." Sara nodded at Orlan's captors.

The right guard swung his "hammer fist" into Orlan's temple. Orlan's neck went limp with a moan.

"Justiciar, do not speak until you receive a direct question," Sara calmly intoned. "Now, Inquisitor Giforan, did you see any guile in Lady Dona's eyes? Do you believe she would prepare the Lord Guardian to break the fast if she believed him departed? Do you believe he would trouble his elderly maid with the affairs of lords? Speak freely, Giforan."

Giforan bowed.

"Your Grace, I saw no deception in her eyes. I am of common stock, and while my lord would dine and sing with us, he never spoke of courtly affairs. So much greater must be the affairs of the

Lord Guardian, tasked by Emperor Taran Solant himself to protect a hostile border."

"Therefore, you do not believe Lady Dona lied to protect the Lord Guardian," Sara replied, her tone neutral.

"I found her forthcoming and truthful."

"As did I, Inquisitor. Let us not forget that I lived alongside the Lord Guardian, supped and bedded there, for two years," Sara reminded all present. "Now Orlan, speak freely. Why did you throttle an old woman? Did you truly believe that you stood above our laws—and His Grace's—so long as you pursued the Lord Guardian?"

Orlan's face twisted into a snarl.

"My belief does not matter. You, the mayor, and his constable saw His Grace's writ. You must consider that Azectrai's guardians of the law would not punish me for an alleged crime against their citizen."

Sara bit the corner of her lips, lest she order the guards to cuff him again.

"The words of those corrupt and venal men mean nothing to me, or imperial law. Captain Orlan, does your writ include the beating of old women? That day, you could have asked me about Lady Dona's character. Instead, I saw joy in your face as you made a fist around her hair. That of a man who seeks out cruelty to, as my once-betrothed would say, 'let out the darkness,' under cover of law."

Sara looked into Orlan's eyes, this time feeling a twinge of pity. *The darkness in Agni's heart,* she thought. *He who impaled a bandit who threw himself at my mercy. Let me show that I surpass him in matters of justice.* The ring warmed itself again.

Orlan looked poised to speak. She raised her hand.

"Orlan, Inquisitor Giforan and I both believe you acted outside your writ. Now, remaining inquisitors, do you believe Captain Orlan acted justly? That seizing Lady Dona's body would further your pursuit of the Lord Guardian? If you do, speak now."

Her wings flared behind her. Lightning seemed to course through her veins—the element of Agni, Anton, Father… and herself.

No man spoke.

"Justiciar Orlan," she said, a chill in her voice, "by the laws of Artania and Kazia alike, you have committed a wrongful death. If you slew her with malice, you will face the pinion-and-drop, or in the fashion of other lands, hang by your neck until you are dead. Did you do so?"

Sara kept her voice flat but fought a smile at making this brute account for his every action.

"Lest Her Grace forget, Dona—a common woman—struck at my groin. I did not intend her death. My palm shot open, and an unfortunate accident occurred."

She did not break her gaze.

"Justiciar, it displeases me that you distance yourself from responsibility for your own actions. You seized a dowager in a gnarled back garden where any fall could take her life. While you may not have intended to kill her, you have still committed a wrongful death. Inquisitors, if you dispute any detail of my account, speak immediately."

Her wings spread to full, clipping the Chief Magistrate. She heard a yelp of surprise.

The inquisitors stood still.

"Captain Orlan," she pronounced, her voice calm, "we find you guilty of a wrongful death. For that, you shall receive one hundred lashes with a switch immediately and lose your command. Whether or not my father deems me in his disfavor, he shall return to find that justice proceeds in his absence. Chief Magistrate, retrieve the jailer and his switch."

The Chief Magistrate looked back and forth at Sara, then at the door to the dungeon. Sara jerked her head at him.

Orlan's face paled as the guards dragged him over a rough stump.

"Your Grace," the burly jailer spoke with a bow. He stood six feet and most of a head more, his muscles rippling beneath his jerkin.

"The sentence is one hundred lashes to this man, for causing the wrongful death of a crone in Azectrai. No, ninety. I will deliver ten myself. Magistrate, count the blows."

Sara watched coldly as the jailer delivered the first blow with a grunt. Orlan's wings jerked. A thin line of blood welled up across his pale skin. The jailer measured him and brought down the blow with a grunt. Orlan's wings jerked.

Ten. Twenty. Fifty. By halfway, Orlan's screams had faded to whimpers and twitches. Sixty.

"Jailer, your switch."

The guard presented it to Sara like a gift.

Sara grasped it like a bastard sword and raised it overhead. A growl rose in her throat as she struck the first. Second. Third. With every blow, her fury deepened.

At ten, Orlan's head hung limp and blood trickled down his spine. Her hands trembled as she lowered the switch. She wanted to deliver a hundred of her own. But a duchess had to control her rage. She handed it back to the jailer.

Lost in thought, she only noticed when the jailer struck the ninety-seventh lash. Orlan's back and wings were a mass of blood and welts.

"Guards," she said, "drag him outside the castle walls. Let him lay with his shame. Let the city see the wages of cruelty."

Sara stepped away, breathing hard. Her wings slowly folded behind her. The men in the courtyard watched her warily, as if seeing her for the first time.

She turned toward the keep.

Would Father berate her or take pride in her, for meting out justice?

Or would Father's reaction hold any consequence, compared to the Voice of Ages?

*In either case, I fulfilled my oath to lash that brute.*

———

That night, her bedchamber felt even grander than the night before. *My first sentence passed. Men of war bowed to me—not Father, not Agni,* she thought.

She ran a finger along her bed frame and saw not a speck of gray. Agni's chamber was one of the largest in Azectrai, but five of them could not fill her room atop the tower. Fine sheer silks draped her bed, making it feel warm and intimate.

Father would return from visiting Duke Rowan and the River Axis in a few days. She had not communicated with him since Azectrai, but his displeasure felt small and distant, like a dim night star. What could he take from her that Anton Kazirian could not gift her ten times over?

Like the Ancient City, Anton's empire was not destroyed, but asleep. Locked away from time. When awakened, it would sweep through the Dragonlands like a mountain storm. A storm that only she and Anton could command.

*And until that day, I only need to wait and live.*

She closed her eyes to feel five seconds pass. Now, time served her as it did Anton. No longer a sentence to the dull East, or a reminder of her fertile years as Father's marriageable pawn.

Father, too, would submit to the Empire Kazia, or be swept away in fate's currents. The currents that she would shape.

As she turned to place Anton's ring on her night table, it pulsed warmly again. Her guardian appeared before her eyes, silver and shimmering against the white silks that adorned her bed.

*"Blessed Ancestor,"* Sara whispered. *"Your will be done. Let your glories ripple forth from the mountains of Kazia."*

It felt like a prayer, so effortless, in a tongue she had not known a moon ago. Bursting with draconic power. She had never felt such pride in her tribe.

Anton's silver eyes gleamed.

*"Sweet Sara. I watched over your journey home. It brings me joy to see you at such peace."*

*"Ai, ancestor. And I, to speak to you in your native tongue. Even the modern Kazian tongue feels so… deadened… next to it."*

Anton smiled warmly.

*"Time sands down even the sharpest blade. But once it finds its whetstone, the years fall away."*

How profound, in a land that forgot it all—its tongue, its sacred beast, its very history.

*"Ai, ancestor. I feel as though I have obtained the power of both Artania and the East."*

Anton's smile deepened.

*"That you have. But you will no longer know the Azectrai Valley as 'Kazia.' That which you call 'Solantia,' you will call, 'the West of Kazia,' and that which you call 'Blevenia,' you will call 'the East of Kazia.' That which you call 'the Ancient City' will one day transcend name. A name carries power but also limits. No name will encompass its splendor."*

Sara felt a chill through her blankets. Even her tutors—men who spent lifetimes studying Anton's conquests—had only unearthed the surface of his mind. How much more had he learned, observing the Mortal Realms—and beyond—for two thousand years?

*"It is already incredible, even if it lies still."*

Anton's figure straightened.

*"You choose your words well, Lady Sara. It has been scourged but stands outside the ravages of time. Mothers with babes, napping dogs, watering horses. Their essences lie outside time."*

*"Outside time?"* Sara frowned, perplexed. *"Does the Dragon God watch over their destiny? Does their fate still weave?"*

Anton's smile sharpened.

*"Their bodies have crumbled, but their essences linger. You saw those of my—soon, our—legions. The curse of that which you call the Ancient City is not just some taboo. Body and essence may be separate, but they long to be united. Just as I do."*

Sara's hand hovered over her ring. *"Does your body lie in the Ancient City, too?"*

Anton's eyes darkened with something she could not name. Regret? Pain?

*"That, even I do not know,"* Anton said softly. *"But only with it can I come into my power. With a lesser body, my powers would return, though they would not be complete."*

She resolved not to disappoint Anton as she had her father. So much more was at stake; she would show Anton how strong of a regent she could become.

*"Then I will find it,"* Sara pronounced. *"Should it take all I command."*

Anton smiled.

*"In time, Lady Sara. Tomorrow, any man would laugh at that order. Your father concerns himself with today's power, not eternity's. But with two years in provincial Kazia, you have tales to recount. He has never traveled east of Eltrazan. Enchant him. Win his heart the same way you would a servant boy's."*

Sara's lips pursed.

*"He wishes to launch an attack from Azectrai, not to explore it."*

Anton's smile widened.

*"He will learn he cannot do the former without the latter. I wish him to do both. Stoke his curiosity like a flame."*

A curious boy. Father once was a curious boy, though she could scarcely comprehend it.

*"I will, ancestor."*

Anton's silver eyes sharpened.

*"Once you discover my body, a ritual will bind it again to my essence. Then, shall I walk the Mortal Realms. This knowledge is forbidden, though not lost, within Kazia. Even I do not know it."*

*"I will find it, ancestor,"* Sara vowed.

*"There will be more,"* Anton said, his voice low, a promise in the dark. *"But for now, concern yourself with that. Turn men's hearts eastward and I will reward you. Now rest. Know that your father will embrace you once again."*

*"Blessed Ancestor, your will be done."*

Anton's specter faded. Sara stared up at the silks where his image showed seconds earlier.

This was not Father's scheme, reliant on petty men; this was the guidance of the Ancient—he who unified the Dragonlands. And she, his chosen agent.

The last time she had felt nearly this powerful was when Father placed her hand in Agni's, ten years ago. What an innocent time, by comparison.

Sara smiled, pulling the silk sheets over her body. Anton's words felt like thunder in her veins.

What was Father's birthright next to true power?

Dear Reader:

You have reached the end of *Son of the Borderlands*—but not the end of the journey.

I wrote this story in quiet hours and long nights, shaped it with my own questions and travails, and the universal human struggle for identity. If Agni's journey moved you, unsettled you, or lingered with you after the final page, then this story did what I intended it to do.

If it did, I would be deeply grateful if you left a review or rating wherever you found this book, or within your favorite reading community. Reviews do not just help authors; they help the right readers find the story when they need it most.

The world of *Rise of the Dragonlands* is still unfolding. More books are coming, along with prequels, side stories, hidden histories, and an ever-growing body of lore. If you would like to walk those roads with me, join the mailing list at **JosephSterk.com** for updates, exclusive content, and early news about what lies ahead.

Thank you again for stepping into this world, and carrying it with you beyond these pages.

For the Borderlands,

*Joe*

## AERIE MARKET

The largest market in Tercera, built into the mountain halfway to the summit—vast enough to rival a small city. Agni ended the Avician Campaign and forced King Theodore to surrender by aiming a nether cannon at this crowded marketplace.

## AGNI KAZIRIAN

The last direct descendant of Anton Kazirian, son of Piro Kazirian and Mara Senotare, former High General of Solantia and current Lord Guardian of the East. As High General, he defeated both Blevenia and Avicia in the Black Moon War. Now, he defends the contested eastern border. Plagued by fits of insight and madness—actually, visions from his ancestor Anton—many believe he is touched by the gods. His given name means "living flame," and his family name means "dragon of the moonless night."

## AIRA

Elder herbalist and healer of Azectrai. At eighty-five years, she is still sharp, spry, and fiercely independent. She cared for Agni's mother and grandparents, and remains close to the women of the valley.

## ALEXANDER

Agni's loyal top bodyguard and counselor. A half-Tarkan, half-Solantian giant, his father raised him on the Great Sea, and in the ports and guilds of all lands. A moral and upright man, he anchors Agni's darker instincts with calm and clarity.

## ALOI (THE LAND OF)

The land of the "tiger tribe" in the northwest of the southern continent, an unforgiving land of scorching deserts and dense jungles. Its capital, Charoi, is a vibrant coastal port, but most cities govern themselves, and nomadic bands range free. Though Solantia lies on its poorly defined southern border, their peoples have been allies for a generation.

## THE ALOI PEOPLE

The strong, lithe "tiger people," with furred ears, forearms, claws, and lower bodies, like their totem beast. While they have cities and noble castes, most are nomadic hunter-gatherers. Often dismissed as primitive by outsiders, they are a fiercely independent people who have never been conquered.

## THE ANCIENT ALLIANCE

The long-standing pact between Blevenia and Avicia which bound each to the other's defense. Agni shattered this alliance in the Black Moon War—razing Western Blevenia, and threatening Tercera, the capital of Avicia, with forbidden nether magic.

## THE ANCIENT CITY

The ruined capital of the long-dead Empire Kazia, obliterated in the divine Scourge two thousand years ago. Entry is a capital crime, and rumor holds that disturbing its ashes will awaken unspeakable horrors. It lies just across the river from Azectrai, cloaked in mystery.

## ANTON KAZIRIAN

The last-born and greatest child of the Dragon God. He united the warring Dragonlands into the Empire Kazia, which was destroyed in the Scourge. In life, he was a mighty conqueror, priest, and sorcerer. Now a shade bound to the Ancient City, he grows in fury as he watches the Mortal Realms forget his empire and his bloodline wither. He awaits a worthy descendant to restore his empire.

## ARKAMA

Agni's massive white stallion, who has accompanied him since the Avician Campaign. Often called "Ark" for short. His name means "white giant" in Kazian.

## ARNO

The bloated, lecherous son of Mayor Goro—lazy, stupid, and repulsive.

## ARTANIA (THE CITY OF)

The capital of the Empire of Solantia, perched atop a mountain crowned by Emperor Taran Solant's palace. A city of wealth, intrigue, and imperial power.

## ARTANIA (THE DUCHY OF)

One of Solantia's four duchies and its political heart. Though the emperor rules the entire empire, the Duke of Artania administers the duchy's day-to-day affairs such as law enforcement and taxes. While the duchies are equal in name, Artania's wealth and proximity to the emperor give it primacy. Duke Verlan Ristana rules it from his castle in Artanport.

## ARTANPORT

The administrative capital of the Duchy of Artania, a thriving port on the Great Sea.

## ARTEVA

A free, multi-ethnic city on the Great Sea, near the borders of Solantia and Aloi. Once an Avician colony, Agni recaptured it during the Black Moon War and made it the stronghold in the Western Defense.

## ASCENSION (THE RITUAL OF)

A sacred ritual to pass to the Dragon God's side in the Lands Beyond. Participants are bound to a mountaintop and struck by Varenox's element of lightning, symbolizing purification and transcendence.

## AVICIA (THE KINGDOM OF)

The wealthiest and most populous kingdom in the Mortal Realms, home of the feather-winged "roc people." Spanning most of the northern campaign—from mountain to plains, forest, and tundra—it is known for its cities and artistry.

## THE AVICIAN CAMPAIGN

The daring final campaign of the Black Moon War, in which Agni's forces sailed north to Avicia, and shattered the Ancient Alliance. A short but bloody campaign, it ended with the Siege of Tercera.

## THE AVICIAN PEOPLE

The tall, graceful "roc tribe," with feathered wings that allow not just gliding but short bursts of flight. They are cultured people known for art, architecture, and learning.

## (Constable) Avro

Azectrai's chief of the guard and law enforcement officer, answerable to Mayor Goro. A short, squat man fond of drink and tavern girls. Quick to assert his authority where it is least needed.

## Azectrai (The City of)

Agni's home, a humble city nestled in the fertile Azectrai Valley between the Spires and Western Mountains. It sits at the intersection of the Great River and the Median Road. Though now a backwater, it sits across the river from the grand Ancient City and was founded by its few survivors. Some say it was built to guard the Mortal Realms from whatever lies within.

## Azectrai (The River)

A great waterway and trade route that divides the southern continent, running from Sivatrai and the Beachroad the north, to the Far Coast and the Dragonroad at the south. While often called "the Azectrai River," "Azectrai" literally means "great river" in Kazian.

## Azectrai (The Valley)

The fertile lands surrounding the Azectrai River, part of the Borderlands.

## Azri of Azectrai

Agni Kazirian's false peasant identity, with a tragic story.

## Ballista

A massive crossbow that fires a spear-sized bolt capable of piercing dragon scales. Common in Azectrai, the Spires, and Western Blevenia, they are mounted on rooftops to defend against dragon attacks.

## THE BEACHROAD

A vital trade route that hugs the northern coast of the southern continent. It stretches from the Solantian port of Sivatrai to the eastern capital of Blevenia, Tonda. It has easy terrain but is frequented by bandits.

## THE BLACK MOON WAR

The decade-long conflict that reshaped the Mortal Realms. It was so named when a young Agni Kazirian torched a Blevenian patrol, sparking open war. It ended with the Siege of Tercera and the sundering of the Ancient Alliance.

## BLEVENIA (THE KINGDOM OF)

The eastern realm of the Dragonlands, comprising all land east of the Spires "from where the hills stand higher than a stallion's head." It is a diverse land of plains, deserts, jungles, and even volcanoes. Once prosperous, it has struggled to recover after the scorched-earth tactics of the Black Moon War.

## THE BLEVENIAN CAMPAIGN

The first campaign of the Black Moon War, an unrelenting guerrilla conflict over the Spires. Agni rose from scout to general, endured moons of grueling captivity, and ultimately led devastating raids to cripple Western Blevenia.

## THE BLEVENIAN PEOPLE

One of the two "dragon tribe" nations with long blue hair, gliding wings, and a proud legacy. Anton Kazirian condemns them for forsaking the ways of the dragon. Many bob their hair or grow beards in the Avician style.

## THE BORDERLANDS

The volatile border between Blevenia and Solantia. Often referring to the Azectrai Valley and Spires. Its mountains and rivers have seen centuries of scheming and bloodshed.

## THE BOUNDLESS SEA

The vast western ocean, part of that which encircles the Mortal Realms. It contains some Aloi fishing isles called the Pins. As one sails west, the winds die, stranding vessels in eerie silence until sailors die of thirst.

## CHAROI

The capital of Aloi. The name means "City of Charos" in the native tongue, trade and tribal tradition meet in its port.

## CHAROS

The tiger god, patron of the Aloi, the sun, and the direction of West. A primitive, warlike god hated by the other three. His rituals are grueling and painful, but he gifts his followers with agility, endurance, and keen senses. His Chosen are superlative hunters and feral warriors.

## THE CHOSEN

"Living saints" of their god, selected from birth to serve their divine will. They exemplify their god's traits and seek deeply to please them. Agni's mother was a Chosen of Varenox.

## CRYSTAL THRONE

The throne of the Emperor of Solantia, carved into the peak of the mountain. Figuratively, it symbolizes imperial rule.

## (DUKE) DANAN

Ruler of the Far Coast and one of four coequal dukes of Solantia. A Silverdrake, he appears to prefer tranquility to imperial intrigue.

## THE DESOLATOR

A title used in Blevenia and Avicia to curse Agni Kazirian, remembering the lands and lives taken in his ruthless campaigns.

## DONA

Elder cook and housemaid of the Kazirian family for four generations. Nearly ninety, she has survived war, plague, and heartbreak with quiet cheer.

## DRAGON

Also called a nighthunter, for its deep-blue scales and preference to hunt at twilight. Highly intelligent and territorial, these ultimate predators are rarely seen near cities unless desperate. An adult has a fifty-foot wingspan, razor-sharp claws and teeth, and a breath of lightning that can stun its prey or kill it outright. Anton Kazirian claims that they and humans once lived as brothers.

## THE DRAGONLANDS

The collective name for Blevenia and Solantia—so called for the mountains where dragons still dwell. Once united as the Empire Kazia.

## THE DRAGONROAD

The perilous trade route along the Unending Sea, it links the southern Blevenian city of Bethen with the Solantian Far Coast. Named for the dragons of the southern Spires, many of which will attack caravans.

## EBONDRAKES

Blevenians of the southern deserts and volcanic regions, named for their darker hair, skin, and wings. They are fierce, insular, and distrustful of outsiders.

## ELTRAZAN

The provincial capital of Kazia, a relatively large city north of the Western Mountains, home to Duke Hauran.

## ESSENCE

The animating force of life—the spirit that survives death.

## FALUAN

The orca god, patron of the islands of Tarka, the waters, and the direction of East. He grants more subtle gifts like physical strength and camaraderie, but they are perfect for a seafaring people. His Chosen are master traders and sailors.

## FALUANIA

The capital of Tarka, a sprawling port city of coves and markets.

## THE FAR COAST

Solantia's province along the Unending Sea; a tranquil land of fine wine and song, dominated by the willowy, artistic Silverdrake people. It is ruled by Duke Danan.

## FAR SIGHT (THE RITUAL OF)

A sacred rite that allows one to glimpse the Lands Beyond and see if someone resides at the Dragon God's side. It requires priests, braziers, a life-size effigy of the Dragon God, and someone with strong emotional ties to the subject.

## FIREGLASS

Obsidian, a rare, sharp volcanic glass mined from Blevenia's volcanoes.

## FRAZI

One of Agni's elite bodyguards and a decorated veteran.

## GARI

Azectrai's High Priest of Varenox, once a decorated warrior, now a devout man of vision.

## GERVO

Inquisitive servant boy to Duke Hauran.

## GIFORAN

One of Justiciar Orlan's inquisitors.

## (BARON, MAYOR) GORO KAZIMANA

Baron of Azectrai and the most prosperous manor in Kazia. A giant, muscular man, he was once the greatest knight in the valley; now a calm, formidable lord. His surname means "dragon of magic."

## THE GREAT SEA

The ocean that sits between the northern and southern continents and holds the islands of Tarka. Sailing it requires a great ship and a moon.

## (DUKE) HARKON LAMATA

Duke of Western Blevenia (also known as the Leeward Plains). Once proud, now broken by the Black Moon War—he lost his land, men, and even his two sons.

## (DUKE) HAURAN

Duke of Kazia, a Westerner (evident by the name ending in "-an") and not a Kazian by descent. An unremarkable man and a follower of Duke Verlan Ristana.

## HERALD

A messenger trained in the use of speaking stones—magical devices used to transmit voice of vision. Typically, the child of a smith or artisan (not a noble, for nobles are loyal to their lords, not the message)—they must recognize the voice of their lord and the direction of the message's origin. They speak with the authority of the lord that conveyed their message, often wearing their crest.

## HIGH GENERAL

The highest military rank in Solantia, granted directly by the emperor. Agni received this title after his crushing victories in Blevenia in the Black Moon War.

## (EMPRESS) IMRA

Empress of Solantia and wife of Emperor Taran Solant.

## THE INFINITE SEA

The great ocean to the north of the Mortal Realms. Sparse islands dot its icy surface, but further out lie furious storms, frigid winds, and eventually impassable ice.

## JORA

A priestess of Varenox and a gifted seer.

## KALI

Agni's longtime lover, a seductive, silver-tongued thief, tavern singer, dancer, and fighter, they met in Arteva during Agni's Western Defense. She won over Agni's men, who call her "Dear Tigress." She lives in uneasy coexistence with Agni's betrothed, Duchess Sara.

## KAZIA (THE DUCHY OF)

A proud and often overlooked duchy of Solantia encompassing the Spires, the Azectrai Valley, and the Western Mountains. The name means "land of dragons" and carries the legacy of the lost Empire Kazia. Some call it "Little Kazia" to distinguish it from the old empire, but this epithet will draw blows. It is governed by Duke Hauran, an ethnic Westerner.

## KAZIA (THE EMPIRE)

The ancient Dragonlands united under Emperor Anton Kazirian. After the Scourge destroyed its capital, the empire fragmented into factions, which were eventually united into the Kingdom of Blevenia and the Empire of Solantia. Anton is obsessed with restoring it, and his throne.

## KERON

A surly Blevenian bandit, barber, and trusted member of Rem's band. He harbors an unspoken hatred for Agni and often lashes out.

## THE LANDS BEYOND

The eternal residence of the gods; a paradise for the faithful and pure who pass to their god's side. Some rites allow one to see into this realm.

## LONTAK

A once-thriving port on the Blevenian side of the Beachroad. It has fallen into decay.

## LESDRAN

The distant capital of the Far Coast, it produces the finest wines in Solantia.

## LORD GUARDIAN (OF THE EAST)

A title bestowed on Agni Kazirian by Emperor Taran Solant himself. It tasks him with the defense of Solantia's eastern border. He has spent two years fortifying this region with traps and relays of speaking stones.

## LUBO

A lawless land in the far northwest, populated by the uninfused (not beast-blooded), outcasts from other lands, and exiles. Lacking a patron god and ruled by no single power, the Mortal Realms regard it with disdain and pity. In Old Avician, "Lubo" means "quarreling."

## (ADMIRAL) MALIA

Solantia's greatest admiral, who piloted Agni's army across the Great Sea to Avicia.

## MARA SENOTARE (KAZIRIAN)

Agni's mother—a paladin (Chosen warrior of Varenox) of unmatched strength, she fought with holy might and once disarmed every fighter in the valley, including Agni's father Piro Kazirian. She died defending her son from a Blevenian raid. Her family name, "Senotare," means "power of the mountain storm."

## THE MEDIAN ROAD

The longest and most important road on the southern continent, it extends from Blevenia's eastern capital to Solantia's, and beyond to Aloi's. While it crosses the difficult terrain of the Spires, it is safer than the Beachroad (bandits) and the Dragonroad (dragons), thanks to Agni's snares. It is called the Midspire Road where it crosses the Spires.

## THE MIDSPIRE ROAD

The length of the Median Road that traverses the Spires, from Azectrai east to the Western Blevenian city of Zarda.

## THE MIGHTY ROC

The god of Avicia, the skies and the air, and the direction of North, whose true name is unknown. Depicted as an immense bird of prey, he prizes wisdom, grace, and arts, and appreciates prayer and contemplation more than others. His Chosen are often eminent artists, artisans, and philosophers.

## NETHER

The forbidden magic element—searing and cold at once, it etches madness and decay wherever it lands. The wicked are condemned to eternal torment in it. Agni threatened nether cannons at the Siege of Tercera, then had the mages who created them ritually burned.

## The Netherworld

The realm of the wicked—a place of eternal torment and horror. Those condemned are frozen in fear and agony, unable to move, breathe, or scream. It is the source of the element of nether.

## Nira

A former tavern girl turned maid to the Kazirian household and Duchess Sara Ristana. Strikingly beautiful and soft-spoken, she is the mother of young Qualo.

## (Captain, Justiciar) Orlan

Chief investigator under Duke Verlan Ristana. A loyalist and zealot, devoid of pity, who executes his lord's will without hesitation.

## Paladin

A Chosen warrior of the Dragon God, gifted with prophetic insight in battle and a blade that gleams like lightning. Agni's mother, Mara, was one.

## Pavlon

Constable of Zarda, loyal to Duke Harkon. A thickset enforcer with a burning grudge against Agni.

## Piro Kazirian

Agni's father. Once a kind nobleman, grief turned him to drink and cruelty after Mara's death. He beat Agni as a child, and one day drowned himself in the Azectrai. A broken man, swallowed by loss.

## THE PORTS (BATTLE OF)

The most lurid battle of the Black Moon War. Solantia's navy landed near the Avician ports of Nearport and Farport, and exchanged fiery winds and flaming oil with the defenders. Many soldiers and horses burned alive.

## QUALO

A poor, scrawny ten-year-old sentry who wins Agni's favor.

## RELAY

A series of linked speaking stones used to convey messages across vast distances. Agni deployed many of these in the Spires, while others connect distant cities and capitals across the Mortal Realms.

## REM (REMON)

Leader of a ragtag band of Blevenian bandits. Small but clever and deadly with knives, he commands fierce loyalty from his crew.

## THE RIVER AXIS (THE DUCHY OF)

Solantia's northernmost duchy, named for the network of rivers and crisscross it. It stretches from the Aloi borders and free city of Arteva south to Artania. A coveted prize in peace or war, thanks to its fertile lands and navigable waterways. It is ruled by Duke Rowan, a wastrel.

## (DUKE) ROWAN

Ruler of the River Axis, one of the four duchies of Solantia. A drunken wastrel with no heir and a preference for young Aloi boys, his barons vie to take his place.

## RUIN OF THE SCOURGE

The blasted cities punished by the gods two thousand years ago as their punishment for wickedness and idolatry. Most lie buried and remote, except the Ancient City where Anton Kazirian resides. None dare venture within.

## (DUCHESS) SARA RISTANA

Heir of Duke Verlan and betrothed to Agni. Her father raised her in wealth and refinement but since assigned her to manage the Borderlands' levies. She dreams of returning to Artanport, free of Agni's philandering and the gritty life in the East. Her father has not yet wed her to Agni, likely to keep other lords uncertain.

## THE SCOURGE

The divine cataclysm of two thousand years ago where the gods, seeing their people grow depraved, let the Netherworld into the Mortal Realms. Empires fell; only ruins remain.

## SILVERDRAKE

A minority race of Solantians native to the Far Coast. They have silver hair and wings, blue or purple eyes, and refined manners. They are more inclined toward craft than combat.

## SIVATRAI

A busy port at the mouth of the Azectrai River. Its name means "north river." It conducts most of the valley's trade across the Great Sea.

## SOLANTIA (THE EMPIRE OF)

The western nation of the Dragonlands, stretching from the Aloi borders to the eastern edge of the Spires. Once the weaker of the two powers, it has prospered since Agni's victories. It is fertile and vast, but vulnerable to internal strife.

## THE SOLANTIAN PEOPLE

One of the two "dragon tribe" nations, they adhere more closely to the traditions of antiquity—they wear their hair long, trim their beards, and practice gifts of prophecy. Anton Kazirian favors them for keeping to their traditions.

## SPEAKING OR SEEING STONE

A polished magical stone that stores speech or vision. An inch-diameter stone, like Agni's, can hold a cherished memory. A larger stone can transmit messages across great distances, especially when linked in a relay.

## THE SPELL OF BINDING

An enchantment that binds magic into a physical object—the stronger the mage, the more powerful the spell. Many mages can create small speaking or seeing stones, but it takes a powerful mage to create a great stone, let alone an enchanted weapon or suit of armor.

## THE SPINE OF SOLANTIA

The mountain chain stretching from the west of the Azectrai Valley to the capital. Those of the Borderlands call them the Western Mountains.

## THE SPIRES

The jagged peaks that form the eastern edge of the Azectrai Valley, long contested by Blevenia and Solantia. Though they yield little but stone, they form a formidable barrier to invasion.

## (EMPEROR) TARAN SOLANT

Ruler of Solantia, third of his name, son of Emperor Zaldan. A wise and just ruler, but sixty-five years of age, growing ill, and without an heir. His death may plunge the empire into chaos.

## TARKA (THE NATION OF)

The islands of the "orca tribe," north of Blevenia and south of Avicia. A nation of sailors and traders, they stayed neutral in the Black Moon War, which they called "a conflict of dragons," and stay friendly towards all nations.

## THE TARKAN PEOPLE

The towering, broad shouldered "orca tribe." They stand a head taller than most races (two taller than the Lubo) and are raised on the sea. Most have darker (often mottled) skin and wild black hair.

## TERCERA (THE CITY OF)

The grandest city in the Mortal Realms and capital of Avicia, home to nearly two-thirds of a million. Built into the side of hills and mountains, it is a city of alabaster temples, magnificent bridges, and fanes in the sky. For decades, people across the Mortal Realms have traveled here to seek their fortune. King Theodore's palace sits at the apex.

## TERCERA (THE SIEGE OF)

The final confrontation of the Black Moon War. Rather than try to starve out Tercera, Agni threatened it with nether, forcing King Theodore to surrender without a drop of blood.

## (KING) THEODORE OF AVICIA

The monarch of Avicia, with long golden hair and broad cream-colored wings. Agni forced him to surrender at the siege of Tercera.

## TONDA

The capital of Blevenia, located east along the Beachroad. It is a thriving port on the Great Sea, named after their first king, Thon Bleven.

## TOVON

One of Rem's bandits, a large and dim-witted but kind-hearted man.

## TRAKO

A shift commander of the Azectrai guards.

## THE UNENDING SEA

The name of the ocean south of the Mortal Realms. It contains one island. Further south, sailors meet their inevitable end from searing heat and terrible monsters.

## (KING) VARDON OF BLEVENIA

The king of Blevenia, who sits in the capital of Tonda.

## VARENOX

The god of the Dragonlands, storms and lightning, vision and fate, and the direction of South. His priests and Chosen are great men and women of war and prophecy. He bestows fated across the Mortal Realms, but by his design, rewards those who defy them. Depicted as a colossal, ancient dragon, he is capricious like his element of lightning. He is regarded as the most powerful and active of the gods.

## THE VAST SEA

The name of the ocean east of the mortal realms, containing the most remote of Tarkan isles. As one sails east, the waves grow monstrous until they split or capsize any man-made ship.

## (DUKE) VERLAN RISTANA

The cunning, ambitious Duke of Artania, second only to Emperor Taran in power. As financier of Agni's campaigns, he gained power, money, and prestige. A schemer who gifted his daughter's hand to the rising general.

## WESTERN BLEVENIA

The duchy of Duke Harkon. Solantia calls it Western Blevenia; Blevenia calls it the Leeward Plains.

## THE WESTERN DEFENSE

The second and longest of Agni's campaigns, in which Agni protected the River Axis and Aloi borders from invasion. Though never conclusive, it set the stage for Agni to invade Avicia.

## THE WESTERN MOUNTAINS

The Borderlands' name for the Spine of Solantia. They form the western edge of the Azectrai Valley.

## THE WOLF OF AZECTRAI

A Blevenian and Avician pejorative for Agni.

## ZAHA

A burly, swaggering Kazian sea captain who fancies himself to be a warrior.

## ZARDA (THE BATTLE OF)

The final battle of the Blevenian Campaign in which Agni's army sacked the Western Blevenian capital lands, drawing out and defeating Duke Harkon's army.

## ZARDA (THE CITY OF)

The capital of Western Blevenia and Duke Harkon's seat of power. Once proud, now scarred by war.

www.ingramcontent.com/pod-product-compliance
Lightning Source LLC
Chambersburg PA
CBHW031238310726
48971CB00004B/1067